"An original take on the famous story, filled with action and excitement, and a fresh look at the ancient world and the legends that haunted it."
　　　—*Science Fiction Chronicle* on *The Book of the Gods*

"Fred Saberhagen's Book of the Gods series offers a unique blend of myth and modernity, with plenty of new takes on ancient and exciting narrative."
　　　　　　　　　　　　　　　—Poul Anderson

"Saberhagen offers classical scholarship, wit, and a brisk sense of pacing in this coming-of-age story that should appeal to readers unfamiliar with the Swords books and attract Swords-familiar readers in swarms."
　　　—*Booklist* on *The Book of the Gods*

"Saberhagen is a masterful storyteller . . . I have every intention of reading the next book in the series. Saberhagen has given us a rich new world."
　　　　　　　　　　　　　　—*Absolute Magnitude*

GODS OF FIRE AND THUNDER

BOOK V OF BOOK OF THE GODS

FRED SABERHAGEN

TOR®
fantasy

A TOM DOHERTY ASSOCIATES BOOK
NEW YORK

This is a work of fiction. All the characters and events portrayed in this book are either products of the author's imagination or are used fictitiously.

GODS OF FIRE AND THUNDER

Copyright © 2002 by Fred Saberhagen

All rights reserved, including the right to reproduce this book, or portions thereof, in any form.

A Tor Book
Published by Tom Doherty Associates, LLC
175 Fifth Avenue
New York, NY 10010

www.tor.com

Tor® is a registered trademark of Tom Doherty Associates, LLC.

ISBN: 0-765-34151-4
Library of Congress Catalog Card Number: 2001059659

First edition: August 2002
First mass market edition: September 2003

Printed in the United States of America

0 9 8 7 6 5 4 3 2 1

. . . the moon embrace her shepherd,
And the queen of love her warrior,
While the first doth horn the star of morn,
And the next the heavenly Farrier.

With a host of furious fancies
Whereof I am commander,
With a burning spear and a horse of air
To the wilderness I wander.

—"Tom O'Bedlam's Song," Anonymous

GODS of FIRE
AND
THUNDER

1

Never before had Hal seen any fire as strange as this one. Its hungry tongues seemed to feed on nothing at all as they went burning and raging up toward heaven from the flat top of a thick spire of stone that rose steep-sided from the broad river valley. Rarely had Hal felt the glow of any blaze this large. The wall of light and heat went up straight, unnaturally straight, into the air for a good thirty feet. To the right and left the wall of fire swept out in a great, smooth convex curve, making a barrier as high and nearly as solid-looking as a castle's outer curtain. For all Hal could tell by looking at it, that might be just exactly what it was, the magic wall of some great god or monarch's stronghold.

The shape of the flaming barricade strongly suggested that it went all the way round the top of the rocky crag in a smooth curve, which would make it an almost perfect circle, and Hal thought that if it did that, it must enclose a space some twenty-five or thirty yards across. From where he was standing now, on a little saddle of land well outside that enclosed space, there was no telling just what might be contained within it.

Ought such a magic wall to have a gateway in it? From this angle he could see nothing to suggest there might be one.

Hal had been standing in the same place for several minutes, getting back his breath after the steep climb, while he studied the amazing flames. He marveled at how steadily they maintained their position, so frighteningly artificial and regular, neither advancing nor retreating, not letting the chilly evening breeze push them even a little to one side, as any natural fire would have wavered. For several minutes now Hal had been certain that the fiery tongues were born of magic, for they were feeding themselves on nothing, seemingly nothing at all but the rocky earth from which they sprang. But as far as he could see, the ground directly beneath the tongues was not consumed, only blackened by the heat out to a distance of a yard or so.

Overhead, the glare of the fire obliterated whatever stars might have otherwise been coming out now that the sun was down. The strange, unnatural blaze created its own local domain of light and summery warmth. This zone included the spot where Hal was standing, and extended for yards beyond him down the broad grassy slopes and rocky outcroppings surrounding the crag on every side. The sound made by the tremendous fire was not really loud, though it was very steady, a muted roar that blended with the background murmur of rushing water. During Hal's long climb up here from the valley he had noticed several small streams, all plunging down steep hillsides to the river some four hundred feet below.

He was a stocky man, standing with his powerful arms folded under a well-traveled cloak. A few flecks of gray showed in his once-fair hair and beard and mustache. His weatherbeaten face was fixed in a thoughtful expression.

Hal was still puffing slightly from his tedious climb. During the final part of the ascent, climbing the last long slope of grass and rocks, he had felt the heat of the great fire grow steadily more intense on his face and hands. Now he was about as close to it as he could comfortably get, and he could tell that the occasional streaks of flame that rose up green and blue were the hottest, while most of the light was coming from tongues of fire that glowed bright orange.

Part of what made the fire fascinating was that its colors were in constant change, varying rapidly from one part of the bright ring to another. Bands of greater heat and greater light were continually changing places, seeming to chase each other around the circle. What caused the variations was impossible to say.

It had been late afternoon when Hal, making his way north through unfamiliar land along the valley, had first caught sight of the strange burning. At that time it had struck him that for all the flame there seemed to be amazingly little smoke. Now, inspecting the scene at close range, he thought there were certain indications that the peculiar blaze was no more than a few days old—there, for instance, a tree stood just at the outer limit of destructive heat. Trunk and branches were now bare and charred, darker on the side toward the fire, good evidence that no tree could possibly have grown in that location while the fire roared.

It seemed the fire was going to tell him nothing new, however long he stared at it. By now Hal had ceased puffing, and he determined to go completely around the ring, getting a close look at it from every side—if he could manage to do so without frying himself or falling off a cliff. He had what he considered to be good reasons, going beyond his usual curiosity. This process of circumambulation proved somewhat difficult, but Hal persisted, though once or twice the irregularities of the slope brought him so close to the object of his study that he might have roasted himself some meat for dinner—had he any meat to roast. The fire was not merely some kind of magic trick, an illusion that a man might be able to pass through with impunity.

At one point he passed the head of a steep, narrow ravine that went plunging down to end exactly on one curving bank of the broad Einar River. The drop-off was so sharp it made him a little dizzy to look down. The polyphonic murmur of a chain of little waterfalls came drifting up—he had taken note of them during his climb. Their noise now blended with the soft roar of the tall flames.

The surrounding landscape was one of rocks and scattered vegetation, and was mostly unpeopled. For miles, in all the directions he could see, there were only very occasional sparks of other flame to see, the signs of settlements or farmhouses lighting up against the night.

Halfway through Hal's pilgrimage around the fire, he was taken by surprise when a certain small object in his belt pouch suddenly twitched and jumped. It felt like a tiny animal in there, but he knew that it was not alive—unless sheer magic counted as a kind of life. Opening the pouch, he pulled out a small object—which to a casual inspection gave no sign of being anything but a scrap of dirty cloth. But the bit of fabric behaved in an extraordinary way, glowing and brightening (though without fierce heat or flame) in the man's hand even as he held it out and moved it about.

When the strange fabric tugged most strongly at his fingers, Hal reached straight down into a tuft of long wild grass at his feet. The thing that now revealed itself to him was half covered by loose sand and hard to see. Hal spotted it nevertheless and picked it up—a broken fragment of yellow, heavy metal. There was enough of the thing to see that when intact, it must have been part of a crescent shape about the size of Hal's broad hand.

A groove ran halfway round one of the thing's flat sides. Holes had been punched through the groove, and one or two of those holes were still occupied by iron nails. The nails were still wedged in place, though this piece of golden semicircle had been somehow torn loose from whatever object they had once held it to. After a long look he stuffed the object into his belt pouch.

He was frowning by the time he had returned to his starting point without having discovered anything like a gate or entrance to the enclosure of flame. The only thing the circumambulation had really accomplished was to remove any lingering doubts that the fire made a complete and regular circle, almost perfect in its shape.

Obeying a sudden impulse, he bent down once again, snatched up a small stone and flung it uphill. Just before the pebble disappeared into the flames it flared incandescent, as if at that point in its flight the heat had truly been great enough to turn it molten.

Hal gloomily shook his head.

Turning his back on the fire at last, frowning more thoughtfully than ever, Hal retreated to a comfortable distance. He took a morsel of dried meat from his pouch, and stood chewing on the tough fibers while he thought things over. Had he had any fresh meat, he wouldn't have tried to cook it on this particular hearth. These flames were too obviously unnatural. He possessed no real skill in magic, but none was needed to see that. The near-perfect regularity of their ring offered good evidence, as did the fact that they showed no tendency either to grow or to diminish.

On reaching the place where he had decided to spend the night, he made his simple preparations for settling in. Winter was definitely coming on in this part of the world, but this close to the great mysterious burning a man ought to be able to stay comfortably warm. In his preliminary scouting Hal had discovered what he thought would be an ideal spot to sleep, on a small saddle of raised land almost as high as the burning crag, and separated from it by only thirty yards or so. There the generous Fates, as if feeling some concern for the weary traveler, had caused soft moss to grow upon a handy patch of soil. On this bed Hal now lay down wrapped in his cloak, shadowed by a small outcropping of rock from almost all the direct light of the untiring fire. Still, by moving his head only a little from side to side, he could see a large part of the slope to his right and left, brightly lit by the fire above. He ought to be able to get a good look at anything or anyone that appeared in the area during the night.

The traveler's peaceful rest behind the rock had not lasted much more than an hour when some subtle change in his surroundings awakened him. He came awake with the inner certainty that he was no longer quite alone. Opening his eyes, he lay for a few moments without moving, his battle-hatchet ready in his hand beneath the cloak. Nothing and no one had come very near him yet. Cautiously Hal raised his head and from his niche of wavering shadow studied the slope immediately below the flames, first on one side and then the other.

In a moment, the figure of a young man had walked into his view, no more than a moderate stone's throw away from Hal, but seemingly unaware of his presence.

The fellow was tall and active, dressed in boots, trousers, and a kind of quilted jacket, but wearing no armor except a plain steel helmet that left his almost beardless face exposed. His movements had a kind of nervous recklessness, as well as the jerkiness of deep exhaustion. At the moment he was certainly not on his guard. A short sword was sheathed at his side, and his clothes were so begrimed and tattered that it was hard to guess whether they had originally been of rich material or poor.

This newcomer's attention was entirely centered on the great fire itself, whose gentle roar went on unceasingly. The youth continued a methodical progression, as if he were intent on making his way entirely around the ring of flame, reconnoitering just as Hal had done. He even seemed to be making the same tentative efforts to approach the burning wall as closely as he could, but of course the heat kept him yards away.

Carefully the concealed watcher sat up, peering first around one side of his rock and then the other, to see more of the steep, rough cone of the hillside. He saw enough to satisfy himself that the young man, who presently reappeared, had come here quite alone. Hal rose to his feet, stretched, adjusted his cloak, seated his hatchet once more in its holster at his belt, and remembered to pick up his horned helmet from where he had set it aside when he lay down to sleep. Then, feeling as ready as could be for whatever might develop, he stepped out firmly, striding back across the little saddle of land toward the fire.

The youth's back was turned to Hal, and his attention remained entirely absorbed in the spectacular wall of flame. When Hal had come within thirty feet without being noticed, he judged it wise to halt and call out a few words of greeting.

The tall lad spun around at once, clapping a hand to the hilt of his sword. Hal was waiting open-handed, arms spread in a sign of peace; but even so he realized that his appearance, that of a powerful armed stranger, could hardly have been very reassuring.

"Who are you?" the other demanded, in a hoarse voice that quavered with some recent and excessive strain. Extreme stress and exhaustion were plain also in his young face. "What do you want?"

"No harm, lad, no harm at all." Hal kept his arms spread wide, and made the tones of his own gravelly voice as soothing as he could. "I'm a traveler, just passing through. My home's hundreds of miles to the north. I was heading that way, following the river, when I saw these flames."

After a pause, in which the other did not respond, he went on. "My first thought was that some farmhouse was burning. Then, when I had climbed halfway up these rocks, I thought maybe it was a castle or watchtower—not really farming country just along here. But now I'd be willing to bet there's no building at all inside that fire. It's a strange one, isn't it? Certainly it has to be more than natural."

"They are Loki's flames." The words seemed choked from the youth by some intense emotion. "They feed on nothing but magic. They need no fuel to keep them burning."

"I see." Hal recognized the name, but took the claim in stride. "So, the gods are involved. Can't say I'm surprised. I never saw another blaze like this one." And he shook his head on its thick neck.

The youth had turned slowly round until he had his back almost to Hal and was staring again into the multicolored, undying blaze. His lips moved slightly, as if he might be whispering a word.

The man from the far north cleared his throat. "My name is Haraldur; most call me Hal, to save themselves a little breath and effort. And who are you?"

The tall one turned slowly back. He relaxed slightly, out of sheer weariness, it seemed. His hand still rested on his sword's hilt, but as if he had forgotten it was there. "My name is Baldur," he announced in his strained voice.

"I see," Hal said again. He nodded encouragingly.

Slowly Baldur went on. "I live—I once lived—only ten miles from here." His words had a wondering tone, as if something about that statement struck him as remarkable. Presently he added: "Some of my family—my mother—still lives there."

Hal, exercising patience, grunted and nodded again. Fortune had now blessed him with a chance to talk to a native of these parts, and he didn't want to waste the opportunity. There was information he desired to have.

Baldur now gave the impression of nerving himself, gathering energy, to make some serious effort. At last he went on: "Do you see—anything—strange about me?" He spread out both his hands and turned them this way and that, presenting them for inspection. "Do I look to you like a dead man?"

Hal strolled a few steps closer, and stood with folded arms, looking the young fellow over from head to foot in the fire's clear light. After a moment he raised a couple of stubby fingers to scratch under the rim of his horned helmet.

"I have seen some strange folk here and there," the northman announced at last. "Yes, a fair number who might be described as really odd. And several others who were seriously dead. But I'd say you don't fit in either category." He held up a cautionary hand. "Mind you, I may not be the very keenest judge. I once spent several months as shipmate to a god, and never guessed who he was until he told me."

But the youth had no interest in some stranger's tales of adventure. He had the attitude of one with more than enough of his own. His cracking voice grew no easier as he said: "Three days ago, I was leading a squad of men in battle when I was cut down." Baldur reached up with large and grimy hands to his plain steel helm, and gingerly eased it off his head, revealing the fact that the steel was dented. When he bent slightly forward, his corn-yellow hair fell free, stained and caked with the reddish-brown of old dried blood. "See my wound!"

Hal grunted again, squinting in the bright, just slightly wavering firelight at the head that loomed above his own. He saw what little he could see without getting any closer. There had certainly been a copious flow of blood, but it had stopped some time ago. The wound itself was quite invisible under thick hair and clots.

The northman renewed his efforts to be soothing. "Looks nasty, all right, but maybe not so bad as it looks. Scalps do tend to bleed a lot. Anyway, you survived."

This soothing attitude was not exactly welcome. "I said I fell!" the youth choked out. Baldur's teeth were bared now in a kind of snarl. "I tell you that I died!"

"I see," replied Haraldur in a neutral voice. "If you say so. That's interesting." He resisted the urge to back away a step, compromising by shifting his stance slightly. Head wounds sometimes brought on bizarre ideas and dangerous behavior.

Baldur was still staring at him, not so much threatening now as if pleading silently for some kind of help. After a moment Hal cleared his throat and asked with polite curiosity: "What happened next? After you—as you say—died?"

"What happened?" Now there was outrage, though not directed at Hal. "When I opened my eyes, I saw that the fighting was over. A Valkyrie came flying over the battlefield to choose a hero from among the dead." The voice of the self-proclaimed dead man was turning shrill. "That is what the sworn servants of Wodan can expect, when it comes their turn to fall!"

"Ah, yes, a ride to warriors' paradise." Hal was really a stranger to this land, but some information about its gods and customs had inevitably traveled beyond its borders, enough to rouse his curiosity. Over the past few days he had been doing what he could to find out more. "So, you are a sworn servant of the god Wodan. I see. And if I remember correctly what the stories say, the Valkyries are handsome maidens, who come flying over battlefields on their magic Horses—"

"Have a care how you speak of her!" Baldur had dropped his helmet to the ground, and his right hand had gone back to his sword. His blue eyes glinted wildly in the uncanny wavering of light.

Brain damage, thought Hal again, and now he did retreat a pace. But he persisted in his quest for knowledge.

He kept his raspy voice as soft as possible. "I mean no disrespect, Baldur. Go on, tell me more. So you got knocked down, in some kind of battle, and when you woke up, there you were, lying on the ground with your head a bloody mess. Right? Then this Valkyrie arrived to carry you to Wodan's feasting hall? Isn't that how the story—isn't that what's supposed to happen?"

"Her name is Brunhild." Now the young man's voice

seemed on the verge of breaking into sobs. Whatever threat had been in him was melting swiftly. "But she rejected me!" His gaze slid away from Hal's, fell to the ground.

"Ah, but you somehow learned her name. So—"

"She chose another man instead! She would not take me to Valhalla!" In a moment Baldur's legs had folded, leaving him sitting on the ground, face buried in his hands, while his shoulders heaved. It was not an attitude Hal would have expected to see in a man who had pledged himself to a god of war. But people were always doing unexpected things.

The northman cast a swift look around him, to right and left over the curving hillside. It was only a routine precaution. As far as he could tell, he and the agitated youth were still alone.

Approaching Baldur more closely, he squatted down in front of him, taking care to stay out of easy lunging distance— just in case.

"Tell me more," repeated Hal with quiet persistence. "I find this very interesting. The lovely and respected Brunhild came to visit you when you were killed—and just the sight of her made you feel better. But then something went wrong, and you were cheated out of a trip to Wodan's glorious feasting hall."

After a pause, during which Baldur said nothing, Hal added: "Well, at least she told you her name."

Hal had to bend closer to hear the muttered answer: "I knew her name already. In spite of everything, she took another man instead!"

"So you were telling me." The northman scratched his head again, trying to make sense of it all. He wasn't sure that the effort was worthwhile—but there was the gold he had just stuffed into his belt pouch. Beings who used gold for horseshoes might well be able to contribute a little more of it, even if unknowingly, to the retirement fund of a weary but deserving adventurer. Perhaps enough to buy him a small farm. "So, who was this other man? Why did your Valkyrie choose him?"

Baldur shrugged.

"All right, it seems he's not important. How did you come to learn her name?"

No answer.

"So, where is the incomparable Brunhild now?"

A cry of agony burst from Baldur's lips, and he sprawled on the earth face down, one arm extended, pointing uphill, directly toward the wall of fire. Now he was screaming. "She is in there, surrounded by the flames, where no man may approach her!"

That was an unexpected answer. The case was only becoming more complicated. Or maybe it really was all brain damage. "She's in the flames, and not in Valhalla? But why . . . ?"

"Not *in* Loki's fire, but hidden behind it!"

"Ah."

"Wodan has bound her away from me forever, in an enchanted sleep!"

"I see," said Hal, trying to sound as if he really did. He decided to keep trying. "So Brunhild is being punished? For what offense?"

"For daring to look with favor on a mortal!" Baldur was still lying face down, talking into the grass.

"The mortal in question being not the man she actually carried to Valhalla, but—you, the one she left behind. Is that it? All right, I think I do begin to see." Now Hal grunted sympathetically.

He changed position so that his own back was to the fire, meanwhile automatically scanning his surroundings again, then sat down on the ground more comfortably. "That's too damned bad, son, too damned bad." He paused a moment before asking: "But how do you know she's in there?" He hooked a sturdy thumb over his shoulder.

"I know!"

Hal persisted. "Were you listening, watching, when Wodan passed his sentence on this girl?"

"Of course I wasn't there, in Wodan's great hall with the heroes. Brunhild cheated me of that!" The final words came out in a shriek of accusation.

"Aha," said Hal, trying to sound wise. He thought things over, shaking his head. So far there had been no mention in the story of any cache of gold, and that was where his interest lay.

But he was curious, as usual, about many things. He pulled a stem of wintry grass, and chewed on the dry fiber. "Still, I keep wondering how you *know* that she's now behind this wall of fire—did the fight, the one that you were, uh, killed in—did it take place here on this hilltop?"

"No, of course not! How could there be room for a battle here?" Shaking his aching head in exasperation, Baldur gestured at the narrow space between flames and the steep drop. "We fought in the valley, miles away."

"All right. Keep calm. Let's go over again what happened. If you don't mind, I'd like to get it all straight. You were struck down in this little battle, and then—"

"Only an hour after Brunhild abandoned me, while I still lacked strength to move from where I had fallen, a messenger from Valhalla brought me the cursed news. As a courtesy to Wodan, Loki had created a ring of fire, inside which those who offend the gods can be eternally imprisoned. Then I raised my eyes to this cliff, and saw the fire, and knew that it was true."

Having finished that speech, Baldur sat up. Now he seemed to be making a start at pulling himself together; a tough young man, Hal judged, who must have been through a few hellish days, whatever the exact truth might be of what had happened to him.

Hal knew from experience how dangerous it could be to

interfere with the gods' business. But it would not be the first time in his life he had accepted such a risk. He thought it couldn't hurt to try to learn a little more.

"What kind of messengers is the old god using these days?" When the youth did not respond to that, the northman prodded: "Maybe a black raven? Or a wolf?"

Baldur looked mildly shocked. "No such thing. Great Wodan's messengers are the Valkyries. Girls. Young women, like Brunhild herself." He paused. "I happen to know that this particular messenger's name was Alvit."

"Alvit, I see—another worthy name. Another Valkyrie you just happen to know—and how do these girls travel when they go on their errands? I've heard that they ride magic Horses through the air." Hal thought that he could feel the heavy little lump of gold in his belt pouch. "Most people in the world have never seen a horse—even the purely natural kind is something of a rare animal. But I have. Horses' feet are not like those of a cameloid or drom. They have hard hooves, and fairly often their owners fit them with metal shoes. Just nail them on. Then sometimes the shoes come loose."

But it was no use now trying to find out what Baldur might know about horseshoes and gold. The youth seemed to be drifting away again, back into his ongoing nightmare of grief and loss. He had regained his feet and was moving restlessly about.

He was mumbling now, and in his raving he kept returning to what obsessed him as a great horror and mystery: the fact that Brunhild had not counted him properly as a worthy hero among the slain, had refused to carry him away to Wodan's hall. The way in which he spoke of Brunhild strongly suggested to Hal that Baldur and the Valkyrie were or had been lovers. Which added to the mystery, of course. Now Baldur was groaning that he had lost both his beloved and his chance at glorious immortality as a member of Wodan's elite guard, one of those chosen to fight beside the Father of Battles in the final terrific conflict, the twilight of the gods at world's end.

"Tell me no more about glorious heroes, lad, no more," Hal muttered in low tones. "Down south I had my fill of them."

That evoked a twinge of interest. Baldur stopped muttering to himself and turned his head. "What do you mean?"

The older man took thought, and sighed. "Does the Golden Fleece mean anything to you? You've heard of Jason and his voyage?"

A blank look. "No."

Hal shrugged. "I thought the news might have reached these parts by now, but never mind. It's a long story. Tell me more about this fight in which, as you say, you lost your life."

He went on with his gentle but persistent questioning, and gradually Baldur disclosed more information, including the name of the lord whose army—or armed band, rather—he had been fighting in, and something of what the fight had been about.

It sounded to Hal like a simple, more or less routine battle between two local warlords. That was something he could understand, and he took this turn in the conversation as a hopeful sign.

Presently he was nodding. "Then the trouble came down to a matter of gold, didn't it? Barons, minor lords of some kind, squabbling about gold." He added, as casually as he could: "I've heard there are substantial amounts of yellow metal to be found hereabouts."

Now for the first time the youth showed even teeth in a ghost of a smile. "That may be, but those of us who live above ground have never seen much of it. The gnomes have all the gold—or they did."

"Gnomes, hey? I know very little about gnomes," Hal added truthfully. "Practically nothing, in fact. Where do they dwell?"

"Underground." Then Baldur shrugged, as if to ask *where else?* "They have their towns and villages, some of them not very many miles from here."

Hal grunted. "And you say they—the gnomes—*did* have all the precious gold—that means they've lost it somehow? Someone else has taken it away from them?"

The youth did not answer; he was swaying on his feet.

Hal stood up, reminded of his own tiredness. He'd had a long day's hike along the valley, then the ascent of a few hundred feet of steep and rugged trail. Now this. His right knee creaked as he called on it to lift his weight, and for a moment the joint threatened to be painful. Not as young as he once was; in a few more years, provided he lived that long, he would have to worry about getting old. But a poor man could not settle anywhere in comfort; a pauper would have no ease and no respect. "How long since you've slept, lad?"

"Dead men need no sleep." Baldur's voice was slurring now in utter weariness.

"But live ones do. You're no more than half dead. Come this way, I know where there's a bed of moss."

"But Brunhild . . ."

"She's probably waiting her chance to come to you in a dream. If you never sleep, how's she going to do that?"

Five minutes later, Baldur, muffled in his quilted jacket, had sunk, like a drowning man, into the deathlike slumber of exhaustion. And a minute after that, Hal, who had pledged to stay awake and watch, was wrapped in his cloak and snoring almost comfortably with his back against the rock.

It was the middle of the morning before Baldur awakened; Hal, who had been up and about a couple of hours earlier, had patiently let him sleep. Meanwhile the northman quietly chewed another morsel of his dried meat and thought things over.

When the youth did open his eyes at last, he looked and sounded more normal than he had during the night. When questioned directly on the subject of life and death, he was ready to admit that he was still alive.

"That would explain it, then," said Hal. "Why the lovely Brunhild did not choose you."

Baldur sat bolt upright, frowning, shaking his head impatiently. "No! No, you see, the Valkyries have that power, given them by Wodan, to decide the fate of warriors. She could have counted me as fairly slain. She should have done so, and then I would have gone to Valhalla." *What more could a warrior ask than that?* his tone and manner seemed to plead. Then again unutterable woe: "But she rejected me!"

Hal grunted and made vague gestures. "I wouldn't blame her for wanting to keep you alive. I'd have settled for a friend who did that. Most men would, I think."

The youth's lip curled. "True fighting men, heroes, do not fear violent death."

"That's fortunate for them, because they tend to find it early on."

Baldur's smile in response was almost that of a dying man—sweetly tolerant, expressing unbearable sadness, confronting someone who had no understanding, none at all, of his grief's tremendous cause. It was hard to tell which bothered the young man most—the tragic fate of Brunhild, or her equally tragic failure to award him a place in Wodan's glorious company. Obviously they had both been stunning blows.

But Baldur was also very young. He might indeed have tremendous cause for grief, but he soon admitted that he was also ravenously hungry. He could not remember eating anything since before the fight, which, as far as Hal could find out, had been at least two days ago.

A long drink at one of the rushing mountain streams served both men for breakfast; Hal said nothing about his own remaining private store of food. Baldur was in no danger of starving to death, and Hal had the feeling that he himself might well be needing the little that he had. Nor did he mention to his new companion the two very unusual objects that he carried in his pouch. But he did persuade Baldur to wash some of the dried gore from his head and clothing before going home—there was no use frightening his mother or anyone else to death when he appeared.

Now it was possible, in sunlight and with careful probing, to get a good look at the wound. Hal observed cheerfully that it would benefit from a few stitches; but he thought the operation could wait till the lad got home. The dented helmet was easier to fix. Using the blunt end of his hatchet, the northman pounded out the deepest part of the depression, leaving the metal almost smooth.

Turning the conversation around to the subject of Baldur's family, Hal more or less invited himself to pay them a visit. In matters not directly connected with Brunhild and Valhalla, Baldur seemed willing to be told what he ought to do next.

Together the two men set out on what Baldur said would be about a ten-mile walk to the small house where Baldur said his mother lived. He made no mention of a father. Well, in families where men took up the profession of arms, there tended to be many widows.

When they reached the place where the trail descending to the valley took a sharp turn down, Hal paused to take one more relatively close look back at the enigmatic and unchanging flames, before descending to where they would be hidden by the shoulder of the cliff. They rose as high and fierce as ever, but now in the morning sunlight were pale and relatively inconspicuous.

Baldur had paused with him. "Somehow I will find a way," the youth pledged solemnly. "A way to join her there."

Hal shrugged. "I think you're right to go home first, take it easy for a while, heal that wound. They'll all be glad to see you there. Likely they think you're dead." Then when he saw how Baldur looked at him, he regretted his choice of words.

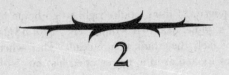

2

Turning their backs on the central valley of the Einar, the two men trudged along on the road pointed out by Baldur. It led them through a countryside of pastures, orchards, and fields, with modest farmhouses visible from time to time. The trees were barren of leaves, awaiting the coming winter, the fields lifeless under dead stubble. Hal's experienced eye could find no signs of the devastation of recent warfare.

As they walked, Baldur described his home—the modest, simple house owned by his mother, evidently a minor land-owner of some kind. Hal got the impression she was widowed, but sufficiently well-off to hire people as necessary to work the land and tend the fruit trees. Baldur spoke in wistful, nostalgic tones, as if he had already been a lifetime away from home and might never be able to go back. It sounded as if he himself had not lived there for many months, or perhaps years.

Baldur was given to long silences, and Hal had plenty of chance to guide the conversation his own way. This included the well-nigh-universal difficulties of farming and the price of land. Presently Hal had brought the talk—cunningly, he thought—to the point at which it was only natural for him to mention certain vague rumors that he had heard—that he had invented, actually. Stories of a great golden treasure hidden somewhere in this vicinity.

He might have saved himself the trouble of trying to be subtle and indirect; Baldur was too wrapped up in his own problems to give a damn for even golden treasure, and only remarked that stories of that kind were always floating around. Which was certainly true enough, in Hal's experience. It was only that he had not been here long enough to hear the local versions. Had it not been for the fragment of golden horseshoe, Hal would have already decided that the stories deserved no more credit here in the valley of the Einar than they did anywhere else.

Around midmorning, the thin road the two men had been following entered a leafless autumnal forest. Shortly afterward they came to a fork in the road. Here Baldur, looking off to their left into a roadside maze of branches, what appeared to be a neglected orchard, observed that some of the trees still held late apples. He announced his intention to make a brief detour and pick some to allay his hunger.

"Fine, lad, you do that. Bring a couple back for me." Hal, looking down the branch road to the right, was less interested right now in wizened apples than he was in information. Some fifty yards in that direction, a small group of people were standing in the middle of the road, to all appearances chatting amiably. He added: "I'll be over that way, having a word with our fellow travelers."

But he had not covered more than half the distance to the little group before he realized that he had come to the wrong place for a peaceful exchange of information. There were two men visible, one of them staying in the background, leaning casually against a fence with his arms folded, as he watched the scene in front of him. Meanwhile, near the middle of the road, a younger and somewhat smaller fellow who wore a sword stood engaged in talk with a youngish woman, who was poorly dressed and had two small children hanging on her skirts.

As Hal came close enough to hear the strained tones of the

quiet voices, and to get a good look at faces, he realized that it was less a conversation than a confrontation. This was no family squabble, but an encounter between strangers that gave every sign of threatening to turn violent.

The woman was obviously in a wretched state of fear. Her barefoot children were shivering in the almost wintry cold. A cheap-looking purse lay emptied on the ground at the man's feet, and the current point of dispute seemed to be whether she was going to be completely stripped and searched. Her feeble gesture toward a streak of color on the arm of the man who stood near her suggested that the bandit had already robbed her of a reasonably good scarf.

This fellow now turned at Hal's approach, hands casually on hips, and gave the newcomer a long look of appraisal. His greeting came in a shrill, threatening voice: "Is this any of your bloody business?"

"No." Hal's voice was quiet, and he remained as resolutely mild-mannered as a hopeful salesman. "I just had it in mind to ask some questions. Nothing personal. You can go on with your conversation. There's a strange fire on a hill back that way a few miles. I thought that if any of you people lived in this vicinity, maybe you could tell me—"

The robber was disinclined to be helpful. "Then turn your fat ass around and march back the way you came—hold on, though, not so fast. Let's see what you've got in that belt pouch before you go."

Hal shot a glance toward the fence, where the bigger man, still content to be an onlooker, was leaning as if from sheer laziness against the top course of some farmer's hard-split rails. He, too, was armed with a sword, not drawn. His gaze was penetrating, and somehow his inaction did not give the impression of any reluctance to take part in robbery. Rather his attitude suggested that he thought neither Hal nor the woman worth his trouble. He might have been a master or a teacher, observing an apprentice at his work.

As if to make up for his companion's near-indifference, the younger and slightly smaller brigand gave the impression of being more than enthusiastic enough. Now he was fairly bouncing on his toes. He seemed not in the least put off, as most people would have been, by Hal's formidable aspect. "You heard me. Let's see what you're carrying today."

Hal chucked the chin of the long-handled hatchet that rode head-uppermost at his belt, loosening the weapon in its holster. The head was of fine steel, the handle seasoned hickory. His voice was even quieter than before. "Doubtless you can tell just by looking at me that I'm really a prince from the Far East, traveling incognito."

While the other was trying to think of an answer for that, Hal added: "It is my duty, as royalty, to carry fabulous exotic treasures with me all the time. But a look at them will cost you something. Maybe an arm or a hand. Does that strike you as a good bargain?" He still sounded almost apologetic.

It was as if the young bandit had received a long-sought invitation. Something had come alight deep in his eyes. "This is your last warning, fat man. Hand over that belt pouch, or I take it from your corpse."

Hal made a soft meditative sound, and his right hand moved again toward his belt. The pouch stayed where it was, but the slender axe seemed to leap from its holster, as if with some purpose of its own. Hal's thick fingers, as practiced as a fine musician's, caught a solid grip on the low end of its shaft. In the same moment, a long knife had materialized in his left hand.

The nearer brigand had drawn his sword, and in the same moment he launched himself in a rush, yelling loudly. But the intended victim was moving incrementally forward, not back, which tended to spoil the aggressor's timing. At the last moment the attack wavered just slightly, and the clang of the bandit's sword against Hal's parrying knife seemed to vibrate with uncertainty.

For a moment, the two men were standing only a little way apart, just out of grappling range. One of Hal's stubby legs shot out straight from his hip in a hard, thrusting kick. The hard leather sole of his buskined foot struck home, and his attacker went down, bent at the middle, dropping his sword. Through the man's clenched teeth there came a shocking, frightening sound that had not been calculated to shock or frighten. He just lay there in the dusty road, eyes shut, his face now clenched like a fist, his body rocking a little back and forth, uttering the strange noise. He hardly seemed to breathe.

Meanwhile Hal had turned to face the brigand's colleague. The bigger man had advanced two paces from the fence, but then abruptly stopped when faced with the surprising end of the fight. He, too, had drawn his sword, and now he began snarling, breathing heavily, as he waved the blade. He gibbered a few words of nonsense, and his arms and fingers twitched spasmodically, offering more evidence that he was going into a berserker rage.

"I've seen that show before," Hal told him flatly. "Are you ready to dance or not? Yes or no?"

The other only growled and twitched some more. He glared, and a thin string of saliva dribbled from the corner of his contorted mouth.

"I'll take that as a 'no.'" Hal sheathed his knife, after frowning at a deep new nick on its edge. Then he looked at the hatchet in his right hand as if wondering why he had bothered to draw it. A moment later it again hung peacefully on his belt.

The woman had snatched up her emptied purse, and then with daring fingers started to unwind her good scarf from around the fallen bandit's arm—he made no move to resist, his thoughts being still fully occupied elsewhere. Hal was about to try questioning the woman about the fire when behind him sounded running feet.

He turned as Baldur came trotting up, one hand on his own

sword-hilt, still clutching a half-eaten apple in the other. He looked ready enough to offer any help that might be needed, but honestly just a little late.

The youth shifted his gaze from Hal to the man still writh-ing on the ground, and back again. "What happened?"

"Little enough." Hal shrugged.

"I thought the people here were only talking with each other!"

"They were." Hal nodded toward the man lying in the road. "But this one and I quickly got into a little wager about wealth."

"Wealth?"

"Which of us might have the most. Let's see how much he's carrying." And Hal bent to take a look. By now the fellow had almost ceased to moan. Hal judged him in the first stage of recovery—to reach the stage where purposeful movement became possible again was going to take a little while.

The man still standing in the background growled again, but fell silent when Hal looked at him. He was still holding his sword, but now the point was almost on the ground.

Baldur stood gazing uncertainly at this onlooker, while Hal continued rifling the belt pouch and pockets of his fallen foe. The harvest was disappointing, only a small handful of coins.

"I win my bet," said Hal. "He was wealthier than I." But when he straightened up, he looked disappointed, and mut-tered to himself: "Nowhere near enough to buy a farm."

Suddenly the woman, who had been hovering a few yards away, stepped forward and dared to make a claim.

Her bony finger stabbed at Hal's broad palm. "Those two coppers there are mine."

The children's eyes were staring at the northman. "Impor-tant to you, are they?" Hal rasped. "Well, take them, then."

The woman snatched up the small coins, her sharp fingers feeling like a bird pecking at his palm. Then she startled Hal by bursting out with what seemed to be a kind of thanks but sounded like an incantation. The name of the god Thor was mentioned, as were the names of Thunderer and Charioteer, which he thought might refer to the same individual. She swore that she knew him, despite his disguise. A moment later the woman had seized Hal's hand and was kissing it. Her last words were: "The common folk will know you, and you will have our worship, always!"

Then she was gone, almost trotting at an impressive speed, her children scampering on bare feet to keep up with her.

Hal could only stare after her in wonderment. "What in all the hells did she mean by that?" he asked the world at large.

Baldur might have offered an opinion, but his attention had been drawn elsewhere. Now he nudged Hal with an elbow and cautioned in a low voice: "That one by the fence shows signs of being a berserker."

Hal looked that way again, then shook his head. "Not he, not any time soon. Or I'd still be running. The same goes for his comrade here on the deck." He hesitated. "You said you'd pledged yourself to Wodan. But you've never seen the real thing, have you?"

For a moment Baldur seemed poised to dispute the point, but then he shook his head. "A true berserk in action? No, maybe I haven't. But I *have*"—he hesitated—"have met some of Wodan's true servants. And they have very little in common with this one you flattened." The last words were uttered with contempt. The man who lay on the ground had ceased to moan, and it looked like he might soon be ready to attempt to stand.

"That far I can agree with you, lad. But I think you mean that Wodan's men are somehow on a higher level, and the truth is that they're worse. Now, which way to your mother's house? Think she could spare me a peaceful cup of tea?"

Again Baldur seemed on the point of arguing, but then he caught sight of something that made him nudge Hal again and point away along the road, in the opposite direction to that taken by the fugitives. "Look what's coming now."

About a hundred yards down the road ahead of them, a group of about a dozen men had come into view, approaching at a deliberate pace. All but one were walking, and all seemed heavily armed; a few wore scraps of armor. One man, near the center of the group and clad in furs, was riding on a cameloid. Hal thought he could see that the rider's body was twisted and deformed in some way.

The man by the fence had seen the approaching band, and the sight seemed to meet with his approval.

"Trouble," Hal muttered.

"Probably not." Baldur pitched what was left of his apple away. He sounded more annoyed than worried. "I know those men—more or less. Some of them. They're not likely to do any fighting unless they're paid for it."

"If you say so."

As the approaching band drew nearer, it became obvious that he who rode in their midst was the leader, and this despite some evident physical handicaps. The others kept looking to him as if seeking approval or direction. He was missing an arm and an eye, and what remained of his body seemed somehow twisted under the furs. Hal judged he might be around sixty years old.

This fellow came riding slowly up on his cameloid, and with a few harsh words called his crew to heel, when some of them began to take a challenging attitude toward Hal. Others were already jeering at the fallen bandit, whose situation they seemed to find amusing.

But Hal paid little attention to any except the twisted leader. The man wore an array of weapons on bandolier and belt, and his clothes appeared to be mostly furs and leather.

Between Baldur and the crippled man in the saddle there passed a brief look suggesting that they knew each other; but at the moment neither had anything to say.

Hal was the subject of many appraising looks; he was relieved to see that at least some of the others who came walking and riding with their chief were well satisfied, considerably amused, to see the robber who had been more ambitious now stretched out on the ground. They recognized Hal's victim, but gave him no respect.

Ī am called Hagan the Berserk," the twisted man announced at last. His voice was low and gravelly, much like Hal's. But generally slower, as if every word were being carefully thought out. Seen at close range, he was younger than Hal had first thought, maybe even less than fifty. But whatever the number of his years, they had all been very tough.

At the moment the man who claimed the title of Berserk looked anything but frenzied, but the northman had no intention of expressing any doubts. "My name is Haraldur."

As Hagan dismounted, Hal could see that the cameloid had been fitted with a special saddle to accommodate his rider's disability.

Standing on the ground, the leader was shorter than he had appeared to be when mounted. Now it was more obvious that his spine was far from straight. His one arm was long and powerful, and the forearm below a short fur sleeve, and his hand with which he gripped a crutch, were marked with old wounds, like his face and head.

In fact Hagan's face was hideously scarred, and Hal watching him soon got the impression that he took a kind of perverse joy or pride in shocking and frightening people with his appearance. There was no patch over his empty eye socket.

Even as Hal watched him now, a kind of spasm, evidently painful, rippled through his body. Now Hal could see that one of the man's legs was also twisted, like his torso. The defect made him lurch when he moved, though his movement did not lack speed. The crutch had a hard, almost spearlike point, which looked as if it might punch holes in a wooden floor.

After taking one look at Baldur, who stared back blankly, the bent one turned swiftly to Hal and regarded him in silence.

At last the northman broke the silence. His voice was not quite as easy as before. "My name is Haraldur. Some call me Hal, to save breath."

"Haraldur," said Hagan thoughtfully. "That's a northman's name. You've come a long way from home."

"I was born in the far north. But I have spent some years traveling round the Great Sea."

"Ah." Hagan nodded. He appeared to be listening attentively. Then he shot an unexpected question. "Do you know Theseus?"

Hal blinked. "The famed sea-rover? Only by name, and reputation. Most people think he is a pirate."

The bent man nodded slowly, managing to convey the impression that he approved of piracy in general. "How about Jason?"

"He was my captain on my last voyage."

Hagan's one eye squinted. "Expect me to believe that?"

"Or not, as you choose."

The twisted man was nodding slowly. It seemed that he was choosing to believe, and that Hal's stock had just gone sharply up. Hagan's voice had a new tone, bordering on respectful, when he asked: "Then you were one of the forty Heroes Jason took with him to hunt the Golden Fleece?"

"There were about that number of us rowing the *Argo*, that much is true. As for our being Heroes . . ." Hal let it trail away. "No one else in these parts seems to have heard of us. I'm a little surprised that you have."

Hagan seemed to take pride in his knowledge. "I have my

sources." He took another long assessing look at Hal, as if confirming his decision to believe him.

When one or two of Hagan's followers showed signs of wanting to test Hal, Hagan with a look and a growl caused them to restrain their aggression. Then, in a surprisingly mild and reasonable voice, he allowed as how he had been favorably impressed by what he had seen, at a distance, of Hal's behavior.

Baldur spoke to the twisted man at last, asking a question. "A member of your band?" With a nod of his head the youth indicated the man who had now stopped writhing on the ground, and was thinking about trying to sit up.

Hagan's tone changed to one of savage contempt. "To join me was his ambition. His and this other's." The man who had been standing near the fence had not come forward to declare himself a member of the band by blending in with it, as Hal had been more than half expecting. Instead the fellow now seemed to be trying to turn himself invisible. Somehow he had translated his body to the far side of the fence, and was edging away into a barren winter hedgerow.

The twisted man was taking no notice of his departure. "But I would not have them," he went on. "I want no play-actors in my company."

Swinging his weight on his crutch and twisted leg, he brought himself a half step closer to Hal. With a new eagerness in his voice, he asked: "You will have seen the real thing? How men behave when the Father of Battles takes possession of their souls and bodies?"

"I have seen them, true Berserks," Hal replied. He was trying to conceal the fact that it cost him an effort to keep looking into the bottomless blackness of Hagan's single eye.

Now the bent man asked, in his urgent voice: "What of yourself, Haraldur? What is your ambition? Have you ever heard Wodan's call?"

Slowly Hal shook his head. "I have seen how others walk

that road, and it is not for me. But let each man choose for himself."

Hagan stared at him a moment longer, then turned his one-eyed stare away. "Well spoken, northman. Great Wodan's way is not for everyone."

Hal felt some of the tension go out of his muscles. Meanwhile the gnarled man glanced with contempt at the figure still sitting in the road. The apprentice bandit's agony had receded to the point where he was now making an effort to get up, glaring about him in his fear and pain and rage. But the only response he got was laughter, from some of Hagan's followers.

In his misery and humiliation the defeated bandit found his voice. "I'll see you again, fat man. I promise you."

Hagan continued to ignore the fellow. "Maybe you can see, northman, how matters stand with me. It is my part to serve in this world for a time yet. When the time comes, I will climb the mountains to Valhalla and join my master there." He turned to give his men a narrow-eyed look of appraisal. "As for now, I have some good lads here," he proclaimed modestly.

"I can see that," said Hal, honestly enough. Looking at the crew the bent man had assembled, he thought that if he himself were going in for banditry he could probably not expect to do much better. Somehow Hal got the impression that they were all fiercely dedicated to serving their master. The least formidable among them looked somehow tougher than the robber he had just beaten. Crippled as Hagan was, he seemed to exert an intangible attraction that could make men want to follow. Hal in his time had known a few others with the same power, and now he himself could feel the tug, though inwardly he recoiled from it as from the taste of some seductive and deadly poison.

"Have you seen Loki's big fire on the hilltop, northman?"

"I have. And it is certainly a wonder."

"You've looked at it closely?"

"Close as I could. Climbed the hill and got within a few yards of it. It warmed me up, but told me nothing. Except that it is more than natural, and I could see that from a distance."

The bent man, who had been listening carefully, now squinted in that direction. "I would like to get a closer look myself. I wonder if a cameloid can climb that hill?"

"The path I found went up a trifle steep for that."

Someone said how long the supernatural fire had been on the hill—it had appeared within an hour or so after the fight in which Baldur had been hurt.

Now Hagan seemed to lose the thread of his discourse. He set aside his crutch and stood rubbing his head, first on one side then the other. At last he said: "Ever since the last time my head was hurt . . . there is a certain god who visits me, now and again . . . did I tell you that?"

"I hope his visits do you some good," Hal told him. "Whoever he may be."

Presently Hagan called his troop together and marched them off, saying he had heard of a local warlord who might want to hire them.

Hal and Baldur watched them go. When the two of them were alone again, Hal remarked: "You and Hagan seemed to know each other."

"We have met before."

"I see."

"He has those spasms . . . in his spine and elsewhere, and sometimes they leave him helpless for minutes at a time."

Hal nodded. "I have seen such things before, the aftermath of head wounds."

"That may be the cause. Or maybe it is a visit from a god. I only know that when it happens, his men seem as afraid of him as ever, perhaps ever more so."

"You seem to know him fairly well."

But Baldur had nothing more to say on that subject. They had walked another hundred yards or so before he began: "Hal, when we reach my mother's house . . ."

"Yes?"

"The people there will naturally want to know what has happened to me."

"Naturally."

"Of course they will see that I have been fighting—this blood on my clothing—and I will tell them about that."

"I suppose they'll be interested."

"But I think it will be better if you say nothing—especially to my mother—about Valkyries."

"I won't if you don't."

They walked on, through a countryside that seemed as peaceful as before.

3

The home of Baldur's mother proved to be a good match for his description. The house was solidly built of timber, though by no means a fortress, and well kept, pleasantly enough sited on a small rise of ground. As Hal drew near, he thought the building must be roomier than his first look had suggested. It had a sharply peaked roof, suggesting that the local climate could produce heavy snows, and was backed up by a few small outbuildings and a sizable barn. Nearby were open fields, now lying fallow with the onset of winter, with leafless woods at a distance in every direction.

Hal took note of a modest stream meandering at the foot of a slope some yards behind the barn. Looking a couple of hundred yards downstream, he could make out, among scattered trees, a few more buildings at what looked like the edge of an ordinary small village.

Dogs erupted out of the farmyard behind the cottage, at first barking a furious challenge, then changing tone to welcome as soon as they caught Baldur's scent. It had been a long time since Hal had seen so many dogs in one place, and he would have commented on the fact, but it was useless to try to talk with all the racket.

In response to the uproar, people of all ages and both sexes, some twelve or fifteen of them in all, began to emerge from the house and several of the buildings in the rear. Children came running in the lead, and Hal took note of the fact that there seemed to be no men of prime fighting age on hand.

The last to emerge from the house, moving very slowly, was one very old man, leaning on a cane.

There was no doubt which of the women was Baldur's mother, from her attitude and the change in her expression when she saw him standing there alive. She enfolded Baldur in a hug that came near lifting him off his feet. In a harsh voice she cried out: "I thought I had lost you too!"

She was a spare and careworn woman, though well-enough dressed, and in general rather prosperous-looking, wearing a couple of items of silver jewelry.

Baldur looked vaguely embarrassed by this attention. Repeatedly he reassured everyone that despite all the dried blood on his clothes, he was not really hurt. Only a scratch, that was all.

Hal was shaking his head. "And there are those," he murmured to himself, "who scoff at the idea of resurrection!"

Baldur's introduction of his traveling companion was brief and to the point: "This is Hal. We met on the road, and he has been of some help to me. He'll stay with us tonight, and maybe longer."

Moments later food and drink were being pressed into Hal's hands, and he was led into the house and offered a place to sit. The names of a dozen of Baldur's relatives were thrust upon him. He thought he might remember one or two, those of the younger and better-looking women. On entering the house he put aside his helmet, and as a sign of peace, his hickory-handled axe, as soon as he could find a proper place to stand it against the wall, where it was not hidden but out of the way. He was careful to retain his belt pouch, and incidentally his dagger—possibly the latter could be useful when it came time to eat.

Hal was heartily welcomed as Baldur's friend, but Baldur himself remained the center of attention. Now some members of the family were eagerly volunteering that they had heard, from other participants in the recent skirmish, that he, Baldur, was dead. Either some member of the family had already gone looking for his body, or someone had been about to go—Hal couldn't quite determine which. No one here had seen any trace of Baldur, living or dead, for months, but apparently that was not really unusual, so the family had continued to nurse strong hopes for his survival.

The names of several absent men were mentioned, and Hal gathered that they were all close friends or relatives currently engaged in various military operations, though not all in the service of the same lord.

Baldur kept trying to change the subject away from war and casualties, and eventually succeeded, though the change was only slight. "Hal and I met Hagan and some of his people on the road. I said hello to him, but not much else."

That diverted everyone's attention, and brought on a brief silence. All the people in the room seemed to know who Hagan was, but no one wanted to talk about him—not just now, anyway. Very soon the focus of attention shifted back to Hal.

The great joy felt by Baldur's mother at his return, almost from the dead, was shared to a greater or less degree by all the other members of the household.

Several people had brought Hal refreshment of various kinds, but only one remained to sit beside him on the bench. This was Matilda, some kind of cousin to Baldur, perhaps five years younger than Hal, and moderately attractive. A little on the plump side, but brisk and active.

Meanwhile several children were also being introduced as either Baldur's cousins or his orphaned nephews and nieces. Hal lost track of which was which. Two half-grown boys, in particular, Holah and Noden, though shy about actual conversation, were studying the scarred and well-traveled stranger with great interest. They seemed to find Hal's axe even more fascinating than its owner, though so far neither boy had offered to approach closer than ten feet to where the weapon stood resting in a corner.

Half an hour after Baldur's coming home with his new friend, preparations for a feast of celebration were well under way. Hal undertook a visit to the privy, which proved to be about where he expected to find it, buried behind the house in a discreet clump of small evergreens. On the way, he paused in several places to take a better look at Baldur's mother's establishment.

Taking inventory as he strolled along, he observed that the house was considerably bigger than it had looked when he first saw it from the road. Farther back, almost hidden from view, were several shanties that he supposed housed workers on the land and in the house.

One of these in particular, almost behind the small barn, suggested in the shape of its large chimney and general configuration that someone in the family was, or had once been, a blacksmith. The smithy had a disused look about it now.

On his way back to the house, along a path that must be flower-girt in summer, Hal encountered Matilda again. She seemed to be waiting for him, and was making no pretense of doing anything else. He noted that there were now ribbons on her dress and some late-blooming flowers in her hair.

She was obviously not given to blushing and stammering when she had something to say. "You've got the beginnings of a limp there, don't you? My late husband walked that way before he died. That's right, I'm a widow these two years. Childless, too. Some say I'll never marry again, being too sharp-tongued to attract a worthy husband, and too hard to please to accept a lesser one."

Hal framed his answer carefully, considering every word before he spoke. "And what do you say when they say that, Matilda?"

"I say they're wrong. I'm not impossibly hard to please."

"I see. Well, people who know me say I am."

"One more thing I must tell you, Haraldur. Ten days ago I had a sign from the gods, telling me that a stranger would soon arrive at this house, whom I must get to know."

"It's remarkable how those things work, sometimes," Hal acknowledged diplomatically.

By now they were strolling together back toward the house. Matilda had not yet taken Hal's arm, but he was expecting the gesture at any moment. She took the opportunity to point out that she owned some nearby farmland in her own name.

Now they were passing the disused building that had once been a working smithy. Matilda saw where Hal was looking.

"I don't suppose you are a smith, or armorer? Too bad. The man who worked there once made fine weapons. Before he felt the call of Wodan," Matilda added.

Before Hal could craft a good response, she was changing the subject, pointing at something far on the other side of the house. "The land up to that ridge and over it is mine, almost as much of it on the far side as you can see on this; I have clear title by inheritance. Good soil, too. By now the harvest's in, of course, or you could see how fine was this year's crop."

"Then you are a fortunate woman."

"That's as may be. My husband's dying was a grievous stroke, but I have my health, and independence."

Hal murmured vague congratulations.

Having explained herself with apparent candor, Matilda was not shy about offering an appraisal of her listener: "I like a man who's old enough to know his way around in the world. Not so old, of course, that his joints and his wind and maybe other powers are failing him."

Hal looked appropriately grim. "I fear I'm practically at that stage."

She ignored the discouraging admission. "And what do you do? Here I talk on and on, and give you no chance to say a thing about yourself. You're not a blacksmith. Are you a farmer?"

He shook his head. "Never been wealthy enough to own a farm. Why, do I look like one?"

Matilda sighed. "You know well enough what you look like. I was just trying to be polite. As if I couldn't see what . . . but you're close enough to some farmers I've known, who were not exactly gentlemen either. You might be one."

"If you mean I might become a farmer, I suppose that's possible. If you mean I might be a gentleman . . ." He shook his head.

Matilda continued to be selective in what she chose to hear. She eyed his arms and face. "I see a few scars here and there, but you're still strong enough for honest work. No disabilities?"

Hal sighed in turn. "None in particular. Except a lack of opportunity for certain forms of exercise. How about you?"

The celebratory dinner was substantial, the long table in the biggest room of the farmhouse crowded with almost twenty people. It was obvious that several neighbors had dropped in. For the first time in many days, Hal truly had his fill of food and drink.

That evening, when some of Baldur's family asked the young man what he meant to do with his life now that he had survived such a close call in battle, he disappointed some and intrigued others by telling them that he meant to find or fight his way to the side of Brunhild.

His mother looked up sharply. "Who?"

"There is a girl, mother. Her name is Brunhild. And she is very important to me. Somehow I will find a way to be with her again, dead or alive."

It was clear from his mother's face that that was not the answer she had been hoping for.

Judging from the silence round the table, and the looks on people's faces, this was the first any of Baldur's family had heard of his affair with a Valkyrie.

It was the very old man with the cane who asked: "Who is Brunhild? What is her family like, and where is she? Is she in some kind of trouble, that Baldur says he will be with her dead or alive?"

As if realizing that he had already said too much, Baldur shut his mouth and refused to utter another word about Brunhild. When it became obvious that Baldur was determined to say no more on the subject, people began to turn to Hal, as if they expected him to come up with some further explanation. He tried to return a look indicating that he had nothing of the kind to offer.

"Not some kind of camp-follower, I hope." That was Matilda's remark, obviously intended as a question.

Hal grunted. Now Baldur's mother, hovering near, wondered aloud if this Brunhild could possibly be from a good respectable family.

Feeling that he had to say something or be taken for an idiot, Hal finally got out: "It's definitely my impression that she is." He could indeed recall Baldur saying something about only the daughters of the nobility being chosen for such exalted roles in Wodan's service.

Matilda pounced. "You know her, then?"

Now the guest regretted opening his mouth on the subject at all. "Never met the girl myself. Baldur's mentioned her name a few times."

By evening, a chill drizzle had set in, and Hal congratulated himself on being snug inside, not seeking some crude shelter on the road.

Not that he or Baldur were in the house. What had once been Baldur's sleeping room as a son of the household had long since been reassigned, since he was almost never home. The rain was drumming harder on the roof of the shed, a small and inelegant but comfortable shelter he and Baldur had been assigned to share. The only fundamental really lacking was a fire, but there wasn't going to be a fire in here, not with all this hay.

As if the subject of fire were on his mind, the youth was groaning to Hal that he, Baldur, should have forced himself through Loki's flames when he had the chance, whatever the cost.

"That's a crazy idea." Hal was keeping his voice low. "Your Hildy wouldn't be pleased to have a great lump of fried sausage fall into her lap. And that's what you'd be when you got through that fire. Not that I think you could get through it at all. Anyway, I say it again, you don't really know that she's in there."

"I know." Baldur was calm, resigned.

"You do? How could anyone put anyone in there, with-out—well—how is it physically possible?"

"You mean to pass through Loki's flames and not be burned?" Baldur shook his head dismissively. "I've seen that done, with my own eyes."

Here was revelation. Hal demanded further details.

Baldur tried to brush his questions aside. "I tell you I have seen it done, by a mere mortal human, never mind how."

"How?" Hal promptly insisted. He waited what seemed to him a decent interval, three or four breaths, then prodded again. "Lad, if she's really stuck up there behind that wall of magic flame, better forget about her. You've seen that fire up close, and so have I. No one's going to get through it." Even as he spoke, he supposed the rain might well be pounding down on Loki's flames, but he doubted it was having the least effect on them.

Baldur's confidence was unshaken. "Someone *can* pass through without harm," he repeated finally. "For the last time, I've seen it done."

"Oh? If you want me to believe that, tell me who and when. And especially how."

After briefly hesitating, Baldur gave in. "I suppose there's no reason I can't tell you. It was another of the Valkyries, on her Horse—I saw them disappear right into the flames, and a minute later emerge again, to tell me the fate of her sister, Brunhild. When she came out, Alvit—her name is Alvit—she told me it was the Horse, and especially the Horse's magic shoes, that made the passage possible. And I saw that she had taken no harm. Not a hair on her head was scorched."

"And when was this?"

"Only a few hours before you and I met, up there on the crag."

Once having got started, the young man was ready to talk on and on. Within a few minutes he was telling Hal that now, seeing no purpose or value in his life apart from the effort to reach Brunhild, he, Baldur, had almost made up his mind to becoming a berserker himself, and prove his devotion to Wodan by achieving a glorious death on the field of battle.

"Why?" Hal asked.

"Why?" Baldur looked at him as if he suspected an attempt at wit. "Because that is the only way a man can ever be truly certain of getting into Wodan's hall."

Hal yawned, reached out a hand to pat and shape the pile of hay behind him. He was looking forward to tonight's soft bed. "Wait a minute. Brunhild's not there, is she? I thought the only object you now had in life was just to reach Brunhild."

"But it's the same thing! You see, Hal, once I am there in Wodan's hall, standing in the presence of the god of warriors, the Father of Battles, I will beseech the All-Highest to set her free."

This seemed to have the makings of an interesting story, anyway. "You think Wodan would do that?"

Baldur stood up from where he had been sitting in the hay. "For a man who stands high in the ranks of Wodan's heroes, anything is possible. Yes, I hope and believe that the god of warriors would grant me that favor. But if he refused, then I would plead to be allowed to join Brunhild. To share her fate, whatever it might be."

The young man remained standing, with one arm raised, as if listening for an answer from above. There was only distant thunder and the sound of the cold rain testing the solid roof.

"I think you mean that," Hal muttered at last, shaking his head. "At this moment you are really convinced that getting yourself cut to bits in some damn fool fight would be a good way to reach your goals in life."

Baldur, sitting down again, gave him his haughty, stubborn look. "Of course I mean it. Were I to die in true berserker fashion, fighting against a dozen men or so . . ." He nodded, as if in private satisfaction.

"Hah!" Hal lay back in comfortable hay, pulling his cloak about him. "Were you to die in true berserker fashion, you'd be mincemeat when you finally fell. The dogs wouldn't want you, let alone your lover. And if Brunhild wouldn't carry you to Wodan the last time you got knocked down, what makes you think another Valkyrie would?"

Baldur didn't want to hear such quibbling. He rolled over in the hay, turning his back. Finally his murmur reached Hal's ears: "I am ready to join Hagan's band."

Hal grunted. "I didn't hear him ask you."

Baldur had the last word, sleepily: "You know, he is my father."

4

On the second evening of Hal's visit, he joined the family group round the hearth in the chill evening. The central hall of the house, heated by two fireplaces, was big enough for quite a gathering. The drizzling rain had stopped, but the sky was still a clammy gray, and a chill wind suggested that the first snow of the season could not be far off.

In conversation, he gradually revealed a little more about himself. Baldur's sisters and his aunt had a way of getting a man to talk without seeming to ask probing questions. The small group included the very old grandfather, who smiled encouragingly but had very little to say.

Hal told his listeners that he had spent the last several years in the far south, round the shores of the Great Sea.

Now and then one of the younger members of the family, reassured by Hal's mild and courteous manners, tried tentatively to press him to tell his stories. The two half-grown boys, Holah and Noden, especially were keen in their expectation of tales of adventure from one who had spent years of his life voyaging round the mysterious and legendary Great Sea. Hal had told them a couple of stories, but the more he talked the more they wanted to hear.

The boys by now were growing gradually a little bolder in their questioning. And it was plain they were still fascinated by the battle-hatchet, though neither of them had ventured to lay a hand on it. Probably they had learned in early childhood that men tended to be touchy about their weapons.

Now Noden pointed at the axe, still standing exactly where Hal had put it on his arrival. "I bet this has seen some fighting, Hal!"

Holah chimed in. "Can you throw it, Hal? Stick it in a target?"

"Has it got a name? I've heard that all gods and famous warriors name their weapons!"

Hal only looked at the youngsters morosely, and they fell silent. One of the elders, who had been half-listening, routinely cautioned the boys to mind their manners, not to pry.

Suddenly Hal couldn't remember whether or not the lads were orphans. Some of the children, maybe a majority, in the extended household were, but he had got the various names mixed up in his mind. Battle-orphans generally want to avenge their fathers, bereaved siblings their older brothers; so it has always been, and so it will be. Hal told them that he had to think about it before discussing such serious matters.

When one of the sisters asked him if he had ever met true royalty, he said: "I have seen enough of kings—and of princes and princesses, as well."

"You really have known such people, then?"

He hesitated, then shrugged. "Here and there."

The night was growing late, the fire was beginning to die down, but it was still warm in the snug house. Now Matilda had joined them, but for once she had little to say.

And Hal, responding to another question: "Yes, since you ask me, I was with Jason. But then I decided . . ." Gazing into the distance, he let his words die away.

"Decided what?" Matilda was all in favor of plain talk. Secrets were a sign of something wrong.

That I did not want to be a Hero any longer, caught up in endless games of blood and magic, gold, and power. Games in which I played with some of the high gods themselves and with the human rulers of the earth. Oh, playing for such high stakes can be great sport. Or so it seemed to me. And the very fact of danger has its own fascination. But in the end even the great prizes meant very little.

How could a man hope to find the words to explain things like that? To Matilda, whose mind was in her farmland. And why should he want to try?

"That I wanted to go home," he finally answered.

He wasn't sure if anyone believed him when he said that. Soon someone asked: "Maybe you can tell us, Hal: did Jason really bring home the Golden Fleece? And then it somehow disappeared? That's what we heard a month ago, from travelers passing through."

"I have heard much the same story myself," was his short answer.

"But you were there. You must have seen what happened?"

"There was a great deal of confusion toward the end."

He had not actually told anyone yet that he was even now carrying with him the muddy remnant of the miracle that had once been called the Golden Fleece.

Yes, he had wanted to see his home again. But he had known all along that the home he had left as a boy would not be there when he got back to it, that the people and things that he remembered could no longer exist as he remembered them.

He had been trudging along through the valley of the Einar, on his way home, contemplating how fierce the winter would be just now, up there in the country where he had been born. A great difference from the summery lands in which he had spent the last few years. When he had looked up to catch his first glimpse of Loki's fire on the high crag, it had seemed for a moment like a summons, a beacon of some kind, meant for his eyes in some special way.

"I suppose you'll have people at home, waiting. They'll be

glad to see you when you get back." Matilda was at last getting into the discussion.

It took Hal a little while to answer. "If they recognize me at all," he said at last. "They'll look at me and tell me I've been gone a long time. And they'll be right." A few faces came and went in memory. Not, he thought, that anyone up there in the north could really be waiting for him now. Not any longer, not after all the years he'd been away. The young girls he remembered would be raising girls and boys of their own by now, and starting to lose their teeth. By the balls and the beard of Zeus, some of them would probably be grandmothers!

That idea had never occurred to Hal before, and now for some reason it shook him deeply. Had a long time spent in those warm climates made him soft?

He knew he was not handsome, that most people found his appearance more frightening than heroic. Baldur had been telling everyone how neatly Hal had disposed of one bandit and faced down another, and the story had done Hal no harm in the eyes of anyone in this house. He could see in the faces of Baldur's family that in general they were all still a little afraid of him—but he could see also that men who caused fear were by no means a novelty in this household.

Other people had retired, rather suddenly, so that before Hal knew it, he and Matilda were sitting alone together by the fading fire.

She had brought some kind of sewing project with her, and her fingers were keeping busy. She said to the fire: "I could see myself marrying a farmer, if he was ready to settle down and work some good land. But never a fighting man again."

Hal had nothing to say to that. Presently he got up and went to find his bed in the soft hay.

Part of Hal's long journey toward home had been accomplished without too much effort, riding a succession of riverboats. Part of it he had endured jolting along in a cart behind a drom, and much had been spent on foot. It had been quite a change from the long voyage with Jason, months of steamy sunburned drudgery at the oar, enlivened with occasional hours of extreme peril. And for Hal the aftermath of the great quest had been greatly disappointing, despite the fact (or maybe because of it) that he had been spending time in the company of gods and kings and princesses and Heroes.

Leaving that all behind him, he had abandoned whatever hope he might once have held of achieving a glorious success in the world. Instead he had conceived what had seemed a much more modest plan, that of accumulating enough gold to perhaps buy a sizable farm in his own country. Maybe a farm, or maybe a couple of stout new fishing boats. With that kind of security, a man could settle down and marry.

One trouble with his plan of retiring to a small farm, as he was beginning to discover, was that unless some unusual opportunity came along, the modest success seemed no more attainable than the great one.

And now there was opportunity, in the form of Matilda, her generous body and her farmland. Practically inviting him to plow and plant them both. And what was really wrong with Matilda, if he really wanted to settle down? If she imagined she heard messages from the gods, she was still far less crazy than many another woman that he'd known.

This wasn't home, of course. But then he was far from sure that he any longer had a home, or that he really wanted to find out if he did.

What was the price of northern land this year? he wondered. Maybe eight or ten acres, in one of the good, rich valleys. And what about the price of boats? How many golden horseshoes would it take to establish himself on a substantial farm? More than one, he would be willing to wager. He thought he would begin to feel comfortable if he had four or five such lumps of yellow metal. To be sure, make it half a dozen.

Having survived the long ordeal of Jason's Argosy, and what came after it, Haraldur had started to be tempted by the thought of starting a new life for himself while he was still young enough to raise a family.

Maybe he was being too pessimistic about the costs, and the golden horseshoe fragment already in his pouch might be in itself enough to make him an owner of substantial property when he got home. Maybe. But more likely not.

He had the feeling that more, much more, might be almost within his grasp now, if he were bold enough to take it. Why not try to gather in the wealth of a dozen horseshoes, or a score? After all, there would be nothing *wrong* with owning two or three big farms and a fleet of boats.

The fact that the thing in his pouch was so laden with heavy magic made him mistrust even the permanence of its common value.

And again, as he sat talking: "But it all comes down to having some modest measure of wealth, enough to do all these nice peaceful things." As he spoke, his eyes met those of the old man sitting across from him, and it seemed to Hal that a kind of understanding passed between them.

In fact it was Baldur's old grandfather, somewhat hard of hearing, who roused Hal from contemplation by asking him: "It's gold, aye?"

"Beg pardon, grandsire?"

"It's gold, I say, that you're concerned about."

Hal had to agree. "Gold is a thing of constant interest, yes. To a man who must try to plan his future. A subject of which few people ever tire."

The oldster slapped a lean hand familiarly on Hal's knee. "Aye, it's always the yellow heavy metal, isn't it? You can understand that, northman, I can see it in your eyes. Jewels can give wealth too, but gold is more than simply wealth. It's light, and life, and warmth. The softness and the beauty, and the glow. The light in sparkling jewels is much too sharp."

And it was practical Matilda, coming in on the end of the conversation, who asked: "Easy enough to say it would be a good idea to have some gold. But how do you propose to get it?"

Hal closed his eyes. He could imagine himself showing his interlocutor what was left of the small scrap of peculiar fabric he had been carrying with him for some months. Pulling it out of his belt pouch, and holding it out.

He could readily imagine what the person he was talking to would say: "Where'd you get that rag? It doesn't look like much."

He saw himself offering it on the palm of his broad hand. "This is gold too, or it once was. Ever hear of the Golden Fleece?"

"It is important magic, then."

"Important, and also exceedingly strange. When I first saw this, it was much larger, and such power as it possessed was of a totally different kind." How could he make a very long story short? Only by throwing most of the story away. "It has—changed, since it came into my hands. First, it is very much diminished. Secondly, it has developed a new power, which astonished me the first time I saw it."

"What power is that? A useful one?"

"A simple one, and tempting. As for useful . . . maybe 'dangerous' would be a better word. Now it shows me whenever gold is near." And it was easy to perform a demonstration on a small golden ornament.

He might of course have told a glorious story, all of it true. Something about how he had picked the little patch of fabric out of the mud of a certain southern beach, on the shore of the Great Sea. The remnant had been lying there ignored, forgotten, after people had died to bring it to that place.

"It was dull and dirty even then. But it was not always so."

"No?"

"No."

And that was all. Hal found that he had suddenly lost his taste for telling stories, even in his imagination.

In real words, Hal questioned Baldur: "Haven't I heard somewhere that the god himself rides on an eight-legged horse?"

"Yes. Or he rides behind one, rather; Sleipnir is the creature's name, and it pulls his chariot."

"You've seen such an animal yourself?"

"No, nor have I ever seen Wodan. But it is true nevertheless." Baldur was firm in his belief, as only those who have not seen can be firm.

After another half-minute had gone by he went on: "I have been thinking, Hal, about the Horses."

"The magic ones, you mean, that the Valkyries ride on? Yes, they seem worth thinking about." *Especially their golden shoes.*

"If one of them can carry a woman in through the flames, to Brunhild's side—why could one not carry me?"

"Oh, we're back on that again?" Hal was about to tell the youth to forget about any crazy plan he might be thinking up for rescuing his girlfriend, or at least paying her a visit. But the golden shoes were still in his mind, and he could not let the subject go.

Yes, Baldur assured him, Alvit had been very clear about the shoes. Even ordinary horses, which were in common use in some parts of the world, wore smooth, curving bands of metal, nailed right on their hooves. "The Horse's hoof, you see, has no more sense of pain than do our hair or fingernails."

"I see." Hal made his expression innocent of knowledge, willing to be instructed.

Baldur was musing. "And in the case of the mounts Valkyries ride, the metal is definitely gold."

Hal had already made sure of that for himself. Delicately, carefully, and in deep secrecy, scratching his secret fragment of a shoe with his dagger's point. He had weighed its heaviness in his hand, assured himself that it was true gold.

Baldur now began quietly and eagerly to explain the plan he had been devising, which involved borrowing at least one Horse from Wodan's stables. Hal's first impression was that it was the kind of scheme hatched by men who had been hit too often on the head.

No one in his right mind would use soft lovely gold to make a mundane horseshoe, and see the precious metal quickly worn away to nothing on hard ground. But gold with a suitable alloy of magic, now—that could be a very different matter.

Hal didn't want to sound too easily convinced. "It strikes me that golden horseshoes would wear out very quickly."

"Not on the feet of a Horse who does most of his running in the air. And of course it isn't just plain ordinary gold, it must be imbued with magic."

Hal had more questions: Exactly why was the Valkyrie riding into the fire, then out of it again, when Baldur saw her at it?

"I thought I had explained that. Because Alvit wanted to— she dared to—visit Wodan's prisoner and see if anything could be done for her. She found Brunhild alive, breathing, seemingly unharmed, but in an enchanted sleep." Baldur's voice almost broke on the last word, and he paused to regain his grim determination. "Hal, I must have the use of one of those Horses."

"Sounds impossible."

"Why? Nothing is impossible, to a true warrior-hero. To a man who refuses to admit impossibility."

"Oh, really? For one thing, you have no idea where the Valkyries' Horses are stabled—or is that another secret you've been keeping?"

"It's true, I don't know where the Horses are, exactly." Baldur admitted. Then he looked up slyly. "Probably they're in Valhalla. But wherever they are, I do know a means of reaching them."

"What way?"

"This must be kept a secret. Have I your word, as—as a warrior and a gentleman?"

"My solemn word as a warrior and gentleman. Oh, of course."

The youth looked all around, then dropped his voice till Hal could barely hear it. "I know who serves as Wodan's farriers. They are gnomes, and I have even visited their village."

Afterward, Hal found it hard to remember whether it was he himself or Baldur who first suggested that they should make a scouting trip to the gnomes' village. Whoever had thought of it first, some such reconnaissance seemed the only way they were going to find out any more about Wodan's Horses—and in particular about their golden shoes, which was the part that interested Hal.

Meanwhile Hal, as usual, kept up his patient search for more information. "Does anyone know what was up on that crag before the fire started? I mean, was there really a castle, watchtower, anything of the kind?"

Even as he asked the question, he was reasonably sure that

the answer must be no. If there had been any substantial structure, then there should have been a road going to the top, or at least the traces of an old one. No one could put up a sizable house or fort atop a steep hill without first making a road, or at least wearing a broad path with all the going up and coming down of workers and materials. And of course there had been nothing of the kind.

Baldur had no particular interest in golden shoes, or gold in any form: what he kept coming back to was that the only known way to get through Loki's fire was by riding a Valkyrie's Horse.

Hal just as persistently kept trying to lead the talk from Horses into the related subject of horseshoes.

Hal kept at it. "So, Wodan's cavalry can really fly, then. Not just fly, but carry people through Loki's fire without harm."

"Oh, no doubt about it. I know it's hard to believe, Hal, but—how many times do I have to tell you? If I had a Horse here now, I could be at Brunhild's side within an hour."

Hal picked his teeth and ruminated for a while. They had recently concluded a very satisfactory dinner. Life on a prosperous farm, like this one, could be quite nice, at least for the owners. On the other hand, farming always involved an enormous amount of work.

Some time had passed before he prodded: "You were going to tell me more about the gnomes who handle the farrier work for Wodan's stable. You said you even visited them."

Baldur nodded, then hesitated, as if wondering whether the further revelation he was about to make was wise. Then he added: "I met the Earthdweller who actually does the work."

"You keep coming out with these surprises. How did that come about?"

"Well—it's a long story."

"I'm not going anywhere."

Still Baldur hesitated, as if he feared to allow the escape of dangerous secrets. At last he said: "Brunhild wanted this gnome, Andvari's his name, to look at her Horse's shoes. She thought one of them was beginning to work loose."

"It's none of my business, really, lad—but how long were you and this maiden acquainted?" He had been about to ask *how long and how well* but at the last moment had thought it best to omit a couple of words.

"Well, it was only about six months." Baldur sounded surprised himself when he came to reckon out the time. "No more than that. But it seemed—forever. It seemed that my life only really began on the day that I met her."

Hal nodded wisely. Then he requested: "Tell me more about the gnomes?"

"I don't know much more about them. Why?"

"Well. It seems to me that getting to know them better is the only way you're ever going to find out exactly where to reach the Horses."

And the only way I'm ever going to get any closer to those golden shoes, and the place where they are forged. But Hal did not say that aloud.

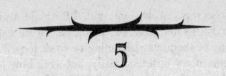

5

Hal was carrying in his pouch good evidence that at least some of Wodan's Horses were truly shod with gold. Possibly they all were. That, he supposed, could easily mean a hundred golden horseshoes nailed firmly on hooves, coming loose, or lying around somewhere as spares. The total ought to buy enough farmland to satisfy a dozen retiring Argonauts. But he was not going to be greedy.

Hal's knowledge of gnomes and gnomeland was practically nil, but Baldur had told him that their towns and villages were generally to be found along river valleys. On the other hand, everyone knew that Wodan's legendary stronghold and headquarters, Valhalla, had to be perched somewhere very high up in some range of mountains. Probably, thought Hal, the gold from which the shoes were made was stored right in Valhalla, or at least nearby. Which suggested that the gnomes who served as farriers for Wodan would have to climb well up into the mountains to do their work.

Of course, any hoard that held a hundred horseshoes worth of gold was certain to be well guarded by one means or another. But in any system of protection there were generally weak points. And Hal had no intention of trying to empty out the divine Wodan's treasury, or even make a noticeable dent in his reserves. No, the northman's ambitions were quite modest, befitting a mere mortal. He would be delighted to just pick up a few more scraps of yellow metal, absentmindedly left lying about by those who seemed to have more gold than they knew what to do with. Just some odds and ends.

For several days now Hal had been incubating an idea in the back of his mind. It was the germ of a scheme which, if successful, should finance the nicest little farm a man could ever want, and maybe the start of a fleet of fishing boats to boot. At first the idea had seemed little more than a daydream, too foolish to be taken seriously; but the longer he thought about it, the closer to the realm of possibility it seemed to drift.

He had to keep reminding himself that he really knew almost nothing about Wodan or magic Horses, and, when you came right down to it, not much about Baldur either. He had no way to test the truth of anything his companion told him regarding Valkyries. So trying to formulate anything like a detailed plan would be a complete waste of time, until he had learned more—a whole lot more. To learn more, he would just have to check out the situation for himself, and the only way he could see of doing that was by beginning with the gnomes.

While Hal kept secretly toying with ideas about gold, Baldur was developing his own scheme for reaching Brunhild and taking Hal into his confidence about it. Now the young man, acting casually and showing a talent for misdirection, so that his family suspected nothing, had begun making clandestine arrangements for his and Hal's planned expedition to the gnomes' village. He was telling everyone that the two of them were going on a fishing trip, just to relax.

Baldur's plan involved finding out from Wodan's gnome-farriers just where the Valkyries' Horses were stabled. Baldur had convinced himself that a Horse could carry him safely through Loki's flames, and once that happened, he would once more be able to clasp his beloved in his arms. Currently he seemed to have no hopes or plans for anything beyond that moment.

Right now, Hal and Baldur were standing on the bank of the stream that ran behind the house, and Hal thought they were out of earshot of anyone else.

As usual, he was playing the role of cautious partner. "We don't have any idea yet where the Horses are kept. At least I don't."

"But certainly the gnomes must know." Suddenly Baldur was ready to offer another revelation; he seemed to dole them out on an average of one a day, like a parent handing sweet-meats to a child. He said: "Brunhild once told me that the farriers' routine work is done four times a year, on the full moon following each solstice and each equinox."

"Is that a fact?" Hal quickly calculated that the next full moon, due in less than two weeks, would be the first after the autumnal equinox. "Then the timing would seem to be in our favor, anyway. How far away is this village of gnomes?"

Baldur, who said he had actually been there once, gave an estimate. Hal thought that with a little effort, they would be able to time their trip so they reached the gnomes' village in a few days. Exactly when the farriers would be starting on their periodic journey to Valhalla was impossible to say, but it would have to be soon, if either departure or arrival coincided with the full moon.

Baldur for once was almost cheerful. "It's a sign, Hal! A very favorable sign, it means that the Fates are with us."

"I'm glad to hear it."

Abruptly the young man turned on Hal. With the air of one who had just reached an important decision and was about to confer a great favor, he announced: "If we can get our hands on two Horses, instead of only one, then you can come with me, when I go to Brunhild." Since Hal was so interested, so ready to join in secret discussions, he must be ready and eager to plunge into the whole bold undertaking up to his neck. What other attitude could a professional adventurer, a former Argonaut, possibly have?

"It will be a glorious adventure!" Baldur added with a grin, inviting his older partner to relax and be enthusiastic.

Hal stared at him. "I'm sure it will."

Baldur had already turned his attention back to planning. "Naturally, our first step must be to think of some good reason to give the gnomes, for visiting their village. We can't just say we were on a fishing trip and decided to drop in."

"Well, we might do worse. But what would you suggest?"

The youth was squinting his eyes, as if his own deep thoughts might be hard to make out. "Tell them you're a merchant, come to trade—no, wait a minute, Hal. That's it. I'll tell them you're a famous warrior, come to commission some kind of special weapon. They fill such orders all the time. They are, as you must realize, the finest metalsmiths in the world."

"I see," said Hal, who hadn't realized anything of the kind. But the world was a big place, and he had to admit that for all he knew, Baldur might be right on this point. "And once we're there, how do we get them to lead us to the Horses?"

Baldur didn't seem to think that that would be a problem. "Either we accompany the farriers when they leave the village—or else we follow them."

"You think we can do either one?"

"Certainly. See, if they don't want company we'll still walk with them openly, part of the way. Then we'll make a show of turning off on a different route. We'll let them get a bit ahead, then follow them secretly until they lead us to Valhalla. Or wherever the Horses might be stabled."

"I see." Hal ruminated for a few strides. "Well, it might work. But why do you assume they're walking? It could be a long journey. Wouldn't they more likely be riding, on cameloids or in a carriage?"

Baldur shook his head decisively. "Gnomes very rarely use such animals."

"You seem to know a lot about them."

And Baldur was suddenly determined to change the subject. Hal wondered silently if the youth might have had a gnomish girlfriend too.

Hal could well believe that Wodan might be a little careless with his gold. He had meditated on the subject for some time, and had decided that probably few gods cared much about wealth in itself—after all, they could pretty much help themselves to what they wanted of the world's goods without having to pay. But magic Horses, like the creatures Baldur had described—such an animal would be a treasure indeed, to any god or mortal.

In their secret discussions, Baldur persisted in talking as if it would be the easiest thing in the world to locate a Horse, hop on its back and ride away. *Brain damage*, thought Hal again, reflecting on his colleague's simple faith. Well, maybe his own plan of picking up some odds and ends of Wodan's gold was no more practical. But he could not be sure of that until he knew more, much more, than he did.

Patiently Hal persisted with his questioning. "Suppose we do find out which individual gnomes are going to do the farrier-work. We still—"

"I know that," Baldur calmly interrupted. "A name, and where he lives."

"You do? How?"

The youth was silent.

After a moment Hal pressed on. "So you not only know which village these farriers live in, but—somehow—one of their names."

Baldur said nothing.

Hal pressed on again. "What if they don't want us to travel with them, even partway? And how do you know that gnomes setting out on a journey won't be riding cameloids or driving a coach with droms? It's pretty certain we won't. We don't have any."

"I told you not to worry about the cameloids," Baldur assured him vaguely. "Of course it may be that the gnomes will want to discourage our going with them." He paused thoughtfully. "But I just might be able to find the Horses anyway, even if the gnomes are no help."

"You might? How?"

Again they seemed to have reached an area where Baldur was reluctant to reveal certain matters to his partner. He did explain to Hal that he had come to know one of Wodan's noble steeds by name, the very one that Brunhild had used to ride. That particular Horse had become Baldur's friend, had eaten lumps of sugar, sometimes apples, from his hand. "Its name is Gold Mane. I think that Horse would come to me, if I should call it."

"Call it how?"

"I mean if I were to summon it by magic—assuming you and I could put together some kind of effective spell—the beast might well come to me, across the miles."

"I didn't know that you were any kind of a magician. I'm not."

"Oh, I'm not either, really. Not on a professional level. But when I was a child, I did manage a spell or two."

Hal thought it over. "Better not try anything of the kind unless we have no other option."

"I agree."

In response to careful questioning, Baldur admitted that yes, he had actually even ridden Gold Mane once or twice—which, of course, was a secret that Hal must promise never to divulge to anyone.

"I promise," said Hal, thinking it was no wonder that Brunhild had got herself into deep trouble.

The details of the plan changed as the two men talked it

over. But Baldur never wavered in his claim that he had ridden on a Horse, that he could ride a Horse again, given the chance, and that any Horse he got his hands on could carry him safely through the wall of fire.

Again he described how he had once seen Alvit, Hildy's friend and sister Valkyrie, perform that very feat. It did worry Baldur somewhat that Alvit had refused to tell him much in the way of detail about Brunhild's condition on the other side. She would say only that the girl was lying in an enchanted sleep.

And so it went. Hal's tentative, private plan, which at the start had seemed little more than a joke, ready to evaporate at the first touch of opposition, was beginning to take on aspects of reality.

Still, there were moments in which it seemed to Hal that he must be brain-damaged himself even to be considering such an undertaking. Even before being hit on the head, Baldur could not have been one of the world's keenest wits. Experience counseled that the only sane thing for a seasoned man of the world to do, in Hal's situation, was to resume his own original northward trek, without pausing to look back. He would say a quick goodbye to the youth with the dented helmet and skull to match, and to all of Baldur's friends and relatives—yes, including Matilda. As far as Hal could tell, none of them had much more sense than Wodan's youthful worshiper.

And yet . . . and yet. There still remained the tantalizing fragment of golden horseshoe, a silent challenge in the form of heavy, real, and lustrous metal. The trouble was that all by itself, that single shard of gold probably wouldn't begin to buy him all he needed for a comfortable retirement. Without any firm idea of current prices, here or in his homeland, Hal could only guess. Maybe his bit of gold would purchase him one plow, along with a pair of droms to pull the plow across the patch of farmland he could not yet afford.

He thought that if he ever saw Matilda again, he might ask her how much she thought her dowry of farmland might be worth in gold. But it didn't take long to come up with several reasons why putting such a question might be unwise.

Alternatively, the piece now in his pouch might pay for no more than one truly glorious celebration—if Hal could think of anything to celebrate.

His real trouble, it crossed his mind to speculate, might be that he still found scheming and struggling to get gold a hell of a lot more fun than farming.

Common sense warned him that there would be only faint chances of success, and probably heavy risks, messing around with the magical property of a god. From Hal's point of view, he might be only picking up a few scraps that their owner would never miss, but Wodan might see the business in an entirely different way. Wodan was not just any god, but one who wanted to be known as the All-Highest, and so far had got away with it.

But on the other hand, when Hal pictured himself returning to his northern home as a poor man in threadbare garments, practically a stranger among folk he had not seen for many years, it was all too easy to imagine the looks of disdain he'd get, the lack of any real welcome . . . the image immediately stiffened his resolve. He could not simply turn his back on what might be a golden opportunity—certainly not just yet. He would have to search and probe a little farther.

For the time being, he would continue to go along with Baldur's plan, just as if he really had some confidence in it. Go along, at least until the two of them had visited the village of the gnomes, and he, Hal, had learned as much as he could there on the subjects of gold and gods.

Baldur, in his desperate craving to rejoin Brunhild, was ready to try anything, and the young man's faith in his own crazy plan now seemed unshakeable. What had seemed a bare possibility only a few days ago was now a certainty in his mind, if only he could come within reach of a Horse.

Hal openly allowed that he had certain reservations about the feasibility of that scheme. But he hastily added that he was ready to go along with it for the time being. Privately he had decided to argue the young man into some more realistic plan as soon as he could think of one; or dissolve their partnership if and when the chance of getting near the gold began to loom as a real possibility.

Of course the idea of just getting on one of Wodan's Horses and riding it away sounded completely crazy. But then, the longer Hal thought about it, the more he realized that as odd and dangerous as the idea sounded, it might not be totally insane. His own experience with gods, admittedly not vast, had taught him a few things. The Face of any deity was bound to confer some great power on its wearer, but it did not necessarily improve intelligence or even guarantee competence in practical matters. The mightiest divinity could, and sometimes had, come to grief through his or her own all-too-human foolishness, forgetfulness and oversight. As it was with ordinary men and women, so it was with gods. A god or goddess, after all, was no more than a human being who had put on one of the ancient and indestructible Faces loaded with odylic magic.

Over the next night or two, as the moon rose later and later, waxing inexorably toward full, Hal and Baldur were careful not even to hint at their true intentions to anyone in the family or village. Meanwhile, they ostentatiously made preparations for a fishing trip—part of the local lore of fishing said late fall was the best time for certain catches.

Baldur told his partner: "We may have to buy a few things—provisions and clothing for the trip. Especially as it seems we will be going up into the mountains."

"I have a little money," Hal admitted cautiously. He had somewhat replenished his otherwise depleted purse at the expense of the would-be robber. "But let's wait, if we can, to buy the mountain gear until we've traveled a way—we still want our departure to look like a simple fishing trip."

"Good idea."

Even if they stayed in the valleys, the strong possibility of cold weather was upon them, this late in the season. There was no telling when the first snow and real hard freeze were going to come along, and acquiring warm clothing and boots gave away no secrets.

Baldur privately remarked that it was fortunate that they would be able to go most of the way to gnome's territory, downstream by water.

Meanwhile, Hal had been casually asking Holah and Noden for information about gnomes, and the boys had been cheerfully telling him some ghastly stories. These tales, of human infants kidnapped and human miners suffocated in subterranean blackness by gnomic treachery, had made Hal wonder if there were not some way to avoid visiting Gnomeland at all. Now he asked his partner: "If we go there, will we be expected to descend into one of their mines?"

Baldur frowned. "No, probably only into their houses. Their dwellings, at least the ones I've seen, are hardly ever dug very deep below the surface. Actually I doubt they'd let us go into a mine, even if we wanted to."

Hal nodded sympathetically. "I can understand why they'd naturally want to keep their gold mines secret."

Baldur looked up at him, as if surprised. "Gold? No, I don't think they really produce much gold. Not any longer. Those diggings were all worked out a long time ago. It's more that they have methods and tools they want to keep secret. When they're in a hurry, they can drive a tunnel through solid rock in no time at all."

"I see." Hal sighed. "So, tell me some more about this place we're going to visit. Don't these holes you say they live in flood out every time it rains?"

Baldur said that in the course of his affair with Brunhild, he had heard her more than once mention the name and location of the gnome settlement where lived the farrier, named Andvari, and his assistant, whose name Baldur did not know.

Hal wondered what else the two lovers might have talked about—apparently they had done a lot of talking.

Then Hal and Baldur began their journey by taking a small boat down the local stream, one of the Einar's tributaries, to the broad Einar itself, which would lead them directly to their secret destination.

Baldur's relatives seemed to accept, largely with indifference, the story he and Hal told them about going fishing. It was hard to imagine weather bad enough to stop a fisherman. So the two men had little trouble in borrowing a cheaply constructed raft from one of Baldur's distant relatives who lived nearby, and who seemed really indifferent as to whether he got it back or not. At one point Hal turned down the offer of the loan of an uncle's trim little sailboat, pleading a lack of knowledge of how to manage one—a totally false plea, but he did not want to borrow any vessel that would be greatly missed if it did not come back. If all did not go precisely well, there would be no use in having an extra set of pursuers on his track.

Baldur had not been entirely truthful with his family, before leaving them this time. His mother and most other members of the family seemed purely relieved that he was undertaking what promised to be an utterly peaceful enterprise.

Holah and Noden, having several times volunteered to go

with Hal next time he went to war, swore they knew where the best fishing could be found, and they wanted to come along on that trip if there was no prospect of fighting. But they were vigorously discouraged.

As they were poling their raft downstream, Hal said to Baldur heartily: "So, tell me more about these people we're going to see. How well do you know them?"

"I don't know that I would call gnomes people." The young man paused. "Though some of them were very good to Brunhild and me."

Here was more news. "Good in what way?"

Now the young man, continuing his progressive series of revelations, disclosed that over the past few months some of the gnomes had actually connived to provide a secret meeting place for Brunhild and her lover. A place underground, where Wodan and his agents were unlikely to discover them.

"Why do you suppose they were so helpful?" Hal asked.

Baldur lowered his voice, though it seemed unlikely that anyone was within a quarter-mile. "Perhaps I should not be telling you this. But it seems that Brunhild had done the Earthdwellers some good turn previously."

Perhaps you shouldn't. I may someday wish I didn't know it, Hal thought. But, curious as usual, he continued: "What sort of good turn?"

"She never told me that."

Maybe that was the truth and maybe not. Baldur was consistently hesitant about revealing his secrets to Hal, but he kept leaking them out anyway, slowly but surely. In concealing his affair with Hildy, he was also hiding the extent of the knowledge he had incidentally picked up about the gnomes. Certainly no one in Baldur's family suspected that the youth had established any degree of intimacy with certain members of the strange race that he and Hal were about to visit.

Hal's persistent curiosity was a good match for Baldur's need to talk to someone about his troubles. Baldur struggled against the need, but not with much success.

The more Hal learned, the more genuinely interested he became. "So, the gnomes secretly found a way for you and Brunhild to get around old Wodan's rules regarding Valkyrie behavior."

Baldur hesitated. "Yes, that's about it."

"Does the god expect all his flying scouts to remain virgins?"

"Well—something like that, yes."

"Never mind, it doesn't matter. But you and she managed to meet underground, by courtesy of the gnomes."

The young man hesitated. "Yes."

"These Earthdwellers don't much care for the Great All-Highest, is that it? Even though he trusts some of them enough to let them shoe his Horses? And gives them access to his supply of gold?"

Baldur shot his companion a reproachful look. "Wodan is the All-Highest, the Father of Battles. No one speaks openly against him. Not even in jest."

"Was I speaking against him? I didn't mean to give offense, I'm sure." And Hal put on an abashed look, and scanned the sky, as if to make sure no instant retribution threatened.

When rain came, the two men sheltered under oilskins as best they could.

They passed several more or less ordinary villages and any number of isolated houses, and exchanged comments with various fishermen on the quality of the catch. Gradually the land on both banks grew rockier, less and less suitable for farming, and the habitations fewer. In the cold mornings, there were fringes of thin ice along the shore and in the adjoining marshlands.

Stopping at a small settlement of humans of their own va-
riety, called by the gnomes Sundwellers, Hal and Baldur
completed their outfitting for winter, including boots and leggings, taking care of such details as had not been done before
leaving Baldur's home.

They had come many miles, and the youth said that he
could now recognize several landmarks. He added that they
were very near their goal.

6

Suddenly Baldur broke off their conversation to point at a muddy hole in the riverbank. It was as big around as a man's leg, just at water level, a dark mouth half submerged. "One of the entrances to their village. There'll be a tunnel running from it inland, just above water level."

The black gap looked to Hal intensely uninviting, like the kind of cave that an otter might call home, or maybe some kind of giant snake. He supposed he might go crawling into such a place, if it was big enough, but only if he was fleeing some great peril, desperate to save his life.

Now Baldur was steering their craft closer to the right bank of the river. They went slowly, and more slowly still. Hal kept studying the slope of land slightly above the shore, which carried what looked to him like nothing but virgin forest.

"If that was really one of their tunnels in the bank," he remarked, "then one of their settlements must be near."

"Oh, it is. But you can see how easy it would be to pass it by and never realize that it was there." Baldur went on to explain that almost everything the gnomes created was underground, where they spent nearly all their time. For extensive settlements they favored sites near rivers, for if the tons of excavated earth could be handily dumped into a briskly flowing stream, very little of their presence would be visible.

Having chosen a place to land, the men tied their raft securely to a handy willow stump—even if they were really indifferent to its loss, it might be suspicious to give that impression. Then they ran through a last-minute rehearsal of their supposed reason for dropping in on this particular village. Hal would introduce himself as a warrior of high status, who contemplated commissioning the forging of some kind of weapon or armor.

At that point Baldur suddenly decided there were a few more things Hal should know about the people they were going to visit.

First of all, the gnomes were sometimes called dwarfs, but gave themselves the name of Earthdwellers. Just why the gnomes, or Earthdwellers, insisted on spending their time and strength grubbing in the earth, instead of coming out on the surface like real people, was more than Baldur could explain.

Hal supposed the main reason was probably just that the gnomes had a lot of trouble with sunlight. So few of the occupations normally open to the children of light were open to them.

Baldur informed him that the gnomes were very clever in some ways, and certainly not lazy. Many or most of them were physically deformed, at least by the standards of surface-dwelling humans. They tended to have pale faces and long beards.

"It's only the men who have beards, of course," the young man added after a pause.

"I am relieved."

By now the two of them were walking slowly inland, through a shallow screen of dead reed-stalks. Baldur said: "We humans, of course, can go down into caves and mines, and they can come up into daylight. But neither of our races can ever be really comfortable away from our own element."

"But where do gnomes come from? How long have they been around?"

The young man seemed vaguely surprised by the question, as if he had never thought about it. "Some say they are formed right in the dust of the earth, just as maggots naturally appear in dead meat. But that's not true," Baldur hastened to assure his comrade. "Those are the kind of things said by folk who really know nothing about gnomes. Get down into one of their houses, and you'll see some big-bellied women, and others nursing small children, just as in any human town."

"Well then, they *are* human, are they not?"

The younger man grunted something, and his face showed his disapproval of that idea. He was not ready to go quite that far with what he considered his liberal attitude.

Hal pressed him: "Do they ever intermarry with—what did you say their word is, for people like us? 'Sundwellers'?"

The expression of disapproval became stronger. "I don't know of anyone who's done that. Married a gnome." Baldur sounded vaguely scandalized. "There are stories about people doing that kind of thing in the past."

"What are the children like?"

"You'll have to ask someone else."

They had come inland but a little distance through an almost trackless wintry forest, a domain of barren limbs and fallen leaves, when Baldur paused and indicated a kind of semi-clearing just ahead, an extensive glade whose grassy floor was irregularly raised and pocked by dozens of low mounds. These ranged in size from no bigger than human heads to the bulk of capacious ovens.

Baldur had come to a stop. "Here we are. I'm certain now, I remember the way it looked. This is the place I visited with Brunhild."

"I still don't see any village."

"But it's there, right ahead of us. You can see the holes in the earth, scattered around, if you look for them. The rooms below ground are bigger than the mounds, which are mainly for ventilation."

Hal studied the rugose surface of the partial clearing. Gradually he was able to make out that there were many small openings for ventilation, mostly near the bases of the mounds, or among the roots of the surviving trees, suggesting some kind of elaborate excavation beneath. Hal thought to himself that the drainage system must be ingenious, to keep them all from drowning when it rained.

Cautioning Hal to follow, and to avoid walking on the mounds as much as possible, Baldur advanced to a position close to the center of the complex. There he stamped one foot on the ground, not too hard, in a small flat area, and called out in a loud voice what Hal supposed must be a traditional word of greeting.

Moments later, heads began to peek up out of several nearby holes, some at the base of tree stumps. Shortly afterward, half a dozen gnomes, of both sexes, emerged from one of the larger apertures, blinking in cloudy daylight. They were all unarmed, Hal noted, unless you counted a couple of the men who were holding what must be their miners' tools. The welcome offered the visitors was courteous enough, no more wary than they would have received at many settlements of Sundwellers.

When the visitors announced that they had come on important business, they were warily invited underground, an apparently solid tree stump being easily rotated aside to make a doorway big enough for them. Hal soon found himself in a kind of anteroom, just underground. He realized that this chamber had probably been designed for entertaining the occasional Sundweller. From here, steep, ladderlike stairs led down again, evidence of at least one habitable level lower than this one. It seemed likely that only a small portion of the extensive underground complex would be accessible to people as big as Baldur and himself.

The guests were offered seats on an earthen bench, and then a tray of food. Hal sampled some whitish roots that had a crisp texture and sharp but pleasant taste, along with several varieties of raw mushrooms. Hal found the mushrooms delicious.

Baldur was chewing too. "I've had these little ones before, they're really good. Try one."

Hal tasted and approved. The gnomes who served the food were glum and businesslike. At least Hal felt reasonably confident that he was not going to encounter any gnomish version of Matilda, ready to encourage him with talk of how many miles of underground tunnels, suitable for root farming, she owned, free and clear in her own name.

The natives of this town were small and lean, most of the adults no higher than Hal's armpit. They seemed to Hal not so much deformed as just built on a slightly different body plan. By the time he had exchanged handgrips of greeting with half a dozen or so, he realized that they were surprisingly strong for their small size. The adult males were indeed heavily bearded. All had pale skins, small and rather sunken eyes, large ears and hairy noses. Most were something like fully dressed, in garments of smooth leather and tightly woven cloth.

On his earlier visit, Baldur had briefly met the farrier, Andvari, who had the honor to serve the Valkyries' Horses. Obviously he was a person of some status and importance among his people.

And when the gnome Andvari now appeared, garbed in what looked like leather and stroking his gray beard, he did remember saying hello to Baldur, the Sundweller man who was the lover of the Valkyrie Brunhild. Visiting Sundwellers must be rare creatures here, and no doubt tended to stick in the memory.

As Hal could see for himself on entering their town, the presence of gnomish children, warped little creatures to his way of thinking, confirmed Baldur's opinion that they were in the habit of reproducing in the same way as anyone else.

Baldur had told him that the gnomes were abnormally sensitive to sunlight, and generally came hooded and wrapped in extra clothing when they were required to be out in full daylight. They also protected their eyes with special goggles. Hal had seen similar devices in the far north, where they guarded against snow blindness. Each eyepiece was a flat, opaque disk of bone or wood, pierced by a single, narrow horizontal slit for vision.

As far as Hal could tell from listening to Baldur on the subject, there had never been a whole lot of intercourse between Sundwellers and Earthdwellers, and there was always a fair amount of mutual suspicion. The visitors were objects of curiosity, though hardly of awe. Only a few gnomes came to look at them, and those who exchanged bits of conversation with Hal were polite enough, but their manners were reserved, and Hal could well believe that they had misgivings about Sundwellers, at least as great as those Baldur had about them. Doubtless Andvari and his tribe considered those who chose to live on the earth's surface as something of an aberrant offshoot of humanity.

In response to their questions, Hal and Baldur were informed that no one in this village was authorized to contract to produce custom designs of weaponry or discuss the terms of payment. Hal was given directions to another village, many miles away, where skilled armorers could be found.

Privately Hal wondered whether the gnomes had a god of their own—it was the kind of thing that might be awkward to ask about directly, and he wished now that he had found out more from Baldur.

Baldur had been certain that only Sundwelling humans could possibly become gods, but now the gnomes seemed calmly certain that that was nonsense. It seemed that the gnomes felt more akin to the great powers of the Underworld, even though those powers were now their bitter enemies.

In conversation, Hal learned that some of the Earthdwellers firmly believed that the current avatar of Hades was also a gnome, in fact that he could hardly be anything else. That only gnomes could wear that Face, or had ever worn it.

Hal was not going to get involved in any argument, certainly not on matters of religion.

Prolonging their visit just a little, mainly out of curiosity, and also on the theory that it would not be polite to immediately rush away, he studied the walls of the underground anteroom where he and Baldur sat talking.

The walls were of what appeared to be a smooth, light-colored clay, and decorated with an extensive series of pictures, or rather carvings in low relief.

Someone pointed out that here on the wall was Jormungand, the world-serpent, doomed in legend to die fighting against Wodan on the last day of the world's existence. And over on the adjoining wall were other creatures of the nether world—great nasty serpents, shown being trodden underfoot, torn apart with picks, flattened with huge hammers, by some obviously gnomic heroes.

When Hal asked about the pictures, he was told: "This commemorates some of our famous victories in the past—and others that are yet to come."

"Hope I never meet this one in a dark alley," Hal muttered, pointing at an image, when he was sure he would not be overheard. He wasn't certain if the creature he was looking at was fighting for the gnomes in the panel or against them.

Suddenly he began to pay close attention to the talk around him. Baldur had somehow worked the subject back to Wodan, and naturally the villagers brought up a matter of which they were obviously proud. Yes, it was confirmed: four times a year, or more often when necessary, two or three of the gnomes made the journey up to Valhalla, to see to the Horses' shoeing, and perform certain odds and ends of metal-work for which Wodan wanted to enlist their special skills.

On hearing that, Hal allowed himself to show some mild interest, thinking it would be strange if he did not.

"I have never seen a god," he lied to his hosts with perfect ease. "What is Valhalla like? There must be wonderful sights."

"Wonderful," Andvari admitted tersely. Contemplating the marvels of Valhalla did not seem to cheer him up at all. "But we tend to our business when we are there, and do not see any more than we have to see, to do our work."

Baldur cleared his throat, and asked tentatively: "I don't suppose human visitors are generally welcome there?"

"No," said Andvari shortly. "They are not."

At that Hal decisively changed the subject, turning the conversation back to the designs of imaginary weapons.

Again he was reminded that he would have to go to the other village if he wanted to contract for such work. The gnomes made no offer of prolonged hospitality, and the visitors soon announced that they must be on their way.

A few minutes later, he and Baldur were out in broad daylight on the surface of the earth, and quite alone. Briskly they tramped away, their footfalls solid on the ground, in the direction where they had left their raft. When they reached their humble vessel, Hal untied it and let it drift away.

Baldur observed: "It wouldn't have been wise to hint that we might want go along with them partway."

"I quite agree."

"What do we do next?"

"Wait for sunset. And we'd better make sure our water bottles are full. I doubt we'll find much water between here and the mountains."

Presently the two adventurers doubled back toward the village to take up an observation post only about fifty yards from its edge, at a spot from which they could see anyone departing in the direction of the mountains.

Before the sun dropped under the horizon, Hal and Baldur had concealed themselves behind some fallen trunks and underbrush, in a spot from which they could keep close watch over the western end of the village. The full moon would soon be rising in a clear sky, giving plenty of light for such a purpose.

A small road nearby, little used and largely overgrown with weeds, curved sharply near the Earthdwellers' settlement, then headed out, running almost arrow-straight as far as Hal could see, toward the sawtooth horizon of the high country.

There came a brief spattering of chilly rain. As they began their wait, Baldur murmured, peering over a fallen log: "I hope tonight is the night when they set out. But you're right, we can't count on that."

"At least we know they're not already gone. I wonder why the time of the full moon was chosen?"

"Probably because full moonlight makes it easier for night walkers to find their way."

The sun fell lower and the air turned cold. Soon Baldur broke a silence to remark: "It is noble of you to help me in this way."

"I've taken a liking to you, lad. You're a little crazy, but you may amount to something yet."

Baldur smiled faintly, knowingly. "And maybe to Matilda, as well?"

Hal cleared his throat uncomfortably. The smile on his face felt false. "Maybe. Besides, I have a yen to see just what's really inside that circle of Loki's fire." And as he said those words he realized that they were true enough.

As they talked things over while waiting for Andvari and his unnamed helper to appear, the chosen subject was still gnomes. "They don't do any farming, of course, or herding,

or anything that would keep them working outdoors all day."
Baldur seemed to consider this a troublesome flaw in their
collective character.

"But what do they all eat?" Hal continued to be curious.
"This village has a lot of mouths to feed. And you say there
are many other gnomish settlements, just as big."

"They eat a lot of roots, I'd say. Mushrooms and other
fungi, like the ones they fed us. Fish. And of course there are
animals and insects that burrow, spend a lot of time underground. And I suppose the Mud-diggers must pick up some
food, somehow, on the surface."

And underground there are also worms, Hal suddenly
thought to himself. And all those grubs and burrowing insects
to consider. It was undoubtedly just as well they had not been
invited to stay to dinner.

Despite all Baldur's theories and claims of expertise, Hal
could not see the Earthdwellers as anything but an offshoot
of humanity, somewhat warped by magic.

"Unless we are the ones warped by magic, and they are
purely natural?"

Baldur only gave Hal a strange look when he voiced that
thought.

"And, by the way, I still wonder how we can be so sure
that they make the journey on their own feet? It would put a
fine knot in our plans if someone suddenly brought them a
pair of cameloids."

"They are walking." Baldur was calmly certain about that.
"I never heard of gnomes traveling in any other way. Long
journeys are difficult, of course, for at dawn each day they
must find a suitable shelter against the sunlight."

Hal thought that probably the cold winds of winter were
more uncomfortable for gnomes than for Sundwellers—under
the surface of the earth, seasonal temperature variations
tended to be small. "So you think you know a lot about
them?"

"Not much. I don't care that much."

"I wonder," Hal mused, "How did these particular gnomes come to be chosen to care for the Valkyries' Horses?"

"I think Andvari might have been chosen because he was the best smith among their people. Probably most of them know little or nothing about Horses, or human maidens either. But as they are in general incomparable metalsmiths, they make great farriers when they set their minds to it."

"What about his companion? The best at working the bellows for the forge?"

Baldur shrugged, as if to say he really didn't know and didn't care. But then he said: "I doubt that. Maybe because he's the best of the gnomish magicians."

"Oh." Hal did not find that reassuring.

Hal, it must be good to have traveled as far as you have, and seen so much."

"It has advantages. I have even seen something of horses, though never before of the kind Valkyries ride—how did you first happen to meet your Brunhild, if you don't mind my asking?" They were making low-voiced conversation as they kept their eyes open for the gnome-farriers' appearance.

Baldur, whenever he began to talk on the subject of Brunhild, seemed likely to keep on indefinitely. No, of course she had not been born a Valkyrie—no one was. They were not a special race, or anything like that—not in the sense that gnomes were. No one was going to suggest to him that Hildy was not entirely human.

"Of course not. Forgive my ignorance."

"That's all right, you are a foreigner and I suppose you cannot help it. No, being a Valkyrie is just something that girls are chosen for when they are very young."

"A very great honor."

"Certainly."

Eventually Hal managed to extract some details. According to Baldur, his first meeting with Brunhild had come about by sheer accident. He had made a long climb to a remote meadow in the hills, where he had been gathering flowers, actually meaning to take them to some other girl.

The image of a would-be berserker gathering flowers gave Hal pause. But he said nothing, only nodding encouragingly.

Baldur went on: "But those flowers never reached the one for whom they were originally meant. From the moment I saw Brunhild . . . all others were forgotten."

"That's romantic."

She had been on some kind of outing with other Valkyries. On a summer day, swimming in an upland pool, while their magic horses grazed nearby—not that Baldur had had eyes for Horses on that day.

Now the voice of the youth was beginning to tremble. "You cannot imagine . . . such beauty . . ."

"I'll try my best." Hal wondered what the chances were of this kid's living long enough to grow up. Well, Hal meant him no harm. He would try to keep him from getting killed, if that were possible. Merely following a couple of undersized metal-workers did not seem particularly dangerous.

Baldur was still lost in his romantic dream. "It was a holy thing," he breathed.

"I'm sure it was."

As the light began to fade and redden into sunset the woods were quiet. They were also uncomfortably cold for fireless Sundwellers who were trying to be as silent and motionless as possible. As soon as the sun was actually gone, a work party of gnomes, not bothering with special protection, climbed out above ground and began to carry out what was apparently routine maintenance on the shallow mounds that collectively formed the roof of their buried village. Hal could hear them moving about in the middle distance, and as soon as the moon peered over the eastern horizon he was able to see them better.

He began to wish that he and Baldur had taken up their observation post at a somewhat greater distance from the village.

Despite his uneasiness and the need to remain alert, Hal had just started to doze off, when suddenly Baldur was poking his arm. "There they are, two of them, on foot. Let's go."

They made two miles along the road by moonlight, then stopped. After waiting to make sure the gnomes were far ahead, they built a fire for warmth, ate sparingly of the cheese and hard biscuits provided for their fishing trip by Baldur's mother, and turned in for some sleep. Sundwellers traveled best by day.

7

At first light Hal and Baldur were on their feet again, shouldering their modest packs and hiking westward on the road toward the mountains. They breakfasted as they moved, munching the remnants of last night's dinner.

The master farrier and his assistant had a long start on their pursuers, and the two men kept up a brisk pace for several hours, thinking there was small chance of their overtaking the pair of Earthdwellers any time soon. By moonlight it had been difficult to be sure, but Hal thought that Andvari and his colleague had been carrying only a couple of modest backpacks, which could have held little more than the necessities of the journey. The tools and equipment required for their work must be waiting up there near the god's stable, somewhere on the higher slopes of the mysterious mountains.

All that was very logical. Still, Hal could not keep from wondering whether the pair of artisans might possibly, even now, be carrying with them the gold they were going to use. How much they needed would of course depend on how many shoes needed replacement this time round. That was something an outsider couldn't even begin to guess; Hal supposed old shoes of gold could probably be melted down, reformed, and used again, just like those forged of common blacksmith's iron. How hot did a fire need to be, to melt gold? Not nearly as hot, he thought, as that required to make the darker, tougher metal flow.

But of course if magic was heavily involved, everything about the metal might be different. Possibly it could even be lighter in weight? But no, the fragment in his own belt pouch was solid and heavy enough.

If only he could contrive to get a look inside the packs of Andvari and his companion, while the gnomes were sleeping at midday!

How many Horses did Wodan own? Baldur had said something about there being only ten Valkyries, which seemed ridiculously few, according to the legends . . . but maybe that meant only ten in her particular group, or squadron . . .

Baldur spoke to his companion sharply, asking if Hal was about to fall asleep as they walked.

"Not yet, lad, not yet."

"What're you thinking about, then? You seemed a thousand miles away."

"I am trying to imagine the glories of Valhalla."

It was around midafternoon, on their first day of tracking, when the men reached the spot where the two gnomes had evidently gone to earth at dawn.

Hal put out an arm to hold back his companion. Hal whispered: "Wait a minute. That looks like a little hut." It was a small, crude construction of stone and wood, its only windows mere chinks between stones and logs. A larger hole at one end looked as if it might serve to let out smoke, and indeed when Hal sniffed he could detect traces of fragrant smoke, blended with fainter odors suggesting cookery.

"They're likely still in there now," he whispered.

"So what do we do?"

"What can we do? Wait till sunset, when they'll set out again."

Withdrawing a short distance down the road, Baldur and Hal made their own cold and uncomfortable camp only some fifty yards away, not daring to start a fire that would give away their presence, though Baldur assured his companion that gnomes had a reputation for being observant only in matters connected with their craft.

Shortly after sunset, they heard a muttering in gnomish voices, and presently the sounds of people breaking camp and getting on the road again.

Hal waited an hour this time before he thought it was safe to build a fire.

When in the morning of their second day on the trail Hal and Baldur resumed their advance, their meager tracking skills were helped enormously by the presence of a light snow fallen overnight. The thin white cover on the ground made it ridiculously easy to track the pair they were following; Andvari and his companion had indeed been in the little hut, they had indeed come out of it and marched uphill, and they seemed to be making no effort at all to conceal their trail.

At one point Baldur caught a glimpse of flying sun-shadows on a low cloud, and pointed them out to Hal, who looked up almost too late to see anything at all.

"Could it have been birds?"

"Far too big." Baldur sounded subdued. "They might have been Valkyries, but I could not be sure."

Hal, who was not sure he had seen anything, was uneasy too. The last large flying creatures he had seen had been the hideous Harpies, which still sometimes disturbed his dreams.

The road wound back and forth almost continuously, tending this way and that, but always came back to point toward the mountains, which were still days away. Soon the river and the forest fell behind them, to be replaced by a more open landscape that gave progressively less evidence of human occupation. Since leaving the gnomes' village they had seen only a few human figures, and those all at a distance, farmers and herdsmen evidently. Now the narrow road was taking them steadily into territory even more sparsely inhabited, lacking all signs of human presence. Close ahead loomed foothills, and beyond those were high mountains, barren and unwelcoming in aspect.

Baldur confessed that he had never been this way before, and there was no way to be absolutely sure that Andvari and his companion were still following this road. But no other range of mountains remotely comparable could be seen in any other direction. If Valhalla was anywhere in this part of the world, Hal thought, it must be there, somewhere straight ahead.

After about noon on the third day, Hal and Baldur kept a more moderate pace and an even sharper lookout. It would not do to inadvertently overtake their quarry. They had no way of being certain how fast the short-legged Earthdwellers might be walking. Around midafternoon the men slowed their own steps even more, and began keeping a sharp lookout for the camp the two gnomes would presumably be making, in which to spend the day. Since they seemed to repeat this journey fairly often, there might well be a series of small huts, conveniently spaced.

Hal continued to be vaguely surprised that Andvari and his companion were not riding or driving droms or cameloids. But Baldur continued to assure him that such animals were practically unknown among the Earthdwellers.

"But somehow they have no trouble dealing with Horses."

"So it seems," the youth admitted. "Though I don't think they ride them. Lucky for us that Wodan didn't choose to provide his workers with magic transport or an escort of some kind."

"Yes, lucky." Hal subjected his surroundings in all directions to one of his routine scans. "I also find it a little puzzling."

Another light dusting of early snow allowed another period of easy tracking, and when that snow melted in bright sun, additional help was provided by patches of mud and dust occurring at intervals along the sparsely traveled road. Traffic of any kind seemed so rare that Hal did not worry about footprints being obliterated by the tracks of other travelers.

Once more the two men continued walking until the sun had fallen behind the western mountains, without seeing the least sign of their quarry. While traversing a long stretch where there were no footprints to follow, Hal had to admit it was entirely possible that he and Baldur had accidentally passed the gnomes, if Andvari and his companion had gone off the trail to rest or for any other reason. There were many stretches of the road devoid of any clear footprints, where something of the kind could easily have happened. It was equally possible that the journeying Earthdwellers were making such good time that their pursuers could not have overtaken them if they tried.

Moving uphill again, on the fourth morning, Hal was practically certain that their whole scheme had misfired, and he would have to start again from scratch, or abandon all hope of being able to pick up scraps of divine gold.

Then suddenly Baldur was pointing at the ground. "Look! Look, Hal, I think these must be the tracks we want!"

Every now and then those promising tracks appeared again, a few clear prints of small, booted feet, plain enough to tell their story to anyone with eyes. The pattern of bootmarks was consistently that of two people walking side by side, in the short strides natural to short legs.

As far as Hal could tell, the Earthdwelling farriers continued to move only during the long moonlit nights. Hal and Baldur did almost all their traveling during the short winter days, pushing steadily to keep up, while always keeping a sharp lookout on the trail ahead, to avoid overtaking their quarry.

Four days passed on the road, then five. The way the two Earthdwellers were following had gradually lost its wagon-track duality, diminished through frequent branchings until it was only a trail. And then steadily the trail grew thinner, and less deeply worn into the ground, as if few people indeed had ever dared to follow it this far. Hal would have had no means of knowing whether he and Baldur were still on the right path, indeed it would have been hard to be sure that they were on any path at all, had they not now reached an altitude where early winter had already moved in, and snow consistently covered most of the ground. Here the four small booted feet of the two gnomes had left plain record of their passage.

Late in the fifth day, the pursuers had stopped to refill their water bottles at a place where a frosty trickle of a stream, still unfrozen, crossed the pathway under a rude log bridge. Hal's curiosity was alive and well, as usual.

"I still keep wondering why the farrier and his comrade did not choose to ride. Anyone who deals in golden horseshoes ought to be able to afford a couple of cameloids."

"How should I know?" Baldur, now that his great adventure was actually under way, was growing nervous and irritable, which Hal thought was a bad sign. "Maybe the dirt-eaters don't like to get as far above the ground as a cameloid's back would lift them. But their being afoot will make it much easier for us to follow."

Hal grunted something. Following the trail was certainly easy enough. Now and then the trackers even caught a glimpse of the distant pair whose footprints led them on. Only occasionally, at dusk or dawn, could the two slight, dark-hooded figures be seen against the snow. Once Hal spotted them no more than about two hundred yards ahead, and the trackers waited for long minutes before cautiously advancing farther. On and up they went, following a slight trail back and forth, working their way higher and higher into what, after the first few hours of real climbing, seemed an uninhabited and practically uninhabitable wilderness of rock.

The deeper Hal and Baldur were led into the foothills by the twisting path, the more difficult the going became. Hills melded together and became the flank of an undoubted mountain. All river valleys were well below them now, and they were no longer walking so much as climbing, hands as well as feet being necessary to get over some of the steep rock ledges.

"Well," the puffing northman told his colleague, "if those two damned moles can climb it, so can we."

"I only wish they would go faster," Baldur murmured back.

Ever deeper they went into the mountains, and ever higher. Steadily receding into the wintry distance was Loki's ring of magic fire, which still sprouted untiringly from the top of its rocky hill. Several times Hal caught a glimpse of the tall flames, hanging on the rim of the sky, like a signal of warning to the world. Now, at a range that must have been more than twenty miles, the god's handiwork seemed no more than a distant candle.

Once Baldur stood looking back at the fire, murmuring Brunhild's name.

At the end of one of their nightly rest stops, while they were waiting for the sky to lighten enough to let them begin a seventh day of tracking, Baldur suddenly asked: "Hal, I keep wondering about Wodan."

"What about him?"

"He is not merciful, that cannot be part of his nature—so if he releases Brunhild, it will be because he is honorable, and generous to his chosen warriors."

Days ago Hal had given up trying to understand Baldur's theology. "If you say so."

"I do say so, Hal—my friend. How much do you know about the gods?"

The northman studied his young colleague warily. "Just what everyone knows, or ought to know."

"What?"

"Well. That Wodan, and Loki, and all the rest are people just like you and me. Except that at some point in their lives, each man or woman of them picked up and put inside his or her head one of the things that we call Faces. And each Face gives its wearer tremendous powers."

"I believe that Wodan must be more than that." The young man's voice was low, but full of emphasis. "The Father of Battles must be something more than just a man with power."

Hal sighed. "Well, I don't want to argue. What makes you think I have knowledge of gods beyond the ordinary?"

Baldur shook his head, as if in disappointment with Hal's answer. "When we first met you told me that you'd once been shipmate to some god, but failed to recognize him."

"Hah, so you were listening after all! But the fact that I once made a fool of myself doesn't qualify me as an expert on the subject."

"You must know something more than you have said!"

"Not much."

"But I have never even seen a god!" Baldur clenched his fists and turned around. "If Wodan should appear now, up there on the mountain . . ." He seemed almost despairing at the prospect.

"You'd deal with the experience somehow. People do. If he appears, then at last you'd get to see what he looks like. Tell me, besides Wodan and Loki, what other deities are most popular around these parts? To which of them do people pray?"

"Well, there's Loki, of course. But I wouldn't say Loki is popular. Feared, yes. He's the subject of talk, not the object of worship." Baldur sounded wistful, adding: "Naturally, those who hope for leadership in battle universally choose Wodan."

"I suppose. Who else?"

The young man meditated briefly. "Thor may be even more popular with the common soldiers—of course he too is a good fighter."

"Of course." Hal was nodding. The mention of Thor had jogged his memory, brought back in sharp focus the face and voice of the poor woman standing in the road with her ragged children, snatching back her copper coins and mouthing the strange prayer, or blessing, with which she had anointed Hal.

He nodded again. "Thor with his hammer, a mean weapon by all reports. As I understand it, he throws it out to kill anyone or destroy anything he chooses. Then back it flies to his hand again. I've heard some stories about that. But what about the ordinary folk? Who do they worship? Not everyone wants to be a berserk warrior, froth at the mouth and ignore wounds."

"Certainly not." Baldur's tone became cool at this irreverence. "As for the commoners who are not fighters . . ." The young man had to stop and think; it was as if he hardly could remember anyone who fit that category. "I suppose Freya is most popular. She's undoubtedly the greatest goddess—and there are half a dozen lesser deities, male and female."

"No more than that?" Hal snorted. "Down south they have 'em by the hundreds."

Baldur's look seemed a polite expression of doubt. If such a swarm of beings claimed divinity, he seemed to be thinking, most of them must be frauds, or at least inferior, and he had no interest in them. "And do the people down there know of Wodan? Are they true warriors?"

"Warlike enough," Hal assured him. "And you may believe me or not, but few down there have ever heard the name of your All-Highest. Round the Great Sea, where I've been living the past few years, everyone would tell you that Zeus is the greatest god of all, practically the ruler of the universe. Of course Zeus frequently has his troubles with Hades, now and then with Neptune. He's chronically at war with Giants. And down there, if you ask who is the god of war, people will tell you it's a fellow called Mars, or Ares."

Baldur shrugged and shook his head, as if there could be no accounting for some people's crazy ideas. "Our gods, with Wodan leading, know that they will face monsters and Giants in the final battle of the world, when fire and flood destroy everything." He sighed. "Giants are another kind of being that I've never seen."

"I don't know about the end of the world. But no one around here has ever raised a temple or an altar to Zeus? Or to Athena?"

Baldur seemed to be trying to remember. "I've heard those names mentioned. But altars and temples? No, I don't think so."

Hal clapped him on the shoulder, an almost staggering blow. "Lad, it is time you got out in the great world, and discovered what most of the people in it are doing!"

The youth was steadfast in his gloom. "Brunhild is the only part of the world I care about. To join her, or to spend my life in the attempt, is the only adventure I am seeking now."

When their journey once more resumed, under a sky grown bright enough to let them identify the marks left by gnomes' feet in the white snow, Hal and Baldur got one more look at the glow of the distant fire-ring, now many miles away.

Drifted piles of old, crusted snow began to appear around the trail as they went on up. The trail itself was covered, and the footprints of the two gnomes were plain to see. The snow was naturally deepest in the places remaining shaded all day long. On and on the two men traveled upward, deeper into the mountains. It was good that they had equipped themselves for cold weather before setting out.

And, since they wanted to avoid freezing to death, a fire was beginning to seem like a necessity, not just a good idea. Hal kept thinking it over, and shivering, until he convinced himself that there was no real reason not to have one, if they built it in a sheltered place and kept it small. At night the Earthdwellers would be intent on their own climbing progress, steadily getting farther ahead, not much caring if someone else happened to be on the trail behind them. Quite possibly, as Wodan's artisans, they felt they had reliable magical protection against assault. Anyway, it was worth a few risks to keep from freezing. As night approached again, they moved aside from the trail, into the midst of a small stand of evergreens, and set about gathering sticks and twigs. Getting out his flint and steel, Hal soon had created a comforting small flame.

There was no game to be had, and even had there been, neither man was carrying a projectile weapon. The little grove offered nothing in the way of nuts or berries.

With the coming of daylight on the eighth day of their hike, they picked up the trail again and climbed on, trying to ignore the growling of their almost empty stomachs. Hal was thinking to himself that if there was a real Valhalla anywhere—and he had no reason to doubt that some truth lay behind the stories—then it would be hard to find a better setting for it than these mountains.

At one spot, a place where the footprints clearly went off the road and came back, Hal and Baldur investigated. At a little distance from the trail they found a kind of campsite, not much more than a small trampled area, where the gnomes must have sheltered during the previous day. Hal supposed they must be carrying a roll or package of lightweight fabric that they raised as a tent to ward off the dangerous sunlight. He searched the area diligently, but unhappily could discover no forgotten food. He and Baldur had been rationing the cheese and biscuits for several days, but now their supplies were almost gone. Right about now, a few roots and mushrooms would taste very good.

While encouraging Baldur to keep thinking about Horses, Hal kept alight the flame of his own secret enthusiasm. It was a good way to keep from thinking of his stomach.

Baldur never mentioned gold but kept speculating about the Horses. He claimed to know the names of several, had various contradictory ideas about exactly where the animals would be kept, how well their stables might be guarded.

Hal was careful not to argue too strenuously against even the most far-fetched details of his companion's scheme. But at the same time he wanted to prepare Baldur, without alarming him, to face the possibility of a sudden change of plan. The young man would have to come to grips with the fact that their chances of even laying eyes on one of Wodan's magic steeds were very low.

Of course Hal's chance of getting his hands on any scraps of gold might not be any better. But he thought that still remained to be determined.

And as for Wodan's Horses—Hal's mind boggled when he tried to visualize himself, or his naive companion, actually getting astride one of those marvelous beasts, let alone using them in a cavalry raid to plunder old Loki's fire-ring of the fair prisoner supposed to have been confined there.

No, if he and Baldur were really on the path to Wodan's stronghold, and he had to admit that now seemed to be the case, then more likely than not they would soon encounter some insuperable obstacle. Probably something—or someone—would appear to turn them back well before they actually got within sight of their goal, and at that point Hal would be ready to give in graciously and sensibly. The trick was in knowing when certain disaster loomed, recognizing the warning signs before it was too late. He had followed a similar plan for most of his life, and so far as he was still alive.

The trouble was, he didn't think that Baldur would calmly accept the postponement, if not the absolute cancellation, of his last hope of reaching Brunhild—not unless the denial came from Wodan himself.

And was there any reason to think Wodan would be even a little tolerant of casual trespassers? But there was no use worrying about that; not now, while the way ahead still lay open. Hal was advancing warily, thoroughly aware that persistent climbing might well bring a couple of mere foolhardy mortals abruptly to the brink of some kind of suicidal confrontation. Of course he fully intended to turn around before they ran headlong into anything of that kind.

And yet, in spite of all the alarms put up by common sense, despite the foreboding of gruesome danger, he was drawn irresistibly forward by the thought that there was still a chance—a slight, magical, insidious, and wonderful chance—that Baldur's scheme was not entirely crazy. The road to full success, to magic gold and magic Horses, to who knew what, might actually lie open—and there was a much better chance, Hal thought, of simply gaining information that could make him at least a moderately wealthy man.

Such trees as still grew at this altitude were sparse, stunted, and twisted with their lifelong struggles against the wind. Now squalls of snow, alternating with freezing rain, came swirling to pester the advancing climbers. Hal found he could no longer tell in which direction they were going, except that it was generally still up. As the howling wind increased in strength, it seemed to him in his more imaginative moments that he could hear laughter drifting down from the still unseen ramparts of Valhalla. He was careful to say nothing of this to his companion.

He was ready to accept that what he seemed to hear was only his imagination. And what he imagined was of course the laughter of Wodan's elite guard, whose ranks had been closed to Baldur by a Valkyrie's whim. They were the pick of the bloody crop, or were supposed to be, men who had been slain in earthly battle but whose spirits had been snatched by Valkyries from the jaws of Hades, saved from the Underworld. By the will of the All-Seeing, they lived on here, above the world.

According to the legends, the courage and ferocity of these warriors had so pleased the great god that he, through his flying emissaries, granted them immortality. They were superbly dedicated fighting men, miraculously restored to life and health after each bout of combat, who could imagine no greater happiness than to spend the remaining ages of the world in a splendid cycle of doing everything they loved, moving perpetually from evening feast and carousal to brief and dreamless sleep, then sallying forth to morning battlefield and staggering, wounded, back again to the hall of feasting, or being carried back by the Valkyries if they were freshly slain.

Trying to picture in his imagination the great game of perpetual slaughter, so lovingly described in many legends, Hal wondered if the players went through rituals and chose up sides anew each night. Or maybe it was just a glorious free-for-all, with no rules to speak of. Wodan's finest should be always honing their martial skills, keeping themselves perpetually ready for the final, world-ending battle in which the forces of good and evil were ultimately doomed to annihilate each other.

Hal could remember hearing, years ago, one version of the Valhalla story in which the Valkyries, when not riding forth on their recruiting missions, served the endlessly rehealed heroes nightly as willing concubines. Hal was not sure how well that system was likely to work, given that there were supposed to be only nine of the young women. Presumably by this time there ought to be thousands of heroes, or at the very least several hundred. Delicately he forbore to raise the subject with his companion.

In any case, Baldur's thoughts must have been running along similar lines—and once more there rose up in the young man his sheer dread of the god he worshiped but had never seen. Easy enough to say that gods were only humans who wore Faces in their heads; but when you knew that you were standing face to face with one, there was a little more to it than that. There were moments when it seemed to Hal that the young man's nerve was going to fail him.

Once, for no apparent reason, Baldur stopped suddenly in the middle of the trail. The youth was staring into the bleakness ahead and shivering seemingly with more than the wintry wind.

Instinct told Hal that a rough challenge would be the most bracing treatment he could administer just now. "What's the matter, young one? Your feet suddenly gone cold?"

The young man sputtered for a moment, then choked out: "What will Wodan do to men who intrude uninvited upon his celebration?"

Hal kept his answer as casual as he could. Demonstrating what he considered heroic restraint, he kept himself from clouting Baldur alongside the head. "You mean, who come to borrow his Horses? Now's hardly the time to start to worry about that. How in the Underworld should I know? If he admires courage as much as the stories say, he might just give us credit for showing a lot of nerve, and invite us in. On the other hand, he might throw us off one of these cliffs—but as they say, a man has to die sometime.

"Anyway, aren't you the same one I heard only a couple of days ago, talking about becoming a berserker?" Trying to come up with some encouragement, Hal added a flat lie: "Even Hagan was looking at you as if he thought you might have the right stuff to join his band. I suppose you ought to take that as a compliment."

But Baldur only shook his head, as if in silent rejection of his crippled berserker father and all his works. Then he cast a long look back, along what was visible of the trail they had just ascended, marked now by four sets of footprints in the ankle-deep snow. Following his gaze, Hal was struck by the thought that if the gnomes started home before that record melted or was covered by a new fall, they would certainly know they had been followed on their way up.

Time enough, Hal told himself, to worry about that later.

Hal had the strong impression that the youth was fighting down an impulse to turn and run. But so far, Baldur was refusing to let himself do that.

At last the young man choked out a few quiet words. "I must see Brunhild again, in this world or the next."

"You know, young one, I really think you ought to make up your mind which it is you really want the most: Brunhild sitting in your lap, or yourself in Wodan's?"

The only response Hal got to that was an angry stare, and for a moment he was afraid that he had gone too far. Probably it was a question Baldur had not yet answered for himself.

Time to move on again. Hal thought that now they must be truly very near their goal.

8

Suddenly there was real evidence that they had almost reached their goal.

Tilting his head back, Hal could now see, through swirling snow and mist, some kind of construction looming above them, see it well enough as to have no remaining doubts of its reality. The fortress, or castle, was so hedged about by sharp, unclimbable peaks and barren crags, and the single path that seemed to offer the only approach lay so intricately wound among these rocks, that the two intruders were almost upon their goal before they got their first good look at it. And at that point the two adventurers were gazing so steeply upward, into such thickly swirling grayness, that they could be certain of very little, beyond the solidity of a smooth, looming mass, the regularity of artificial walls.

Now they had had a glimpse of their destination, but how to reach it still presented something of a question. A light accumulation of new snow, together with drifting of the old, was covering all signs of a path among the jagged rocks, as well as the footprints they had been following.

As it turned out, there still remained almost a mile of winding trail between them and the structure that loomed above. Hal and Baldur had to spend one fireless and almost-frozen night, huddled together for warmth, when it grew too dark for Sundweller eyes to find their way among the clustered boulders. This close to their goal, they did not dare to show a light of any kind. Fortunately, between big rocks they were able to find a niche in which to shelter from the wind.

When the stars in the clear portion of the sky started to fade in morning light, and the mountain landscape began to grow faintly visible beneath the waning moon, the men gave thanks for their survival and started climbing again. Each time they paused to take their eyes from the trail, they strained them looking upward at a dim and distant parapet, still wreathed in what seemed perpetual mist.

Suddenly Baldur came to a halt. He had his right arm raised, aiming uphill with it as if he meant to use it as a spear. The finger that he pointed with was shaking. His voice was practically a shriek when he cried out what he had seen.

"There's a wall up there. By all the gods, an enormous wall. And a sentry on top of it, looking this way! We have been seen!"

Hal jerked his head back, staring upward, catching nothing but a blinding swirl of mist and snow. "Well, if we have . . ."

He let his words die there. If they had been seen by the powers of Valhalla, it was too late now to do anything about it.

His heart had begun to pound, but he was certainly not ready to turn and run. As far as he could tell, they had crossed no marked boundaries, transgressed no warning signs. He and Baldur ought to have as much right as anyone to this deserted mountain path.

Moving steadily, they trudged on. They had climbed through one more switchback, when both stopped in their tracks. Someone, a single figure, was marching down the path from above, coming directly toward them.

Marching was not really the right word. The means of movement looked more like sliding . . .

Baldur cried out: "It is the sentry! Or it looks like the same man."

"It must be . . ." Hal started, but again he let his words die.

He could not tell what it was, this thing advancing upon them. He could only be sure it was no ordinary man.

The man, or image, was following a descending trail, but on drawing near the pair of intruders it ignored them as if they were not there. The appearance it presented was that of a lone soldier whose dress and equipment Hal found completely unfamiliar. The figure's clothing was light, utterly inadequate for the cold weather, and it was carrying a javelin in its right hand, and wearing a shorter, broader spear slung over its back, with a sling knotted at his waist and a net bag of rocks for ammunition.

As the figure drew near, Baldur began an impassioned plea, or greeting, but the thing ignored him totally, and he broke his speech off in midsentence.

Still it seemed to be gliding, rather than striding normally on its two legs. The legs were moving, but not fast enough to account for the thing's rapid progress.

"Hal, is that a god?" Baldur's whisper was tortured, barely audible.

Hal's answer was just as quiet. "It looks like none I ever saw."

"Is it a ghost?"

Whether ghost, image, or something Hal had never even imagined before, when it came to the blockage in the trail, it passed through the rock, as if either the stone or the warrior's body were insubstantial.

Meanwhile, as the thing approached, Hal uttered the best that he could manage in the way of a calm greeting, but unnervingly he and his words were totally ignored. Meanwhile Baldur had resumed his jabbering at the figure, pouring out a mixture of pleas and boasting—but the man, or wraith, in gray still paid no attention to either of them, and strode or glided on about its own unguessable business, until it vanished round a turn only a few yards downhill.

Hal felt a chill biting deeper than the cold wind, but actually no great surprise, when he noted that their visitant had left no footprints in the snow. Up the trail, there were still only the two sets left by the gnomes' feet, here spared from the drifting snow by some vagary of wind or shelter.

Well, having come this far, he was not going to be turned back by a speechless ghost. If Wodan meant to warn them, he would have to be a little plainer.

Baldur was too shaken to notice the lack of tracks, and Hal said nothing about it. Instead he asked: "Was that the sentry you saw above?"

"I—I don't know." Baldur scowled and stared up into grayness, but the weather had thickened so it was no longer possible to see anything.

The two men climbed a half-hour longer, making slow progress, panting their way up one switchback after another, before they touched those mist-enfolded walls. They had seen no one else and heard no challenge from above. They had come now to a section of the trail where less new snow had fallen, and still there were only the tracks of the same four feet, marking the passage of the same two gnomes. By now, Hal was confident that he could have recognized the prints of their small but well-constructed boots anywhere.

Presently Hal and his companion rounded the last bastion of the outer wall, and then went boldly in, entering Valhalla through a huge gateway, passing a framework of metal bars that might have been a portcullis before it was overtaken by utter ruin.

The doors that must once have guarded this entry had entirely disappeared. It seemed that at some time they might have been ripped or burned from the ravaged gateway, for there still remained the twisted remnants of their massive metal hinges, along with some of the overhead stonework. What was left was only an open passage between the frowning walls of stone, empty except for drifted snow marked with two sets of gnomish footprints.

An hour ago Hal had thought he was too far from the walls of Valhalla to get a good look at them, and now it seemed he was too close. In a few more moments, the towering stone surface was actually within reach, and behind it an enormous and vastly higher structure, the latter visible only in hints and suggestions, brief glimpses through swirls of mist and snow.

So far, the only portions of Wodan's home—if such it was—that was clearly visible to the visitors consisted of tiers of enormous blocks of stone, each slab so huge it was hard to imagine how it had ever been lifted and set in place. Certainly forces vastly stronger than human arms and backs must have been at work. But still those great ashlars had been fitted together with consummate skill, the joints all fine and straight.

Following the base of the gigantic wall for a couple of hundred yards brought the pair of intruders to a gateway constructed on a matching scale. Whatever door or barrier might once have blocked this portal seemed to have been long since removed, just as the outer gates had been. Through this broad aperture the footprints of the gnomes marched on and in with no sign of hesitation, not even a change of stride. Now Hal could see that the outer wall was all of forty feet thick.

There might have been a sentry on the wall above, but there was none now. Nor was there any visible guardian at the gate.

Having passed the gateway, the two intruders found themselves in an outer courtyard of a savagely ruined but once magnificent castle, built on a scale that Hal thought truly worthy of the gods. He thought the remaining portions of the inner citadel, or keep, even more than half ruined as it was, must be fully a hundred feet in height.

From up above them somewhere, among the giants' stonework, there came a sudden whine of wind, startling both men. But it was only wind.

"Hal—this is not what I thought we would discover here."

Baldur's voice was awed, and also troubled. He had moved a step closer to his companion. "Not at all what I expected."

For once Hal had no answer. If this was, or once had been, truly the home of Wodan, then it seemed Zeus had a worthy rival for his claim to be the master of the universe. No doubt about it, this structure was very large and still impressive. But a glimpse through some of the narrow upper windows showed slivers of snowy sky, evidence that the great castle too had been unroofed. Now the still-advancing double trail of footprints was bordered, and in one place partially blocked, by regularly shaped ashlars that had tumbled down from above. The snow hid all details that might have offered a clue as to how long ago the tumbling and scattering had taken place.

Hal had never visited the legendary home of Zeus and his most exalted colleagues, nor did he know of any human who had done so, despite all the descriptions in hundreds of detailed stories. He wasn't sure that any such place as high Olympus had ever really existed—but he thought that this might once have been its equal in magnificence.

On the other hand, it looked to Hal like no feasts or ceremonies had been held here in Wodan's castle for many a day. To what height these walls might once have ascended, and what roofs might once have covered them, was impossible to say. Nearly all were fallen in, great beams and stones making vast piles of rubbish, the rubble and the remaining structure alike now half-hidden under mounds of white. On level space, untrodden snow lay inches deep in the mountain's morning sunshine, all across the vast and nearly roofless space that might once have been the great hall of a great god's castle. Here and there, half-shapeless mounds of white suggested snow-buried furniture.

Steadily the double tracks, the same ones Hal and Baldur had been following for many miles, went on, through and around all these wonders. The gnomes had come this way before. Their footprints betrayed no uncertainty on their makers' part, no false turns or doubling back, showing that the farrier and his magical colleague knew exactly where they wanted to go, and had not been tempted to delay and gawk at any ungnomish marvels on the way. Doubtless they were regular visitors to this mountain realm, and to them this was all perfectly familiar.

"Wait!" It was an anguished whisper, accompanied by a hard clutch on Hal's arm. "Look over there!"

Baldur was tall enough to see from their present position, but Hal needed to climb up a step. Raising his head cautiously over the top of a huge tumbled block, Hal saw distant movement in a half-enclosed courtyard—what looked like a squad of perhaps a dozen irregular soldiers, armed men in an assortment of shabby clothes that were not uniforms.

The courtyard was perhaps a hundred paces distant from the place where Hal and Baldur watched, and over most of its considerable area the snow had been trampled into slush and mud. Snow had stopped falling now, and the sun kept trying to extricate itself from scudding clouds, with intermittent success.

Keeping themselves concealed behind huge blocks of stone, Hal and Baldur spent a minute or two gaping at a squad of drilling soldiers in the distance. Hal felt mixed emotions at the sight. It would have been unreasonable to hope that the place where the gnomes were going to work would otherwise be entirely deserted. The soldiers were practicing formally with their weapons, while the harsh, penetrating voice of a sergeant, which doubtless sounded much the same forever and in all armies, nagged and berated them. A thin line of men, no more than a dozen or so, lunged with spears at imaginary opponents, and then withdrew raggedly. At a distance they looked more like sick call than dominating heroes.

The sergeant bawled again, and his squad paired off, one

on one, obviously intending to engage in some kind of fencing or sparring practice.

Baldur found the spectacle disturbing. "Those can't be . . ." He let it trail away.

Hal kept his voice low. "Can't be your blessed heroes, enjoying their daily brawl?"

"No." The young man shook his head emphatically. "They can't. Not possibly."

"Then what are they?"

The youth was almost dancing in his worry and frustration. "This can't be it. This must be only some outpost, where they stable Horses. But if this *is* Valhalla, I want to—"

Hal took a hard grip on Baldur's upper arm, shook him into momentary silence. "Keep it quiet. If your girlfriend actually had to carry someone to this godforsaken ruin, filling her quota or whatever, it's clear why she didn't want it to be you."

Judging from the look on Baldur's face, the youth might just have received his death blow. "But I . . . no, that must be wrong."

"Just look around you. The gnomes are real enough. And probably their magic is, for it charms golden shoes, giving Horses the power to fly and carry Valkyries, even carry them unharmed through strange fires. And some peculiar power is producing things like that image of a warrior that met us on the path.

"But you can have the rest of Wodan's glorious domain. It doesn't look to me like any place I'd want to live. Anyway, we shouldn't be arguing about this now. Now get a grip on yourself, and let's see if we can find some Horses."

Baldur turned pale under his soldier's tan, at words that must have sounded in his ears as something very close to blasphemy; but it was hard to argue with the evidence of his own eyes. His manner became a kind of frenzied timidity. At last the youth choked out: "I say the real Valhalla must be somewhere else. And this is only some outpost, where Wodan stables Horses."

Hal was eager to accept that theory, or any theory, if it let them get on with business. "I think you've hit on it, lad. All the better for us if Valhalla's somewhere else. Then its master will likely be there, not here—if he's anywhere right now. So pull yourself together. I thought you were ready to risk all for a chance of seeing Brunhild."

Privately Hal was thinking furiously. The many signs of ruin and neglect and poverty around them strongly suggested a lack of management, to say the least. Hal could readily imagine that Wodan was currently dead, his Face lying lost and forgotten somewhere, unworn by any human. If that was true, the implications were tremendous. If anyone, Valkyrie or not, was really imprisoned behind Loki's fiery curtain, it would not have been Wodan who put the prisoner there; he or she had run afoul of some other power.

Again Baldur was peering back in the direction of the drilling men. "It can't be," the youth murmured.

"You mean those scarecrows with sticks are not your chosen Heroes. I'm sure you're right. It could be they're only— well, enlisted men. Auxiliaries of some kind."

"Yes, that could be." Baldur sounded slightly relieved.

"Or Heroes on sick call," Hal added as a private, murmured afterthought. Other possibilities were whirling through his brain. Gods did die, and for all he knew, Wodan might be really dead. Maybe one of the local warlords had secretly taken over the stewardship of Valhalla, gold and Horses and all.

Not having to contend against a god should make their expedition vastly easier. Whoever was master of the marvelous Horses and their blessed shoes, the farriers' smithy would have to be here somewhere . . . that part of the legend couldn't be entirely a lie. It couldn't be. Because he, Hal, was still carrying a fragment of a golden shoe.

"Auxiliaries." Baldur was still chewing on that word. It did not really satisfy him, but it gave him something to bite on. "That must be it." Then a renewed note of awe crept into his voice. "Hal, look at this."

Hal looked. Another squad of men had appeared from somewhere, to practice against . . . but hold on. Were those in the new detachment men at all? Their gliding movements and stiff poses reminded Hal of the "ghost" that passed them on the trail.

The visitors observed in fascination. Hal, watching as closely as he could at the distance, soon realized that the weapons carried by the gliding images only stung and did not wound, when employed against live flesh and blood. When a weapon in the hand of a live man struck a wraith, the effect seemed even less consequential.

But all this spying was essentially a waste of time. Now he and Baldur turned their backs on the distant drill and withdrew from it, under cover of the scattering of huge tumbled blocks. Meanwhile the blanket of old snow surrounding them remained almost untrodden, so the castle could hardly be swarming with people.

The trail of the gnomes remained as plain to see as ever, but now Hal began to move ever more slowly forward. He paused before he crossed each open space, peering cautiously around each corner before advancing.

He was just at the crucial moment of one such step, when Baldur's touch on his arm made him jump. When Hal looked around, the youth was pointing skyward, whispering fiercely: "Look!"

Half expecting to see an armored maiden straddling a flying Horse, or maybe a truly remarkable ghost or two, Hal raised his gaze. From some unseen base no more than fifty yards ahead, a band of greasy smoke had begun to mount into the sky; it appeared that Andvari was getting his forge working. Moments later there came a preliminary clang of heavy metal, as if a smith might be warming up his arm with a swing or two against an anvil. Hal thought any golden horseshoe that caught *that* blow, the way it sounded, would have been mashed flat.

Working iron ought to need a lot more heat and force than working gold—but of course when magic entered the picture, common sense was often driven out.

Hal's imaginative conception of an underground workshop, created for the convenience of the gnomes, had vanished in cold morning daylight. Soon the two intruders had got closer to the forge-fire, which glowed behind the closed shutters of a small building. They were so close that Hal could hear the master farrier tell his assistant to throw in a handful of salt, "to keep the fire clean." It was a heavily accented voice, filled with dark overtones, and he thought it was Andvari's. Certainly it sounded like the speech Hal had heard in the gnomes' village.

A strange, whinnying sound, unfamiliar to both men but not entirely strange to either of them, carried in the clear morning air.

"Listen!" Baldur's breath puffed like steam from a kettle when he whispered again. This time it was obviously not the whinnying horse that he had in mind.

Hal listened, standing in shadow. All the while, despite his warm coat, he kept shifting his weight and swinging his arms, fearing that he would stiffen if he stood still for very long in the fierce cold. Soon he could hear a few more clangs, of a slightly lighter tone, as if the smith who wielded it were now getting down to serious business. Maybe, Hal thought, there was urgent work on iron and steel to be got out of the way, repairs to harness or armor, before the artisans could get to working the rare and valuable stuff.

"What do we do now?" Baldur was gripping his sword-hilt, and his voice held an agony of fear.

Hal kept his own whisper quiet. "We sneak around there,

and try to get a look at what they're doing. Well, we've come to see the Horses, haven't we?" He made a savage pointing gesture. "They must be over there somewhere."

And, he thought to himself, if golden shoes were being forged right here, then the raw material could hardly be very far away.

9

Cautiously the two men kept working their way, a step at a time, toward the small building that poured out sounds of industrious activity. Hal, moving a step or two ahead of his companion, thought the little shop or smithy could not have been part of the original construction of the citadel, because it was so roughly built, mortared together of much smaller stones than the towering walls surrounding the courtyard. This structure also enjoyed what seemed to be quite a rarity in Valhalla, an intact roof. As Hal crept closer, he took note of the fact that the covering of the smithy was a fairly recent construction of poles and thatch. A few small birds, their winter nesting evidently disturbed, now flew out screaming.

Energetically, the black smoke continued to pour out of the short stone chimney. Each visible side of the small structure boasted one small window, and each opening was protected by a crude wooden shutter, roughly wedged in place. Hal decided that the building probably served as housing for the visiting gnomes as well as their workshop. Naturally, gnomes would require more shade against intruding daylight than any of the surrounding ruins seemed likely to afford them, all well-ventilated as they were.

Once again, as when he had picked up the fragment of horseshoe in front of the wall of flame, Hal became aware of the twitching of the Golden Fleece in his belt pouch. Elated, he sneaked a look into the pouch, and saw that the bit of special fabric that he cherished was glowing as before.

"What are you doing?" Baldur breathed.

"Nothing! Never mind." With a gesture commanding full attention to the job at hand, Hal led on.

Hal saw that the building had at least two doors. The small one, which he could see, was tightly closed. The other was big enough for large animals to pass in and out, and was guarded only by a tattered canvas that was doubtless meant to keep in warmth and block out the dazzling daylight from sensitive gnomish eyes.

Moving with what seemed to him infinite care, Hal got close enough to the gnomes' forge to get a look inside, peering through a chink at one edge of one of the uneven shutters. He could see and recognize Andvari's face, but not that of the gnome who worked beside him.

The gnomes had removed their outer clothing in the heat of the interior, exposing most of their pallid skin. The master artisan was frowning with concentration as he bent over his anvil, hammer raised in a big hand at the end of a lean arm gnarled with muscle. The assistant was a vague shadow, moving briskly in the background.

It was pretty much the scene Hal had expected to see, and the only trouble with it, from his point of view, was that there was no gold to be seen anywhere. He caught a brief glimpse of something on the anvil—but all he could tell about the workpiece was that it was glowing metal.

The raw material for magic horseshoes had to be somewhere nearby—but where?

He opened his pouch again to sneak one more look at his fragment of Fleece, and discovered it no brighter and no warmer than before. His talisman was going to provide no further help.

Where in the Underworld would the guardians of golden

treasure put it, to minimize the risk of theft? A strongbox of some kind seemed likely. Or it could be simply buried in a hole in the ground, almost right under the forge-fire. And where were the guards? Hal thought there would simply have to be guards standing by, and he had noticed none. That of course raised the ominous suggestion that Wodan might be depending on sheer magic, or invisible beings of some kind, to protect his treasure—and that would be bad news indeed.

Baldur was nudging him. Suddenly it was necessary to temporarily abandon all attempts at spying, and try to conceal themselves in the inadequate shelter offered by a corner of the building, because the crunch of feet on snow and gravel signaled someone was approaching. Here came a scrawny youth who looked no more like one of Wodan's Heroes than he did a gnome, leading one of the strange four-hoofed animals through daylight from a nearby stable to the forge. This individual was ill-clad and shivering, moved at a shuffling pace, and looked almost as blank-eyed as the ghost Hal had encountered on the trail. He guided the willing Horse along with one hand gripping its mane. The farriers' operation had begun very recently, but already a broad trail had been trampled into the snow between the stable and the smithy.

Hal and Baldur both froze into immobility when this attendant appeared. They were only half-hidden, and it seemed inevitable that the fellow was going to see them, yet he did not. His eyes were fixed in a hopeless stare on the ground some little distance ahead of him.

As soon as the youth had once more passed out of sight, Baldur, whispering something Hal could not hear clearly, something about finding the Horses, began a nervous slow retreat. But Hal had not come this far to be easily scared away. He waited until he felt sure the gaunt fellow was out of the way, and then carefully worked his way closer to the window, thinking that in this case the bright sunlight outside would protect him from observation better than midnight darkness. Baldur took courage and with his hand on his sword-hilt crept up close to Hal again.

Between the intervals of hammering, there were other sounds from inside the workshed, as of some large, hard-footed creature moving on a floor of hard-packed earth. And there were smells that might have issued from a cameloids' stable—but it was not exactly the same smell, with which practically everyone in the world must be familiar.

With each passing second, Hal became less and less concerned that the gnomes, with their poor sight and their concentration on their work, were going to catch sight of the intruders. Nor, with the noise of fire and hammer going on inside, were they likely to be heard. And even discovery would not necessarily be disastrous.

At last Hal could peer in round the edge of the crude canvas drapery shading the doorway. He got one good look at And-vari, and then at last he was granted an eye-shocking glimpse of the glow of gold. With one wiry hand the farrier was fitting an aureate shoe onto a broad hoof, while holding the animal's fetlock clamped between his knees. First it was necessary to scrape the bottom of the hoof, using a rasp or sharp iron tool made for the purpose.

Standing slightly in the background, the assistant gnome, who was really a skilled magician, gestured and muttered at each curved piece of metal before it was nailed into place.

The shoe itself went through some slight variations in color until it was securely fastened on. It grew blurred and dim as the nails went in, one after another, and Hal thought it lost all special radiance the instant the last one was clinched tight.

There was another roofed building nearby, evidently a kind of stable, from which the gaunt assistant was leading the animals one by one to be shod. The pair of intruders looked into that next.

Baldur repeatedly kept whispering: "Gold Mane, Gold Mane." Hal recalled that that was the name of the horse that Brunhild had ridden. Meanwhile, Hal kept silently but fiercely scanning every inch of the place for gold.

Naturally enough there were stalls in the stable, besides sources of food and water that Hal thought might very well be magical. And still there was the strange and half-familiar smell, very earthy and mundane. Hanging on the walls were clusters of leather straps, some kind of harness evidently, but none of the metal attachments to the straps were gold.

Of anything resembling a treasure vault, there was no sign at all.

When Hal had completed a stealthy progress through almost the entire complex of stables and barns, he had actually seen no more than about a dozen Horses in all, in space adequate for many more. The animals present were housed in two different buildings, the majority in one barn where they were waiting to be looked at and worked on by the farrier. Only a couple of Horses were in the other group, standing about restively on their new footwear. Hal was no judge of quality in the rare species, but to him, all the animals looked strong and healthy.

Gesturing silently, Hal led his companion around the smithy where the forge-fire burned, and from which issued the occasional sounds of metallic hammering. He had convinced himself by now that there was no need to be exceptionally quiet. One creature snorted as the strangers passed through the stable; and the straw littering the old wooden or earthen floor of its stall stirred and crumpled and jumped, disturbed by heavy hooves.

Half-expecting at every moment to encounter someone, Hal was ready with what he hoped might be a halfway plausible story; and as a last resort, his battle-hatchet. But they found no human presence other than their own.

This stable, like the others, was a dim place, with a broad central aisle, from which a number of finely built, commodious stalls diverged on each side. Baldur began to look into each of these in turn. Hal thought he had seen a lot of human habitations that were not as comfortable.

Hal could see no droppings in the occupied stalls; maybe some magical power was cleaning the stables as fast as they were dirtied.

There was a strange sound from the next stall, and Hal looked over to discover Baldur in a paroxysm of delight, which he was somehow managing to keep almost entirely silent. At the moment he was kissing a large, pale-haired Horse on the muzzle, and it was obvious that the young man had at last identified the animal he had been seeking. Baldur kept stroking Gold Mane's head and shoulders, and murmuring feverish endearments, almost as if to Brunhild herself.

The Horse seemed pleased by this treatment, as far as Hal could tell, and Hal himself was pleased as well—any confirmation of the wild stories that Baldur had been telling him was more than welcome.

Just as Hal was turning away again, his foot inadvertently nudged a battered metal or wooden bucket, which made a weighty rattling sound. He looked down, and his breath caught in his throat. For once, it seemed, the Fates might be truly with him!

Jumbled carelessly in the bottom of the bucket were at least a dozen golden horseshoes, full-sized and unbroken.

For a wild moment Hal was tempted to grab the container by its rope handle and run for the open gate and the descending trail. But any such mad try would of course be hopeless. Even if his dash to get away went unmarked by any of Wodan's creatures, Baldur would certainly yell after him, maybe even jump on his back and tackle him, for committing such a staggering blasphemy as stealing from the great god.

A second look into the pail convinced Hal that these were the worn shoes, pried from the horses' hooves and casually tossed into a bucket, ready to be melted down, then, with some addition of new gold to replace what had been worn away, reworked into new ones. Now he estimated there were more than a dozen, as many as fifteen. Why they should be here, yards away from the forge and out of the farriers' reach, was not immediately obvious. But a lot of things in the world were awkward and illogical.

Blind greed, surprisingly strong now that it had a real chance, urged Hal to snatch up and carry away the whole bucket, heavy as it was. But the instinct for self-preservation insisted that he not try that. Half a dozen shoes would be plenty, or at least he was willing to bet they would, and he thought he had room for that many in his pouch.

As fast as his hands could move, Hal began stuffing twisted little curves of gold into his pouch; they were heavy, but there seemed little danger of his falling into deep water, so he would be all right.

There was a strange little noise, a kind of choking, and he looked up to see Baldur staring at him. The youth was almost stunned. "What are you doing?" he quavered, in evident horror.

"Providing for my future, lad." Hal kept his voice to a hoarse whisper. "For yours, too, if you like. Let's get on with it!"

"But you cannot *steal* from Wodan!" Baldur was almost hissing with outrage. "I should have known, because all along you have talked of gold, gold, nothing but gold! I should have suspected—but still I thought—"

"I'm only taking a few—"

"You *cannot!*"

Hal drew himself up and tried to speak in a paternal voice. "My son, a great god, a glorious deity like your Father of Battles will never miss a few small metallic crumbs." But he had to heed the look on Baldur's face, inflexible already and getting worse, practically ready to commit murder.

Right now they could certainly not afford a serious argument, much less a brawl. Hal pulled most of the gold from his pouch—carefully retaining his original fragmentary find— and dumped the rest quietly on the ground beside the bucket, thinking the clanging metal would make less noise that way. Even as he sacrificed his treasure he was marking the spot mentally, intending to come back later for what he had already begun to think of as his own property.

Horror and rage were fading from Baldur's face, and he quickly regained some of the happiness that had been his only moments earlier, when he was embracing Gold Mane. In the ecstasy of his excitement he seemed to forget and forgive Hal's attempted crime.

The fact of an exotic stable awoke old memories. "Let me tell you a story about Hercules sometime," Hal whispered to his companion, trying to distract him from his outrage, meanwhile chuckling to himself.

But the youth was in no mood for distraction now, and seized him by the arm. "Hal, do we dare, after all, to do this?"

Hal stared at him. Maybe it was finally dawning on Baldur that Wodan might consider the taking of one of his Horses as great a crime as the pilfering of discarded shoes.

Drawing a deep breath, Hal became heartily encouraging. If it was truly possible for men to ride these creatures, they would provide an excellent means of getting away. "Of course we dare. We are going to borrow—not steal, you understand—a couple of these excellent animals. You will help me find one I can ride. Then they will carry us to a safe spot at some convenient distance. When we are there, you and I will discuss what our next step ought to be."

"*Right now?*"

Hal mastered an impulse to club the young fool down. "Yes, right now! What did you think? Before someone comes nosing around and discovers us. When d'you think we'll have a better chance?"

Hal's sporting blood was up. It seemed that Baldur, though now his will was wavering, had not been entirely crazy after all. In situations fraught with danger there were times—and Hal thought he had learned to recognize them—when the least dangerous thing to do was to move fast and straight ahead.

Experience had given Hal a great respect for the powers that god-Faces bestowed on men and women; but it had also completely freed him of the commonly held notion that gods, especially the truly great ones, could see everywhere and find out everything.

The lord of this ruined fortress might still be formidable—but on the other hand there were certain indications suggesting he might not. Certainly the place had been allowed to go to rack and ruin. It would have come as no surprise to Hal to learn that whoever wore the Face of Wodan now had not visited this scene of embarrassing deterioration for a long time. It was easy to believe that he might never come back. It even seemed quite possible that the most recent avatar was dead, and no one else had yet picked up the Face. Hal had never laid eyes on a naked Face, few people had, but he had no trouble imagining the Face of Wodan lying somewhere, lacking all power and purpose in itself, until, as would inevitably happen, another human being should pick it up and put it on.

If Wodan *was* truly dead, and the gnomes knew it, they were successfully keeping the secret. And if the Valkyries knew it too . . . ? The implications were too complicated and far-reaching to be immediately grasped.

B ut right now the only thing to do was to climb on a pair of Horses, as quickly as they could, and get away before they were discovered by a stablehand—or by some being far more dangerous. If the Horses could really fly, then they would leave no trail of hoofprints in the snow—and it ought to be much easier that way to carry a truly substantial weight of gold.

Baldur was still dithering. Hal shook him by the shoulder and demanded: "How are you going to reach Brunhild, otherwise?"

Spurred on by this reminder of his beloved, the youth joined Hal in the effort to decide which Horse Hal was going to attempt to ride.

"Of course Gold Mane might carry us both."

"Without a saddle, and a hundred feet in the air? I'd rather not take that chance, let's try for two." Hal had not abandoned his determination that when he left Valhalla he would be carrying some gold—far from it. Which meant he would probably find it convenient to separate from Baldur shortly after they reached their next stop. Of course he hoped, he really did, that the lad would somehow succeed in recovering his beautiful Brunhild.

And still, the methodical clanging racket from the forge went on; evidently the gnomes were unaware that anything was happening outside their door.

While the men were in the stable, deciding which Horses they would take, Hal was looking about for actual saddles, such as he would have employed on any ordinary cameloid. One or two devices of that kind were visible, but stored high up, as if for display rather than for practical use. He looked into another room of the big barn. There was a pile of hay, looking quite mundane, and stuck in one side of the pile a pitchfork, of no use to Hal at the moment.

Hal pointed urgently. "Don't we need saddles?"

Baldur shook his head. "Hildy never used one, nor did Alvit. She said that courage and kind words were all she needed to control her mount."

"We don't have any magic," Hal reminded his colleague succinctly, and began to lead his own chosen Horse away, the fingers of his left hand firmly tangled in its mane. It was a large and capable-looking animal, and did not seem to have taken an immediate dislike to him—he wasted no time worrying about other details. There was a name, Cloudfoot, presumably the Horse's, burned into the worn wood of a railing at the stall's entrance.

A collection of leather straps, their iron clasps and buckles finely worked enough to be considered objects of art as well as function, were hanging on a wall, but Hal dreaded the idea of fumbling around to put strange harness on an unfamiliar animal—that might take him half an hour, if he could do it at all.

He took a close look at some of the harness. Hanging on the planks of the adjoining wall were fat leather pouches that had to be saddlebags. The two pouches in each set were connected with a simple network of straps that must be intended to hold it in place on an animal's back, almost like the saddlebags an ordinary cameloid might wear. Each pair also included a strange addition on one side, in the form of a deep leather cup, that it seemed a rider might use to ground the butt end of a lance or spear.

It raced through Hal's mind to wonder why riders should be furnished with saddlebags when they used no saddles. But of course the Valkyries were not gods, and like the rest of common humanity they must sometimes need practical help in routine matters—there would be missions, journeys, on which they had to carry their own food supplies.

Hal climbed and stretched to reach one set of saddlebags, and snatched them down. A faint cloud of dust came with them, almost provoking a sneeze.

"What do we need those for?" Baldur wanted to know.

"You never know what we might have to carry. Food, for instance."

Baldur looked distracted. "Yes, you're right, we desperately need food. I ought to have a set of those too." And he scrambled to help himself from the display on the wall. Having done so, he announced: "Now we must be on our way."

"Yes, I think we'd better. But wait a moment." Etched indelibly into Hal's brain was a memory of the precise spot, just around there in the stable, where stood the bucket of golden shoes; now if he could only distract Baldur, somehow, for a few moments . . .

"Food," Hal reminded him again. "We must have food. For the Horses, if not ourselves!"

"You're right, I'll find some," the dashing young warrior volunteered. Hal's stocky body could move with surprising speed when it was called upon to do so, and Baldur's brief absence gave him the chance he needed to quickly gather up the gold and load it into his new saddlebags. After picking up the shoes he had earlier dumped on the ground, he scooped a few more from the bucket—maybe farmland in the north would prove more expensive than he thought.

That done, he pitched the empty bucket away into a pile of straw, where it landed almost noiselessly. He strapped the saddlebags tightly closed, to minimize any clinking and jangling when they were shaken. A moment later Baldur was back, timing his return perfectly from Hal's point of view, and carrying his own set of saddlebags stuffed with whatever kind of Horse-fodder he had been able to snatch up.

Hal threw the leather baggage on the animal's back, and then at the last moment, when his gold was loaded and the way seemed clear, fear of the unknown held him back. Bravely defying an absent god was one thing, but climbing onto the back of a creature whose like he had never touched before, in hopes that its wingless bulk would somehow magically carry him into the gray sky like a bird—an adventure like that presented dangers all too clear and present. He hesitated just a moment too long, until the animal caught his uneasiness and started to shy away. Another problem was the simple fact that this Horse had no stirrups. He needed something to stand on, to give him a leg up ...

Baldur just sprang up on his long, young legs, and with a twist of his body had gained a rider's seat.

That was inspiring. Hal's legs were shorter, but they still had a good spring in them. Still, it took him an extra moment or two to pull himself up into proper riding position once he had gained the animal's back.

Hal and Baldur had just got themselves aboard their respective Horses, with a set of saddlebags strapped on each, when animals and men alike were spooked by a frightening distraction.

There came a great swooping, half-visible rushing in the sky, a swirl of noise and cloud reminding Hal of whirlwinds and waterspouts he had encountered in the warm waters of the Great Sea.

He was just starting to say something else to Baldur, when the thought was dashed from his mind by someone or something making a loud noise, accompanied by a dazzlingly great flash of light.

Hal spun round. As soon as his vision cleared he could see, supported by some invisible force a dozen feet above his head, a golden-haired young woman in dazzling silver clothes suggesting armor, sitting a magnificent Horse, whose movements she controlled with her left hand in its mane. In her right armpit she held braced the butt end of a very competent-looking spear, strongly resembling a type of cavalryman's lance. Her fierce blue eyes were stabbing at Hal like darts.

The northman froze in his tracks, and something in the pit of his stomach abruptly knotted. Again there came a powerful swirling in the air—this time it was a whole lot more than smoke.

Baldur evidently recognized the Valkyrie at first glance, for he called her by name: "Alvit!"

She in turn recognized Baldur. Her voice was clear, imperious, speaking the common tongue in what sounded to Hal as a strange but elegant accent.

"Are you insane, Baldur? What do you and this one think that you are doing?" With the sharp tip of her spear, the Valkyrie savagely jabbed the air in Hal's direction.

The young man's answer was drowned out by the Horse's snorting breath, and also by a roaring sound of unknown cause that was now swelling swiftly in the background; but the name of Brunhild was a part of that reply.

Then her gaze turned round on Hal, and to him it looked coldly murderous. He grabbed instinctively for his axe, but the tip of the woman's long spear swung round on him with startling speed, so that before he could even try to parry or dodge the mere touch of it shocked his arm and sent his weapon flying, threw him sprawling in the snow, like a child flicked by some great warrior's blow. He came down hard, on bruising rocks waiting close beneath that cover of deceptive softness.

In a moment Hal was up, flexing his right arm, scrambling instinctively to recover his lost steel. His eyes fell on an axe-shaped imprint in the snow where his weapon had buried itself. His right arm, as he used it to reclaim the axe, was unbroken, not even cut, but tingling in bone and muscle as if he had been sleeping on it for a week.

For the moment the Valkyrie was ignoring him. But she was still holding that spear ready.

Baldur had not tried to draw his sword. Instead, he greeted the mounted girl as if he knew her. When she grounded her flying steed, he tried to grab the animal by its mane, but it pulled swiftly away, freeing itself from his clumsy grasp.

Hal, having recovered his axe, was trying to grab with his free hand for his own animal's bridle, forgetting for the moment that it did not wear one. It took a moment for his fumbling fingers to find the long mane again, and fasten themselves in that.

With shouted warnings and cautions Baldur let Hal know that this Valkyrie was one who had proven herself sympathetic to Brunhild and her affair with a simple warrior.

Baldur sounded as if he had crossed over into panic: "Hal, hold back! Put down your weapon!"

Panicked or not, that sounded like good advice. With a broad gesture, wanting to make sure that everybody saw, Hal slipped it back into its holster, glad of the chance to demonstrate his preference for a peaceful resolution of this misunderstanding. The spear in the Valkyrie's hand was still ready, and he was not going to try to compete with it again. Not unless he had to, to save his life.

When Alvit once more turned his way, he warily introduced himself. His arm still seemed to be on fire, though functioning, and he resisted the urge to rub it.

Something in the Valkyrie's attitude as she confronted Hal strongly suggested that she had seen him stuffing two saddlebags with golden horseshoes, and the hard stare of her blue eye made him feel guilty about it.

In a moment Hal's instincts were proven correct, for she contemptuously charged him as a thief. "And this one has come along to steal gold."

Baldur was lagging mentally a step or two behind, as usual. Reassuringly he told the Valkyrie: "No, I made him put that back."

There came an interruption from an unexpected source. From the direction of the smithy, now out of sight behind some other sheds, came the gnomes, the pair of them stumbling and wincing in daylight. They were pulling on additional clothes and shielding their faces as they cried the alarm. Both small men were crying out in their harsh, accented voices, and struggling with the strings that held their bone-disk goggles on, as they forced themselves to brave the outdoor sunlight. Hal needed a moment to understand what they were saying.

"Someone has carried off the bucket of old shoes!"

Fortunately Baldur once more failed to get the point. "We saw it in the stable," he assured them.

The Valkyrie was briefly distracted as she tried to reassure the two gnomes.

They protested some more, but she had at least temporary success, despite the obvious presence of mutual suspicion.

For a moment at least the gnomes were staring straight at Baldur and Hal, but it was possible, Hal supposed, that in the glaring, show-reflected light they failed to recognize the recent visitors to their village. Moments later the Earthdwellers, at Alvit's urging, had turned away to grope their way back to the smithy.

Now the Valkyrie turned back to Hal and Baldur, and in a low voice urged the foolish intruders to flee.

"Get out of here, and quickly. Yes, you had better take the Horses. I'll get them back later, and think up some explanation. How did you reach this place? On foot? Fools!"

Hal needed only a moment to recover from his astonishment. "Thank you, my lady," Hal bowed deeply. She was welcome to call him whatever names she wanted, for he had never heard sweeter words. "We're on our way at once. Let me just give you back what we have taken—"

But Alvit interrupted, cursing at him. "Never mind that. Take what you have, I say, and go!"

When Baldur showed signs of being unable to move until his mind had been relieved regarding the mysterious problem of the gold, Alvit relented and tried again: "If there is not enough gold to make the shoes, that will get the attention of the All-Highest. Then maybe I can get him to confront our greater problems."

"Greater problems than missing gold?" Even now Hal could not restrain his curiosity.

Alvit's answer burst forth as if she had been holding it back for a long time and could no longer do so. "The guard is greatly under strength, there are shortages of equipment, clothing, even of food—" She broke off, looking anxiously back over one shoulder.

Baldur, who now seemed determined to explain his conduct, began to say something, but she silenced him with a fierce gesture. "Wodan is coming! I will try to delay him, but—no, it is too late." Her last words were almost inaudible, her voice sinking in what sounded like despair.

Baldur took a step closer to her, and for a moment he had Alvit's full attention.

Hal seized his chance. Winding his fingers into a mane of coarse dark hair, he clutched it tightly and leaped astride the Horse, fear lending an extra spring to his legs this time. From the corner of his eye, he could see clearly enough that Baldur had mounted too. As soon as Hal felt himself firmly aboard, he kicked hard with both heels into the animal's flanks.

The next few moments were total confusion.

Using stirrups and saddle, Hal had climbed onto the backs of cameloids and droms more times than he could count. But this bareback experience was every bit as different as he had feared it would be. The beast beneath him seemed harder, bonier than any he had ever clamped between his legs before, and was surely as strong as any cameloid that Hal had ever ridden. In two bounds they were out of the stable and into the air. He caught a glimpse of Baldur near him in the sky, legs forked as they clamped hard round the thick body of a running animal. Both Horses had left the ground in giant leaps, and neither showed any sign of coming down.

Someone, in a voice that sounded remarkably like Hal's own, let out an outcry, as if of fright.

The Horse with Hal aboard was moving quickly, but he had not left the Valkyrie and her steed behind. Their flight had covered only a few yards when in the next moment Alvit, with what seemed a single sweep of her flashing Spear, knocked them both out of their saddles, and sent them sprawling on the snowy ground.

Baldur seemed to have been flattened utterly, but Hal came up from the fall with a bloodied knee and elbow. He also had acquired a mouthful of snow, muffling the words of rage that he was ready to spew forth. His anger was chiefly at himself, for making what now appeared as a long chain of stupid decisions, getting himself into this, and it was doubly fierce because of that. "What now, in all the hells—?"

In the moment it took him to regain his feet, the warrior girl had changed her mind as to what she wanted them to do—her attitude, her shouted commands, showed that they had become her prisoners. And in a moment Hal understood why.

It was already too late. Hal saw with a sinking heart that it was far too late now to attempt flight—because now another airborne marvel had come into view, a single figure riding a black chariot that thundered through the sky behind a pair of Horses, somehow harnessed in tandem rather than side by side—no. Hal rubbed his eyes and looked again.

Pulling the chariot was one monstrous animal, that in fact appeared to be an eight-legged Horse.

One moment this fantastic equipage was hurtling through the air directly toward them. But a moment or two before it ran them down, it abruptly descended until the wheels spun in snow. A moment after that, the chariot had pulled to a stop on the ground no more than twenty feet from Hal, sending up a spray of snow and gravel from the vehicle's two wheels and the eight hooves of Sleipnir. That, Hal now seemed to remember from some legend, was the name of Wodan's Horse.

The Valkyrie and the young man seemed both frozen in position like two statues. Baldur had just dragged himself erect, while Alvit sat astride her own Horse, spear held firmly with the point raised, as if to offer a salute to the new arrival.

Looking at the great god leaning toward him from his chariot, Hal saw an imposing man apparently about fifty years of age, his one functioning eye, locked now in a stare at Hal, deepset under a jutting brow under long hair of silvery blond. A black patch covered the other eye. Wodan was clad in rich furs, and there was a definite resemblance to Hagan, so that the two of them might have been brothers. The big difference that Hal could see with his first look was that except for the missing eye, Wodan's massive body was that of a hale and hearty man.

Baldur was whimpering like a lost child, and he had fallen on his knees.

10

With a sense that the youth's behavior was utterly unseemly in the eyes of humanity and the gods, Hal grabbed Baldur's collar with one hand and yanked him to his feet. Meanwhile a fragment of some old parody of a drinking song, learned in some exotic tavern from some fellow Argonaut, had begun running through Hal's head. It was something about:

. . . marching with the heroes . . .

Some part of his mind, as usual, kept finding jokes even when the situation was far from funny.

He couldn't remember the next line of the song, and at the moment it did not seem to matter. He was feeling even less heroic than usual, but at least it seemed that he and Baldur were not going to be thrown directly over a cliff. Wodan was staring at them both, but Hal had no sense that the god was particularly angry. Beside Hal, Baldur was keeping silent too, both of them standing there panting and disheveled, about like a couple of boys caught stealing apples. The young man seemed not much worse off physically for having been knocked off his Horse, but his helmet was still dented, and Hal was bleeding freshly from a couple of minor scratches. Anyone who gave them a cursory inspection, as Wodan seemed to be doing, might be easily convinced that they had just fallen on some battlefield.

As far as Hal was aware, only the two gnomes and Alvit

had as yet noticed that gold was missing, and only the Valkyrie had connected the loss with him. For her own reasons she was keeping silent about it.

Meanwhile the All-Highest was still directing his one-eyed glare at the pair of intruders, his broad, bearded face betraying not much in the way of interest despite the steadiness of his regard. When at last he spoke, he apparently saw no reason to doubt that they were newly harvested heroes.

"And where are these two from?" The voice of the Father of Battles seemed fully appropriate to his reputation. It gave the impression that if he raised it, it ought to be audible to the farthest corner of any field of war.

Alvit bowed her head and uttered what sounded like a place name, one that meant nothing to Hal. But Wodan accepted it without apparent surprise.

"Have you seen the god Loki anywhere?" was the surprising first question Wodan now shot at the newcomers to his realm.

"No sir, I have not," said Hal clearly, and kicked Baldur in the ankle so that the youngster was roused sufficiently to second Hal's denial.

Silence fell again. The god maintained his dour look, but his gaze was wandering, so maybe his mind was elsewhere. At first Hal kept expecting him to make some comment on the shabby appearance of the two new members of the corps of Heroes. But then Hal remembered under what circumstances the Valkyries generally did their recruiting.

Somewhere behind Hal, in the middle distance, a dozen human feet or so came shuffling and tramping through the snow. He didn't turn, but he thought he could identify the source: a small squad of human soldiers, moving at route step, still some distance off.

Again the god seemed to have drifted away into some shadowy realm of rumination, chewing his substantial mustache and staring now right at Hal, now at something over the northman's shoulder. When Hal looked around at the squad marching toward them, perhaps to escort the two new recruits to the barracks, something about them struck him as odd. As far as he could tell not one of the men was really wearing a uniform, proper or not.

Hal kept expecting rough hands to seize him, strip him of battle-axe and dagger, and probably dump out his belt-pouch too. Wait till someone hefted the saddlebags—then the fun would start. But nothing of the kind happened. All that happened was that Wodan commanded that the two new arrivals be conducted to the barracks.

The tramp of feet grew louder, then shuffled to a halt. Now Hal took a closer look at the squad that had just arrived. He was not impressed. There were only six of them, armed with a miscellany of what looked like second-rate weapons, and none of the men looked really formidable. On neutral ground, and with some other companion than befuddled Baldur at his side, he might have seriously considered trying to fight his way free once the god had ceased to stare at him. Here, under the eye of Wodan, there was no point in considering resistance.

Again the god was speaking, in his voice of rolling, muted thunder. "You are the sergeant—?"

"Sergeant Nosam, *sir*!"

Hal thought there was probably no reason why Wodan had to know the name of every noncom in his army. Still, a god ought to be able to do that, if he made the effort. If Hal were a god, he would have done as much.

Wodan was rumbling. "Nosam, yes. You are to take charge of these two recruits . . ." The volume of the thunderous voice declined, the words trailed off.

The sergeant did not seem to be surprised at his commander's vagueness. "The recruits, yes sir. They will be inducted and indoctrinated according to standard operating procedures."

"My army," Wodan was saying now. "My army needs more men."

"Yes, sir. That has been—that has been my opinion for some time, if I may say so."

Wodan apparently did not care if the man said so or not. Eventually the god grated out an order. "Sergeant Nosam, see that the new members of the guard are issued proper uniforms."

"Yes, my great lord, at once." The sergeant, snapping to attention, saluted and acknowledged the order with military precision. None of the men were wearing any insignia of rank, as far as Hal could tell.

Wodan's rambling voice kept running, on and off, like intermittent rain. Hal would have liked to concentrate more fully on what the god was saying, but he could not. All he could think of was the purloined gold still packed into the saddlebags on the back of the Horse he had been trying to borrow. So far, no one had discovered the theft—no one but the gnomes, and they seemed not to count. Hal was beginning to hope against hope that the matter might somehow, incredibly, be overlooked. But he knew he was not out of the woods yet.

The presence of the animals, as if waiting to be ridden, had suddenly caught Wodan's wandering attention.

"Why are these other Horses here?" the god demanded, pointing with a huge forefinger at Gold Mane and Cloudfoot.

Alvit, bless her, was sticking her neck out to try to save the trespassers. "The heavenly farrier is making his regularly scheduled visit, my lord." Hal hadn't really expected any more help from the Valkyrie, not after she had almost killed them with her damned Spear. But he wasn't going to argue. Still, he feared her noble effort would be wasted. As soon as someone else discovered the stolen gold, he was as good as dead anyway.

"About time," Wodan grumbled.

To Hal's dismay, the gnomes were back. Andvari was even daring to approach the god directly, while his colleague trailed behind. The daring Earthdweller was babbling to the god something to the effect that the supply of gold was almost entirely missing.

If Wodan heard the plea at all, he ignored it totally.

Alvit looked utterly discouraged. She eyed the two small workmen fiercely, and ordered in a low voice: "Look around carefully. Things are forever being misplaced."

"Yes, my lady," the gnome who had spoken to Wodan rasped, in tones of fear. Then he and his more timid associate began to retreat, walking slowly backward and bowing repeatedly, like dancers or magic toys, until they had passed around the corner of a building.

Suddenly Baldur had fallen on his knees again, and was making preliminary noises in his throat, as if about to utter some impassioned plea, or worse, a miserable confession. Once more Hal grabbed him roughly and jerked him back to his feet, this time twisting his collar and choking him into silence in the process. Wodan had no reaction to this incident; the mind of the All-Highest, if he really had one any longer, still seemed to be elsewhere.

Meanwhile Hal was thinking furiously, or at least trying. The two Earthdwellers ought to have been able to get a good look at Hal and Baldur, and ought to have recognized them from their meeting in the gnomes' village. Yet they had given no sign of knowing them. Possibly the gnomes had been unable to identify the men here in the glare of daylight—or possibly they had simply thought it safest not to recognize the intruders, who were obviously in deep trouble of some kind.

Thinking seemed quite useless at the moment. Wodan was mumbling something into his beard, and Alvit was busy being deferential and soothing to her master. "As you say, lord. I will see to it that the Horses are kept under better control."

"See that they are," said Wodan in a voice that was suddenly clear and sharp. A moment later he picked up the reins of his chariot, and with the sharp tug of an expert driver induced the eight-legged horse to turn the vehicle around, the animal demonstrating fancy footwork in the process. He drove off slowly, staying firmly on the ground, in the direction of his stronghold's massive, towering, half-ruined central keep.

While Sergeant Nosam was trying to get the squad's formation into shape, Hal favored Alvit with his best effort at a pleading glance, hoping she would understand his silent request that she somehow arrange to get them free again. If for some obscure reason she *wanted* him to steal the gold, well, that could certainly be managed; if not, he could live with that decision too.

When she only glared at him, he tried to talk to her again, keeping his voice low.

"That is impossible," the young woman snapped, in reply to his first few words. "Now Wodan knows you are here."

"He does? I mean, with all respect, he doesn't seem to—"

"Here you are, and here you must stay."

"For how long?"

That provoked a savage look. "For the rest of your lives. What did you expect? But take courage, northman. Your life may be over much sooner than you think."

Then the Valkyrie must have signaled to the squad of soldiers with a gesture, for the squad gave up on trying to dress itself into a tight square and loosely surrounded Hal and Baldur, as if officially taking them into custody.

"Forward, march! Route step." Sergeant Nosam might not look like much, but he had the knack of issuing crisp commands.

Dazedly they moved away, the escort looking and sounding

as awkward as the two recruits, or prisoners. It was an uneven march, and one of the men somewhere behind Hal,
seemed to be straggling, almost unable to keep up. There
came a sound of hard breathing, with the slight exertion of
this simple walk. Again, Hal thought he could almost certainly outfight any of them, maybe even any two, but it would
be berserker madness to take on all of them. Whether Baldur
would help him or swipe at him with his sword would be
about an even bet. And he doubted that he could outrun any
but the slowest.

There was no air of pride, or even of menace, about their
escort. Their guide had little to say to his new captives, or
recruits; it was as if his thoughts had joined his divine master's, brooding in some distant world.

Their destination, reached after a minute or so of circuitous
route-stepping through the sprawling ruins, proved to be a
kind of armory or barracks, built into a lower level of the
great keep.

Baldur became aware of the low doorway just in time to
duck his head. The interior was a shabby place, with makeshift barriers of straw and rags propped with boards over
holes in the wall, where they fought to keep out the cold.
Better help came from a roaring fire in a makeshift hearth,
positioned below another hole that served as chimney. Hal
noted with a start that the flames in the crude fireplace seemed
to be consuming nothing, just like those on the high crag.
More of Loki's magic, he supposed, here in Wodan's headquarters as a gift or on loan.

The sergeant took note of what Hal was staring at. "Never
seen a fire like that one, have you? Once Loki was welcome
in Valhalla. Some of the flames that he gave Wodan, when
the two of them were friends, are burning still. Thank Loki,
or we'd none of us survive the coming winter."

Hal was curious. "But Wodan and Loki are friends no
longer, is that it? How about Thor? What's his attitude now?"

Now that the god was no longer in sight, Baldur had regained his powers of almost normal speech and movement. He murmured to Hal that this might be a kind of training station where new recruits were kept until they could prove themselves.

"See, Hal, it is only a kind of outpost, as I thought. The stables are here, and a few men to guard the stables. The All-Highest must be only visiting. We won't be here long." He seemed to be doggedly trying to convince himself as well as Hal.

Hal only grunted in response. Alvit's parting remarks, whether they were meant as curse or warning, hadn't offered much ground for hope. And with every passing moment Hal expected a great outcry, a shout from whoever had charge of the Horses now—whoever was going to discover the gold in the saddlebags. And soon horrible vengeance would fall upon the thief.

But moment after moment passed and there was no outcry.

Shortly after their arrival at the barracks, Baldur's outpost-with-stables theory suffered a distinct setback when Sergeant Nosam pointed out to the recruits what he said were the god's regular living quarters, high up in the solid remnant of the still-impressive keep.

When Hal ventured to question the mild-mannered sergeant on the subject of Valkyries' housing, he learned that they were quartered in an upper floor of the same building, very near Wodan's private domain.

There was another entrance to the keep, at ground level, through which the young women came and went, as a rule, without their flying Horses. Even as Hal was watching, he saw a couple of them flying in, the Horses landing on and taking flight from a high terrace, up near the highest level of the still-palatial remnant of a building.

Moments after those maidens on Horses landed, a bright light, like a large lamp newly kindled into flame, suddenly came on in those high rooms. Maybe that was coincidence, thought Hal, or maybe evidence that Valkyries' duties did not end when they put down their Spears. He doubted they were held strictly to their pledge of perpetual virginity.

"The old man's turning in for the night," one of his new comrades in arms observed.

Baldur turned his head sharply. "Who?"

"The old man, I said. Who do you think that is? Our lord and eternal master, Wodan." The tone in which the words were spoken was far from reverent, and the hero let out an ugly laugh through broken teeth.

Baldur rose up as if determined to object to such a sacrilegious attitude, but then remained silent, as if he were either afraid to speak, or didn't know what to say.

Suddenly everyone wanted to avoid the subject.

Hal had not been in the barracks for an hour, when he was surprised to be summoned to take a turn at guard duty. The sergeant led him to a deserted courtyard not far from the smithy and the stables. Was this some kind of trick, to see if he would try to grab the gold and flee again?

Nosam had turned his back and started away when Hal called after him. "Can I ask you a question, Sergeant Nosam?"

Turning, the sergeant was agreeable as usual. "Fire away."

"No one's told me what I'm guarding, or who I'm supposed to challenge if they come this way."

Slowly Nosam shook his head. "Maybe I didn't make it clear. I wouldn't challenge anyone, Haraldur. Just stay on your post, and look alert, in case Wodan or a Valkyrie comes by. Maybe a guard is needed here, maybe not. But there's a standing order to post one, going back a long way, that's never been countermanded. Our job is to follow orders."

"I see."

Hal had not been on guard for more than half an hour, when he was surprised by Alvit, who appeared, on foot and unarmed, and stopped to talk with him.

"Well, northman. What do you think of Valhalla now?"

"So far I am surviving. Give me a little time and I might get used to it."

"Is that all?"

"If you want my opinion of it as a prison, well, I've seen worse. As a military outfit, I have to say it stinks." In fact he had already noticed that the latrine behind the guardroom had a particularly evil smell, despite the fact that it was even colder than the barracks. The walls of both facilities were full of holes and crevices, some of which had been stuffed with straw and rags in a futile attempt to shut out the rising winter wind.

Somewhat to Hal's surprise, the Valkyrie only nodded thoughtfully. "I suppose you were brought to this country as a mercenary?"

"Then you suppose wrong. I was very much on my own, just passing through."

"So you can tell me very little about the intentions of any of our local warlords?"

"Never met any of them, so I can tell you nothing. But I'd think you must know them fairly well. You visit their battle-fields, don't you?"

Alvit shook her head. "Battlefields are not good places to discover what people are thinking."

"I am curious," Hal said, taking advantage of the young woman's evident willingness to talk. "I know very little about Valkyries. Do you really make an effort to collect the bravest and the best when you go out recruiting?"

Alvit was shaking her head, as if she marveled at his ignorance. "Haraldur, I believe just this much of what you have told me so far—that you really are a stranger in these parts."

"I am."

"Well, just stop and think about the problem of recruiting

heroes. The rankest cowards have run from the battlefield before we Valkyries get there. The brave but ineffective have been slaughtered, unless they are very lucky. Others are trapped, just fighting for their lives. So how are we to know who among the survivors is the bravest? Personally I always look for a man not too badly hurt, but no more than about half conscious, so he won't put up a fight when I drag him aboard my Horse."

"Presumably he should not be dead, either; though the legend has it that you bring the dead to Valhalla."

"Of course, not dead!" Alvit gave a harsh laugh that did not indicate amusement. "Wodan needs fighting men, not corpses."

Hal chuckled too. "I think Baldur more than half believes the legend."

"How do you mean? Believes what, exactly?"

"He's idealistic about Wodan and Valhalla, but doesn't have the details worked out very well. He seems to think that if Brunhild had gathered him in, his dead body would have stayed on the field, while only his spirit would have been carried here to glorious—"

The Valkyrie interrupted, snorting. "Baldur is a fool! And so are you, or you would not be here."

"I won't argue that point. But tell me more about your work on the battlefields. What if you need recruits but can't find a good candidate?"

"We always need recruits, as you can see by looking around you. And it's true, acceptable men, let alone ideal ones, are hard to come by." She sighed. "More often than not we ride home empty-handed after these skirmishes. But Wodan insists we do our recruiting in the traditional way. Some of those we bring back here are failures. We are granted no magical insight. But more likely than not, those struck down in battle have some bravery, or they would not be on the field. I always try to avoid the men who are really trying to run away."

For once Hal had no comment. Alvit ruminated briefly, then turned away and started to leave. Then momentarily she turned back. "Maybe, Haraldur, you will live longer than I thought."

Baldur and Hal had been assigned a pair of neighboring bunks, poor berths hardly more than pallets on the stone floor, in a dim-lit, cheerless barracks or guardroom, with a row of some ten or a dozen bunks down each side. Despite the welcome presence of Loki's magic fire, the room was cold.

Hal looked, and pulled his cloak around him. "Damn those holes. Is there a better barracks than this somewhere around?"

A man who was sitting two bunks away looked over. "This is it, friend."

Everything that Hal had seen and heard since his arrival was forcing him to the realization that the Heroes of Valhalla comprised a total of something less than twenty men, most of them not very heroic.

He turned to his companion. "Baldur, do you know what I am beginning to suspect? That this handful of misfits in this barracks are all the army Wodan has."

"That can't be." Baldur looked over as if he suspected Hal of cooking up a joke.

"Maybe it can't be," put in the tired-looking fellow from two bunks away. "But it is."

Other men around them wearily confirmed it.

The tired-looking one sat up; the movement seemed to cost him a great effort. "When did you die?" he asked Baldur. Despite the evidence of illness, there was a glint in his eye that told of joke-making.

Baldur only looked at him, but Hal replied. "It was so long ago, I can't remember."

Then he looked back at Baldur, who seemed to be in shock.

Staring at him, Hal asked in a whisper: "What are you worried about now?"

Baldur only looked at him.

"By all the gods!" Hal couldn't keep his voice from getting louder. "You haven't really been thinking that we're dead?"

Slowly the expression on the youth's face altered. "No. Not really. Though for just a moment, when Alvit swiped at us with her Spear . . ."

Hal was shaking his head. "Look, Baldur . . . I'm not sure how to try to tell you this . . . but none of us here are dead."

Baldur was dignified. "If we are not, we ought to be."

The man from two bunks away was listening now, and went through a kind of spasm, gripped by almost silent laughter. "Dead? Dead? You're not yet *dead*, you clodpate! Though you might soon wish you were." He turned his body and let himself fall face downward onto his bunk, where the sounds of his laughter grew louder, until they turned into convulsions of desperate coughing.

Hal studied his companion. "You have the damnedest eagerness to be dead of anyone I've ever met!"

"So I admit that now we are still alive." Baldur took a long, shuddering breath. "But that being so, I don't know where we are. It should be Valhalla, because Alvit and her sisters are here, but . . . what does it all mean?"

"For one thing, it means that all the old stories about Valhalla have got it just a little wrong."

The man on the other bunk had lain down again, and turned his face away. Baldur was silent, contemplating the impossible. At last the youth got out: "But if this is truly not Valhalla—what should we do?"

"Well, let's not be in any desperate hurry to make up our minds. This is . . . not *too* bad. Let's give them the chance to feed us a couple of square meals first. A little food, a little knowledge—that's what we need right now."

And a little gold, Hal added in the privacy of his own thought.

At the dim far end of the large room were two closed doors. Hal pointed toward them and asked a veteran: "Where do those go?"

"Private rooms, for our two corporals, Corporal Bran and Corporal Blackie. You'll know Blackie by his white hair. All white though he's not old."

"So where's the sergeant sleep?"

The man gestured vaguely toward the keep. "Just outside the old man's quarters, where he can be easily summoned at any time. Being sergeant in this outfit is not a job I'd want to have."

On their next morning in Valhalla the men were wakened at first light, and Hal and Baldur, as they had expected, were told that they were going out to drill.

Nosam had their names down on a roster. "Couple of new ones for you, Blackie."

Blackie, in his slyly indifferent way, gave Hal and Baldur what he said was the same warning he gave all new recruits, that there was no use trying to get away. There were only a couple of dozen live heroes on hand anyway, and the Valkyries ruthlessly pursued and brought back any who tried to get away—except for those who died in the trackless mountains, trying to find their way out.

Hal and Baldur exchanged a look. When it came to planning an escape, they were conscious of having a special advantage shared by none of the other men in the barracks—they had not been carried here on Horseback, but had walked into Valhalla on their own two feet, and therefore they knew the path that could carry them out. It seemed that no one but Alvit knew of their advantage.

The joking man from two bunks down, whose name was Baedeker, now seemed to have taken to his bed more or less permanently. The sergeant had excused him from all duty, and he did not look at all well. In fact the more Hal studied him, the worse he looked, and Hal soon decided that the fellow might well be dying. The victim did not appear feverish, and so Hal thought there was probably little risk of contagion. But to be on the safe side, he avoided getting too close, anyway.

During their first morning drill session, Hal and Baldur took part in the scene they had earlier witnessed from a distance: the daily combat drill, including the charade of dueling, in which breathing Heroes were pitted against wraiths.

Hal sparred very cautiously at first, guarding and striking as if he were in a fight against solid metal and solid muscle. He had to begin by assuming that the wraiths, with their fierce aspect, had some real power to inflict harm. But this proved not to be the case.

Fairly often during drill and marching these disobeyed the sergeant's orders, or rather simply ignored them, as if they were listening to commands from someone else. The result was that he gave them specific orders rarely; there was after all no way to punish them, by whipping, confinement, or deprivation of pay or rations. The noncoms had long ago given up trying to shout them into obedience.

On the positive side, several veterans assured Hal that these seemed to have no power to do serious harm. If you saw them from a distance, or squinted at them with your eyes nearly closed, they did lend a great air of military bustle and purpose to the establishment. When Hal was matched against them in the practice drills, he soon realized that their weapons were as insubstantial as their bodies, and only stung and did not wound, when employed against live flesh and blood.

"Doesn't seem that they would be of much help in a real battle," he remarked while getting back his breath.

"They do a great job of rounding up deserters," Corporal Blackie assured him with a smile.

"How do they manage that?"

"You felt the sting just now. Their swords and spears carry power and pain enough to harry and drive men of solid flesh back up the trail. Though one or two have chosen suicidal leaps instead."

Some other Hero demonstrated the essential harmlessness of their wraith-opponents by allowing one of them to strike him several times. But such playful negligence seemed to be against orders. When Bran and Blackie bellowed at the offender, he went back to treating his opponents seriously.

The only one who never seemed to slack off during the drills was Bran, though sometimes he would fake a withdrawal. Then with a yell he'd spin around and rout his insubstantial assailant with a powerful blow.

Panting with the effort, he smiled at Hal. "Hit a wraith a real good lick and he disappears for good. Just like a real man in that respect. Like most men, that is."

"If you keep exterminating ghosts, don't they all get used up after a while?"

"Wodan has a device that produces more." Apparently the answer was meant to be taken seriously.

Gradually Baldur was forced to the understanding Hal had already reached—that Wodan's fabled honor guard contained less than a score of living men in all, and most of those were in poor physical shape, hardly able to do more than go through the motions of drilling and practicing at arms.

There were a few exceptions, most notably Corporal Bran, a great physical specimen who seemed to genuinely feel a tremendous devotion to the god. Fighting, even against ghosts, seemed to awaken something deep and terrible in the man's nature. When the drill was over, he seemed to be awakening from a trance. This man seemed to take a liking to Hal, and suggested that the two of them spar sometime with dulled blades.

"Don't think I want to dull my axe."

"That would truly be a shame. By the way, I like that helmet that you wear."

Hal thought that there was something lacking in Bran's eyes, as if he were already dead. Outside of that, nothing in the man's appearance or behavior made him seem particularly threatening at all, at least at first glance, though he was physically formidable enough. Several inches taller than Hal, with sandy hair and beard, he owned sloping shoulders and powerful arms. He walked with a kind of eager, energetic shuffle and carried nothing extraordinary in the way of arms or armor. He was usually smiling, in a way that could easily be taken for mockery. But Hal soon decided that the man really had no thought of mocking anyone.

Minute followed minute in this strange new existence, hour followed hour, a full day went by, and then another, and still Hal had heard nothing about stolen gold. He kept making up imaginative scenarios to explain to himself what seemed a remarkable stroke of good fortune. The most optimistic of these said that whoever had found the treasure had simply decided to keep it, and that even if the loot should somehow be recovered, at this stage there would be no clue to show that Hal had ever touched it.

But then he changed his mind and decided the gold was

probably still in the saddlebags. Routine care of the Horses must be sadly neglected here, like so much else, but probably the animals' magic, or that of their golden shoes, allowed them to survive anyway, even to flourish. But sooner or later someone would go to lift those containers off the Horse, and be astonished by their weight. And then . . .

But still there came no alarm, no accusations. It was as if the absence of a few pounds of mere gold was likely to pass entirely unnoticed.

Among the breathing men now quartered in Valhalla, the later arrivals, being better nourished, usually had an advantage in drill and practice, if they were not badly hurt when they came in. But there were some recruits who, seemingly in some kind of shock when they arrived, withdrew into themselves, ate and slept little, and had trouble talking or even understanding orders.

"Those kind never last more than a month or two," was one of the veterans' comments.

Others, usually men of lower rank who had been collected by Wodan's flying girls because no higher were available, took a philosophical soldier's attitude that one outfit was not essentially different from another and life was bad in all of them. These tended to last longer than men of any other category.

When the sergeant summoned Baldur to stand guard duty, he was more insistent than Hal had been, about having the formalities spelled out. "Is there not to be a password, then?"

One of the veterans, overhearing, called out an obscene suggestion in jest.

Baldur ignored the jibe, and in his anger criticized Nosam as being a poor noncom. "When I chose men to lead into battle, I chose none who were like you!"

The sergeant's reply was quiet and unthreatening: "Baldur, I just told you to shut up about passwords and such stuff. That's an order, I want to hear no more. Disobey me and I'll put you on report, and you won't like what happens to you then. You're young and hard, you could probably kill me if we fought, but then Bran would kill you. Or if he didn't—" Nosam's lips smiled thinly. "You might be promoted to sergeant."

Baldur slowly lowered his raised fist. "What do you mean?"

"Just what I said. And you wouldn't want my job, young one." The white-haired Corporal Blackie was shaking his head sadly in the background, while Nosam went on. "Twice a day—and sometimes twice a night, if Wodan's sleep is restless—have to report to the god in person."

Time dragged on, in drill and guard duty and boredom, and Hal began to lose track. Had they now been Wodan's guests for four days or five? And did it matter?

And meanwhile the intermittent presence of wraiths made the armory and barracks seem much busier, more fully occupied, than they really were. At least they consumed no food and filled no sleeping space.

Bran, in his normal mild and almost wistful way, frequently expressed a wish that Wodan would snap out of his listlessness and inattention.

Bran thought that the god must be the victim of some enemy's sly magic. "If only a man could find out who it was . . ."

Loki was a prime suspect, in Bran's thought; and even Thor was not above suspicion.

Bran when he hung around the barracks was a mild-mannered sort, with a tentative and almost gentle smile. His nominal rank seemed to mean little or nothing to him, except that he was never detailed to clean the latrine. But Hal noted that the veterans all went out of their way to avoid antagonizing him.

As soon as Hal and Baldur were able to talk privately, Hal said: "It seems that we can walk away, the gates are seldom guarded. If we time it right, no one will miss us for a few hours. But walking won't get us far enough or fast enough. I think we really need the Horses."

Baldur agreed. "If we walk, Valkyries could overtake us quickly."

Hal looked around. "And Valkyries might not be our worst problem. They say that sometimes Wodan sends out his best berserker after deserters."

"You mean Bran? There would be two of us."

Hal did not reply. Corporal Blackie had suddenly appeared, from around a corner, and as if he knew what they had been saying, began in his gently taunting way to talk about escapes.

"Maybe you've been wondering why we don't guard the gates."

"It's not for us to question such decisions," Hal said nobly. Baldur looked at him.

So did Blackie. "No one who tries to leave us can get far. A few who attempt to desert are simply lost in the mountains. The others are hunted down and brought back, the very lucky ones by flying Valkyries. Those who are simply fortunate are harried and driven back by wraiths."

Hal was curious. "Why do you call them fortunate?"

"Because sometimes Wodan sends out the berserker instead—you know what a berserker is?"

"I've heard the name."

Blackie appeared to be reminiscing. "I remember well one such group. There were three men, all recent recruits, all desperate, and well-armed." A pause. "And when they were reported as deserters, Bran volunteered to bring them back, and

Wodan granted his request, and sent him out alone." Blackie nodded solemnly.

"Well, what happened?"

"Bran returned, wounded but alive. Not so the others."

Baldur asked it: "Bran brought them back?"

"Not altogether."

"What do you mean?"

"Only their heads."

As far back as Hal could remember, he had understood that two of the most important things about any military organization were the name and nature of the commanding officer. Ever since he and Baldur had been so irregularly drafted, Hal had been looking around and listening, trying to gather information on the individual, whoever it might be, who held that position in Wodan's divine guard. But for all he had been able to discover so far, the job might be wide open. Hal had yet to hear of anyone who outranked Sergeant Nosam—unless it would be Wodan himself, as supreme commander.

When Hal questioned the sergeant, he was told that for the past year the rank of general had in theory been held by one of the mere ghosts. The sergeant could not remember ever hearing the General—as this wraith was generally called—give an order to anyone, or even speak.

The sergeant's mild attitude encouraged Hal to question him further. "If this General says nothing and does nothing—why is he commander?"

"Because the Father of Battles says so."

"Oh."

"Haraldur, it's not your place as a new recruit to criticize our methods of organization. Rather, you should be learning them, and doing your best to fit in. You don't want to be promoted, do you?" The question made it sound like some exotic punishment.

"No, I don't think so. Since you put it that way, Sergeant, I don't believe I do. So I will try to learn your ways, as you recommend. If in the process of learning, any more questions should come up, I suppose I can bring them to you?"

The sergeant gave him a severe look. "First, just try to forget the things that bother you. Let that be the first thing you learn."

"Right."

Sergeant Nosam relaxed a trifle. "This really isn't a bad outfit, Haraldur. I've been in a lot worse in my time."

"You must tell me about them some day, Sergeant."

"I may do that. Here, if you just go along, as a rule nobody will bother you."

"What more could a man ask?"

Hal and Baldur soon learned that none of their living colleagues had been here in Valhalla for more than a few years, and their average length of service was probably less than a full year. There were probably many real deaths among them, but few of these were casualties from actual fighting. Hal supposed it would be easy to get lost when attempting to escape.

On the evening of their first day of duty as members of Wodan's guard—or as Wodan's captives, but it didn't help to view things that way—Hal and Baldur got their first look at Wodan's great hall. Baldur at first refused to dignify the place by that name, but it was the chamber where the Heroes were expected to put in an appearance every night, for a meal that was often a poor excuse for a feast, enlivened by some sad revelry.

This chamber had thick stone walls, like most of the rest

of Wodan's stronghold, and like the rest was well on the way to falling into ruin. Hal thought it must have been designed and built many long years ago, and for some lesser purpose. There was a distinct lack of grandeur. This portion of the stronghold did have the great advantage of a nearly intact roof. Two functioning fireplaces, with one of Loki's roaring, fuelless fires in each, kept the worst of the freezing cold at bay. Hal could see that one good reason for coming to the great hall each night was that two fires made it marginally warmer than the barracks, despite the ruinous condition of the walls.

Half a dozen trestle tables, long, worn, stained, and old, were not only carved with many initials, but much hacked and battered around the edges, suggesting that mealtime was not always peaceful. Sixty or seventy men could easily have been accommodated around the tables, but less than a third of that number were on hand. Once in a while the sergeant urged them to spread out, occupying a greater number of benches, as if he wanted to make it look like the whole room was truly occupied. Here and there the figures of wraiths appeared, filling in empty seats.

Veterans informed the latest recruits that Wodan himself was usually, though not always, in attendance at the nightly gatherings they called his feasts, not at any of the wobbly tables, but sitting gloomily on a high, thronelike chair positioned midway between the fires. Old hands said that the quality of the food and drink would vary wildly and unpredictably from one night to the next. At intervals poor music squawked and wailed, provided by serf attendants with stringed instruments and horns. Hal thought he saw a wraith musician or two, but could not tell if their instruments were making real sounds.

"This can't be *all*, can it?" Hal murmured when he had looked the place over. "This is supposed to be Wodan's entire

162 ——— Fred Saberhagen

harvest of Heroes, going back to the beginning of time?"

Baldur shook his head decisively. "It cannot be. This is some elaborate device for testing us."

Sometimes the wraith figures responded when spoken to, lips moving and producing hollow, distant voices. Hal never heard more than a word or two from them, not enough to let him decide if what they said made sense; but he had the impression that no real thought or feeling was behind their words. And when he steeled his nerves to touch one, his hand passed right through, his palm and fingers appearing brightly lighted when inside the spectral body.

To Hal the most realistic of them suggested reflections in a fine mirror, rather than flesh and blood.

Sometimes Baldur was greatly bothered by the wraiths, and kept nagging Hal with unanswerable questions. "If these ghosts come from some strange device, what power sustains it?"

Now and then Hal saw in a wraith some resemblance to someone he had known in life, once to a man he knew to be dead. But he told himself firmly that it was not truly the man himself who walked, but only an image, like a reflection in a pond.

Hal realized that this explanation tended to leave uncertain the fate, the nature, of other individuals . . . he told Baldur he had heard wild stories of certain folk down in Tartarus, people once alive who had passed through the gates of death but still retained their solid, breathing bodies. Sufficient life remained in these dwellers in the Underworld to allow them to move and speak. And Hal had even heard one tale to the effect that when some of these were able to regain the surface of the earth, they were not much the worse for their dread experience.

"Who has ever visited the Underworld and returned, to bring such reports?"

"Not I." Hal shuddered. "I told you that these are only wild stories."

On almost every evening (excepting only those occasional times when Wodan for some unexplained reason did not attend) events in the great hall followed pretty much the same routine. Several times during the course of each nightly carousal, Wodan urged his followers to stand on their feet and laugh, to empty their flagons and sing a rousing song. There arose a thin chorus of broken and wavering voices, creating echoes that soon were lost, drifting away through the cracked stonework high above. Even with one or two men roaring loudly, the overall sound of the song was never more than feeble at its best. The serfs, or the wraith musicians, were still making most of the noise.

Something made Hal look up, into the dim, broken vaulting high above; he felt slightly cheered to see that a bird had flown in, but a better look convinced him that it was a bat.

Now and then a chunk of stone, perhaps disturbed by bats or birds or gusts of wind, or simply coming loose, came falling from the heights to strike with a vicious crack on floor or furniture. Hal decided he'd keep his helmet on.

Strong drink, generally mead, was magically provided, though not on any dependable schedule, and never served by wraiths or soldiers, but only by creeping, starveling serfs. The servers staggered and stumbled as if they were helping themselves when out of Wodan's sight, for which Hal could not blame them. On some nights, the casks and flagons on the tables were filled with all the fermented honey that any man could drink.

After his first cup, Hal made a face. "Is there never any wine?"

"No wine," one of his new mates told him. "Wodan does

not consider it a proper drink. Mead is for true Heroes."

On other evenings there was nothing in the men's flagons but weak beer or water. When there was enough mead to let them do so, most of the men generally drank themselves into a stupor.

All too often, the new recruits were told, the rations of real food tended to be scanty. Wodan's quartermaster department was nonexistent, except for the occasional magical efforts of the god himself. Wodan simply never made much of an effort to equip or strengthen his captive army. His magic had grown as erratic as his thinking.

Wodan himself always drank mead, as befitted his legendary reputation, according to which he never ate. Hal was vaguely relieved to note that in practice the god speared some of the choice food morsels for himself—it made the All-Highest seem more human and therefore more fallible.

Though the food varied wildly in quality, the dishes and knives and goblets were consistently magnificent. Hal thought some of the plate might be worth as much as the damned disappearing horseshoes; but the dishes would be harder to carry and more readily missed.

None of the Valkyries ever showed up for the nightly feast, and no one seemed to be expecting them. Hal saw no reason to hope that any of them would accept the idea that solacing the Heroes was part of their duties.

Wodan, when addressing his troops, spoke to his poor handful as if they represented a mighty host. He repeatedly announced it as his own sacred duty, and also his solemn fate, that he must do his best to amass an army for some climactic battle against an opponent of shadowy reality. The god of war was convinced that on that day the treacherous god Loki would be one of his opponents.

At least once an evening he broke off to ask: "Have any of

you who feast and drink with me tonight learned aught of the whereabouts of Loki the Treacherous?" And with his one eye Wodan searched the thin ranks of his guard.

On each of the several nights that Hal heard this question asked, the large room remained profoundly silent.

Some members of the guard of honor talked of Loki, as of some being with whom they were almost familiar.

He was a god, that much was certain. But he had now become the enemy of his former colleagues.

Each night, when Wodan had finished with his futile questions, and produced from somewhere an ancient-looking scroll, and unrolled it, a silence fell in the great hall.

Presently the god began to read:

". . . in that evil day, Loki's wolf-child Fenris will lead the monsters of disorder to blot out the Sun and Moon.

"Rising from the sea, the great snake Jormungand will try to swallow up the Earth."

Hal raised his head and began to listen. He had heard that name before.

". . . meanwhile his demon officers will sweep out of the Underworld with an army of ghosts and monsters. Then will follow a tremendous battle, in which the great gods and their enemies will destroy each other. The dead bodies will be consumed in a terrible fire that will engulf the universe and drown its ashes in the sea of anarchy."

Obviously Wodan took his legends very seriously, and this one was fascinating in what it suggested; but still Hal's attention kept being drawn away from Wodan's words to Corporal Bran. Bran always sat listening to the reading with rapt attention, eyes shining, his broad shoulders swaying slightly, as if he dreamed of swinging weapons. This was evidently the high point of the corporal's day, every day. Tonight Bran was murmuring something, in a kind of counterpoint to the reading itself; the sound of his voice was so soft it was smothered by Wodan's stage-whisper, but something gave Hal the impression that the corporal was whispering some kind of prayer.

Meanwhile the god's voice rumbled on. "Know that before these things can come to pass, there will be savage wars all across the world, and a time when each man seeks revenge upon another. The ties of kinship will be dissolved, and the crimes of murder and incest will be common . . . the stars will fall from the sky, and the entire earth will quake and quiver . . . all monsters bound beneath the world will be set free. The . . . sea rises to engulf the land, and on the flood the ship Naglfar is launched . . . fashioned from the fingernails of dead men. It carries a crew of Giants, with Loki as their steersman."

Hadn't the gnomes included Giants in their catalog of enemies? Hal thought he could remember something of the kind from his brief visit to their village.

Wodan had concluded the night's reading, and sat staring into space, as if in contemplation of the horror and glory of the events to come. Looking round his own table, Hal was struck by the absence of two men. "Where's Baedeker?" he asked the man next to him in a low voice. "And Baldur?"

The other whispered back: "Baedeker was too sick to make it out of the barracks tonight. Baldur stayed with him. If anyone should ask, they're both on special duty."

Soon the evening had frayed out to nothingness in its usual way. Wodan had departed and all were free to leave the great hall, Hal returned to the barracks.

There he found Baldur, sitting beside the dying man. Sergeant Nosam had also come in and was standing by. As Hal entered, the man on the bunk murmured a few words, something that made Baldur burst out with: "Wodan will not let you die!"

Hal and the sergeant looked at each other, but neither of them bothered to contradict Baldur. Baedeker, his breath rasping in his throat, was gazing off into the distance, through the stone walls, into some country that he alone could see.

Presently Corporal Bran came in and joined the group. Standing at the foot of the bunk, Bran in a firm voice but with gentle words tried to urge the prostrate man to pull himself together and return to duty.

Baedeker gave him a fleeting glance, and got out a few words: "It's no good, Corporal."

Bran looked nervous. "That is no way for a man to die. You shouldn't just lie there like that, on a bed of straw." With a sudden movement he unsheathed a knife, and held it out, hilt first. "Here. Get up and fight me, I'll give you a proper end."

Baedeker did not try to move. He had resumed his staring into the distance, as if he and Bran were now a million miles apart.

Sergeant Nosam intervened. "Bran, I want you to go up and take the high lookout for a while. I mean on top of the keep. Relieve whoever is on duty now."

Bran only looked at him, as if his mind were far away. Then he looked back to Baedeker on his bunk.

It was the first time Hal had seen Nosam nervous. "Do you hear me, Corporal? I have given you an order."

At last Bran nodded. "I hear you, Sergeant. The high lookout." Obedience to orders was part of the great scheme of things, ordained by the All-Highest, not to be disputed. Bran slowly turned and took himself away.

The sick man's breath, already labored, began to rasp and rattle in his throat.

And then, before Hal had really been expecting it to stop, it stopped.

No one put the event into words, but no one had any doubt of what had happened. Baldur sat stunned on the edge of the cot. The sergeant stood by with nothing to say for the moment, only looking a little grimmer than usual.

Hal drew a deep breath. "What's the usual procedure now?"

Nosam seemed grateful for this practical attitude. "Simple rites are usually conducted around midnight." The sergeant looked all around him, into darkness, as if seeking some sign that would tell him how far the night had progressed. "Guess there's no use waiting. Just wrap him up in his blanket and bring him along."

Baldur was shaking his head slowly. "Is there to be no ceremony?"

"If you want some ritual, make one. But I wouldn't want to remind the Old Man—or Bran—that people actually die here. They know it, but they don't want to know it, if you know what I mean. They manage to forget the fact, in between the times it happens."

Baldur did not respond to that. Hal thought: *Who would he pray to, if we did have a ritual? Wodan?*

Hal moved to pick the body up, but Baldur stepped ahead of him, and gathered up the underweight corpse, wrapped in a thin blanket, to carry it in his arms.

"Follow me."

The sergeant led them out of the rear door of the barracks, through cold and darkness, past the malodorous latrine, then through another unheated vault of stone and out of doors again.

As they walked, Hal's guide pointed with a hand out over the parapet.

"The plain of Asgard's out there. Had we proper light now, you could see it."

"The plain of Asgard?"

"You know, it comes up in the Old Man's readings. Or maybe he hasn't gone through that part of the book since you've been here. That's the great stretch of flat land where the last battle will be fought."

The night was well advanced by now, and Hal took note

of the stage of the waning moon. It had been just full, he recalled, on the night when he and Baldur began their walk from the gnomes' village to glorious Valhalla. Somehow he had lost track of the days, but there could hardly have been a great many of them.

Presently they came to a dim, chest-high parapet.

"Here's where we usually put them over," the sergeant said. "The deepest drop is just below. So lift him up, and let him find his rest. Then we'd best be getting right back to the barracks. I've got to see the Old Man yet tonight, and we're due for an early drill tomorrow."

Hal asked: "You're going to see Wodan about—?"

"Not this. No, never about anything like this. Unless he heard it from someone else. Then I'd have to answer questions. Somehow come up with answers."

Someone was still holding the body. "Where do I put—?"

The sergeant patted the top of the parapet. "Just set him up there, I say. Then give him a little shove. There's a good thousand feet of air to cool his fever before the trees and rocks will catch him."

Baldur complied. Then just at the last moment he reached forward with one nervous hand, to tuck in a fold of blanket, as if in the name of neatness or of comfort. It was the sergeant who stepped forward to push the bundle off the wall, over the precipice, to vanish in dead silence. Hal found himself listening for some faint sound of impact, but then he turned away before it came.

Next morning, immediately after the early drill, Alvit appeared, and after a few words with the sergeant took Hal aside to talk with him.

He was half expecting to be questioned about Baedeker's death, but Alvit did not mention it.

"What do you think of Wodan's army now?" Alvit asked

when the two of them were alone, walking through one of the snowy courtyards. The sun was out this morning, and the trampled whiteness underfoot was turning into slush. "Have you perhaps found the place you have been looking for, here in Valhalla?"

Hal gave the Valkyrie a hard stare, trying to figure her out. "I thought you were willing for us to escape."

"I was, but I have changed my mind."

"I don't understand."

"I have been watching you, Haraldur, and I think you are a real soldier, not just a thug or an unlucky drifter, like most of these. You probably have it in you to be a real leader. To command troops in combat."

Hal stopped walking, and shook his head. "My present position does not afford much scope for leadership."

"Having experience as a common soldier in Wodan's ranks should work to your advantage. You must know the organization before you can be placed in command of it."

He had started to walk again, but now he stumbled and almost fell. "What are you talking about?"

"I am thinking, hoping, praying to all the gods I know, that there might be time to turn this feeble remnant into a real army before it must enter battle." Alvit looked back at the remnants of the morning's drill, a small mob slowly breaking up, and shook her head. "I know it will take months, at least, but we might have that long. Perhaps even a year, if we are lucky."

Hal's curiosity was growing. "Tell me more."

"The point is that we need leaders as well as men. Nosam is too thoughtful and cautious, Blackie too sly, and Bran—I think could not be trusted. And they are all too small in mind to be commanders. Baldur may perhaps someday grow big enough."

"And you think I'm big enough now?"

"I think you may be if you try. In good time we will see. For now, be patient."

Alvit's hints gave Hal something to think about as he trudged back to the barracks. It came to him that she might be the true commander here, managing things for Wodan in his dotage. Was the Great Game of power Hal thought he had abandoned about to catch him up again? He was still tired of trying to be a hero.

But Alvit, herself, now . . . she was something for a man to really think about. He could well imagine himself trying to talk her out of keeping any foolish vows of virginity she might have made . . . as Baldur must have done with Brunhild.

12

On the night after Baedeker's death, the evening feast was delayed, and when the food and drink at last were served, both Wodan and Sergeant Nosam were absent.

Corporal Blackie had been left in charge. He and Bran were sitting two tables away from Hal and Baldur, facing in Hal's direction.

Hal thought the food was a little worse than average tonight, though plentiful enough. But the mead was of reasonable quality, and fairly plentiful. The music seemed even feebler than usual, though Bran several times ordered the musicians to play louder and faster.

When the faint hum of talk in the big room suddenly ceased, Hal looked up to see that the pair of gnomes were standing, unbidden and unexpected, in the entrance to the great hall. It was the first time he had ever seen them here.

Blackie growled at them. "Well? What is it?"

Moving a step forward, Andvari asked pardon for intruding, then said they had come not so much to complain as to beg for food, because no one was feeding them lately, and they were still forbidden to leave Valhalla. He doubted that Wodan really wanted to starve them to death. They were almost ready to run out, to just leave anyway.

Hal stood up and scraped food from serving dishes on his own table onto two clean, incongruously elegant plates. Then he carried the plates over to the gnomes, who thanked him profusely, sat down at once, and began to eat.

Baldur tonight had consumed more than his usual share of the drink of true Heroes. When Hal came back to his own table, Baldur waved an arm to indicate the scene before them. "I am now certain of it, Hal. This—all this nonsense we have here—it cannot be the real thing—all this—it must be a test, I tell you, Hal."

"You've said it, youngster." Looking over from two tables away, Bran vehemently agreed. "I don't believe a man can really die here, the straw death, in his bed. Some kind of lousy magic trick was worked on us. And I don't think Wodan's really sick." His voice was challenging, belligerent, and none of the eyewitnesses to death corrected him. No one was going to try to force Bran to face anything.

"We are being tested," Baldur repeated.

It seemed that Bran, too, had been having more than usual to drink. He slammed a big fist on the worn table. "That's it, you're right, I've said it all along, we are being tested. Those who prove loyal will win to the true reward at last. True Heroes should be fighting every day and every night. Not this . . ." His face and his gesture spoke eloquently of his disgust.

Corporal Blackie, seated at yet another table, had a contribution to make. "If we're being tested, though, how long is the trial to go on? I've been here a year, and all who were here when I arrived are dead now. All of those who tried to escape are dead, and so are many who did not. What kind of a test is that?"

Blackie looked round, as if seeking an answer to his question, and his gaze fell on the unusual visitors. "What's this? Who invited in these bloody dwarfs? Why are they eating our food?"

Hal looked over at him. "I gave it to them, Corporal."

There was a sudden tension in the room, to which the

gnomes seemed utterly oblivious. Ivaldr, usually silent, raised a plaintive voice to complain that someone had taken away their essential gold. Without it they could not complete their work, and until their work was finished they could not leave.

He concluded: "We tried to explain all this to Wodan, but he just walked past us as if we did not exist."

Andvari chimed in, shaking his head unhappily. "And all the great god said to us was: 'You are always complaining about something of the kind.' "

Ivaldr was nodding. "I don't know about calling him 'the great god.' Wodan did not look healthy."

That got Bran's attention back. "Careful what you say about the All-Highest," he rumbled.

The Earthdwellers must have heard the words, but they seemed deaf to tone, insensitive to tension. They were busy gulping mead and belching.

"But what can you expect," Andvari concluded, speaking to the room at large, "from a god of crazy berserkers?" The little man threw the word out very casually, as if he had no idea of what it really meant.

Hal held his breath. From the corner of his eye he had seen Bran's head turn round. Suddenly Bran had started breathing deeply and heavily, and when he spoke again his voice had changed. It was as if a different man now looked out of his scarred face.

"You have blasphemed my god. And for that you must die, small man."

This time the message was in the simple words, and came through clearly. Open-mouthed, the two gnomes sat there looking numbly back at Bran.

On the bench beside Hal, Baldur seemed not to know whether to laugh or take alarm.

Hal was very far from laughing. His brain was working rapidly, trying to calculate the chance of summoning a Valkyrie before someone got killed. He could see no chance of any other kind of help. There would be no use trying to reach the sergeant, who was almost certainly busy attending the god.

The music had long since faltered to a halt. Standing up, Hal called Bran's name, sending the one word clearly into an aching silence. The big man's head turned.

Hal told him in a flat voice: "The little one you challenge would not be here bothering you, were it not for me. So bring to me any complaint that you might have."

When Bran said nothing, but only continued to stare at him, Hal added: "You said you admired my honored helmet? Take it, and welcome. A gift." That was the best distraction Hal could think of. He pulled the helmet off and tossed it across the width of the two tables, so it bounced on the table where Bran was sitting, and then onto the floor.

He might have spared himself the effort. Bran's gaze did not turn to follow the clanging, bounding thing at all.

Without another word Bran, moving slowly and steadily, got to his feet. He stood much taller than Hal, though as Hal had already noted, there was not that much difference in length of arm.

Hal wanted to try more soothing words, but he could find none, and suddenly there was no time. Bran was standing on the table at which he had been sitting. From Hal's position he looked about twelve feet tall; and when Bran pulled the short sword from its scabbard at his side, that made him look no smaller.

Without a pause he charged across the tabletops at Hal, sword raised and howling like a winter wind out of the north.

When a man came leaping through the air at you, the traditional effective counter was to get out of his way by stepping sideways. Hal's first concern was getting his feet and legs clear of tables and benches.

Bran's weight splintered a bench when he came down on it. By that time, Hal was out of reach, axe in one hand, knife in the other, trying to find some open space.

Bran came bounding after him, quick as a bouncing ball. This time Hal stepped into the rush, blocked sword with axe, feinted one way and thrust another, feeling his dagger go deep into the big man's side, sliding through tough cloth, digging on into meat. The cut would have brought down any normal man, but it had little immediate effect on a berserker's strength or energy.

Hal had to break away. The next rush forced him backward, and in the swift exchange that followed he neatly broke Bran's sword-blade, catching it in the angle between the head and the tough handle of the war-hatchet.

But to berserker Bran a broken sword meant nothing. He still came after Hal, in one hand the stump of his snapped blade, the other armed with a yard-long wooden splinter, snatched up from a broken bench.

Men were yelling, scrambling desperately right and left and backward, falling to get out of the way. The howling Berserk kept on coming, too fast for Hal to make a conscious plan. He parried, and struck, and struck again. It seemed like two swords coming at him, not one broken one. His forehand swing with the axe was blocked with Bran's forearm on the shaft, the impact feeling as if he'd hit a piece of wood. But then, backhanding with the blunt end, Hal got home solidly on flesh and bone.

A broken leg was not going to stop death attacking, but perhaps would slow it down a bit. Now Hal could see a jagged end of white bone, sticking right out through skin and cloth above Bran's knee. Blood from a wounded arm spouted at Hal, and he realized that Bran was spraying him with Bran's own blood, trying to blind his vision.

Fine dishes, goblets, crashed and clattered underfoot, scattering their contents. In the background, Hal saw another fight had broken out, a skirmish anyway. Baldur, his sword drawn, seemed to be holding off Blackie—and another man was down, not moving.

Hal's foot slipped, whether in spilled soup or blood it mattered not, and in a helpless instant he went down hard on his back. Death leaped upon him, still spraying blood but never weakening, grappling with inhuman strength. The face of death was inches from Hal's own. Teeth tore at Hal's collar, trying to reach his throat. With an all-out surge of effort, Hal got his hickory axe-handle wedged into the open mouth.

In his paroxysm, Bran had screwed one of his eyes shut, as if in unconscious imitation of Wodan's one-eyed glare. Bran's wounded arms still clutched and tore. He howled no longer, but his breath sobbed like a great wind.

Somewhere inside Hal, his own berserker fury had come alive. Enough of it, perhaps. Slowly, slowly his arms straightened, gripping the axe-handle near both ends, forcing the frenzied killer up and back, throwing him violently off so Hal could move again.

His own breath sobbing, Hal staggered and scrambled to his feet. Bran came up right after Hal, almost with him, still quick on his broken leg.

Hal could see it, looking into the one open eye: Bran was dead but he would not fall.

Baldur, you stupid sod, now is the time to hit him from behind with all you've got. If Hal had had the breath to speak, he would have roared the words aloud. But what he could see now and then in the corner of his eye assured him bleakly that no help was on the way. Baldur seemed to have his hands full at the moment, holding other men at bay, those who would have come in on the berserker's side.

Bran had lost his remnant of a sword, but had somehow rearmed himself in both hands with more splintered wood. He still came on relentlessly, stumbling and lurching on broken bones. The lungs of the dead man were still laboring, forcing in and out the air the dead man's muscles needed for their work. This would be Bran's last fight, but while an opponent still faced him, it seemed the spirit of Wodan would not let him fall.

Hal gripped his axe in two hands now . . . a weapon so heavy that it seemed to need two hands to lift . . . and Bran, his body still moving, though no man could say how, was coming after him again. Hal wondered if berserkers had to breathe at all . . .

Later, Hal could not even remember what final blow had brought the monster down to stay.

Berserkers were not gods. And in the end mere human flesh and bone must find its limits and fall down.

Hal dropped the axe and fell almost on top of him.

He was gasping, gasping, gasping, and thought he could not have made another move to save his life; Baldur's grandmother could have finished him, right there, with a knitting needle.

He dared not wait until his breath came back, he had no choice. As soon as he stirred and tried to move again, the world immediately started to turn gray before him, as in the beginning of a faint. But he could not allow himself the luxury of anything like that.

Slowly, laboriously, Hal picked up his knife, which had fallen nearby, With his good dagger in his hand, he began the process of slicing and chopping off the berserker's head.

Baldur's hand was tugging at his arm. "What are you doing, Hal? He's dead. He's dead!"

Hal was shaking his head *no*. That was easier than trying to talk. The job done, Hal heaved his grisly trophy into Loki's fireplace. Automatically he sheathed his knife. Breathing was still a full-time job, but now he could make words. "It's the only way. To make sure. Doesn't get up again. And come after us."

Baldur had put away his own sword and was retrieving Hal's helmet for him, putting it on Hal's head. No one else was moving to interfere. Now Baldur was handing him the axe. Hal noted dimly that one of Bran's teeth was still embedded in the handle.

"Hal, you're all blood. Can you walk?"

It took Hal two more breaths to be able to spare the air for two more words: "Not mine."

Both arms still functioned, and both legs. By some miracle he wasn't hurt, not really hurt apart from scrapes and bruises caught from floor and furniture, and from the sheer gripping strength of the berserker's hands.

Someone must have run for Sergeant Nosam, because here the sergeant was, staring in cold horror at the ruin, the dead and wounded men. *Let's see you keep all this from Wodan, Sergeant.* But then maybe he could. Maybe he could.

So far Nosam was saying nothing, and Hal stepped over a body he did not recognize, brushed past the sergeant and the surviving corporal, Blackie, white-faced and clutching at a wounded arm.

"Baldur, this way." Now Hal was almost ready to breathe and talk at the same time. "We go to the Horses."

At last the sergeant found his voice. He only asked: "What happened to the gnomes?"

It was Baldur who turned to give the answer: "I saw them running out. They'll be on their way home."

In the stable, Baldur went immediately to start checking out the Horses. As soon as he was out of sight, Hal, now able to walk unaided and almost straight, moved with deliberate speed to recover the golden saddlebags. Miracle of miracles, almost as soon as he looked for them, there they were! He could only think that someone—quite likely Alvit—had simply lifted them from the Horse and set them down against a nearby wall, where they were inconspicuous though not exactly hidden. In the madhouse that was Valhalla, nothing like a thorough search had been conducted.

Besides being equipped with a spear holder, each set of saddlebags came with a water bottle made of some treated skin. The bottles were empty now, but once out of Valhalla it ought to be easy enough to get them filled.

Baldur soon returned, leading the almost-familiar Gold Mane and Cloudfoot. While the young man soothed the animals, Hal quickly strapped on two sets of saddlebags, making sure that Cloudfoot got the gold. He was about to announce that they were ready, when a glance through a nearby doorway spotted something that made him risk delay.

Quickly he muttered to Baldur: "Hold it one second, I'll be right back!"

The doorway led, as Hal had instantly surmised, into what had to be the Valkyries' armory, or at least a branch thereof, conveniently situated here near the stable. What he had glimpsed from outside was a high rack, in which half a dozen of the Valkyries' Spears stood waiting, unguarded and available.

Hal needed only a moment to snatch a Spear and stumble on his bruised legs back to the courtyard. But it was a moment ill-spent, or so it seemed. When Hal emerged, almost staggering, Spear in hand, he saw a sight that made him draw in breath for a desperate yell.

Baldur, not hearing Hal's last words or choosing to ignore them, had mounted the wrong Horse, the one that bore the gold, and was already on his way. But Hal choked off his yell before it could get started, for Baldur was too far away to hear, and too far away to turn back if he did. Besides, an all-out bellow might bring discovery and destruction on them both.

Hal had just dragged his battered frame aboard Gold Mane when Alvit suddenly appeared, on foot and out of breath. For a moment Hal was ready to use his borrowed Spear against the Valkyrie, but her first words convinced him that there was no need.

"There is no help for it, Hal, now you must flee. The sergeant will tell Wodan that Bran and the other man who fell are chasing two deserters." When Hal would have turned his mount away, her hand fell on his arm in a hard grip. "Where are you going?"

"To Loki's fire. Baldur won't go anywhere else."

"Then follow him, and I will meet you when I can. I'll try to bring some food."

13

Baldur was urging his Horse to its best speed, Cloud-foot's long legs working at a hard gallop, reaching out with each stride to take their magical grips upon huge chunks of air and pull them back. Every time the soles of the two hind hooves turned up toward Hal, the gold shoes on them caught dull gleams from the first horizontal rays of the rising sun, seeming to symbolize his vanishing fortune.

Vaguely Hal realized that if the sun was up already, last night's ritual feast must have started some time well after midnight. It seemed that time itself, like many other things, was coming askew in Valhalla, or at least in the minds of its inmates. Meanwhile he was yelling in Gold Mane's ear, kicking the animal in the ribs, in an effort to overtake his colleague. The trouble was that Hal's mount was slower, though not by much. Trusting that a Horse could be controlled in the same way as a mundane beast, he kicked Gold Mane some more, and shouted out a string of oaths. Their speed increased.

For Hal, the strangest thing about the ride, at first, was not the visible emptiness beneath him. He had been expecting that. It was that his ears kept anticipating the beat of hooves and metal shoes on hard ground—and there was no sound but only the whisper of the passing wind, soft as a woman's breath, and now and then the jingle of an iron buckle on a saddlebag.

In cold blood he might not have been able to force himself

to dare this ride. But now with the dead berserker and Wodan and slavery behind him, he was ready to dare anything to get away.

By the time Hal had taken a few gasping breaths, Wodan's stronghold had fallen completely behind them, while ahead and below almost nothing was immediately visible in the gray light of dawn but jagged rock and terrifying space.

As if to avoid some unseen obstacle, maybe a passing bird, Gold Mane shifted his flight path abruptly, so sharply that Hal's horned helmet, so narrowly saved from the berserker, tilted clean off his head. His instinct was to make a grab for the helmet before it got away, but somehow neither of his hands was willing to let go its grip on coarse Horsehair. Over the next few seconds Hal grew dizzy watching his prized headpiece grow smaller and smaller, becoming a barely visible dot before it disappeared into a distant cloud.

The falling body of a man, just like the helmet, would take a long, long time to reach even that cloud. Hal slumped forward, clasping his arms around the racing Horse's neck.

But he was not going to fall. He was not going to fall.

What was he *doing*, trying to fly like a bird on the strength of unknown magic? Had he gone completely mad, ready to kill himself trying to regain a few handfuls of stolen gold? Helplessly he yearned after the modest treasure so neatly packaged on the back of Baldur's Horse. And Baldur of course was completely ignorant of the fact that Cloudfoot was carrying gold—or was he? No, Hal had to believe he was. By this time he was certain that he knew Baldur pretty well.

Sternly commanding himself not to look down, Hal managed to overcome his vertigo. Now, glancing back over his shoulder as the clouds flew by, he was heartened by being able to detect no signs of immediate pursuit. To his surprise, they had already covered so much distance that he could no longer see Valhalla at all, but only the mountain peaks among which it nested. As far as he could tell, Alvit was the only one in the disorganized stronghold who knew that they had gone.

Hal's next shout to Baldur died out awkwardly as Hal's throat spasmed—on reaching a break in the fluffy clouds beneath him, he was suddenly able to see only too clearly the immense altitude that he had now reached. Far, far below him sprawled a wilderness of jagged rock, a scene that lurched and jiggled with the onrushing movement of his steed. Thousands of feet, maybe a mile of empty air, loomed below, a distance that made his gut tighten in anticipation of a fall.

Once again he clutched desperately with both hands at the animal's mane. The strangeness, the unfamiliarity of the Horse that he was riding made the experience all the more terrible—he had to close his eyes again to reassure himself, concentrating on the solid feel of the galloping animal between his thighs.

But voluntary blindness was not going to ease his terror for more than a moment; his imagination was all too ready to furnish the space in front of him with objects of dread. Hal opened his eyes again and saw nothing but rushing clouds ahead, and the galloping figure of Baldur's Horse. This time he did not look down.

The world spread out before the flying riders in the dawn of a clear winter morning was an amazing sight, and Hal was awed by this borrowed, secondhand power of the god—for a moment he was utterly terrified by his own audacity.

But his situation as a captive in Valhalla had been bad, horrible to the point where he would have tried anything to escape. Even fighting a berserker, though that had not been his conscious plan when the fight started.

He thought there was no telling how Wodan was going to react on learning of the violence and death erupting in the mess, costing him at least his favorite berserker. Probably the Father of Battles had already been informed. Or even now someone might be bringing him the news. Of course, in the legendary version of Valhalla, beating a true Hero to death and cutting off his head should cause him no more than a little pain and inconvenience—nothing to lay him up for long. Combat in Wodan's realm, as it was so widely celebrated in song and story, was never more than playacting.

There was one more considerable difference between romance and reality. In the legends, no one ever thought of trying to escape from Valhalla. Well, at least this time Wodan would not be able to send out his favorite berserker to track down and dispose of the fugitives.

Which might mean that this time, the god would be conducting the chase in person. But maybe not. To Hal it seemed quite possible that Wodan would prefer the comfort of remaining in his private dream-world, would refuse to consider the fact that his best berserker was gone for good. Instead the All-Highest would probably be looking forward to tonight's feast, anticipating a good discussion between the winner and loser of last night's rousing fight. And even the absence of both principals in that contest might not matter much; if neither man appeared tonight, the All-Seeing would be perfectly capable of imagining they were there.

Wodan's general ineffectiveness, his wandering attention whenever there were decisions to be made, gave Hal strong reason to hope. Unless someone forcibly brought the fact to his attention, it might be a long time before the befuddled Lord of Valhalla realized that two of his magic steeds were missing from their stalls and faced the fact that two of his exalted band of Heroes had forsaken their eternal reward for the fun of stealing a couple of Horses and a few pounds of gold.

And even if Wodan was ready to confront the truth, he might not be capable of doing anything about it—if only Hal and Baldur could get far enough away.

Looking back over his shoulder again, Hal's heart sank when he beheld what looked like a swarm of giant insects on his trail, great wings churning the air in flight. So much for his hope that there would be no pursuit. The insects looked like nothing he had ever seen before. But at least it was not a chariot that now came speeding after him, gaining ground—or air—seemingly with every vibration of what looked like a hundred blurring wings, propelling scores of bodies in a cloud. He could hope that it was only wraiths that followed, and he rejoiced that he had managed to borrow one of the Valkyries' Spears.

Rapidly the vague cloud of semitransparent entities drew nearer, traveling at truly frightening speed. When a whirling vortex of spectral wingbeats swirled around Hal, he resisted the impulse to draw his axe, and put his borrowed weapon to good use—at each touch of its point, an image exploded into nothingness. Though the Spear was unfamiliar in his hands, it proved formidably efficient, and what had been a whole formation of the speeding wraiths soon dwindled to a scattered few that gave up the chase and turned aside.

Before he could relax, he realized he was being pursued by yet more apparitions, traveling every bit as quickly as the first.

As this second wave of pursuit drew nearer, he was soon able to identify a pair of huge unnatural Ravens, with ten-foot wingspans. These came hurtling at him from both sides at once, pecking and slashing with huge beaks, evidently intent on forcing him to land or knocking him off his Horse.

Again he thanked all helpful gods for the mighty Spear. A mere touch from that glittering point produced an almost soundless explosion, obliterating one bird and then the other in a cloud of raven feathers, fragile debris dispersed at once by the rushing winds of the high air.

Still, only a brief time had passed since the Horse first carried him aloft. The sun seemed to have advanced only a few of its own diameters above the eastern horizon, but Valhalla had fallen completely out of sight, and many miles of air had passed beneath their Horses' flying hooves. The mountains were distant, the valley of the Einar spread out beneath, and Baldur and Hal were drawing near their goal.

Despite Hal's efforts to catch up with his young companion, he had actually lost a little distance, and his shouts for Baldur to slow down a little had either gone unheard or were being ignored.

Studying the object of his pursuit, Hal noticed to his consternation that Baldur was now even slightly farther ahead of him, the young man's Horse still galloping through the air in the direction of the flaming clifftop, which was already noticeably nearer. After only an instant's hesitation, Hal urged his own mount in the same direction.

Of course Hal was looking forward to getting his hands once more on Cloudfoot's saddlebags, stuffed with gold; he thought he deserved that much compensation for long days of unjust imprisonment. But he had other goals in mind as well. Soon Loki's flames would be visible ahead.

Hal was also gripped by a vague, instinctive fear that Baldur, if left to his own devices, would be sure to make some horrible blunder that would result in their both being overtaken and punished by a vengeful god.

Every time Hal looked over his shoulder he was faintly encouraged, because he could see only a rolling, low, uneven sea of clouds and distant mountains. Let more wraiths come if they would, and he would fight them off with his beautiful Spear; there was still no sign of the one pursuer he truly dreaded, the airborne chariot, pulled by an eight-legged Horse and occupied by Wodan himself.

Then a time came when his head turned again to look and his heart sank, when his eye was caught by distant movement in the sky. There came in view some flying object much too big to be a bird, and looking too solid to be another wraith. Something, just faintly visible between himself and the site of vanished Valhalla, was cruising along briskly on an angled course. What gave Hal hope was that fortunately it was not following directly on his and Baldur's airy trail. The distance was so great that Hal could barely make the object out. But he could tell that it was moving very fast.

Unhappily, Hal soon felt completely certain that it was a solid object, not a wraith, and also that it was indeed a chariot. But he could still hope that the speeding conveyance was not Wodan's. For one thing, this vehicle was of a lighter color than the black Hal remembered.

Every time he looked back, the chariot was somewhat closer, though it was still, thank all the Fates, not in direct pursuit. Hal thought he could see now that there was only a single occupant. It was being pulled by something—what appeared to be a pair of somethings . . . not cameloids or droms . . . certainly not an eight-legged Horse.

Whatever the vehicle was, and however it was being propelled, its course kept diverging more and more from Hal's and Baldur's. But still it was a worrisome sight.

Baldur must have caught sight of the same disturbing presence, and only moments after Hal did. For now the young man suddenly changed course, urged the speeding Cloudfoot in a different direction, heading away from the circle of flames.

Then Hal noticed another possible reason for Baldur's change of course: a small squadron of Valkyries were flying on their Horses near Loki's flames, actually circling them like half a dozen or more huge and glorious silver moths. One or two others were sitting their magic mounts on the ground of the clifftop, very near Loki's great ongoing demonstration.

Possibly these young women would share Alvit's cooperative attitude, but Hal was not ready to bet on it. Unless mortal men were armed with something much better than their own mundane weapons, they could expect no success at all in fighting against Valkyries. Hal did have a Spear, but still the odds would be prohibitively heavy against him.

When Baldur's mount went diving lower, Hal kept close behind him. Uncertain of how to order his Horse into a descent, he tried pushing gently forward on the animal's long neck. To his great relief he found that that technique worked beautifully.

Down they went, racing through deep vaults of vapor, to burst out at last through the lower surface of a broken layer of clouds. Presently they were quickly skimming low in the valley, about a mile from the cliff of fire.

Baldur, with Hal now very close behind him, guided his mount to a landing on the near shore of the broad Einar, on a bank thickly forested enough to offer some hope of concealment.

A few moments later, Hal guided his own mount to a soft landing at the same spot. At the moment of his own landing, Hal shut his eyes again and gripped his Horse's mane, but Gold Mane managed the business as complete routine. The long-missing sound of hoofbeats came almost as a shock to the ear. He resisted an impulse to immediately leap from his Horse's back and kiss the ground.

Here it seemed to Hal that they ought to be pretty effectively screened by the canopy of some tall evergreens with overhanging branches, long and thick enough to offer effective shelter against aerial observation.

Both Horses were as unexcited by the adventure of flight as if it had been a mere canter through a mountain meadow. Nor did they seem at all exhausted by the terrific speed they had achieved while airborne. They were ready to take a good drink from the shallow eddies of the Einar, and to enjoy some of the long soft grass that grew on the adjoining shore.

Hal, watching Baldur keenly as he approached him, could detect no evidence that the youth suspected anything about the treasure in his saddlebags, or that he had been seriously trying to leave Hal behind. Instead, Baldur looked up almost calmly as the northman appeared at his side and began a congratulatory greeting. The young man's eyes widened only when he caught sight of the stolen Spear that Hal had grounded in the handy holder strapped on with his saddlebags.

"What are you doing with that?" The joyous expression faded from Baldur's face, and his voice was grave.

"Oh, this little thing?" Hal seized the shaft of the Spear and shook it. "Don't let it upset you. I just thought I might need something of the kind. It really seemed of considerable importance that we should get clean away, even if someone tried to stop us. And it came in handy when I met those ghosts and the Ravens."

"What are you talking about?" It soon turned out that Baldur, intent as he was upon his goal, was not even aware that they had been pursued. When Hal had explained about the wraiths and Ravens, Baldur still frowned at the long weapon Hal was carrying.

"Yes, but . . ." he objected. "Alvit won't like it, that you took a Spear."

"You think someone will mistake me for a Valkyrie? Don't

know what the Heroes on the battlefield would do if they saw
me coming to carry them away."

"I should think they might be inspired to go on fighting."

"Huh. Well, this sticker saved our lives, my lad. But still
I'll give it back, next time I see her. I'll gladly give her more
than that, we owe the girl a lot."

Half-expecting Alvit to come in sight at any moment—she
had said she'd meet them—Hal looked up at the rude canopy
of pine branches, through which the sky was visible only in
spots and fragments. "I'd say you picked a reasonably good
place to land."

"Yes, I thought we had better wait until those Valkyries
got out of our way—I'm not sure if they saw us or not."
Baldur made no mention of seeing a chariot in the air. Hal
hesitated over whether to tell his partner about it or not, then
quickly decided to abide by his general rule: in case of uncertainty, keep quiet.

But there was one point he had to raise. "By the way—I
thought you were going to take this Horse. The one I'm riding."

Baldur was gracious. "Why, I thought to leave Gold Mane
to you. Being more or less used to real humans, he would be
less likely to throw off a total stranger. Is there anything
wrong with that?"

"No. Oh no, nothing. I see. Thank you. I appreciate it."

In any case they had got away, were free, and no harm
done. Now Hal felt free to turn his thoughts to getting at the
gold. Looking at Baldur, Hal was sure that the youth had no
idea what was hidden in his saddlebags. He could think of no
convincing reason to suggest that they switch Horses, and
tried to come up with some more subtle method of regaining
his lost loot. Meanwhile, both men had dismounted and were
crouching by the river to fill their water bottles. Then, sprawling belly down on a flat rock, they drank directly from the
stream.

Whether Hal was ever really going to be a rich man or not, the water of freedom had a good taste; he sat up, wiping mouth and beard with the back of his hand. It was, in a way, tiring to have to think of gold again. But he was spared the effort. Before he could decide on the best way to raise the subject with his companion, a lone rider in a flying Chariot burst out of a low cloud, descending rapidly toward them.

14

The Horses had been quiet, but now they froze, heads turned in the same direction. Hal and Baldur, both on their feet again, stood beside their respective mounts, staring at the one who had just arrived.

The chariot in itself was almost ordinary in appearance, little more than a big cart—but it was pulled through the air by two animals that Hal could only have described as giant goats, the size of cameloids. It was the same strange object that Hal had earlier seen flying at a distance. No more ordinary was the single figure occupying the vehicle. Thank all the Fates, it was not Wodan. But it was certainly not the shape of a mere mortal human either.

"It is Thor." Baldur's whisper was almost as awe-stricken as if this were the first god he had ever seen.

And Hal had to admit the young man must be right. The Thunderer in his goat cart came casually coasting down, steering easily in under the canopy of trees, the wheels of his vehicle spinning just as if they worked against a solid road, instead of air.

The figure in the chariot was male and powerful-looking, to say the least. Red of hair and beard, and with ruddy cheeks that gave him a vaguely jovial look. His head was covered by a broad-brimmed hat, and he was otherwise dressed in sumptuous furs, similar to those that Wodan generally wore, but better cared for. Thor's arms, almost inhumanly thick with bone and muscle, were each encircled by metal bracelets, one gold, the other silver. The god was also wearing dark gloves that seemed to be made of iron, all joints and scales like the finest armor, for when he pulled one off and threw it down, it landed with a metallic thud.

Having brought his vehicle to a stop, Thor looked at Hal and Baldur without surprise, as if he had been more or less expecting to find this pair of mortal humans here. But his interest in them seemed to be only incidental.

Thor's voice was incongruously light and high. "I noticed you fellows galloping across the sky on Horses, but somehow you don't have the look of Valkryies. Is there serious trouble in Valhalla, or what? I'd go see for myself, but I might not be exactly welcome."

The two mortals looked at each other. Baldur's chin was trembling, as if he were trying to speak but found himself unable.

That was all right with Hal, who readily assumed the role of spokesman. "Wodan still occupies his throne, my lord," he grated out. "So I suppose it depends what you mean by serious."

Thor made a little dismissive gesture with one huge hand, as if to say the business was not worth worrying about. "Really none of my affair what goes on in Valhalla," he assured Hal. Then his voice took on a keener edge. "I don't suppose either of you've seen anything of that bastard Loki?"

"Not that we know of, sir," said Hal. And Baldur silently shook his head.

Thor sighed. Just like any ordinary man who had been riding too long in a cramped position, the god descended from his chariot, letting the reins fall carelessly to the ground, and demonstrated to the onlookers that he was not overly tall, at least not for a deity. As the god enjoyed a good stretch, Hal took note of the heavy Hammer, bigger than a blacksmith's sledge, that hung at his belt just as the hatchet rode on Hal's.

Myelnir. Hal stared at it, seeing no signs of awesome power. The handle seemed incongruously short, and he wasn't even sure that it was made of wood. Could the whole Hammer possibly be one piece of forged metal?

Oblivious to the scrutiny of two pairs of human eyes, Thor chose an ordinary riverside rock and sat down on it like an ordinary man. Hal did not really see him draw the heavy Hammer from his belt, but suddenly Thor had the weapon in his hand, and was idly spinning it, head down like a top, on the stone surface.

In his impressive voice he said: "Loki in his capacity as fire-god can whip up a really toasty blaze. I don't suppose anybody here would know exactly why he set fire to that tall hill? Or where he's got to now? At this moment he's of more interest to me than Wodan is. Considerably more."

"No sir," said Hal. Almost in unison with him, Baldur pronounced the same two words. Then Hal added: "That fire's surely interesting, though."

Thor grunted a kind of agreement, and looked very thoughtful. "I've been over there a couple of times, and taken a look around."

Suddenly Hal realized the god was looking steadily at him. "I think you better put that down," said Thor quietly.

"What?" Hal asked, then felt his ears burn with the sound of his own stupidity. There was the borrowed Spear, its butt grounded in his Horse's harness, but the shaft actually still clutched in his right hand.

Thor hefted his short-handled Hammer ominously.

Hal with a flick of his wrist plucked the Spear from its rest, and hastily cast it down at his side. Distantly his mind registered the fact that he did not hear the weapon hit the ground. A moment later he noticed that it had somehow come to be part of the equipment aboard Thor's chariot.

Meanwhile Myelnir had gone back to rest at Thor's belt. The god continued to regard the two men steadily. "Well? Either of you got anything else to say?"

Baldur seemed to be gradually giving way under the strain of the divine presence. Now he was hanging on to his Horse's mane as he stood beside the animal, as if without support he might faint and tumble over.

Hal was hardly at ease, but neither was he about to collapse. He cleared his throat. "Tell me, Lord Thor," he invited, "what the general subject of conversation is to be?"

Whatever Thor's chief concern might be, it did not seem to be the conduct of the two frightened men before him. The god looked grim, but, thank all the Fates, the cause of his grimness seemed to have nothing to do with the puny mortal men before him. "We were talking about Loki," he reminded his interlocutors, gently enough. "I suppose you fellows do know who Loki is?"

"Yes sir," said Hal. "In a vague, general way, that is."

"Well then, let me be more specific. It's important. Either of you see him anywhere, within the last few days? Now remember; he's a great shape-changer. Did either of you see anyone—or anything—that struck you as especially remarkable?"

"I can't remember anything like that, my lord," said Hal. "I mean, considering we've been in Valhalla until very recently. There were some strange things there—but I think not of the kind you mean." He looked at Baldur, who silently shook his head.

Hal was beginning to feel some of the strain that was paralyzing Baldur. In a way, Thor, in his matter-of-fact sanity, was more frightening than Wodan. People had described similar sensations on confronting Apollo. Whatever this god might decide to do, it would not be out of forgetfulness, or befuddlement. But there was a reassuring aspect too. Thor did not seem much interested in who Hal and Baldur were, or what sins they might have committed against Wodan—he only hoped that they might answer some questions for him.

Silently Hal was cursing himself again for getting into this at all. For being so greedy for gold, so big a fool, that he would stick his nose into gods' business for the sake of some farmland and fishing boats. How could he, with his experience, have fallen so completely for the ancient lure of greed?

Meanwhile, Hal's and Baldur's Horses, in the presence of Thor and his two huge, incongruous goats, had almost ceased entirely to move. The beasts were still standing as if frozen into sleep.

Thor seemed to have decided not to press his questioning any further. "Looks like a hard battle coming soon," he observed, to no one in particular. After studying the horizon in several directions and listening carefully—he briefly held up one huge hand for silence—as if to sounds that mere human ears could not expect to hear, Thor waved an abrupt farewell, climbed back into his chariot, and clucked to his outsized Goats, who scrambled into action. In a moment the god and his strange equipage were airborne and out of sight.

Hal mourned the loss of his borrowed Spear, but there was nothing he could do about it. "Let's see if the Valkyries are still in sight," he suggested. Baldur agreed, and volunteered to climb a tree—his joints and limbs were, after all, younger than Hal's.

"I won't argue with you there." Hal's body was starting to stiffen, in the aftermath of the battering he'd taken in the fight with Bran. He ached when he tried to move and ached when he did not. If he was still alive tomorrow, he thought, he would be lucky if he could stand on his feet without help. It was as if some enchantment had suddenly advanced him to about eighty years of age.

Baldur had done some fighting in Valhalla too, but had fortunately escaped without wounds, and he seemed to feel no aftereffects. Vaguely Hal could remember what it felt like to be that young. Now the young man nimbly shinnied up a trunk, and presently was peering outward from the upper branches.

"What word?" Hal called up to him.

"Looks like the Valkyries are all gone," Baldur reported. "I don't see them near the flames or anywhere else. We can go on at once," he concluded.

Moving with the agility of youth, Baldur had dropped from the tree again before Hal made any move toward the saddlebags on the young man's Horse. A moment later, the young man was once more astride Cloudfoot's back. His knees were practically touching the packaged gold, though plainly he had no suspicion it was there.

"Maybe," Hal offered, "we should wait a little longer to make sure that Wodan's not coming after us." If only he could think of some reason to get Baldur away from his Horse for one nice, full minute . . .

At this point the young man, thoroughly disillusioned by his experiences in Valhalla, seemed not even to care whether or not an angry Wodan might be pursuing them. Baldur was not going to be distracted now. He did care enough about one subject to say something before becoming airborne again. "I have been thinking, Hal, and now I understand the problem."

"Oh. You do?" By now Hal had hauled himself aboard Gold Mane again. He was going to make very sure that Baldur did not get away from him.

"Yes." Baldur had the air of announcing a great discovery. "It is not really Wodan who has turned senile."

Hal stared at him. "I got a very strong impression that he was about as crazy as two monkeys with—"

"No, what I mean is, the problem lies only with the avatar, not with the essence of the god. A Face cannot become senile, can it?"

"Well. I don't know. I never heard of anything like that."

"Of course it can't." Now Baldur was as certain as if he had been dealing with gods' Faces all his life, turning them out like cheap helmets in the smithy behind his mother's house. "Which means that the problem can be solved. It is just that the time has come for another man to put on Wodan's Face."

The northman stopped to consider. "I hadn't thought of that." True enough, he hadn't, because such a possibility hadn't seemed worth thinking about. Unless, of course, something were to happen to Wodan, which so far had seemed about as likely as the Einar drying up. "But you may well be right."

Their argument, or discussion, was interrupted by the arrival of Alvit, who as she rode up announced that she had been watching from a distance.

"I rejoice to see that Thor has not taken your Horses or your lives," was the Valkyrie's next remark, as she slid off her barebacked mount to stretch, in unconscious imitation of Thor. Then she looked at Hal. "What happened to your helmet?"

He shrugged. "I'm lucky I've still got my head."

Alvit had not paused to listen to the answer. "I have warned all the Valkyries to keep clear of the Thunderer," she told them. "I feared he might be grown contemptuous of Wodan, and would confiscate the first Horse he saw, and ride it into the flames, to see for himself just what Loki's fire is hiding. But what did he want of you? Was he curious to know what was happening in Valhalla?"

Hal shook his head. "Not very," said Baldur. "He was asking about Loki."

"In the tone and manner of one who tries to locate an enemy," Hal amplified. "But of course we could tell him nothing. Then he said that some kind of battle was about to start. Any idea what he meant by that?"

"The reasons for it I do not know, except that the creatures of the Underworld hate gods, especially Wodan. But the evidence that we will soon be fighting is very strong."

Hal said: "But you and the other Valkyries remain loyal to him."

Alvit was obviously troubled. "Most of my sisters are loyal—when they are loyal—only because they are afraid. The All-Highest devises terrible punishments for those he thinks have betrayed him. That is why you did well to flee."

"But you wanted us to go for other reasons. Why are you helping us?"

"I had thought there might be time to strengthen our forces before we had to fight, but it is too late for that. Wodan must fight for his life, and he will have no time for distractions. And you would be a great distraction now, so it is better that you simply go."

In the presence of the Valkyrie, Hal dared not say or do anything about the gold hidden in the saddlebags. He couldn't even suggest breaking out the food Baldur had packed, for fear that someone would open the wrong containers.

Baldur was obviously growing restless, impatient with all this talk. Now the young man insisted that he could delay no longer, and was going to ride immediately to Loki's Fire, and clasp his Brunhild in his arms. "You cannot stop me, Alvit, before I have done that, unless you kill me. When I have done it, I will give back this Horse."

"I have no intention of killing you, young man, and you

may both keep the Horses yet a little longer. I have no need of them at the moment, nor does the All-Highest. What we need now is not more Horses." On the last words her voice came near breaking, in something like desperation.

Then she pulled herself together, thinking matters over in her serious way. "Yes, go to Brunhild—or get as close to her as you can. Stay there with her, and in a little while I will come in through the Fire and tell you whether Wodan has abandoned his pursuit."

"Could you bring us some food?" Hal asked. "That last feast was a little thin."

"Yes, I will try to do that," she agreed, and noted with approval that they had their water bottles.

"We thank you, Alvit," said Hal. "I still don't understand why you are doing this for us."

She hesitated before adding: "Long I have loved Wodan, too. But now there are things . . . it is strange, almost as if he has determined that his life will end. For his own good, some of us must disobey him." For a moment the Valkyrie seemed on the brink of weeping.

Hal wished that he could do something for her. He also wished that he could think of some excuse, any excuse, for swapping mounts, or saddlebags, with Baldur. But before he could come up with a good idea, Baldur was again on Cloud-foot's back, urging his mount toward the flames. This time Hal had to watch in silence as his farm and his fishing boats seemed about to vanish into the distance. All he could do was jump on Gold Mane and try to keep up with them.

In less than a minute the men were riding very close to where the flames still burned, and quickly they brought their Horses down to land, side by side, on the high hillside not far from the spot where they had first met.

Looking cautiously about, Hal made sure the Valkyrie was

out of sight. Now he ought to be able to get his gold back in one way or another—without doing Baldur any damage, if that was possible.

The young man, his face working with some deep emotion, said to Hal: "You have been a true comrade, and I owe you more than I can ever repay."

"Never mind about that—wait! Hold up!" Hal had to force his own mount right next to Baldur's, and jostle him aside, to keep the headstrong youth from plunging right into the fire.

"Let me go!"

"Not yet! By all the gods and devils, man, hold off a moment! Can't you see we must think of what we're doing, before we attempt this? I might have some interest, too, in what's inside the flames." *If you must plunge in there, give me my gold first. Then maybe I'll follow.* But he could not quite bring himself to say that in so many words,

"What more is there to think of? Brunhild is in there, she may be dying, and I am going to—"

"You're still absolutely convinced she's there. Then—"

"Of course she is there. You heard Alvit."

"Yes, yes, but she's already been there for several days—how many is it now?—and she can wait another minute or two. Will you listen to me a minute? I propose we first try riding near the flames, and make sure the heat won't scorch us, that these magic mounts offer us protection." And Hal reached out and caught his companion by the jacket.

"Hal. Let me go."

"Look, I know you saw a Valkyrie do this trick, but it also might be a good idea to drench ourselves in water before plunging into that kind of—wait! Hold up, damn you!"

But Baldur had wrenched free, knocking Hal's arm away with a swinging elbow. The young man kicked his mount in the ribs again, and he was off, headed straight into the wall of fire. The Horse, as if accustomed to such a practice, did not balk or shy away.

Hal's cry went unheeded, and Baldur's mount bore its rider straight into the wall of flame. At the last moment the young man bowed his head so that his face was hidden between his arms, his shoulders in the tattered jacket tensing in the instant before the fiery tongues closed around them.

Raising his head along with his clenched fists, to hurl an oath of anger at the sky, Hal caught sight of something in the distance that stilled his outcry in his throat.

His vision was ordinarily quite good at long range, uncomfortably good in this case, and he had little doubt that the approaching object was a two-wheeled chariot. For some reason he felt vaguely relieved to see that the animals pulling it through the air did not look at all like goats. Then relief faded. At first he had thought there were two Horses, but now he could see that there was only one, and it had eight legs. There was a single rider, who seemed to be carrying a long Spear, a weapon even longer than the Valkyries', and ominously stouter.

Hal hesitated only briefly, taking one last look around. Baldur and his steed had disappeared right into the fire, and they were not coming out. Not immediately, anyway.

Hal's imagination presented him with an unwelcome sensation, the smell of cooking meat.

But Wodan was coming after him, and Wodan was angry. No doubt about it now. The man could feel the radiation of that wrath, even at a distance, and it felt even hotter than the fire. Like the approach of a piece of red-hot iron, or the imminence of a thunderbolt from a black cloud. Choking out a strangled oath, Hal closed his eyes, kicked his Horse savagely in the ribs, and went plunging straight into the flames after his companion.

15

For just a moment Hal's ears were buffeted by a huge noise. In his imagination it was equal to the roaring of all the flames that Loki in all his avatars had ever kindled. In the same moment, a fierce light came glaring at him, forcing its way in through his closed lids in the colors of blood and gold, far brighter than any natural fire.

But he felt nothing of the blasting heat that he had expected and instinctively tried to brace himself against. The motion of his bounding, airborne Horse kept on unchanged. Then the great light was gone as quickly as it had appeared, and the noise of the divine fire had faded to its usual muted roar. The plunging motion of Hal's mount stopped abruptly, and he thought he felt the Horse's four legs all come down on solid ground.

Opening his eyes, Hal nearly fell from the beast's back in astonishment. He had come through one fire only to confront another. He and Gold Mane had come to a standing stop in the middle of a corridor of clear space, some ten yards wide that ran curving away in two directions, between two concentric walls of fire, so that the strip of free space between them was shaped like a wheel's broad rim. The flames on each side were equally tall and bright, and for just a moment he feared that he would be roasted between them. But this fire was the work of a god, not ordinary nature, and the god had designed this curving space to be habitable by mortal humans.

The air immediately surrounding Hal and his mount was clear, free of smoke, and cooler than many a summer's day he could remember.

The ground on which Hal's Horse had braced its legs was mostly rocks and scattered tufts of grass, much like that he had observed outside the outer ring of fire. The chief difference was that in here the surface was almost flat.

The breath Hal had been holding broke from his lungs explosively. His mount had landed quietly and easily, and as if it found this environment familiar, was already tasting some of the grass that struggled to grow here just as it did outside the outer burning ring.

Within this narrow sanctuary, bounded inside and out by Loki's glowing barricades, the air was so quiet that Hal could hear the slight ripping sound made by his Horse's teeth as they worked calmly on the scanty grass.

A pebble's toss ahead of him stood Baldur's mount with Baldur still aboard, facing toward Hal. Cloudfoot was also calmly cropping winter grass. Both animals were behaving as if this little space of rocky soil were some ordinary pasture—somehow, Hal thought, the beasts must be able to distinguish Loki's handiwork from ordinary fire, and they felt no dread of it at all. Or perhaps—and this idea raised new questions—it was as if they had visited this place so often that Loki's handiwork was quite familiar to them.

From where Hal perched on Gold Mane's back, he could see no sign at all of Brunhild. Baldur, also failing to discover his beloved anywhere, shot one haggard, desperate look at Hal, then tugged at his mount's golden mane and kicked the animal into action, so that it bore him quickly away. In only a moment, beast and rider had vanished around the sharp curve of fire-bounded space. And in the next breath the youth and his Horse were returning, coming around the bend of narrow corridor from the opposite direction.

Raising both arms in a despairing gesture, Baldur gave a cry: "She is not here!"

Hal had already reached that conclusion and only nodded abstractedly. At the moment he was less concerned about Brunhild than he was about the fact of Wodan's furious pursuit. Hal found himself holding his breath, expecting at any moment the noise and fury of an angry god to come bursting in through Loki's outer fire-ring. Listening carefully now, the northman could even hear (or imagined that he could) the All-Highest out there somewhere, bellowing in a kind of rage that matched berserker Bran's.

Hal could only pray to the Fates that eight-legged Sleipnir could not breach Loki's barrier as easily as the Valkyries' Horses had. Of course Gold Mane and Cloudfoot had not been harnessed to a chariot. Now if it should occur to Wodan to borrow a Valkyrie's Horse . . .

If Hal was ready to forget Brunhild, Baldur seemed to have already forgotten Wodan. The young man's fears were of another kind entirely. Again he shouted: "She is not here!" And he waved both arms at Hal, as if he expected his mentor to tell him where she was.

Hal shook his head. "I kept trying to tell you it would be better not to get your hopes up—what're you doing now? Wait!"

Baldur wasn't listening. Instead, he had flung himself from his mount and was dancing and scurrying back and forth, getting as close as he could to the inner barrier of flame and trying frantically to see through it. If Hildy was not to be found in this wheel-rim space between the fires, then maybe she was in there, somewhere deeper inside Loki's sanctuary. There was a kind of logic to the idea. Bending and crawling, her lover brought himself as close to the ground as possible, evidently seeking a favorable angle of sight.

Muttering blasphemies against a whole pantheon of gods,

Hal scrambled after the young man, trying with practically no success to get his attention.

In this fashion the two men had made their way almost halfway around the inner barrier when suddenly Baldur froze in position and let out a hoarse scream.

"Here she is! I see her! Hal, look at this!"

Baldur was crouched down, his head only three feet from the inner barrier—about as close as he could get without burning himself—trying with both hands to shade his eyes from the yellow glare, even as he stared intently at something near ground level and just in front of him, on the other side of that incandescent wall.

Hal squatted beside the youth, cupped his hands round his own eyes to shade them from the omnipresent flames as best he could, and studied the indicated region. Then he rubbed his eyes and stared again.

The object Baldur was focusing on was hard for Hal to make out at first, behind the glare and slowly swirling color, but when he had concentrated on the place for the space of a few breaths the thing seemed to come a little clearer—enough to allow him to perceive the outline of what might well have been a supine human shape.

Given the obscuring glare, colors and other details were almost impossible to determine. But there could be no doubt about the general configuration. It did indeed appear to be either a young woman or the statue of one, lying on her back on some kind of bed or slab. She seemed partially clothed in some tight-fitting, reflective stuff that might have been metal armor.

Squinting even more intently, Hal thought he could make out a pale mass of gold, just where the recumbent figure's head ought to be resting, as on a pillow. But as the fire bathed everything in its own bright yellow, it was impossible to be sure.

Abruptly Baldur broke off his contemplation of the image beyond the sheet of fire. Next moment, with a bound and a wild cry, the youth had regained his seat astride his mount. Ignoring Hal's urging to stop and think, he urged Cloudfoot straight at the inner burning wall. But to the surprise of both men, the Horse refused the barrier at once, as simply and conclusively as it had accepted that of the outer ring.

It occurred to Hal that if Wodan himself had carried Brunhild into this nest of fire, then the god must have had some means of getting in and out unharmed. On the way in, he must have protected his prisoner also, unless the terms of punishment had been broadened to include incineration. Of course Hal could not be sure of the exact sequence of events. The girl might have been brought here before Loki called the flames' fierce circles into existence.

Or, and this seemed more likely as he thought about it, the Firegod himself could have carried the disgraced Valkyrie here as a favor for his colleague, the All-Highest, just as Loki had furnished Valhalla with some hearth-fires. That would mean that the two gods had been on good terms until only a few days ago.

It would be something to ask Alvit about, Hal thought, when he saw her again. If he ever did.

"Do you remember, Baldur?"

"Remember what?"

"Back in Valhalla, Wodan asked us several times what we knew about Loki, any contact we might have had with him."

"Yes, of course I remember that. And Thor asked the same thing. What of it?"

"I'm not sure. I was just trying to figure things out."

Hal let it drop. There was no use trying to talk to Baldur, who was growing more frantic with every minute. Again and again he tried desperately to urge his Horse to join the motionless figure half-hidden behind the flames.

Repeated efforts accomplished nothing. The animal showed

no reluctance to approach the inner wall of fire, or even to stand near it—only within a few inches of the glowing wall did the heat become unbearable. But Cloudfoot could not be induced to try to pass through it, no matter what Baldur did. The burning inner curtain might as well have been a wall of stone. When Baldur persisted in trying to force the great Horse forward, it reared and finally threw him off.

On his feet again a moment later, he borrowed the mount Hal had been riding and tried again, with exactly the same result.

After being thrown the second time, Baldur lay for a long moment without trying to move. At last he croaked: "Maybe it is my fault—maybe I am unworthy. Hal, you must try!"

Hal argued with him uselessly for a few moments. Then, more to pacify his colleague than in any hope of success, he made the same attempt, and managed to keep from being thrown. But his half-hearted effort achieved no more than Baldur's all-out try.

Now, after stumbling about uncertainly for a few moments, the young man crossed his arms over his face and, before Hal realized what he intended, went lurching blindly forward, trying to reach Brunhild on his own two legs. Heat met him like a solid wall, and his effort accomplished nothing but slightly burning his arms and hands, and scorching some of his long hair until it smoked.

Beaten back once by the intense heat, which when you got close enough was as fierce as that of any fire, he was still ready to try again.

Seeing the expression on Baldur's face, Hal felt compelled to grab him and hold him back to keep him from a suicidal plunge.

"Let me go! Let me go!" The young man struggled frantically, but Hal was stronger.

When the youth attempted a desperate kick, Hal tripped him and slammed him expertly to the ground, knocking out his wind. Then he straddled him to keep him there.

"Let me go!"

"As soon as you get back your wits, I'll let you go. Can't you see, you're going to fry yourself like an egg if you keep on? What good'll you be to her then?"

The youth broke down in helpless weeping.

Releasing his prostrate partner and slowly regaining his feet, Hal looked about him. The brief struggle had not been very intense, but it had worsened every ache in his body. It would be too bad to leave Baldur here in this state, but he might have to do so. Still, Hal was in no immediate hurry to stick his nose outside the outer fire-ring, where an angry Wodan might well be waiting to pounce. Alvit had said that she would come to them here, and maybe she really would, bringing food and information.

Meanwhile, *something* must be preventing Wodan from simply bulling his way in. Loki's defensive magic must be powerful. Sleipnir perhaps lacked golden shoes, and Wodan probably could not think straight enough to borrow a properly equipped Horse.

And Hal thought he had better take advantage of Baldur's collapse before the youth revived. Hal himself was nearly exhausted, but he retained the strength and energy to switch the saddlebags from one Horse to the other, strapping the heavily laden pair firmly onto Gold Mane, the animal he had himself been riding, and the light pair on the other. He was assuming that Baldur, when he had pulled himself together, would continue to ride Cloudfoot. But right now Hal's companion did not question what Hal was doing or even notice it.

It eased the aches and pains of battle wonderfully, to think that he had now secured his fortune as best he could. Now, Hal thought, the only thing really preventing his immediate departure was the strong possibility that Wodan was waiting for him just outside the flames. His stay could not be prolonged indefinitely, but he could afford to wait a little longer.

Loki's refuge might be proof against certain angry gods, but it was notably short on such amenities as water and food. Now Hal opened the lighter set of saddlebags, in search of whatever Baldur had managed to snatch up before leaving Valhalla. Hal sighed at what he found. A few handfuls of nothing better than fodder for the Horses, some of it stale-smelling stuff probably left over from some previous Valkyrie ride. Hal decided to postpone trying to eat any of it now—Alvit had definitely said something about trying to bring them food.

Shaking first one water bottle and then the other, to ascertain just how much might be left, he stood over Baldur and spoke to him sharply.

"Look here, young one. Give up this whining and bawling and pull yourself together. Sit up like a man and share a little Horse-fodder with me. Thinking and eating will be better than banging your head against a wall of fire."

Baldur sat up. If his assortment of minor burns, cuts, and bruises were paining him, he gave no sign. Ah, youth! Hal thought again. Sitting down to rest his legs, he groaned with the pain in his chronically sore knee. He wished there was a solid wall that he might lean his back against.

Baldur stirred. He rubbed his head with both hands for a while, then asked: "Where is Alvit? Didn't she say she was going to meet us here?"

"She did say something like that, yes." Hal could feel his eyelids trying to sag shut. It was a long time, years, since he had felt as tired as he did right now. He was going to have to rest before he tried to flee, or made an effort to do anything, for that matter. Not that he wasn't proud as well as tired. Few men—very few—could boast of killing a berserker in single combat.

Still thinking about Alvit, he added: "But she's done a lot

for us already, and now she may be caught up in whatever damn fool battle this is that the gods are getting into. We oughtn't to expect much more from her." Privately he was thinking that Alvit would be lucky if Wodan did not discover everything she had been doing for his prisoners and deal her out some terrible punishment.

"I suppose." Baldur had run out of tears and groans for the moment. Now he sat slumped beside Hal, just staring at nothing.

"Let us think," Hal repeated. "How we are going to reach behind the inner flames. There never was a barrier without some kind of a way to get through it." As soon as those words passed his lips, he had serious doubts that they were true. But he let them stand. Baldur needed all the encouragement he could get. And for that matter, so did Hal himself.

At last Baldur said, in a weakened voice: "We need some rest; I don't think I can think straight."

"Truer words were never spoken. Who wants to stand the first watch?"

Later Hal was never sure which of them had volunteered for the first turn of sentry duty, if either did. As things turned out, it did not matter. The two men were exhausted after putting in a day of duty in Valhalla, getting through the nightly feast, then fighting a deadly brawl in the early hours of the morning, and after that a desperate flight. In less than a minute they were both asleep, sprawled on the hard ground.

Hal woke up with a shock, half-strangling on a snore. But he knew it was something more than snoring that had awakened him. There had been a sharp burst of sound, a briefly stuttering, ripping, slamming kind of noise like nothing he had ever heard before. It could have issued from no human throat—but could it possibly have been a dream? The sound had repeated itself once, he thought, and then had come no more.

Now fully awake and sitting up, he listened, as carefully as he could. But everything was quiet, save for the endless murmuring of Loki's surrounding fire, which burned on undisturbed.

"Now what in all the hells was that?" Hal muttered to himself, not really believing the jolt of sound had proceeded from a dream. No one answered him. Baldur was still sprawled out and snoring faintly. A whole team of eight-legged horses could have galloped in through the firewall and trampled over him, and he would not have cared.

Groaning, Hal stood up and forced himself to move about a little. He had a distinct feeling that hours had passed since they had fallen asleep. He was both thirsty and hungry, and his muscles and joints were stiffer than ever from sleeping on the hard ground. But the two confining walls of fire showed no change, and he realized that he had no idea how long he had been asleep. In here, he thought, it would always be impossible to distinguish day from night. This time they had arrived at the crag in the early morning. For all he could tell, the day had passed, and night had fallen; day or night, things would probably look exactly the same in here.

The two Horses were only a few yards away along the curving corridor, still browsing the scanty grass that endured in spite of magic fire. Hal opened a water bottle and took a swig. The Horses were going to have to wait for theirs. He opened the heavy set of saddlebags and checked the gold again, to make sure that something strange and evil had not happened to it while he slept. Then he told himself his nerves were making him inordinately suspicious.

Well, if he had really been sleeping for many hours, that

would seem to make it much more likely that by now Wodan had got tired of waiting in ambush outside the fire. Or the Father of Battles might have forgotten about his victims, and gone off to fight an important battle somewhere. Hal was in no hurry to find out. Speaking gently to Gold Mane and Cloudfoot, petting them as he passed, as he had seen Alvit and Baldur do, he took a complete slow turn around the little circle of their flame-protected sanctuary, stretching his arms and legs.

When he had reached a point diametrically opposite to Baldur and the Horses, Hal opened his belt pouch and got out his scrap of Golden Fleece. The little swatch of cloth grew brighter, very definitely brighter, when he held it near the inner circle of flame.

Don't be greedy, he told himself sharply. *All you need is the several pounds of yellow stuff you already have put away. If you can get clean away with that, you'll have had all the good luck that any man could dare to hope for in a lifetime.*

And yet, and yet . . . now the Fleece was indicating a much vaster hoard nearby. For Hal the real lure of great treasure was not so much to possess it, but simply to know about it. To fathom all the secrets of the rings of fire . . .

By the time Hal had put away his talisman and returned to his starting point, his companion was also awake, drinking from a water bottle.

W hat we need," said Baldur, when the two began to plan again, "is a skilled magician for an ally."

"Of course. I should have thought of that. Better still, why don't we just enlist one of the great gods as our partner— Loki himself, wherever he is, would be about right."

Irony was lost on Baldur. "Why do you suppose both Thor and Wodan are angry with him?"

"Who knows? If Loki's unavailable, we might instead employ some powerful tool of magical power, something so simple that it can be used effectively even by clumsy clods like us." Hal paused. "Any idea how we can do that?"

Baldur was the picture of gloom. "No. My only clear idea is that I must reach Brunhild, and hold her once more in my arms."

"Then we'd better come up with a different kind of plan. Maybe something totally practical, for a change. How about a scheme that requires us to do nothing outside the realm of possibility?"

What felt like a lengthy period of silence dragged past. At last Baldur offered: "Magic *would* seem to be our only chance. Some kind of magic."

"I hope that's not true," Hal meditated. "Because, as I keep pointing out, neither of us is able to do magic worth a fart. I learned a long time ago that I have no skill along those lines."

There passed another lengthy interval during which no one spoke.

"Clues to magical difficulties are often concealed in riddles," Baldur suddenly announced.

"Are they indeed?" Hal snapped awake; he had been on the point of dozing off again, a vision of a bushel of golden horseshoes drifting in his mind. What was the young fool babbling about? Riddles? Magic riddles? Hal couldn't remember ever hearing anything of the kind.

"Of course!" Baldur was emphatic. "I've heard any number of stories. And I did hear a certain riddle in Valhalla—from one of the kitchen workers—"

Hal made a disgusted noise.

"Wait a moment." Suddenly Baldur stood up straight, rejecting one theory to push another. "Riddles, no, that's nonsense." He raised an arm to point dramatically at nothing. "Gold rings!"

"Brain damage," Hal sighed.

"What?"

"Never mind. All right, gold rings. What in the Underworld have gold rings got to do with anything?"

Baldur had recovered himself sufficiently to begin pacing in the confined space. Once more he looked and sounded full of energy and hope. "Rings are famous for being used in the most powerful magic. I could tell you a dozen stories—"

"Yes, and I could tell a score. But how about a few facts instead?" Hal paused. "You mean a ring like one that Alvit has been wearing?" Come to think of it, he had seen something of the kind on her hand.

Hal did what he could in the way of encouraging suggestions, but soon Baldur's enthusiasm faded. They could not even agree on whether Valkyries generally wore rings or not, or whether Alvit had been wearing one or several.

Hal thought privately that if Baldur were suddenly to insist on some plan that involved their returning to Valhalla in pursuit of some strange magic, that would be the moment when he, Hal, decided he had waited long enough. He would encourage his young partner with some inspiring words, jump on the gold-loaded Horse—yes, that would now be Gold Mane—checking just once more, at any cost, to make sure his treasure was still in the right place—and strike out alone for freedom and security.

Baldur was struggling, as he said, to recall the exact words of some spell that a certain enchantress had tried to teach him as a child, when without warning something large came bursting in upon them through the outer firewall, no more than fifteen feet away. Both Horses started, but only momentarily.

For the space of half a breath, Hal was certain that his doom had come upon him. But he was not lost yet. The intruder was only Alvit, mounted on her own Horse, whose gold-shod hooves came clattering now on the hard rock.

The Valkyrie looked tired, but seemed genuinely pleased to see the two men, and glad to dismount.

"I bring you one item of good news," she began without

preliminary. "Wodan has not laid siege to your sanctuary. He is nowhere in sight."

Hal had jumped to his feet, momentarily uncertain whether Alvit had come to skewer them on her Spear or bring them help. Now he relaxed. "That is good news indeed! Then we can leave."

"*Leave*?" Baldur was dumbfounded. "But Brunhild—"

Alvit said: "I suppose you may. But I should tell you, before you go. There is a strange—phenomenon outside."

Hal's surge of relief was abruptly tempered. "What kind of a phenomenon?"

The Valkyrie made awkward gestures that seemed to suggest an object spinning in the air. "There is a glowing circle round the crag, at a distance of about a hundred yards."

"A glowing what?"

Again she moved one hand around. "As if some burning coal, some particle of fire, were speeding steadily in a circular path, revolving around this blazing hilltop, keeping always at about the same distance. I was careful to avoid the thing, whatever it is, as I arrived."

Hal and Baldur looked at each other fearfully. At last Baldur said: "It must be some magical device of Wodan's. As soon as we emerge it will slay us—or at least it will follow us and lead more of Wodan's berserkers to us."

The Valkyrie was shaking her head and frowning. "I do not think that this—thing—belongs to Wodan—I have never seen anything like it in Valhalla. Or anywhere else."

Then she brightened and reached into one of her saddlebags, producing a package that looked and smelled unmistakably like a loaf of fresh bread. Moments later she brought forth a flask of mead and some meat.

Baldur and Hal both expressed their profound thanks.

"How long have we been in here now?" Hal asked, sitting down again, mumbling his words past a mouthful of bread and sausage. Food and drink always made a man feel much more human. Now it seemed the world was going to go on for a while yet, and he would still be in it.

She reassured the men as to how much time had passed—outside the sun was setting, on the same day of their flight. And she reported incidentally that, to the best of her knowledge, Andvari and his comrade had not been seen in Valhalla since Hal and Baldur had fled. She assumed the gnomes had started for home, and she knew of no pursuit.

"And what about the battle?" Baldur asked. "Is Thor taking part?"

"I have not seen Thor since I saw him with you. As to the battle, it's hard to say. I have not been near the actual fighting, but I think so far there have been only scattered clashes. Not all the forces have yet been mobilized on either side. Wodan is grim and determined as usual."

"Has he forgotten about us?" Hal asked hopefully.

"For the moment. He has much greater matters on his mind—and as long as he concentrates on them, his mind is keener than it has been for a long time."

"In a way, I am glad," she added slowly. "It will be better for him to fight, even if he must die, than to go on . . . as he has been, these last few years."

"Then do you think he'll lose this battle?"

Alvit catalogued what she knew of the forces arrayed against Wodan and his few allies. Aside from some local human warlords, it was a roll call of giants and monsters, including certain names Hal could remember from Wodan's reading in the great hall.

She said that Wodan had gathered his handful of living troops around him, including whatever Valkryies were in range of his summons, and made them a speech, while an army of wraiths hung in the background and appeared to listen also. He had delivered to his assembled forces a version of his usual sermon, about the Twilight of the Gods, and of monsters of unspeakable horror being called up from the Underworld by his demonic enemies to overthrow his rule.

"But make no mistake, though his mind is confused, it is still powerful." She stared at Baldur's look of disbelief, and added: "You have not seen his powers in use, and I have."

After a little silence, Hal asked: "What will you do now, Alvit?"

The Valkyrie shook her head slowly. "If I can think of any way to save him, his honor and his life, then I will try. If he is at least partly right about this battle, despite all his delusions, and the monsters of the Underworld are really going to overwhelm him, then I wish to die with him." She paused. "I loved him once."

After a little silence, Hal said: "I think you love him still. But whether gods or monsters win this round, I do not think the world will end."

Alvit only gave him a sad smile.

Now Baldur was saying: "Can you be sure this final conflict isn't all in Wodan's imagination? Possibly there is no real attack at all? He doesn't have a lot of real force to mobilize, as I recall."

"Thor, too, spoke of a great battle brewing," Hal reminded him.

Alvit was shaking her head. "The attack is real enough, I have seen evidence of that. And Wodan's power is greater than you think, when all the wraiths are called to duty. You never saw anything like their entire number."

"But what can they do?"

"They are more effective against certain of the Underworld creatures than they are against humans. At least that is what we are all hoping." After a pause, she asked: "What are you two doing now?"

Baldur had an instant answer ready. "We are of course going to reach Brunhild, somehow, or die trying." Then, looking at Hal, he amended. "*I* am going to die trying. I do not require such sacrifice from my friends."

Hal winced. "Baldur, I hope you find a way to get your girlfriend back. I really do. If I could think of any way . . ."

But Baldur had turned back to the Valkyrie, and was saying: "We had been talking riddles, and were about to go around in rings." When Alvit looked puzzled, Baldur amplified: "The gnomes are supposed to have forged gold rings of great power in the past. The Earthdwellers have powers that are truly legendary."

Hal put in: " 'Legendary' isn't going to do us much good right now. What we need are powers truly practical. And what the gnomes may have . . ." He suddenly fell silent.

"What is it?" Both of his companions asked at once.

But the northman was not listening. He had risen to his feet, and was staring at the mysterious base of the blazing inner circle. Especially he was concentrating on the way its tongues of fire kept rising, like those of its outer counterpart, seemingly from nothing. He scuffed his booted feet on the solid rock where he was standing. Then he stamped both his feet hard, first left then right, one after the other. He let out what sounded like a battle cry, a kind of screech of triumph.

"*What—?*" Baldur recoiled from him, but Alvit remained standing just where she was, leaning on her Horse, as if she were too tired to be excited by anything short of a physical attack.

Hal gripped his companion by the front of his worn quilted jacket. He said: "Yes, the gnomes. The Earthdwellers do have great powers, and they just might be able to do us some good. But sometimes the simple method is the best."

"What do you mean?"

Hal waved his arms. "How might we attack the problem if this fire were a solid wall, too hard to break?"

"Well, how?"

"If we are going to take the risks of making a foray back to Valhalla, I have a better goal in mind than ransacking the tyrant's rooms for rings that probably would be of no use to us anyway. I want a juicier bait than a few gold rings before I put my head in the mousetrap."

Baldur and Alvit looked at him in bewilderment.

Once more Hal stamped his right foot hard on the hard ground. "We're going to liberate ourselves a pair of gnomes, along with whatever tools they think they need to do a little job."

"What job?"

"I think they'll do it, out of sheer gratitude. I think they'd better, if they know what's good for them."

"What job?"

"What do you think? Andvari and his friend are going to dig a little tunnel for us!"

16

We must waste no more time," Baldur said after another silence. His voice was alive with renewed hope. "If we are going to find the gnomes, and make them dig a tunnel for us—" He suddenly turned his head and shouted, as if he expected her to hear him: "I'm coming to you, my Brunhild!"

Alvit remounted her Horse, and promptly disappeared through the outer wall of fire. Half a minute later she was back again, reporting that the way seemed clear—there was still no sign of Wodan, or of any entity that she thought might be an agent of the god. She added that the strange phenomenon she had observed earlier still persisted: a faint, sharply curving streak, traced out by something like a spark of flame. Still the spark maintained its course, circling the crag at a distance of about a hundred yards.

The Valkyrie also assured the men that the All-Highest would very likely be distracted now, and for some time to come, by the needs of combat, so he would not be likely to interfere with their endeavor to recruit gnomes, even if their search carried them near Valhalla. "But if you see Thor, or even Loki, remember that my lord needs help desperately. Even when gods have quarreled, they should stand together against the Underworld."

"I'll remember," Hal said.

Impulsively Baldur grasped her by the hand. "We owe you

our lives," he said. Hal, standing beside him, solemnly agreed.

"You were never Wodan's enemies," she sadly observed, looking at them in turn. "Nor was Brunhild."

"Then help us save her!" the young man pleaded.

Alvit shook her head. "It may be that you will be able to reach her, with the help of gnomes. I can be of no more help— but I do wish you success. Now I must hurry away."

As soon as Alvit was on her way again, Hal and Baldur hastily conferred, sketching out a plan for the mission they were about to undertake. Then they mounted their Horses and rode out separately through the outermost ring of fire.

It was Hal's idea, at the last moment, for the two of them to take their departure simultaneously but not together, emerging from opposite sides of the outer circle of fire. Then if, in spite of everything, Wodan or one of his creatures was waiting to pounce on them, either Hal or Baldur might have a chance of getting away.

Keeping a sharp eye out as he urged his mount back out through the flames, Hal emerged into the glow of late sunset. He and Baldur were immediately confronted by the strange phenomenon that Alvit had mentioned. Hal could think of no better way to describe it: a small, fiery object of unknown nature, whirling around the crag at about the speed of a thrown stone, while keeping a steady distance from the center of the curve.

The flying spark did not react to the appearance of the two men on their Horses. It made no move to approach or attack, as Hal and Baldur had been at least half expecting, but only maintained its smooth and rapid revolution.

More ominous were certain loud rumblings in the far distance, accompanied by a trembling that must have come through the very bones of the earth, for it made the wall of Loki's flames shiver slightly. There was also a strange glow along the edge of the visible world, in the wrong place to be either sunrise or sunset. Along the far horizon, in the direction of Valhalla, Hal observed strange flashes of light that could hardly have been lightning, flickering as they did where the sky was clear.

Even Baldur was distracted from his great purpose for a moment. "Then it is true," he muttered. "The gods must be already engaged in serious battle. But who are they fighting? Each other, or their common enemies?"

"Either way it ought to keep them out of our hair," said Hal. "Come, I want to get some digging done, so we can reach Brunhild—and also I want a better look into Loki's secret sanctuary."

Sometimes Hal had trouble understanding his own behavior. Here he was, mounted on a steed that few or none could overtake, and with the package of undefended gold in easy reach. Why not simply take his treasure and ride away?

Well, for one thing, Baldur had probably saved his life when he was fighting the berserker, and deserting Baldur now would not be honorable. Honor did mean something to most northmen. Sometimes to this one it meant a lot. Hal thought stealing gold from strangers was about as respectable as most forms of business, but letting down a shipmate who depended on you was another matter altogether.

Besides . . . having entered the outer room of Loki's sanctuary, had a sampling of its wonders, Hal knew he would regret it for the rest of his life if he retreated now, without even trying to probe its inner secrets.

Tugging his Horse's mane, he made the animal rear and turn around. This riding through the air at terrific speed could get to be fun, as addictive as certain drugs, if a man were granted the chance to practice it a little.

To Baldur, whose mount was galloping beside Hal's—it was still amazing, how quiet hoofbeats were when they fell on air!—Hal said: "It will be safer, I think, if we keep to the interior of clouds as much as possible."

Baldur nodded. "As long as we don't get lost. Now, we must decide which end of the trail to start at—near the village, or near Valhalla."

"Starting halfway between should do the job. If the gnomes ran away from Valhalla at the same time we did, they've only been on the trail for one night—maybe a little more. They can't have made many miles just yet."

Finding the proper road at night was not too easy, even with their Horses trotting through the air only a few yards above the ground. The broad curves of the Einar tended to be confusing in the darkness, but the light of the waning moon led them at last to Andvari and Ivaldr's village. From there it was easy to pick out the right road. Soon Baldur and Hal were cantering briskly along the way to Valhalla, covering in mere hours distances that had taken them days on foot. Yet they dared not go too fast, for fear of missing the men they were trying to find.

"If Wodan sent Valkyries after them . . ." Baldur left the thought unfinished.

"All the pursuit he could scrape together probably came after us. But if we don't find our gnomes on the trail, we'll go to Valhalla. I'd bet the place is undermanned, if Wodan's got his army out in the field. But I'm afraid that in this gloom we'll miss our quarry. They'll see us riding the air, and think we're Valkyries, and hide."

Baldur agreed. Moments later, the two men landed near the trail, tethered their Horses, and allowed themselves the luxury of sleep.

At first light they were up again and in the air. No more than half an hour passed before Baldur stretched out an arm and cried: "There they are!"

Two weary, goggled gnomes looked up from where they had just turned off the trail, evidently in search of shelter against the rising sun. For a moment Andvari and Ivaldr were poised to run, but then they harkened to Hal's bellowing and waited for the riders to arrive.

The two Earthdwellers were also hungry, and made short work of the food Hal brought out from his saddlebags. Of conditions in Valhalla they knew no more than Hal and Baldur, having fled at the same time. And they were much relieved to learn that little of the blood that stained Hal's clothing was his own.

When Baldur offered them a ride, they were more than willing to be rescued. "Our hearts hunger to see our village again!"

Hal promised them: "And we will take you there, my friend, in good time. But there is something vitally important you can do for us first."

"Of course, anything—anything within reason. Twice now you have saved our lives." But still Andvari seemed a little wary. "What are we to do?"

"It is only a little job of digging. I will explain while we travel," Hal rasped in his best soothing tone.

Despite all their experience in handling Horses, neither gnome had ever flown before. Both admitted they were terrified of riding through the air, but they now feared Wodan even more. In a matter of moments, each was astride a Horse, clinging on behind a massive Sundweller. On becoming airborne, they both groaned and cried out in amazement and alarm.

Hal thought he was able to appreciate the courage this

flight must have required of them. If the Earthdwellers found the act of simply venturing out into the open air from underground something of an adventure, how terrible must it be to risk their bodies at such a distance from Mother Earth?

The gnomes said that if digging was required, it would be necessary to stop first at one of several mining towns inhabited by Earthdwellers, where the essential tools would be available. Hal had to agree; even gnomes could not do much with their fingernails. The equipment the miners wanted to obtain included short-handled hammers, chisels, scoops, and shovels. Filter masks were also on Andvari's list of essentials. These were woven of some fine cloth and served to protect the miners' lungs against dust and dirt. Some minerals were notably more poisonous than others.

"Is the digging in a mine?" Andvari wanted to know.

"Well—no," Hal admitted.

"It's right out in the open, then? And I suppose if the need is so urgent, you'll want us to start in daylight? Maybe even with a lot of snow lying about, reflecting sun?"

Baldur was about to answer, but let himself be hushed by Hal, who framed his answer carefully. "The site is pretty thoroughly illuminated."

Andvari sighed. "Well, we have our goggles, and can wrap ourselves against the sun."

When Ivaldr asked him what kind of rock they would be expected to tunnel through, Hal had to admit that he didn't know, being no expert in such matters. Baldur was no help either. About all they could do was warn the Earthdwellers that it wasn't sandstone, or anywhere near that soft and crumbly.

The gnomes received this confession of ignorance in silence, leaving Hal with the feeling that they were too well-mannered to comment on their clients' appalling lack of knowledge.

But as long as they were available he thought he might take advantage of their presence to ask them a couple of very casual questions about matters involving gold. Of course it seemed that his stash of horseshoes would provide all the gold he really needed . . . but he was curious.

"This animal's the first I've ever ridden on that wore shoes made of gold," he began, with what he considered ingenious subtlety. The first with shoes of any kind, he might have added.

"And probably the last." Andvari, clinging on behind Hal, did not sound inclined to enter into any lengthy conversation.

On the other hand Ivaldr seemed ready to discourse on the subject—though Hal had trouble hearing him across the gap of air between the Horses. Gold, said Ivaldr, was the Earth-dwellers' sunlight, the only brightness that many of their race ever saw. No punishment was too severe, he proclaimed, for thieves who stole the yellow metal. All gold, and, to tell the truth, all metal, by rights belonged to gnomes, and it was only by courtesy that they let anyone else use it.

Getting to the mining settlement required a journey of many miles, but at the speed of Valkyries it did not take long, and was happily uneventful.

They landed at a little distance from the miners' village, amid a raw, scarred landscape, marked by many mounds of excavated dirt and rock, some fresh, some very old. There were reddish piles of crumbled material that Hal could recognize as iron ore. Sentries had been posted at the village entrance, and Hal got the impression that regular work had been suspended, as the people mobilized for self-defense as best they could.

The sight of the Horses landing immediately drew a modest crowd, all goggled against exposure to the morning sun.

Hal and Baldur remained on the surface, trusting to Andvari and Ivaldr to return from a quick trip underground to gather tools and arrange for an urgent message to be sent to their home village, informing their relatives and friends that they were safe.

By midday they were all four on their two mounts again, the gnomes hooded and goggled against the sun. They were carrying stout canvas bags of stubby-handled mining tools, as well as a new supply of gnomish food.

Hal thought he was definitely beginning to develop a certain skill in riding a flying Horse, and he realized he was going to regret the loss when the day came for him to give the animal back. Trying to hang on to it would be tempting, but he understood that it would be hopeless for an ordinary man—certainly if he wanted to retire to anything like an ordinary life.

"What're you thinking about, Hal?"

"Not much. Just trying to imagine Cloudfoot and Gold Mane pulling a plow . . ."

"What strange ideas you have." Baldur looked at him with the sympathy one might reserve for the brain damaged.

Hal had planned to wait until the last possible moment, when they were inescapably airborne, to let his new helpers know that they must be carried through a barrier of magic flames to reach the site where they were required to dig. Then, as the last possible moment came and went, he decided it would be best not to tell them at all.

"What is that?" Andvari suddenly demanded, clutching hard at Hal with one hand, and pointing a wiry arm ahead.

"That's where we're going." Now ahead of the cantering Horses appeared the crag where Loki's flames still went soaring and roaring up to heaven, the whole still encircled by the path of the mysterious flying spark.

17

To Hal, the smoothly rounded fire on the crag looked no different than it had when he first laid eyes on it. And the only change he could detect in its surroundings seemed minor, having to do with an alteration in the appearance of the object, whatever it was, that gave the crag a halo. The revolving spark still maintained a good, hurtling pace, but Hal thought its glow had been slightly dimmed since he last saw it. He had been privately evolving a theory about the peculiar thing, a theory he now wanted to put to the test.

Andvari, with a bag of short but heavy tools tied to his belt, was still clinging on tightly behind Hal. The gnome now turned his head, averting his goggled eyes from the towering flames as they flew near, and muttered a stream of what sounded like prayers and imprecations.

Without giving any warning of what he meant to do, Hal tugged on his Horse's mane to change direction slightly, then halted Gold Mane in midair. He had chosen a spot where, if he had calculated correctly, the hurtling object in its regular course must pass almost near enough for him to touch it.

Meanwhile, Baldur (who also still had a mumbling gnome, complete with tool bag, clinging on behind him) had seen Hal pause, and had tugged Gold Mane into a short circling pattern, some fifty yards away.

Now Baldur called across the gap of empty air: "What is it, Hal, what are you delaying for?"

"You know my curiosity." Hal called back. He eyed the mysterious object carefully as it shot past him in its orbit. It came so close that his Horse recoiled slightly, but not before Hal had been granted the look he wanted. At close range Hal could recognize the thing easily enough; now he was sure that he had seen it before.

"Damn your curiosity!" Baldur was yelling at him. "We must press on to reach Brunhild! Are you with me or not?"

"I'm with you, and I'm ready." Hal wasn't going to try to explain his discovery now. He tugged Gold Mane around to face the flames. Then, over his shoulder in a low and cheerful voice: "Ready, Andvari? Got your goggles on?"

"I do." The voice of the gnome was somewhat muffled against Hal's shoulder. "We're coming down somewhere near that huge fire, then?"

"Quite near it, but it's perfectly safe. Baldur and I have been there before. Just hang on to me and hide your face. We'll be through in a moment, with no harm."

"*Through?*" Andvari squeaked. "Through what?!"

When they were no more than a hundred yards from the fire, galloping straight toward it, Andvari screamed aloud: "By all the fiends of the Underworld, we're going to be roasted alive!"

Hal was calm and firm. "No we're not. Believe me, Baldur and I have done this before. And forget about the powers of the Underworld, we're too high above the earth for them. The only god who might be involved in this business is Loki, not Hades, and Loki's not objecting."

But by the time Hal had finished saying that, Andvari was no longer listening.

The dreaded experience was over in a moment, and when it proved harmless, the two Earthdwellers recovered rapidly from their fright. Despite the steady glow of the burning walls, the fact that space around them was now tightly enclosed must have been deeply reassuring. Soon the two gnomes had their feet planted firmly on solid ground, and presently, still keeping their goggles firmly in place, they were able to concentrate on work.

At that point, Hal and Baldur had little to do except stand back and keep out of the way.

As soon as they had reentered the curving corridor, so stoutly guarded by two towering rings of fire, Baldur jumped from his Horse and hastened to peer through the inner fires once more at the figure he assumed was that of his beloved. He cried out at once, rejoicing that her blurred image was still visible, and spent a few moments in eager contemplation.

Hal and the two Earthdwellers followed him, somewhat more slowly. Yes, the gnomes agreed. Squinting through their goggles, with eyes barely open, they could see the figure too.

Hal immediately began to issue instructions for what he wanted, the excavation of a small tunnel through the solid rock.

Andvari tugged at his straggly beard. "For what distance?"

"For no great span at all. Just down a couple of feet where we are standing, then straight in that direction." Hal accompanied his words with expressive gestures, pointing toward the hidden center of the flames. "You needn't go far, just make sure you get under this second ring of fire—the flames must be of only modest thickness, since we can see right through them. Then up to ground level again on the other side. We're sure there's a clear, safe space over there." Of course Hal was not really sure of anything of the kind, but he thought there was no use introducing unnecessary complications. "Naturally you must dig the tunnel wide enough for me to get through it."

Andvari, professionally cautious, looked at Hal and seemed to be measuring his breadth and girth. "And nothing will happen to us if we dig under the fire? The god who made the flames has not—defended the ground beneath them?"

"Nothing at all will happen, you have my solemn pledge." Hal did not look at Baldur as he made that promise.

"How quickly must this be done?"

"Quick as you can. Will you be able to manage it in any reasonable time?"

Andvari squinted at his companion, who spat, and nodded. He reviewed the plan. "Straight down here—you say we don't have to go very deep?"

"No reason that I can see."

"Good. Down a couple of feet, then bore horizontally, ten feet or so in that direction"—he pointed inward, then slanted his long gray fingers to the vertical—"and then straight up again? That's it?" His shrug was almost contemptuous. "That shouldn't take long at all. Maybe not even an hour."

"Then do it! Please!"

The next step was for Andvari and his companion, standing alternately close together and far apart, to undertake a round of preliminary testing and probing, tapping and listening, scraping and peering, obviously in search of essential information about the quality of the rock. From time to time this was interrupted by a rapid discussion in some gnomish dialect, promptly followed by another burst of activity in which the two skilled miners took soundings of the ground beneath their feet, one of them tapping on the surface, now with his heaviest hammer, now again with a light one. Meanwhile his colleague, moving to various places, sometimes halfway around the corridor, listened with an ear to the ground.

Progressing in this way, the gnomes finished a complete circuit of the corridor before they agreed on the best place to dig. The spot Andvari finally selected was some four or five feet from the inner wall of flame, and only a few strides from where Hal, on first penetrating the outer ring, had landed on his Horse.

Having determined the exact site of operations, the gnomes wasted no time. They adjusted their goggles, spat ritually on their hands, and then snatched up their tools to begin alternately scraping and pounding on the rock with incredible rapidity.

Watching the speed with which his new allies tore into the earth, Baldur's excitement grew, and Hal could feel his own spirits rise. The Earthdwellers' thin arms flowed in ceaseless motion, and the bones of the world beneath them rang solidly from the impact of their tools. They fractured rock with a hammer and split it with an iron wedge. Hal first squinted and then turned away, protecting his eyes from flying fragments.

"Things seem to be going well," Hal cautiously commented.

Baldur looked strained, as usual. "I will agree that they are going well when we have reached Brunhild."

Hal turned his head from side to side in a futile effort to hear whatever might be happening outside the outer wall of flames. Out there, somewhere, by all accounts, the gods were fighting a great battle, an event that must ultimately be of great importance. Just what the fight was all about was still a mystery to him—well, most wars were like that. But in any case it was no great surprise—it was common knowledge that gods and Giants often clashed.

Though Baldur hated Wodan, he was unable to bring himself to hope that the vile creatures of the Underworld would win. Even though the death of Wodan's present avatar would make it possible for another human, hopefully of clearer mind, to put on the Face of the All-Highest.

———

Hal would have willingly passed on what he had discovered regarding the mysterious aerial token, the whirling dot of fire that seemed to guard the flames. But Baldur obviously was not interested.

When Hal tried to force the subject on him anyway, the young man brushed it away. "As long as it does not interfere with my reaching Brunhild, I care not what it is."

Hal sighed. "All right. Probably won't make a whole lot of difference to you." To himself he added: "But it gives me something to think about."

Meanwhile the diggers were scooping away the fractured rock and loose earth in an almost continuous stream, first with their strong, outsized hands and then with the blades of short-handled scoops or shovels. Hal thought they were making amazingly rapid progress.

When they had dug down the distance of a full handsbreadth, they begin singing or chanting as they worked, spouting words in some rhythmic rhyming tongue that neither Hal nor Baldur could understand, words blurring against the eternal muted roaring of Loki's flames.

This had not gone on long when, without warning, there came another bursting intrusion through the outer wall. Again, all Hal's muscles tensed—again he relaxed gratefully when he recognized the Valkyrie's familiar face.

The gnomes might not even have been aware of Alvit's arrival. They kept working without a pause as she dismounted from her Horse.

Quickly Alvit brought Hal and Baldur up to date on the latest news from Valhalla.

She also remarked that she could not understand the Earth-dwellers' chanting either. "But I have heard it before. Someone has told me that it has something to do with gold."

"A subject that seems never to be far from their thoughts," Baldur commented.

"Or from the thoughts of certain other people." She was looking at Hal. "Have you discovered Loki's whereabouts?"

He shook his head. "No. Why?"

"Because Wodan, at a time when his mind was clear, has assured us—myself and the other Valkyries—that he is ready to be reconciled with the Firegod. I can tell you that he hopes to recruit Loki for his side in the battle, or at least to keep him from joining the other side."

"We will certainly let you know if we encounter any god. What of Thor? Has Wodan found him yet?"

Alvit shook her head. "There is a new rumor that Thor is dead—but as far as I know, that is no more than a rumor."

"No big surprise if it proved true," Hal commented.

"Alive or dead, no one can locate him. It is a strange and terrible time for all our gods." Then Alvit added, unexpectedly, "You look very tired, Hal."

He had been listening with his eyes closed, but now he opened them and nodded. He thought that her voice had a new tone in it, almost tender. "And so do you," he observed.

With the gnomes out of sight, he could easily imagine from the rapidity of the dull thudding and scraping noises that four or five men were hard at work.

Baldur and Hal in turn had both made some effort to help the gnomes during the first few minutes of the digging, but each time Andvari shrilly ordered the Sundwellers to keep out of the way. In any event, both men were soon busy trying to soothe the Horses, who were growing nervous in the unaccustomed atmosphere of noise and dust and flying gravel. At last Baldur, saying he was worried that the animals might bolt, led them gently around the curve of cleared space until they were as far as possible from where the digging was in progress.

Hal was on the verge of thinking up some objection to this move, but he held his peace. It just made him vaguely uneasy, seeing his bagged gold being once more conveyed out of his sight. But he told himself that his prize remained very near. Only he knew where it was, and he had no reason to worry.

Under the impact of the gnomes' forged steel and driving energy, what only minutes ago had been a mere marking on the scraped rock had now become a hole. The hole grew deeper with amazing speed, so rapidly that within a few more minutes the foremost of the two diggers was working entirely below the surface of the ground, almost out of sight, his slitted bone goggles left aboveground.

While one pale, wiry figure, turned even whiter with rock dust, battered away at the face of the lengthening tunnel, usually with a hammer driving a chisel of the hardest, finest steel, the other skillfully cleared debris while keeping out of the digger's way. Every few minutes Andvari and his companion swapped places, keeping a fresh man at the hardest job, while the scattered piles of excavated rock and earth rapidly grew higher.

There soon followed an interval in which both gnomes were completely immersed in what had now become a tunnel, though it was hard to see how even their small bodies would find room to work in such a confined space. Hal wondered if they might be employing serious magic of their own, if they were worried that Loki had, after all, set up some different and invisible barrier.

Presently he and Baldur were tersely summoned, and commanded to help in the task of scooping away the pieces of fractured rock that were rapidly accumulating, being passed back through the tunnel from the swiftly eroding face.

Then, almost before the Sundwellers had begun to hope that the job might be soon completed, the gnomes shouted at them to stand clear of the tunnel's entrance, and Andvari soon came scrambling out of it, closely followed by his colleague, covered in rock dust. Both of them had taken their goggles off for the moment, and were rubbing their eyes, circles of sallow skin not powdered with with rock dust.

"We have broken through," the senior Earthdweller informed his clients tersely.

"What did you find?" Baldur demanded frantically. "Is she there?"

"See for yourself." The gnome's gnarled features were unreadable as he stood aside. Hal took that as a bad sign.

Groaning and rushing ahead of Hal, Baldur threw himself headfirst into the narrow tunnel, barely allowing the protesting diggers time to get entirely out of his way.

Moments later, Hal followed, thrusting himself ahead of Alvit, who seemed in no great hurry to finally learn her beloved sister's fate. He found the excavation an exceedingly tight fit in several places; the struggle to get through cost him a couple of small patches of skin, but he persevered.

After some ten or twelve feet of scraping and squeezing his way forward, he came to where the passage turned up, and gradually was able to force his way, sweeping some debris with him like a broom, up through the rising curve to the newest tunnel mouth.

When his head reemerged into direct firelight, he was not entirely surprised to find himself again between two concentric rings of fire. He was in yet another wheel-rim of clear space, somewhat narrower and more tightly curved than the first had been. What had been the inner wall of the first rounded corridor was now of course the outer wall of this one.

Now Hal was able to confirm the existence of something he had more or less suspected: a third wall of flame. Very likely, he thought, this latest discovery was the innermost and final one, for there didn't seem room for another wheel-rim corridor inside it. The third wall looked no different than the other two, except for being more tightly curved, surrounding as it did a smaller area.

Nor was Hal really surprised to observe that there was no more metallic gold to be seen here in the second corridor than there had been in the first.

Consideration of any further details would have to wait. Only a few feet from where Hal was half-emerged from the tunnel, Baldur crouched at the side of a simple bed that seemed to have been formed from a spread-out cloak, occupying a central position between the inner and outer walls of flame.

Pulling the last sections of his aching body out of the hole in the floor, Hal crawled closer to the couple. The impression he had gained by trying to look through the flames had been essentially correct. Lying on her back, upon this rude catafalque, was a slender young woman wearing partial metal armor, loosely fitted over simple cloth undergarments. This outfit left her lower legs, forearms and part of her midriff exposed.

The top of the girl's head was covered only by her golden hair, so long and thick that it spread out in a great fan—this was obviously what Hal had seen from outside the barrier, what had suggested in his eyes a pile or pillow of yellow metal.

Hal's fragment of the Golden Fleece remained quiescent in his belt pouch, not leaping or twitching as he came near the girl. Whatever magic inhabited the Fleece was not going to be deceived by golden hair.

Baldur raised a face transformed and wet with tears of joy. His voice rang out: "She lives, Hal! She lives!"

"I rejoice to hear that," Hal said wearily, painfully getting to his feet. And truly he was relieved to see that the lovely face of the unconscious Valkyrie had the peaceful look of one who only slept, and that a faint blush of life showed in her cheeks. He hoped that that meant something more than skilled magical embalming. But he could not be sure the girl was breathing at all—if she was, the rise and fall of her breast beneath its light steel armor was too slight for Hal to see.

Baldur was clutching one of the young woman's inert arms and pressing his face to her motionless hand. Now his body was again racked by sobs.

Weary of all these demonstrations, Hal got slowly to his feet. "She's not dead," he reiterated in a dull voice, now feeling reasonably confident of the fact. Good news, he supposed—at least now Baldur ought not to absolutely break down—but another complication. Hal had the feeling that he was being battered by events, new things to worry about, first on one side then the other, the impacts coming too fast for a man to cope with them. Was he, after all, getting to be too old for this sort of thing? Shouldn't he already be standing behind a plow, staring at the rear ends of a couple of droms who were content to plod a field and never thought of flying?

Well, maybe he should. Right now the prospect did not seem all that inviting.

Baldur meanwhile had dropped his beloved's hand—her arm just fell limply to the ground—and was trying all sorts of things to wake her up, calling her by name, kissing her one moment and then in the next slapping her—though never very hard. But whatever he did, the young woman's eyes stayed shut, and she showed no sign of regaining consciousness.

Something small, very small indeed and very white, in darting motion, caught Hal's eye and he looked up. Once again light snow was falling, and somehow the soft flakes were managing to escape melting in the air high above the guardian flames; they came drifting down unscathed, to melt only when they touch the enchanted earth within the circle, or more swiftly on the maid's armor.

Alvit had come crawling through the tunnel to join the men. She remarked on the fact they were all standing between fires so large and so close to them that they should be roasted in a short time, yet none even felt uncomfortably warm. The others nodded agreement.

Cautiously experimenting with one hand, Hal decided that the heat within the flames themselves had to be at least as great as that of any normal fire. He could move his own toughened skin to within a few inches of it without being actually burned, but no closer.

"What use are all these speculations?" Alvit asked.

Hal did not answer directly. "I have been watching the snowflakes. If they can fall this far, come down here in the midst of the flames, without melting . . ."

"Ah, I see. Then it might be possible for a flying Horse to do the same? No, Hal, I tried that days ago. It was one of the first things I thought of, when I wanted to see Brunhild. But it will not work. Seen from above, Loki's magic makes this whole clifftop look like one solid mass of fire."

After a pause, she admitted: "Clever of you to come up with the plan of going underneath, right through solid rock. I suppose it never occurred to Loki that anyone would try that."

"Thank you. Maybe he just thought it would take them a very long time if they did."

Hal watched several large flakes settle in the blond hair of the unconscious girl, and several more come down in Alvit's hair, almost exactly the same color as Brunhild's, where they persisted briefly before sparkling into droplets. Another met an even swifter doom, landing on the soft red fullness of Brunhild's upper lip.

Baldur was not interested in snowflakes. He was groaning over his Valkyrie, alternately kissing her passionately, and pleading with her to awake. Again and again he had sworn that all he wanted was to hold her in his arms, but now that he could do that, he wanted more. Well, that was only to be expected. Hal still felt confident she was not dead, but she might as well have been, for all the sign she gave of waking up.

As far as Hal was concerned, Brunhild could wait a little longer. He still believed that Loki must have had some greater purpose here, and was still fascinated by trying to discover what it was.

Suppose that Loki—traditionally the master of fire, and of treachery as well—feared both Wodan and Thor. And suppose, with his knack for making enemies, he had come to be at odds with the powers of the Underworld as well—well, that would be a dangerous situation for even the greatest deity. Loki would have to depend entirely on his own powers, his own skill, for his survival. At least temporarily, until he was able to fashion new alliances. If Loki had wanted to create a defensive stronghold for himself, what better place than here, triply protected by his own wonderful fire?

The gnomes had now followed their Sundwelling clients in through the tunnel, thin wiry bodies accommodating easily to its narrow curves. On emerging from the dark passage, Andvari and Ivaldr put on the goggles they had removed while actually in it, and with their eyes hidden behind opaque disks it was impossible for Hal to even guess what they might be thinking.

Joining the Sundwellers, the gnomes sat down, establishing themselves solidly on the rocky ground as if determined to claim a well-earned rest. One of them helpfully suggested looking for a poisoned thorn, or something similar, embedded in the girl's flesh.

Baldur seemed to be sliding into helplessness. "What should we do if there is one?"

"Why, pull it out!"

Alvit and Baldur began carefully removing more sections of the girl's armor, while Hal sat back, watching and thinking. Baldur's hands were shaking as he set aside, one after another, pieces of metal and cloth.

Alvit seemed ready to take over the operation. "You might turn her over and examine her back."

But there was no need to do that. In the end it was Alvit's keen vision that saw it first: a black dot, coarse but tiny, so small against Brunhild's fair skin, so like a tiny mole, that it might easily have passed unnoticed.

She murmured: "This looks like it. It could be just the end of a thorn that's causing the trouble."

Brushing Alvit's hand aside, Baldur took it upon himself to try to remove the thorn, if thorn it was, stuck so cruelly and outrageously into her tender flesh, near the side of her right breast. With shaking fingers he fumbled for a grip and finally found one.

The thorn was amazingly thin, and horribly long, a couple of inches at least. Baldur cast it away with a shudder.

The pinpoint wound where the thorn had been was marked now by a single drop of crimson blood. Almost at once, the recumbent girl drew a deep, shuddering breath and began to stir. Baldur kept pleading with her, clutching her in his arms.

Brunhild's eyes when they opened were dazzlingly blue. She was at first completely bewildered and naturally frightened to find herself enclosed by walls of flame, which she did not remember seeing before. But her recovery proceeded with almost magical speed, and she greeted Alvit joyfully.

Only then did she realize who held her in his arms. "What is this—Baldur? What are you doing here, where are we?" Her voice was thin and weak at first, but soon gained strength.

Her lover was beside himself with joy at her recovery, and did his best to reassure her.

A moment later Brunhild became aware that there were strangers present too. She modestly tried to recover her clothing and her armor. Dressing herself for action, she naturally wanted to know how much time had passed while she remained in her enchanted sleep.

Baldur was horrified when she muttered something about having to prepare herself for combat. It occurred to Hal to discourage her by pointing out that she had no weapons available—and no use trying to borrow any, because probably the only weapon with which Hildy had any familiarity would be the magic Spear.

She was naturally relieved to learn that only a matter of days had gone by since Wodan had sentenced and punished her.

And Brunhild confirmed that she had earlier refused to take Baldur to Valhalla because she wished to save him from an unpleasant fate.

When she learned that he had been there, she was frightened and relieved at the same time. "Thank all the gods you have survived! I wanted to save you from Valhalla—I ought to have told you what it is really like—but I was afraid. And I knew you would never believe me."

At last her gaze focused on Hal.

"Who's this? One of your father's men?"

Hal made a little gesture of salute. "I'm just a type of wandering savage, miss. No more Hagan's man than you are."

At that Brunhild gave him a strange look; but Baldur hastened to vouch for his comrade.

The gnomes had been resting, listening to Sundwellers' talk, for only a little while when they surprised Hal by getting to their feet again, showing signs of renewed energy.

"I hope none of you will mind if we dig another tunnel?" Andvari asked the four Sundwellers, indicating with a gesture that he contemplated burrowing under the second ring of fire just as they had the first.

Brunhild only shook her head, not understanding. Alvit seemed surprised, but too tired to take any real interest. Baldur, as if he thought he might have misunderstood the gnome, told him: "You have our eternal gratitude."

Hal also shook his head, not particularly surprised. "No, no, go right ahead and dig. In fact I will be delighted, provided that you make a passage big enough for me to get through. Just a little wider than the last one, if you please. I'd like to see what's in there."

The gnomes nodded silently, their eyes hidden behind goggles. In a minute they had chosen their starting place and work was under way, with fragments and rock dust flying as before.

Baldur and his Valkyrie were clinging together as if they both feared to let go. She murmured dreamily: "Whatever happens now, we two will always be together."

Obviously the young couple had no interest in further exploration, and were eagerly, deeply absorbed in planning their own futures. What were they going to do now, where were they going to go? There was evidence of serious disagreement, though so far nothing like a quarrel.

Hal and Alvit both began to urge them to make up their minds quickly.

Hal said: "If I were you, I'd argue about my destination after I was on the road. Head anywhere you like, as long as it's not toward the war."

Baldur seemed too happy to bother to listen closely. "Some day maybe I will go to war again. Right now I do not see the need."

Suddenly Alvit recalled the Horses. "We must make sure they are still safe. We'll need them to get out through the outer ring of fire, it wouldn't do to find ourselves trapped." And one after the other the four Sundwellers slid and scrambled back through the tunnel.

When they had all rejoined the Horses in the outer corridor, Alvit again exhorted the couple to get going. Now, while the battle still raged, was the time to flee the wrath of Wodan. If the Father of Battles was strong enough and lucky enough to survive his current fight—and if he then remembered Brunhild at all—he would certainly try to inflict some extra punishment on her for her escape.

Hal too urged the lovers to move on while they could, while the All-Highest was still distracted with battle.

At last Baldur and Brunhild mounted, on a single Horse, their two bodies molded together and whispering in each others' ears. It was as if, now that they had found each other again, they feared to be out of sight or out of touch for even a moment. Baldur murmured that it would not be the first time the animal had carried them both swiftly.

This time it was Baldur who, automatically assuming the role of leader, sat in front where he could grip the Horse's mane and exert control. And his beloved, Spearless now, no longer a Valkyrie, yielded the place of leadership to him without a murmur. So closely did she cling on behind her lover that it looked like he was sitting in her lap.

At the last moment, Baldur turned his head and swore eternal loyalty to Hal, pledging his honor and his help if Hal should ever need them.

"Thank you, I may need that pledge some day. Meanwhile, get the hell out of here." Hal urged the lovers on their way with a violent motion of his arm, ending with a hard swat on the Horse's rump. The couple and their mount vanished through flames, carrying Alvit's shouted blessing.

Hal's blessing went with them too, silent but just as sincere, since he had first made sure that his gold remained behind.

When Hal looked around again, Alvit was already astride her own mount. But she lingered long enough to tell Hal that she meant to accompany the young lovers on the first stage of their flight.

"And there, your Horse is waiting for your departure." She pointed at the remaining beast.

"I'm looking forward to my next ride," he assured her.

Still Alvit delayed. "Where will you go?"

"I'm not sure yet. What about you?"

The Valkyrie pulled at her golden hair, which was dull and tangled now, evidently from want of care over the last few days. Her cheeks looked hollower than before. "I have already told you, Hal. I mean to return to Wodan, and fight beside him when the enemy draws near—so far I have been unable to do any real fighting."

She reached out a hand to grasp her grounded Spear. "Until now the great powers on each side have only bombarded each other with their terrible weapons at long range. There has been little that ordinary humans like you and me could do. But that will change." The Valkyrie's voice sounded suddenly uncertain. And after a moment she added: "Whether the mode of fighting changes or does not change, whether my god lives or dies, I want to be with him at the end."

Hal said: "I don't know about your sisters, as you call them. But I think you've already done all that the All-Highest could ask of you, and more. Loyalty should work both ways."

Her face and voice were grim. "I have not been truly loyal. I broke my oath to Wodan, in setting you and Baldur free."

Hal had to think that over. At last he said: "I would want all my friends, if I have any, to be as faithful to me as you are to your god. Friends mean more than oaths."

The Valkyrie was shaking her head. "I was all ready to let you steal Wodan's gold—and now I think that was a mistake."

"You only did that for his own good, you were trying to wake him up and save his life. If he was in his right mind, he'd thank you . . . of course he'd probably kill me."

"I hope you are right, I mean that he would thank me. In any case, Hal, I am going to say goodbye to you again." There was something tender and regretful in her manner.

He bowed slightly.

Alvit started to move away, then turned back and said: "We are much alike, northman, you and I. Somewhere under all the differences."

He thought it over, and nodded slowly. "For one thing, it seems that we are neither of us farmers."

She frowned at that. "Farmers? Why should we be farmers?"

He shrugged.

"If I had time, I would ask you to explain."

"I will explain, if you come back to me as soon as you have the chance. I think I'll be here for a while."

Again Alvit was on the brink of leaving, when he added: "And there's another reason I'd like you to come back."

"What?"

"Just so I can see that you are still alive. And, now that I think of it, there's yet another reason after that: I like the way you say goodbye."

"What?"

Hal felt relaxed and confident, the heavy bulk of gold right under his hands in the saddlebags. He could feel it through the leather. Maybe it would never turn into farms and fishing boats, but it meant that he had won. He said: "I'd like to hear you say goodbye to me, oh, another hundred times at least."

He thought that the request pleased her. "If I can, I can, I will." And with that, she was gone.

Now he was all alone, as far as he knew, except for three rings of fire and two gnomes. He could hear the muffled sounds of their tireless digging, only a few yards away.

And a single Horse, of course. But given the fear the gnomes had so far shown of heights and Horses, he wasn't worried about their making off with this one.

18

With Alvit gone, Hal went back to the inner corridor and put his head down into the new tunnel to talk to the gnomes.

"Have you finished digging?" he asked.

"No, but we must rest again." From what Hal could see in the dimness, indeed the pair of Earthdwellers looked just about worn out. Andvari also seemed worried about something. "Hal, you will not leave us here, will you?"

"No, why would I do that?"

"I don't know. Of course you wouldn't. It's just that we would never be able to manage the Horse by ourselves. We would certainly perish in the attempt."

"And the heights," his companion chimed in, from somewhere deeper in the tunnel's darkness. "I keep remembering how high we are above the valley. If the flames were gone, it would be a terrifying view."

Hal generously agreed. If things here now went as well as he hoped they might, he would owe the little men more than he was ever likely to repay them. So he readily pledged that he would not leave without them, and that he would carry them gently to safety. He didn't expect the Horse would have any trouble carrying him and the two gnomes for a modest distance. It would be awkward but quite possible.

The little men seemed reassured. Soon, after resting for only a couple of minutes, they went back to hammering and scooping away relentlessly at their new tunnel. Still they had offered no explanation of why they were doing it. Hal thought he knew the reason, and he was waiting to find out if he was right.

Sitting down again in the inner corridor, he enjoyed a brief rest, looking around him at the curving walls of fire. The flames were always going up and up, and at the same time they were unchanging, like a magical reversed waterfall. With the gnomes on the job he thought he might actually succeed in probing the mysteries of Loki's stronghold and sanctuary.

Now that the Earthdwellers were out of sight, working away like fanatics in their new tunnel, Hal seized the opportunity to test his fragment of the Golden Fleece in the inner corridor. What he saw confirmed his previous observations: the closer to the center of the concentric rings he brought the Fleece, the more dramatically it glowed and twitched. The talisman was even more active here than it had been in the outer corridor.

He paused to listen to the sounds of a steady hammering, accompanied by a clattering of broken rock, that came drifting out of the near mouth of the tunnel. Despite the eagerness with which the Earthdwellers had undertaken the new task, they now, in spite of all their industry, seemed to be taking a comparatively long time about it.

When Hal called down into the tunnel to ask what was going on, he received answering cries in tense voices, telling him that they had run into especially hard rock.

There was both strain and weariness in Andvari's voice. "The edges of our tools are blunted, from the work we have already done. There is granite just beneath the surface."

"Are you encountering magical interference?" Hal demanded.

He heard a mumble as Andvari and his comrade conferred between themselves in their strange dialect. Then one called back: "We do not think so. Just some very hard rock." The sounds of hammering resumed; Hal thought they seemed to be coming now from a greater distance.

Hal chafed and grumbled to himself, but there was nothing he could do to speed up the digging. Then an idea struck him, and he sat for a time in silence, thinking.

He was still sitting there when at last Andvari and his companion appeared to announce the job was finished. Having emerged from underground, the little men stood aside, and silently gestured that the way through the tunnel was open for Hal. He noticed in passing that the hands of both gnomes were sore and bleeding. But he made no comment.

Seeing light at the other end of the tunnel, Hal started through at once, headfirst. For all the time that the miners had spent in digging it, this passageway was no longer than the first one, and he thought it might be even slightly narrower, as if perhaps the diggers had hoped to discourage the passage of anyone stouter than themselves, without quite daring to make it impossible, against his direct request. He had a real struggle, and once he heard his clothing tear.

When Hal's head came poking up out of the exit, he was at once able to confirm what he had suspected: that the third circle of fire was indeed the innermost. He was emerging from underground very nearly at the center of the final ring. From here it was possible, as it had not been from anywhere else inside the fires, to see a circle of sky directly overhead. This took the form of a disk of orange-washed blackness. He thought he was beginning to lose track of time. Either night had fallen, or this was some strange effect of Loki's light, that the sun's illumination should be kept out even though snowflakes could drift in.

The light in this round chamber was peculiar, somehow not nearly as bright as it should have been, considering the luminous nature of the encircling wall. In fact the whole surface underfoot for some reason lay under a kind of blight of shadow, making it hard for Hal to tell just what he was stepping on, or looking at. There was a small litter of digging tools.

The circular space enclosed by the third ring of fire was no more than about five yards in diameter, and basically level. But further details were hard to see, for the darkened ground was thickly scattered, all across its width, with the loose material of the gnomes' digging—for some reason, in carving out this most recent tunnel, they must have carried much of the excavated material through with them, along with their tools. Hal found that puzzling, but just now he had no attention to spare for such puzzles.

At one side of the enclosed circle, the rocky floor of the space rose up slightly, just enough to accommodate a low mound of something that despite its earthy hue was neither rock nor soil. Whatever hopes Hal might have had for an immediately visible heap of gold went glimmering. But he had not really expected to see spectacular treasure at once. The gnomes would have seen it first, immediately on breaking through.

Suppose they had. What had they have done then?

The answer was simple and obvious. The Earthdwellers would have tried their best to hide the treasure so that no one else, on entering this inner sanctuary, would be able to see it. The only way to conceal a mass of metal would have been to bury it, which meant Andvari and his comrade must have dug yet another hole in solid rock. The surplus material dug from the new treasure pit must have been scattered round evenly with the rest. No wonder the diggers were in state of near-collapse, with bleeding hands, and no wonder this round of work had taken them so comparatively long.

Hal had dragged his thick body only halfway out of the tunnel when his attention was sharply distracted from the mound by a sharp movement in his belt pouch. The jumping vibration was so intense that it startled him. His fragment of the Golden Fleece was twitching and jumping more violently in his pouch than he had ever felt or seen it do before. It grew relatively active every time he brought it into Loki's stronghold. Overall it had been giving him stronger and stronger indications the closer he brought it to the center of the rings of fire.

But at the moment it was not signaling him to move toward the mound, but in the opposite direction.

Slowly Hal tugged and scraped himself completely free of the tunnel. Getting to his feet, he studied his surroundings in puzzlement; the Fleece was hopping in its pouch like a live thing, but there was not the smallest spark of bright yellow to be seen anywhere. Squinting, he scanned the basically level floor of the enclosed space, which was everywhere heavily littered with loose dirt and chips of stone.

Hal's fragment of the Fleece seemed to be trying to tug him, direct him, to the side of the inner chamber farthest from the mound.

Pulling the talisman from his pouch, he held it in his hand, gripping it firmly so it could not jump clear of his fingers. Then he moved it from side to side, letting the strength of its activity guide him. Quickly he was led to one particular spot of rubble-covered ground, exactly opposite the shadowy mound. Here the scrap of fabric was glowing so that it seemed it must burn his hand, but in truth there was no heat. Hal tucked the fragment back in his pouch, the better to do the necessary digging with both hands.

He had to displace only a few inches of loose rock fragments before the unmistakable glint of gold came into view. Now his hands began to work with great excitement.

The treasure had been hastily but effectively buried, and Hal realized he would never have imagined it was there had it not been for the feverish activity of his fragment of the Golden Fleece.

The uncovering of the treasure went very swiftly now.

In the quarter of an hour or so they'd had available, Andvari and his comrade had carved into the solid rock a repository about two feet in diameter and of unknown depth, just big enough to hold the gold that must have been lying on the surface when they entered this inner chamber.

Hal knew he was looking at what amounted to a king's ransom—no, make that an emperor's ransom, or a god's. He had little doubt that before him lay the legendary treasure of the race of Earthdwellers.

Tugging at the upper layers of heavy treasure, lifting a few of the larger items completely out of their latest hiding place, he was able to see that the cavity was as deep as his arm was long, and fairly solidly packed with gold.

The treasure was in several forms. There were huge raw nuggets, as well as refined bars, and pieces of jewelry (though he could not see a single gemstone or any metal that was not yellow). Here and there, mostly sifted toward the bottom of the pit, were handfuls of minted coins, bearing faces and script Hal could not recognize, filling up the interstices. How such a great hoard had originally been gathered, and by whom, was more than Hal could guess.

Altogether there was so much gold that he could hardly have encircled it with his two arms, far more than he could possibly have lifted. The sheer bulk of the find made it seem somehow less real than his own secret hoard of thin little horseshoes.

But it was real enough.

Hal's first elation swiftly turned to gloom. He had probed Loki's stronghold almost to its final secret, and his success seemed to present him with only another problem.

Who but a god was likely to succeed in accumulating such

a mass of treasure? It would seem to represent the hopes and efforts of a whole tribe or race. Actually Hal thought most gods would not bother to go in for hoarding precious metals. What need had deities for gold, when all the things that humans needed gold to buy were effectively theirs for the taking?

With a grunt, Hal lowered himself to sit on the littered and stony ground, close beside his find. Aching as much as ever, feeling more tired than elated, he sat there staring morosely at it. This was what came of being cursed with insatiable curiosity—whatever fine things you might discover, you were sure to be saddled with new problems. Somewhat to his own surprise, he found himself seriously considering the idea of simply covering up the hoard again.

But even before he made his decision on the hoard, there was, he was almost certain, one more treasure to be discovered here. A thing that might, he feared, have a greater impact on its discoverer than even a ton of gold.

The sight of the immense trove had momentarily knocked everything else out of his mind. But only momentarily, because now the thought of the even more important object trumped everything else.

Turning back to confront the dimly, strangely shadowed mound, Hal suddenly wished he had had more chance to talk with Alvit, discuss the situation with her. On the other hand, he was now somewhat easier in his mind knowing that Baldur was already far away.

Before he could even approach the mound, he became aware that the gnomes were calling something to him through the tunnel. He called back to them to wait, and then went to take a closer look at what else lay on the other side of this inner, triply-defended room.

Looking closely, Hal could see that the dim little mound was something more than earth. Those were bones, he could see now, as he had suspected, and bones of a special kind, part of a body that had once walked on two legs.

Standing right beside the corpse, Hal confirmed that it was little more than a ruined skeleton, so disjointed that it was hard to say whether it lay curled on its side or stretched on its back. There were a few remaining tatters, burned and shredded, of what had once been clothing. The front of the skull grinned fleshlessly at Hal. Those particular bones were still more or less intact, as if something had halfway protected them from the impact that had shattered most of the rest of the body. The remainder of the head was entirely gone, not even enough of it left to tell what the hair had been like.

There was nothing special about any of the bones—not in their present condition, anyway—to tell him if he was looking at the body of a man or a woman. The ruin of a human body, yes, but also of one that had been more than human. Had it not been for the nearby hoard of gold and certain other indications, Hal would have assumed that the remains must be those of another of Wodan's prisoners.

If you assumed that this unfortunate was only another prisoner, then he or she had evidently been triply confined, inside three rings of fire instead of only two; and so perhaps she or he had been judged guilty of some offense even more serious than Brunhild's.

But it would not be "she." Hal felt certain of that now, and certain the individual's confinement had been voluntary.

Loki had been trying to hide. Hal had no real doubt of which god would have sought safety within a triple ring of fire.

The appearance of the body testified eloquently to the force of the blast or blow that had driven the life out of it— Hal didn't see how any merely natural blow, struck by any mortal human hand and weapon, could possibly have mashed a human body, let alone a god, the way this one had been mashed. Not even if the masher had been Hercules. Somehow

258 —◦— Fred Saberhagen

all the fires and all the magic that this Firegod and Trickster could put up had not been enough to save him.

Hal needed just a moment longer, in the strange, dim light of magic fire, to locate the confirming evidence, but it was there all right. Holding his breath, he bent lower to examine the Face of Loki.

Looking at the first god's Face that he had ever seen, Hal realized that there was nothing intrinsically impressive about it, compared with a pile of gold. All the essentials of Loki's divinity resided in an object no bigger than Hal's hand, and no more conspicuous than a piece of dull glass. It lay close beside the body, near what little was left of the head. There it had come to rest after the skull of Loki's most recent avatar was shattered by some god-blasting impact, an overwhelming force that had come smashing right through the triple rings of fire, penetrating what must have been very impressive magical defenses.

In his wanderings over the past few years, Hal had learned a little about the strength of gods and their magic, and now he shivered slightly when he sought to visualize just what had happened here, tried to imagine the forces involved.

Probably the gnomes had not even noticed the small, dull, ordinary-looking thing lying on the ground—they had been dazzled into ecstasy by finding what they did find, just what they were looking for, and consumed by their anxiety to hide the glorious treasure. Possibly they had looked right at the Face in passing, and simply had not realized what this inconspicuous object was. The Face of Loki, god of fire, and . . .

A Trickster-god as well.

Very few people had ever seen the Face of any god. Probably not many people in the whole history of the world, he reflected, for no Face was likely to be lying about, naked and unworn, free for the taking, for very long before someone picked it up. History seemed to confirm what legend taught: powerful forces of magic tended to prevent the Faces from going long unused. When the death of an avatar stripped away the human flesh from some god's divinity, supernatural powers came into play, bringing a suitable human replacement to the exposed Face, or somehow conveying the Face to a man or woman who would put it on.

After looking at the Face for a long moment, Hal shot out suddenly unsteady fingers and picked it up. He was holding what appeared to be a fragment of a carved or molded image of a human countenance, broken or cut from a mask or statue. It weighed almost nothing.

Hal drew a deep breath, and said a prayer to several gods—for years now he had been convinced such prayers were useless, but the habits of youth were hard to break.

Suddenly he knew that he had to make sure the find was genuine, and not some Loki-trickery. Setting the Face back on the ground, he tried to cut it with his battle-hatchet, tapping the object warily at first, then winding up with a full swing. The only result was a recoil that bounced the weapon back, so that it almost hit him in the forehead.

The Face itself jumped only a little on the hard surface where he'd set it down, and when he picked it up for close inspection the cloudy, translucent surface showed not the smallest sign of any damage.

So, it was genuine, the handiwork of whatever unimaginable power had made the gods. Talk about treasure. Compared to this, a pile of gold was worth little more than a pile of lead.

Enormous as the value of the hoard of gold must be, Hal suspected that the market price of this small object, so easily held in one hand, could be greater. There were surely men and women in the world who would pay staggering sums, give value on the scale of treasuries and kingdoms, for the small object Hal now held in his hand. He observed with a kind of awe that he could feel a tingling in his hand, almost a burning in his fingers where they touched the smooth surface.

The eerie impression of life that the thing gave was quite accurate. For certainly something inside it was engaged in rapid movement, reminding Hal of the dance of sunlight on rippling water. Inside the semi-transparent object, which was no thicker than his finger, he beheld a ceaseless, rapid, internal flow, of—of *something*—that might have been ice-clear water, or even light itself, if there could be light that illuminated nothing . . . but when he looked a moment longer, his impression shifted, until it was more one of dancing flames, as if it mirrored the encircling barrier of heat . . .

Again and again Hal kept coming back to the fact that Loki was one of the Trickster-gods, and you would expect his Face to have something uncertain, something deceptive, about it.

It was practically impossible to determine the direction or the speed of flow. The apparent internal waves seemed to be unendingly reflected from the edges, and they went on and on without any sign that they were ever going to weaken.

The thickness of the strange object varied from about a quarter of an inch to half an inch. It was approximately four inches from top to bottom, and six or seven along the curve from right to left. The ceaseless flow inside it, of whatever it was that looked like dancing flame, went on as tirelessly as before.

Whether the modeled face was intended to be masculine or feminine was hard to tell, except that there was no representation of beard or mustache . . . the most prominent feature of the fragment was the single eye that it contained—the left—which had been carved or molded from the same piece of strange, warm, flexible, transparent stuff as all the rest. The eyeball showed an appropriately subtle bulge of pupil, and the details of the open lid were clear. No attempt had been made to represent eyelashes. An inch above the upper lid, another smooth small bulge suggested an eyebrow. A larger one below outlined cheekbones. No telling what the nose looked like, because the fragment broke off cleanly just past the inner corner of the eye. Along the top of the fragment, in the region of the temple, was a modeled suggestion of hair curled close against the skull.

Around the whole irregular perimeter of the translucent shard, the edges were somewhat jagged . . . now when Hal pushed at the small projections with a finger, he found that they bent easily, springing back into their original shape as soon as the pressure was released. Everything about the piece he was holding suggested strongly that it was only a remnant, torn or broken from a larger image, that of a whole face or even an entire body.

The god who had fallen and perished here had once been on such friendly terms with Wodan that he invited the All-Highest to use one compartment of his stronghold as a prison for recalcitrant Valkyries. The same god who had somehow, somewhere, taken possession of the golden treasure the gnomes were now trying to reclaim. The same god who had brought the vast hoard here, in an attempt to hide it, keep it for himself.

The northman knew roughly what powers the Face of Loki would bring the human being who wore it. But he was not in the least inclined to put it on.

Instead, he tucked it into his belt pouch, where he imagined he could feel it burning against his belly. Faintly smiling, he took an inventory of the digging tools the gnomes had left scattered about in here—he thought the whole of their equipment was pretty well accounted for.

Then Hal put his head down into the tunnel and called sharply for Andvari and Ivaldr to come through to him. He was reluctant to go out to them, lest they assume he had found the gold, and be tempted to murder him while he in the vulnerable position of emerging from the narrow passage.

After a pause, Andvari's voice came back, politely asking

Hal to first pass their digging tools out to them.

He made his own voice neutral, sending it back through the ten-foot tube. "I think you had better come in here and get them. We have some matters to talk over. And as soon as you have tools available, I wish you'd make this tunnel a little wider."

When Andvari and his comrade reentered the innermost chamber of Loki's stronghold, they found Hal sitting casually right beside the pile of gold.

For a long moment no one spoke. Then Ivaldr said in a weary voice: "So you have found it."

Hal was letting one big hand rest almost carelessly on the glowing pile. "I suppose this was just lying on the surface in here, and you somehow caught a glimpse of it when you looked in through the second ring of fire? No wonder you just had to dig the second tunnel." He grabbed up a few coins, and let them trickle through his fingers.

Ivaldr started to react angrily to Hal's fingering of the hoard, but then subsided into gloomy silence.

"Well?" Hal prompted.

The two little men exchanged an exhausted look, then nodded in agreement. Andvari said: "Yes, looking through the flames with our goggles we could see it from out in the second corridor. And when we came up through the floor here, it was spread out on the ground at the feet of the skeleton—this second prisoner."

"As if," the other gnome put in, "the prisoner had been gloating over it before she—or he—died. Much good did it do him, or her."

Hal was curious. "Did it ever occur to you to wonder who this second prisoner was?"

Clearly it had not. The pile of gold was what Ivaldr and

Andvari cared about. And now that they had handled it, and buried it with great expense of energy and effort, they were probably ready to kill to keep it.

Standing, Andvari drew himself up to his full height, a little over four feet. "The treasure is ours, you see. And now that we have found it, we are not going to let it go." His voice quavered slightly as he confronted the giant warrior before him with this declaration.

"I do not dispute that it is yours," said Hal, mildly. He still sat relaxed. "Others may, but that will be your problem."

They only blinked at him distrustfully. Here in the strange dimness they had taken their goggles off again.

Now in a rush of candor Andvari confessed that he and his comrade had thought of fighting Hal for the gold, but decided against that course. It would be much better if they could trust each other.

"You have been our friend, and saved our lives. And we are miners and metalworkers, not hardened fighting men."

Ivaldr gloomily chimed in: "Also, if we fought, you would probably kill us both in no time."

Hal nodded judiciously. "There is that."

"Besides that, we will need your help. We must all remember," Andvari pointed out, "that we Earthdwellers are unable to manage Horses by ourselves, and without your help we would certainly kill ourselves in a fall from this high place, even if we managed to get out through the outer ring of fire . . . you don't even ask for a share?"

"Would it make you feel better to give me one? You'd be getting no gold at all if I hadn't brought you here."

The two little men looked at each other. "We will have to talk about that," Andvari said.

Ivaldr nodded. "Discuss it with our elders."

Hal had about decided that he didn't really want a share, but still their attitude annoyed him.

The two gnomes, saying they wanted to talk the matter of sharing over between themselves, gathered up their tools, left Hal in the central chamber and went out again through the newest tunnel.

If he hadn't been dead certain of their inability to ride the Horse without him, he would have followed closely. As matters actually stood, of course—

Now in through the tunnel—through two tunnels, actually—there came the abrupt sound of hoofbeats, golden shoes on hard rock, followed by terse scrambled dialogue in gnomish voices—followed by sudden and utter silence. Hal jumped to his feet. As clearly as if he could see them, he heard the gnomes somehow scrambling together aboard the one remaining Horse, and riding outward through the fiery curtain.

They were already gone, successfully making their escape. And, whether they knew it or not, they had his pitiful small trove of golden horseshoes with them. He had been utterly wrong about the Earthdwellers and their supposed dread of Horses. The little bastards had tricked him, and now the disaster he had feared had struck.

The strangest thing was that he hardly felt the impact of the loss. Somehow having the Face in his possession had driven all real worries about mere gold out of his mind.

He said aloud: "Well, if they have my treasure now, I still have theirs. Until they get back with their army to collect it. And that will take a while." Hal looked from the huge pile of gold back to the skeleton, and it grinned back at him. "Didn't do you much good, did it?"

The skeleton made no reply.

"Yes, I have theirs. Along with something even better."

Hal listened, for a sound coming from outside the flames, he wasn't sure exactly what. He thought he could hear several kinds of noise. Whatever he heard, he made no move, but only waited.

19

Several minutes had passed, but Hal was still standing there in almost the same position, except that he had taken the Face of Loki from his pouch, and was once more holding it in his hands, when Alvit came writhing through the second tunnel to confront him.

Her blond head popped into view, and she regarded him without surprise. "There you are, Hal. Did you know the gnomes had gone? As I approached I saw them in flight, both of them with their sun-goggles on, clinging desperately to the back of one Horse. The same Horse I left here for you."

Hal let out a great sigh, as if he had been unconsciously holding in his breath. "I realized that they were gone," he said.

"I suppose," Alvit replied after a pause, "that somehow gold is once more at the root of the trouble?" Pulling herself up out of the hole, she stood with hands on hips and glared at him. She was just a little taller.

Hal nodded.

"Where is the gold this time, northman?"

Forcing his hands to move slowly and casually, Hal opened his belt pouch and put away the essence of the great god, so that Loki nestled right beside the Golden Fleece. At the same time he watched the young woman carefully, trying to judge by her reaction whether she recognized the object he had just concealed, or whether she had even bothered to look it at all.

Alvit was staring at him, but her thoughts were obviously not on Faces at the moment. "So, do you wish to discuss the situation? The gnomes have ridden away on your Horse, and left you trapped in here. And I once thought you might be leadership material. Or were you counting on using their tools to dig your own way out, under the outer ring?"

"No—I mean, I didn't know they were going to take the Horse, but I'm not absolutely trapped."

"You're not? Just how would you propose to get out through the outer ring of fire, lacking a Horse?"

"I'm all right, Alvit. Don't worry about me—not just now. What about you? By the way, I'm very glad you accepted my invitation and came back."

She sighed. "I seem to do a lot of riding to and fro."

"What's going on with Wodan?"

"I think he is happy that his great battle has begun, but he is not well." She went on to report that, since leaving Hal only a little while ago, she had been with Wodan on his not-so-distant battlefield. Her chief reason for returning to the high crag now was that Wodan had dispatched her and all the other available Valkyries to search everywhere they could for Thor.

"And you thought Thor might be here?"

"He was not far from here when last I saw him. You remember when that was."

"What happens when you've found him?"

"We are to appeal to the Thunderer's honor, and to his better nature, for aid against the monsters of the Underworld."

"So Wodan is actually appealing for help? I didn't know he could."

"Of course the All-Highest would not put the matter in those words, he is far too proud—but yes, he needs help and is asking for it. Unlike some men, who can be effectively trapped and need a Horse, but refuse even to admit the fact."

Hal grinned. "I admit that a Horse is likely to be of substantial help to me in getting away from here, when the time comes."

"In that case you may use mine—if I am here when the time comes." Then she dug something from a belt pouch. "Here—I wouldn't want to see you waste away." She handed over another small package of food.

Hal murmured thanks and opened the package. Looking at the food, he remembered his last meal, a nibble of gnomes' roots, and realized that he was hungry.

Alvit's gaze had now moved past him to probe curiously at the modest mound. From the way her face altered, he could tell the precise moment when she recognized that it was largely made of bones.

Her voice took on an edge. "Who's this? Another prisoner? A couple of other Valkyries are unaccounted for."

Brushing crumbs from his fingers, Hal moved that way a step or two, so he was once more standing close beside the remains. "The gnomes, too, thought this was another of Wodan's prisoners. But he wasn't."

"He? It is a man, then? Who?"

When Hal didn't answer immediately, Alvit turned, looking all round the inner chamber. Her gaze fell on the golden hoard, and the question of the bones was momentarily driven from her mind. For the space of two or three breaths she remained frozen in silent astonishment. Then in a hushed voice she said: "I see now why you could be so casual about losing a few horseshoes."

"There seems to be a curse of some kind on me. I'm never going to be rich."

She moved a little closer to the yellow pile. "Surely you will try to take a part of this, at least?"

"It seems the gnomes are determined to have it all. Actually, I've been thinking about another problem."

From the corner of his eye he saw Alvit's pale face turn to

look at him. But when he turned to see her expression, her handsome face was unreadable.

Now Alvit was looking from bones to gold and back again, as if an idea had struck, and maybe the truth was beginning to dawn on her. At last she asked again, in a more demanding voice: "Who is this, then?"

Hal gave the skeleton a brief glance. "Not much of anyone right now. But I'd be willing to bet that whole pile of gold that this was the last avatar of Loki."

"This?" And for a moment she drew away, as if in awe, or perhaps fear of some contamination.

"Sure. Gods die, or at least their avatars do."

It took only a second for Alvit to come up with the next thought. Then she was suddenly down on her knees beside the body of a man who had been a god, digging and scraping with eager fingers at the rocky soil around the broken skull. She looked up to see Hal shaking his head.

He told her: "I've looked for the Face too. That was the first thing I did when I discovered him." Now Hal had clasped his hands behind his back, keeping them well away from his belt pouch. If Alvit even suspected where the Face was now, he knew she would try anything, including physical attack, to get it from him, without stopping to heed warnings or explanations. She was desperate to help Wodan, and she would want to stuff the damned thing into her own head at once, turn herself into Loki and go dashing off to save the life of the god she loved.

The Valkyrie was on her feet again. "Hal, if one of us could become a god, we could immediately tip the battle in Wodan's favor. Hal, I beg you, if you have any idea where—" Then abruptly her shoulders slumped. "But no, if you knew where the Face was you'd already be going after it. And if you'd picked it up you'd have become Loki by now."

Hal gave her a wry smile, a slight shake of his head. "You know me pretty well," he said. Then he changed the subject, nodding toward the body. "I have a good idea what killed him. Beyond that it becomes harder and harder to be certain about anything."

Alvit looked at him sharply. "What killed him, then?"

"Understand, there are not many weapons, in this world or the Underworld, that can destroy a god so thoroughly. Not a god as great as Loki. I believe Thor threw his Hammer at him."

It might well have happened, Hal supposed, even without Thor knowing for certain where his rival had concealed himself. Probably the Thunderer needed only to murmur his victim's name to Myelnir, and let it fly; overpowering magic would do the rest. Thor might have believed that Loki was here, but assumptions regarding the behavior of a Trickster could only be tentative.

Again Alvit considered the ruined skeleton. "That may well be. But Loki's Face is not here, which means someone must have picked it up. Who? Did Thor actually come here, inside the flames? Or did he just throw Myelnir from outside?"

"I believe Thor cast his weapon from outside, and I don't think he came in to pick up Loki's Face. Maybe someone took it who—who was in no hurry to be a god."

Alvit was puzzled. "I don't understand. Do you know anyone who would *not* want to be a god?"

Hal drew a deep breath. "I have met the enchantress Circe, who is one example; remind me to tell you more about her sometime. And I myself, like Circe, have seen divinity at first hand, more than once. And never in the countenance of any god have I seen great happiness."

"Are you turning into a philosopher in your old age, northman?"

Hal grimaced. "I hope not. Leaving matters of philosophy aside, I can think of a very practical reason not to be Loki at the moment."

Alvit was not going to be distracted. She shook her head.

"I am forgetting my duty. Whatever happened here, Loki is not available. Where is Thor now? I tell you, Wodan is in desperate need of strong allies."

Hal was looking at her intently, trying to find the right way to explain certain things that had to be explained. He said: "I am practically certain that Thor is dead, too."

She stared at him. "Why are you certain?"

"Because I have seen his Hammer." Just at this crucial moment, he was distracted by noticing how—how *pretty*, that was the only word for it—Alvit looked, when her mouth came open in astonishment. He went on: "In fact I've seen it twice. The first time was when Thor's last avatar was still alive and it was hanging on his belt. You've seen Myelnir too, not long ago, though I believe I've had the closer look."

Alvit was now regarding Hal with something like awe. She murmured: "I've never seen the Hammer of Thor, save at a distance, when it was in his hand. That was days ago."

"You are wrong. We've both of us seen it within the past few hours." Hal put out a stubby finger to draw a circle in the air. "It's whirling in a kind of orbit round this crag. You're the one who pointed out the mysterious flying spark."

"That—is Myelnir!" Alvit breathed.

He nodded. "First I suspected, then I made sure. I rode my Horse close to the glowing circle, close enough to get a good look as it flew by. It was Myèlnir, all right, but Thor was nowhere near."

Privately, Hal was wondering how effective Thor's Hammer would be in the hands of a mere mortal, supposing he could get his hands on it. He might try to ride his Horse near it again, as it whirled in midair, and try to grab it as it went spinning by.

He might attempt that kind of stunt if he were forced to it, but he was afraid of what the result might be. He didn't want to suggest it to Alvit.

Myelnir's physical dimensions were quite modest, but some

of the stories suggested that just lifting it might be more than an ordinary man could do. In the hands of a mortal, assuming he could wield it at all, Hal thought it would still crush other weapons, and kill adversaries. But he doubted that any mortal—Hercules was always an exception in these matters—could throw it effectively; and if he did, once thrown it would not come flying back in perfect obedience to his hand.

Alvit was silent, trying to digest his revelation.

Hal went on: "Some time back, when Baldur and I were lying exhausted in one of these corridors, a strange noise woke me up. I think now that what I heard was the sound of Myelnir coming in through all the firewalls, killing Loki in his hiding place, then flying out again.

"Myelnir did its work on Loki. But then for once it failed to dart right back to its master's hand. I can imagine only one reason for that—because Thor himself had been slain, in whatever little time there was between his hurling the Hammer and its striking home. Loki and Thor must have died at almost the same instant."

Alvit interrupted. "But then, who killed Thor?" In a moment she had answered her own question. "Of course, it must have been one of those mighty Giants or demons of the Underworld. They have their own means of long-range killing, just as the gods do."

"I expect you're right."

Now Hal, though he could not have said what he was looking for, studied the corpse more closely than before.

"What puzzles me is why would Loki, why would any god, want to hoard gold?" Why would a god, with practically all the riches of the earth lying open and vulnerable to his plundering, fight and struggle to maintain possession of a mere yellow mass of metal? One reason Hal could think of was that Loki might have done it just for fun—for the same reason he, Hal, had been so intent on penetrating all the rings of fire. Otherwise, he could only think that the god was Loki, and Loki's knack for troublemaking was as great as his skill in making fire—that must have had something to do with it.

In some ways, gods were no better or more able than any human. And Hal had known mortal men to die, risking their lives to steal something they did not truly need.

The two other gods he had encountered over the last few days had both been looking for Loki. They had each mentioned him more than once, and not in any friendly way.

The dead skull grinned its grin, as if proud of how very good it was at keeping secrets. The blasted ruin surrounding the bones was good at keeping secrets too. And now an unmelted snowflake came drifting down, to give it the same blessing as another flake had given Brunhild's ruby lips.

Well, you may contemplate your dead bones, northman. As for me, I must report this find to Wodan."

"Of course."

Alvit had already plunged into the near tunnel, making her way back to the outer corridor. Hal kept right behind her, and Alvit called back: "I don't understand. Are Loki and the Trickster the same god, the same being, or are they not?"

"There's more than one Trickster among the gods, and I think it will be very hard to get a simple answer to any simple question about any of them. Stop and think who you are dealing with."

That answer gave Alvit pause. By this time she was standing beside her faithful Horse.

"For the last time, are you coming with me, northman? We can ride double out through the fire, and then I will set you down anywhere you like, before I go on to Wodan. He would not be pleased to see you."

"I would like to go with you, Alvit. Actually I would like very much to spend a considerable amount of time with you, somewhere where there are no battles to be fought . . . but before I can go anywhere with anyone, there is another matter I must think out for myself. So let me stay where I am, for now."

"Has this other matter anything to do with Loki's Face? Or with the gold?"

"With one of those at least."

"But you are determined to remain trapped inside these flames?"

"If you want to look at it that way."

She shook her head slowly, as if chiding him. "There is too much gold in that pile, Hal, for any one man to carry." Then she suddenly raised her head, to all appearances listening intently. "My god is calling for me," she informed Hal in a tense voice.

In a moment she was astride her Horse, and in another moment after that she and her Horse were gone.

Now Hal was completely alone, standing in the smooth, narrow curve of the outer corridor, surrounded by the enduring magic of a dead god. Not even a gnome remained for him to argue with. Not even a Horse on which to get away.

Turning, he gazed at the outer entrance to the first tunnel, as if pondering whether it could be worthwhile to drag himself through it again. But he had not decided anything before another Horse came bursting in through the outer flame-ring.

For a moment, Hal believed that Alvit had turned round and come back to him, and his heart leapt up.

Then his hopes fell, and his hand moved to the blood-stained hatchet at his belt. This time the mounted intruder was Hagan, with another man, who could only be one of his band of robbers, clinging to the Horse's back behind him.

20

Strangely enough, Hagan on first entering the fire-sanctuary showed no particular surprise at discovering Hal was there before him.

The Berserk's first words offered a kind of explanation. "Hail, northman! I had word from our mutual acquaintance that I would probably find you here." Then he looked curiously at the second wall of fire. "What is this? Rings within rings?"

Hal nodded slowly. He had been looking forward to getting some sleep, as an aid to thinking out his problems, but clearly rest and sleep would have to wait. "Our mutual acquaintance being your son Baldur?"

"So, the brat told you that he's mine?" Expertly Hagan slid off his mount, keeping his one-handed grip on the Horse's mane. The man who had been riding behind him got off more awkwardly. Hagan went on: "He'll never make a real warrior, and I have serious doubts about his parentage, though his mother was my wife when he was born." He gave Hal a look of frank admiration. "He'll never be a fighter good enough to soak himself in a berserker's blood."

"Baldur acquitted himself well. He saved my life." Hal glanced down with revulsion at the dried stains on his own garments. "But I think your son is done with praying to Wodan, if that's what you mean."

So far Hagan had been balancing, on one good leg and one

bad, without his crutch. But now he accepted the aid when his silent attendant handed it over. "Speak no more to me of sons, Haraldur—I'll never get another one on any woman. Wodan, in his tender care for his servants, has seen to that as well." And with the upper end of his crutch tucked into his armpit, Hagan pointed with a jerk of his thumb at his own crotch.

Then Hagan had a question. "You've seen that flying thing out there, northman? Looping in a circle around this rock, like some demented bird?"

"I've seen it."

"I made sure to keep well clear of it as I approached. What do you know about the thing?"

Hal shook his head as if the question were beyond him. "It's every bit as strange as you say." Then, as if just struck by a thought, he added: "I wonder if it has something to do with the Valkyries."

Hagan seemed intrigued. "Why should it?"

"Some of them have gone to fight at Wodan's side. Are you going to join them?"

The twisted man looked over his shoulder, making sure his acolyte was temporarily out of sight. The man had gone off along the circular corridor, evidently exploring. Then Hagan snarled, in a low voice: "I am going to tear out Wodan's bloody guts, if I can ever find the means to do it." When Hal only stared at him, he grabbed Hal by the arm. "Haven't I been dropping enough hints for you to understand? It's he, the grand All-Lowest, the Father of Shit, I have to thank for what I am today. The great Wodan, who has robbed me of all human life!"

Hal was staring, fascinated. But he shook his head. "No, not robbed. You laid your life on his altar, willingly, when first you went to worship him."

"I was only a boy then."

"Of course. It is the kind of thing that children do." Hal

started to say something else, but then his eye fell on the Horse. Jarred out of his own thoughts, he demanded of Hagan: "That's the mount that Baldur rode. Where is he now?"

The man gave a twisted shrug. "Who knows? I did the brat and his woman no harm."

"You have the Horse that they were riding."

"Is that what worries you?" Hagan laughed. "I got this beast in a fair trade. I gave Baldur two nice cameloids for it, and he and his girl were happy."

"The two of them just rode away?" Hal was not quite convinced.

"I told him he'd do well to ride clear of war, and he gave me no argument."

Hagan's attendant had returned, having completed his circle of exploration. Now the man put into operation what seemed a prearranged plan, backing the Horse into the outer circle of flame, in which its magically protected body seemed to suffer no discomfort. At once, more of Hagan's men began to appear inside the corridor. They were using the beast as a kind of bridge or conduit to bring them safely through the flames. One after another came stumbling through, eyes closed, sliding close along the animal's side and arriving safely, to open their eyes and blink in wonder at the strangeness.

Hal supposed the one Horse could hardly have carried them all here, so most of these new arrivals must have climbed the crag on their own springy legs. Each man of them was young, disgustingly young in Hal's estimation, and he could easily picture them all bounding swiftly up the rocky path, probably not even needing to stop for breath. Their youth and vigor made them all the easier to hate. And now, how proud they all were of having dared the flames.

When about half a dozen had come through, and there seemed to be no more, Hagan interrupted his confrontation with Hal to count heads. He seemed satisfied that everyone he had been expecting had now arrived.

Then he turned back to Hal. "Do you enjoy taking revenge, northman? You look like a man who knows something about that subject."

Hal shrugged. "It's like some other things in life—I find I enjoy it less as I grow older."

Hagan did not seem to be listening. "But how can a mere man ever manage to revenge himself upon a god? Did you ever ponder that question, northman?"

Slowly Hal shook his head. "That's one problem that I've never tried to solve."

"Oh, but I have! I have tried indeed. I've thought and thought about it, northman. And when I had thought enough, and sacrificed enough of my own blood, eventually understanding came. The only practical chance a man can have to be revenged upon a god—*is by becoming a god himself.*"

Hal murmured something and tried to keep himself from backing away a step. He didn't like what he thought he was beginning to see in Hagan's single eye.

"That's why I have come here." Hagan stood closer to Hal and lowered his voice so only Hal could hear him. "I want to get my hands on the Face of Loki, for I have reason to believe that Loki has died here somewhere, inside these rings of fire."

Hal nodded. "Others have had the same idea. Loki is suddenly a very well-liked fellow. Nothing like death to make a god more popular."

Hagan's one-eyed stare was boring into each of Hal's own eyes in turn. "I don't suppose you've seen the little trinket that I'm seeking, northman—? No, of course you haven't, or it'd already be inside your head. And I can see in your eyes that hasn't happened."

Hal had to struggle to keep his own voice steady. "Are you quite sure you'd know the Face of Loki if you saw it? He's one of the Trickster-gods, you know."

That set Hagan back for only a moment. "Oh, I'd know it. Don't try to fool me, northman. You do not wear the Face of any god."

"You're right, I don't."

"But you're right too, there may be trickery." Hagan looked taken aback, as if he had not thought of that before. "Loki's a Trickster, among other things. "His Face may change its look from time to time, for all we know. Maybe it can even move itself about, without the help of any human hand."

Hal nodded silently. In fact he remembered how, just as he was stuffing it in his pouch, the Face had twitched like a small animal in his hand, startling him so that he almost dropped it.

Hagan seemed about to say more on the subject, but he was distracted by a call from one of his men.

"Chief, come look at this! Someone's really been digging! Digging like gnomes, through solid rock."

Naturally Hagan went to look. After inspecting the outer entrance of the first tunnel, and snarling at those who had failed to inform him of the excavation sooner, he said: "This work is very new, the dust still drifting in the air." Then he turned on Hal a glare that burned with new suspicion. "Who dug that hole, and when? Where does it lead?"

"Your man there is right, gnomes did the work. Look into it, and you can easily see where it leads." Hal gestured. "No farther than just inside this second ring of fire. Crawl through, and you'll discover a third ring that looks just the same, and a second tunnel going under it. Inside the third ring of fire, at the core of Loki's little stronghold, you'll find an open space, maybe three or four strides across."

Hagan was studying him intently. "And what have you discovered there?"

Hal gestured minimally toward the hole. "Might as well go see for yourself."

Commanding his men to stay where they were, and guard the Horse, Hagan plunged in headfirst. He had less trouble than Hal would have expected, dragging his twisted body one-handed through one narrow passage after another and even managing to bring his crutch along.

Presently the two men were standing side by side inside the inner sanctuary, with Hagan eagerly taking in its contents. At first disregarding the exposed surface of the pile of gold, he spotted the skeleton, and went immediately to search near it for the Face that was no longer there.

When Hagan raised his head, he was bitterly disappointed. "So, I will have to find some other way . . . who took it?"

Hal was standing back with folded arms. "I am curious, Hagan. Which would you rather have, the Face of Loki, or this pile of gold?"

Hagan's eyes turned in the direction of Hal's gesture. Slowly the expression on his scarred face altered, as he began to appreciate the full magnitude of the hoard.

At last he said: "So, it's real gold? And what a heap! Yes, very interesting indeed. With that much—with half that much—a man could hire and pay an army."

"And even hire wizards, to help him fight a god. If a man had time."

When the bent man had probed the surface of the treasure, he straightened up, as well as he was able. "This gold is now mine, northman. I am here, with my men, and in possession. Unless you want to dispute the rights of ownership with me?"

"Oh no." Hal shook his head. "I wouldn't if I could." He had trouble understanding why everyone besides himself seemed ready to fight and die for the tremendous treasure. What bothered Hal more than missing out on gold was trying hard to win something, coming close to success, and then being denied the victory after all. It was a discouraging thought, but he was beginning to wonder if all of life might not be like that.

To himself he thought: *Maybe I'll still go for one handful of those yellow coins, if I can get the chance.*

Aloud he mused: "That great pile might buy a man his dearest dream. But for some dreams, it still would not be enough."

The ravaged face before him showed puzzlement, followed by a flash of understanding—no, misunderstanding, as it turned out. "Are you trying to tell me there's some way to trade this gold for Loki's Face? I'd do that in an instant!"

Hal was taken aback. "No, I didn't mean that at all."

"Then what?"

"Nothing. Listen to me, Hagan, I—"

"Tell me, damn you to the Underworld! Tell me!"

Hal tried to turn away, but with impressive one-armed strength the bandit grabbed and spun Hal's massive body back.

Hagan's face was evilly transformed. "A god is speaking to me right now, northman. He tells me that you're acting strangely, you must have weighty matters on your mind." The twisted man took a step closer. "You know where the Face is, don't you? *Tell me!* The gold is yours, all yours, if you can somehow put the powers of Loki into my hands!"

Before Hal could answer, they were interrupted. The first of Hagan's men had found his way through the second tunnel into the central area. Others were right behind him. One after another they came pouring up out of the ground, weapons ready in their hands, in response to the sound of Hagan's raised voice.

"Having any trouble, chief?"

Something in that voice caught at Hal's memory, and when he took a second look at the speaker, the face was unpleasantly familiar too.

Their master seemed about to order them back, but then

he stuttered and stumbled. Hagan raised his hand to his head and tangled his gnarled fingers in his hair. Suddenly his voice held hollow desperation. "Ever since the last time my head was hurt . . . there is a certain god who visits me, now and again."

"That's interesting," said Hal in a small voice.

"Ever since the last time my head was hurt . . ." Hagan repeated. A moment later, he sank to the ground in a kind of trembling fit.

"Remember me, fat man? We met once before."

Again Hal heard the voice that he had almost forgotten, and turned to see a countenance to match. When last he saw that face, its owner had been sitting in a dusty road, and it had been contorted with great pain. But now it wore an evil grin of triumph.

Hal said: "I remember."

"I told you, fat man, that this day would come. Now take that hatchet off your belt and set it down—and your knife, too."

Hal took a long look behind him, then in front of him, evaluating the grim and eager faces, the ready weapons. Then he shrugged and followed orders. Greedy, grasping hands picked up axe and dagger as soon as he cast them down. Eager eyes examined the beautifully made if somewhat battered weapons with the proprietary interest of new owners.

By this time Hagan had regained consciousness. In another moment he had pulled himself to his feet, and stood leaning on his crutch, looking thoughtfully from one of his men to another. It was as if he wanted to make sure he knew what had happened while the fit was on him, and what was happening now, before reassuming control. Evidently his men were used to these interruptions of command, for at the moment none of them were paying their leader much attention.

Meanwhile the short bandit was taking his time; obviously he meant to enjoy his moments of power to the full.

Now he said: "In a minute I'm going to pay you something that I owe you, fat man. Give it back with interest. But first, let's see what's in your pouch. This time I think you'll let me have it."

Again Hal hesitated only briefly before he unfastened the pouch from his belt and tossed it over. "That's twice in a row you're right. You're having a good day."

Three men who had been standing behind Hal pushed forward, around him, to join the others. One of the bandits snatched up the oilskin package and dumped out the contents on the ground. A circle of grimy faces stared uncomprehendingly at something they had never seen before. The Face of Loki had fallen among some trivial oddments, including a few crumbs of food—so had the scrap of fabric that once had been the Golden Fleece, but no one even noticed that.

As Hal would have been willing to bet, the bent man still had the wit and spirit, the unthinking berserker readiness, to move faster than any of his followers. Uttering a hoarse cry, Hagan lunged forward with a terrible surge of strength, thrusting with his crutch to knock aside a couple of his followers who were just an instant too slow. His strong hand snatched up Loki's Face, and without a moment's hesitation he pressed it over his own eyes and nose.

Hal had thrown himself down in the same instant that Hagan moved, but in the opposite direction, stretching his body away from the Face as far as he could go. He hugged the hard rock, and wanted to close his eyes, but somehow his private demon of curiosity would not allow him to do that—he had to see what was going to happen next.

Then it came. Again Hal heard the sound that had once wakened him from an exhausted sleep.

His diving body had hardly struck the ground before the air around him seemed to ring like a great gong. Hagan had put on the Face and was just in the act of reaching with both hands—Hal saw dazedly that the Face of Loki had already restored the new avatar's missing arm—eager to embrace the gold.

But before the new god touched the yellow metal, there was a blinding flash, a sense of surging power, ending in a stunning detonation. A small drop of something struck Hal on the forehead, with force that made a spattering of blood feel hard as stone.

Hagan had achieved his apotheosis, and now the body of Loki's latest avatar lay still while a halo of small flames went dancing harmlessly around it. Hagan in his bright momentary life as Firegod might have willed to cut off the magic feeding the three burning curtains, for now they abruptly sputtered and guttered out. The calm daylight of late afternoon ruled the hilltop, and the world surrounding it had abruptly sprung into view. Not even Wodan could have blown those fires out so quickly, like so many candles. But Hagan/Loki had time to do nothing more than that.

No, one thing more. Blooming momentarily back into existence, Loki's giant billows of fire reached out, dying powers only half-alive at best, doing their best to defend the newest avatar. Incidentally they incinerated a pair of bandits unlucky enough to be standing in the wrong place. But the flames of Loki were too late, and too relatively weak, to save their master.

Hal, raising one arm to shield his eyes and squinting into a radiance of yellow light, caught one memorable glimpse of the Face of Loki spinning briefly in midair, after being blasted out of yet another human head. Now the small translucent oval was falling free again. Right into the pile of gold Hal saw it go tumbling, even as that pile melted under the last spasmodic output of the avatar's dying will.

For a moment the glaring glow, the blasting heat, was such that Hal was forced to close his eyes. As he did so, it crossed his mind that Hagan/Loki had just been granted the most glorious cremation that any warrior or Trickster could ever want.

When Hal was able to turn back, and dared to open his eyes again, he watched as the molten pile, seeming to boil with something more than mere natural heat, poured itself fuming down the slopes and crevices of the clifftop, to collide at last with the river at the bottom in a glorious explosion of steam that rose from a deep pool.

The entire bandit crew had been scrambling for the Face. The two or three who had survived the blast, who had not been burned to death or hurled right off the crag, now went tottering and stumbling away in terror and shock. Scorched and blinded, one after another lurched scrambling across the clifftop and over the edge. Their screaming had a thin and hollow sound in the shocked stillness of the air.

Hal was truly alone, and Loki's stronghold was no more. All of the tongues of fire were gone, save for a thin glowing channel in the rock, burned out by molten gold on its way to go trickling over the cliff's edge.

Once again the Hammer of Thor had done its work. Now from atop the crag the view of the sky was completely open. Hal looked up—the fiery dot circling the crag had disappeared at last.

As far as Hal could see, every last ounce of gold was completely gone. Not a drop of it, not a fragment, was left on the hilltop.

Inching his way forward, avoiding the spots where naked, blackened rock still smoked with heat, Hal got his chin over the cliff's edge. He was staring down, hundreds of feet, to where a cloud of steam still hissed. The yellow metal would be undergoing a prolonged quenching and tempering in a deep pool of the river. The heat in several hundredweight of molten gold must have been awesome, but the Einar was bringing endless, irresistible resources to put it out.

Even as Hal watched, the steam-clouds soon dispersed, and the river flowed on as before, the surface troubled only by occasional huge bubbles, showing something was still stirring in the depths. And presently even that disturbance ceased.

One detail remained etched, brighter than all others, in Hal's memory—the Face of Loki going over, caught up in the flood of useless wealth. If Hal could rely on what his eyes had told him, the end result was going to be a god's Face embedded in the middle of a huge, crude nugget.

Still looking down, he saw with fascination that the flying spark that was Thor's Hammer now circled over the deep pool—in which, even as he watched, the last bubbling and steaming ceased.

Then Hal blinked. Abruptly the Hammer had gone out of sight again—where was it now?

Pulling his head back from the edge of the cliff, he rolled over on his back and sat up, hearing the quick trampling of another Horse's hooves upon the flat, scorched rock nearby, followed by a familiar voice.

"Hal, you are alive!" The gladness in Alvit's words was marvelous to hear.

"So far. Just barely." He rubbed his head, which still felt as if a river of molten gold might be running through it. His eyes were dazzled, but he could make out Alvit's face and form as she bent over him.

She was saying: "As I rode up, I saw something go—pouring—over the cliff. Something tremendously hot it seemed, burning, steaming all the way down—what was it?"

Hal turned slowly to look down at the river again. "A farm and two fishing boats. All gone for good."

"Will you talk sense?" Now the woman sounded unreasonably angry. "Stop gibbering about farms! Or have you been hit in the head too many times, like Baldur and Hagan?"

And like Wodan too. But he did not say that aloud. "Hagan's dead," Hal began to explain. Then, straining his ears, he raised a hand. "Hush! Did you hear something?"

Both of them froze, listening. Hal found himself intently focusing on a sound that might be the rumbling approach of the Chariot of Thor, carrying no passenger—or no living one at least—pulled by its two magic Goats. For a moment his imagination pictured the vehicle arriving at or near the crag, so he would be able to scramble near it somehow and look inside.

But that was not happening. He could imagine any presence that he liked, but there was no sign of any Chariot.

Quite near at hand, though, another noise startled Hal. He grabbed at his belt for an axe that was no longer there, then looked around him for a weapon, any weapon. A rapid, bouncing, scraping noise, like something hard on rock. Then he saw what it was. No, not Chariot wheels.

The Hammer of Thor was no longer circling the crag or skimming the deep pool either. Having now entirely lost its glow of burning heat, it was bounding and skipping around the newly opened and exposed surface of the crag, from which Loki's fires had only moments ago been banished. The rocks were still marked with neat concentric rings where magic fires had blackened them. The four open holes of the two tunnels looked utterly pointless now.

Again Hal was struck by the fact that Myelnir's handle seemed incongruously short, and he wasn't even sure that it was made of wood. Could the whole Hammer possibly be one piece of forged metal?

Hal heard no voice, and yet had the distinct impression that he was being sent a message: *You wanted a weapon. So here I am.*

His fighter's instinct, which he trusted more than any conscious plan, took over. Wodan, or the gods knew what, might be coming at him even now. Spurred by fear of what could happen if he did not act, Hal lunged for the Hammer and managed to seize its incongruously short handle in his right hand.

A moment later he was hanging on for dear life as Myelnir yanked him to his feet, then right off his feet, as if he were a child trying to hold onto a god's hand. But the stubbornness that won in combat had sprung to life in Hal, and he would not let go. Before he had time to draw another breath, he was being swirled away, dragged up into the clouds in a flight at screaming speed. This time there was no Horse beneath him, and his whole weight hung on one hand.

Alvit was crying out in fear. She had been standing right beside him only a moment ago, but now her cries came faintly to Hal's ears, from a great and growing distance.

A plunge into the deep river from the height of the crag's top would have been terrible, but that he might possibly have survived. But before he could wonder whether it was wise to hang on an instant longer, he was at such an altitude that it would have been sure death to let the Hammer go. Besides, now he was no longer over water.

The wind of his passage was roaring in his ears. His weapons that he depended on had all been left behind, just like his gold. Just like his imaginary farm, that now he would never see. He could do nothing but hang on for dear life.

21

ow Alvit had completely disappeared from Hal's
sight, her screams swallowed by the rushing wind of
his passage as the Hammer dragged him upward.
The Hammer was the one thing in the world Hal could claim
as a possession now, outside of a few rags of bloodstained
clothing, cloak and leggings torn by the savage wind with
every moment of his soaring, roaring flight.

No prospects of a peaceful farm for Hal the Northman
now—he could not even reach a handful of dirt. No fishing
boats, not even a few splinters from a waterlogged hull. And
not an ounce of gold. There was only the rush of air that
caught and tore his breath away.

His insane hurtling flight seemed to prolong itself for hours.
Had he not earlier begun to accustom himself to flight on
Horseback, sheer panic might have broken his stubborn, life-
saving grip upon the Hammer. But as it was, his fingers stayed
clamped tight. Presently he thought that if he tried, really
made a great effort, he might be able to swing himself up one-
handed, against the screaming pull of speeding air, to lock his
left hand also on the Hammer's handle. Short as that shaft
was, there certainly ought to be room for a man's two hands.

With a gasping exertion he managed, on the third try, to
accomplish that. Now his right arm had some ease from the
killing strain of his full weight, and his dread of being torn
loose at every moment was eased a little.

In his current situation, he had gone far beyond being upset by looking down. Numbly he watched as a layer of broken clouds streamed by beneath him. What little he could see of the earth below, streaked with long slanting shadows as the time neared sunset, strongly suggested that he was being carried into regions that he had never been before. There were no mountains below him, or immediately nearby. At least he could be sure that he was not being borne back to Valhalla.

How long the journey really lasted was impossible to say. After a flight wilder than any Horse had given him, Hal felt the terrible speed begin to lessen, and he could see that he was coming down. During the descent, the flying Hammer shifted its orientation so the handle was still pointing toward the earth.

Land spread below him, dark and flat and unfamiliar. Trying to see where he was going to alight, Hal saw a flat dull expanse, and in the middle of it an object, dead ahead, that was soon close enough to be recognizable as Thor's chariot, the two Goats still in harness.

Around the motionless vehicle, rapidly growing larger as he flew toward it, there spread what he now perceived as a vast, roadless and unnavigable marsh, clinging to the rim of some great river. Was it the Einar? He couldn't tell. This might well be some other river altogether. Just how many miles had he flown?

At almost the last moment, he realized that his present trajectory would land him not just near the chariot, but right on top of it, and at a dangerous speed. He had no way to steer, no means of control of the force that bore him on. At the last moment, when a crashing impact seemed almost inevitable, Hal forced his cramped fingers to let go of Myelnir's stubby handle. His body went plunging down a few yards away from the hard wood, with a large but anti-climactic splash, head-long into a waist-deep chilly swamp.

The Hammer, released, went bumping and thumping right down into the open vehicle, its landing loud and hard enough that you might think it would have gone right through the floorboards. But no, it simply banged and rattled to a stop—evidently those boards were made of sturdy stuff.

The pair of huge Goats looked round with curiosity, then went on patiently cropping whatever their immortal jaws were managing to dredge up out of the swamp.

Half-wading and half-swimming, spitting and snorting foul-tasting muck, Hal soon got his feet more or less under him. Around the chariot there stretched, for at least half a mile, a seeming forest, practically an ocean, of tall reeds. No one was going to walk to this spot or ride here on a cameloid. Forcing a passage through the masses of vegetation by boat would be a weary job. So no ordinary humans, unless they came somehow flying over it, would find Thor's Chariot here.

Hal took note of the quiet, the loneliness, and the reddening light of approaching sunset. At least there were no sounds or sights of fighting anywhere nearby—it was hard to imagine how anyone could ever organize a battle here. It looked like a place where a man might easily drown, or starve, but he would not be attacked, at least not by his fellow humans.

He hoped that the watery muck engulfing him was too cold to nurture snakes. Wading and swearing, scraping malodorous mud from his eyes and beard, Hal dragged himself right next to the Chariot—it was floating delicately, magically, with only a few inches of each wheel submerged, showing not a spot of mud—and looked inside.

There on the floorboards lay not only the Hammer, now inert, but the body of Thor's previous avatar. The late embodiment of the god was still wrapped in exotic, spotless furs and still displayed enormous metal armbands and iron gloves. The countenance had changed, but it was the same man who had once spoken to Hal and Baldur, and spun his Hammer for them.

At least Hal was reasonably certain it was the same. The body that Hal remembered as so mighty now lay sprawled on its back, shrunken, shriveled, almost mummified, though it was neither mangled nor decayed. There was no sign of spilled blood. The arms no longer came near filling the broad decorative bands. Doubtless the strange appearance of the corpse was some result of whatever Underworld magic had struck Thor down, at a moment when his most potent weapon was miles away. Automatically Hal looked for the Spear that Thor had taken from him, but could not find it. Perhaps Thor had turned it over to some Valkyrie.

Anyway, the northman had little attention to spare for such details. Right beside the body's desiccated forehead, just where you would expect to find it, lay the great god's Face. To Hal's mortal eyes, the small translucent slab looked practically indistinguishable from Loki's.

For a long moment Hal did not move to pick up this new treasure. This time it was not fear of any immediate catastrophe that held him back, but something deeper and more subtle.

"Why me?" he muttered aloud, and one of the Goats turned an inhuman face to look at him.

In all his years of wandering the world, he had never seriously thought that this choice would ever be his to make, but now it had come leaping out at him like a wolf from ambush. And not once, but twice in one day.

What surprised him was that this time the wolf should be so toothless. Because, in truth, Hal had already made his decision, long minutes ago when he moved to pick up the Hammer. And Myelnir in some way had also chosen him.

It was a sobering moment, not entirely one of joy. Before him lay a forcible reminder that becoming Thor's avatar did not guarantee survival. As in the case of Loki, whatever power had demolished the last avatar of Thor might be ready and waiting to destroy the next one too.

Both Goats looked round this time, as if made curious by this strange mortal's actions. Still they seemed to be waiting patiently for something meaningful to happen—something that would call them back to duty. Maybe, Hal thought, they were wondering why this particular human seemed so reluctant to become their god.

Not that it should make much difference to the Goats. Because if he didn't become Thor, someone else soon would. The same magic that preserved Faces from destruction also saw to it that they did not long remain unused. One variation of that magic had brought him here, and if he refused the offer, the challenge, the invitation, the same eldritch power would bring someone else. Or, perhaps, the Goats would somehow be inspired to move the Chariot to a place frequented by people. Either way the result would be the same. The very nature of Faces prevented them from remaining for very long out of the reach of human hands. He thought the Face of Loki, locked in gold at the bottom of a river, would probably be out of reach for some time to come—but it was hard to make any safe predictions about a Trickster.

Hal could remember very plainly how, in his last moment high on the crag, when he had reached to grab the Hammer for himself, he had known an inner conviction that Myelnir had chosen him as well.

He wondered how many humans, down through the centuries, had covered their own human faces with these strange god-things, just out of fear of what would happen if they did not.

Holding the strange, masklike shape in his hands, Hal studied it, even though he already knew all that he had to know about it, and all that he was likely to find out—until he put it on. He had roamed the wide world for some twenty years without seeing the naked Face of any god—and now, in the course of a single hour, he had held two of them in his hands. Well, it came as no news to him that life was strange.

Hal was afraid, knowing that from the moment he pressed Thor's Face over his eyes and nose and let it sink magically into his brain, Haraldur the northman would permanently cease to exist. Oh, not that he expected to die. Not exactly. Hal's memories, his hopes and fears, the things that made him who he was, would all go on. But never again would he be alone in his own head. With him inside his very skull would be all the powers and cravings of the great god, along with all the memories mighty Thor had amassed over many centuries. Those things would henceforward be as much a part of Hal as his own nature, and he thought he could almost feel the pressure of them already, more than enough to fill his old head up to bursting. Over the hours and days to come, they'd stretch him into a new and different shape.

—if the Underworld powers that had killed Thor should allow his new avatar to live that long.

As simple and direct as putting a sharp dagger to your own throat—someone had said that, about the decision to put on a Face.

But what else could he do? And besides . . .

Hal was curious.

Raising the object toward his own face, Hal let out a startled little grunt. Despite all his foreknowledge, at the last moment he had the feeling that the Face attacked him like a striking snake, leaping at him across the last few inches. At the same moment he'd felt it melting in his fingers, dissolved like a piece of ice in flame.

A moment later, the Face had totally disappeared, and Hal knew a burning sensation that told him it had run into his head. He'd felt it go there, penetrating his left eye and ear, flowing right into his skull like water into dry sand. The first shock had been an ice-cold trickle, followed quickly by a sensation of burning heat, fading slowly to a heavy warmth . . .

there was a long moment when his vision and his hearing blurred . . .

Then he knew that it had happened, and he was still Hal, after all.

Still Hal, yes, but . . . now he was different. At the moment, the most profound change was that he was no longer on the verge of physical exhaustion. Hagan had grown a new arm within an instant of putting on a Face, and now Hal thought he could feel himself twenty years younger.

Now his enhanced senses could pick up the distant sounds of battle, a groaning and roaring, and now and then a real clash of arms. His eyes were now keen enough to pick out subtle variations in the strange glow near one side of the horizon.

He also saw, in the far distance, a Spearless Valkyrie, who seemed to be urging her airborne Horse rapidly toward him.

There was the Hammer, now docile and available, and he picked it up at once, knowing it would never dare to play tricks upon him now. Hal hung Myelnir on his belt, where once an axe had hung. Legend, current among gods and mortal humans alike, said that Myelnir had been made for Thor by gnomes, some of whom were as skilled with magic as they were with metal. Was the legend true? Even now, with centuries of divine memories to call on, Hal could not be sure, so ancient were the god and his great weapon.

Even gods, Hal supposed, must have had a birth or a beginning somewhere, sometime. But Thor's origins were lost in the mists of his most distant memories.

In other ways, the memories of a god's lifetime were more helpful. Hal could now at least dimly begin to understand the reasons for the current battle—although those reasons were still far from perfectly clear to either man or god.

Hal's stomach, which the god now shared, was ravenously hungry, and Thor remembered several things that he could do about that. In the air there moved a certain power, whose mere existence Hal alone would never have discovered, and on the railing of the Chariot there suddenly rested a pair of delicious-smelling oatcakes, steaming slightly as if fresh from the oven.

Hal tried one and found it very tasty.

The galloping Horse bearing a Valkyrie was somewhat closer now, only a few miles away.

His new memory did offer him one definite assurance: that what he ought to do before anything else was dispose reverently of the body of his predecessor.

Thor's voluminous memories also assured Hal that cremation was the preferred method, in line with some ancient tradition whose origin was probably older than Thor himself.

It took only a minute to straighten out the almost mummified corpse, decently close the eyes and clasp the hands upon the breast. There was no memory suggesting that the god's favorite weapon ought to be burned with him. The Hammer in its present form had outlasted many avatars and would probably outlast many more.

The new god thought, and his old memory confirmed, that Wodan would be pleased to know that this was being done by and for his eminent colleague.

In the swamp it might not be easy to arrange the proper fuel and heat for a funeral pyre. But if he did not take care of this matter now, the body of his predecessor would have to ride with Hal in the Chariot when he set out on his next task, which could not be long postponed; and that was an intolerable thought.

The same servant powers that had brought the cakes now set about the job of arranging a suitable funeral pyre, stripping the dead body of the god's accouterments, and when all

296 ——— Fred Saberhagen

was in readiness, igniting flame. Nowhere near the spectacular display that Loki could easily have managed, but it would do.

The pyre had been burning fiercely for half a minute, when the rider Hal had observed in the far distance at last arrived.

The rider was Alvit, of course: her Horse came cantering at low altitude, skimming over the swamp. She had done her best to catch up with Hal in his mad flight, but the flying Hammer had outsped even the best that her mount could do.

He was still just standing in the chariot, when she drew near and tugged her Horse to a standing stop in midair. She gazed at Hal for a long moment.

"So, northman, I see you have survived again. I saw the smoke from a distance, and when I saw the Chariot, too, I thought that Thor was here. What are you doing in . . . ?"

The truth was slow to force itself upon her, but presently it did. Then, while her Horse stood quivering in the air, she gave a long gasp and nearly fell off its back. She let out a little shriek, for once a very girlish sound. "My Lord Thor! You are . . ."

As Alvit fell silent in confusion, Hal reached out and gestured. He was glad he had not yet put on the iron gloves. In a moment the Horse had brought Alvit near enough for him to touch her hand, and a moment later she was with him in the Chariot.

"Never a lord to you, Alvit. I am still Hal." Still Hal, and always would be.

But—not the same Hal that he had been. New differences were coming into view in rapid succession. It was like watching his reflection in a mirror and observing alterations. Thor's new body was not going to stay mud-covered for long, not if the god did not want himself to look that way. Rapidly the stuff of the marsh was drying on his body and falling away like loose dust, along with remnants of dried berserkers' and bandits' blood. He would be able to readily change his clothing, too, just by thinking about it, into something more appropriate for divinity. As soon as he got around to such details.

"Be at ease." He thought his voice still sounded pretty much like his own, like Hal's. "It's all right, I am still Hal, I tell you. Talk to me, Alvit, tell me what's happening."

She was standing close beside him in the Chariot, with her fists clenched nervously at her sides. "I am to tell you, my lord—I am to tell you, Thor—Hal—"

"Yes, call me Hal. Take it easy. Calm yourself."

Presently Alvit was able to inform him that Wodan strongly suspected that Loki was dead. Naturally the Father of Battles was ready to go to any lengths to get control of Loki's Face, so he could have that weapon delivered into the hands of one of his, Wodan's, worshipers.

Alternatively, if there was already a new avatar of Loki, and if the reborn god should still be Wodan's foe, Wodan (or Alvit, serving by default as his strategist) was thinking that it would be best to fight the Firegod early, while he was still relatively ineffective in using the tools of his divinity.

On the other hand, if there was a new Loki and he was inclined to be a friend to Wodan, then Loki might need immediate help in their shared fight against Giants and monsters.

But whatever the true situation was regarding Loki, Wodan was still hoping to recruit Thor.

Now Alvit could carry good news back to her god: that Haraldur the northman has picked up Thor's Face and put it on.

Alvit's countenance showed the hint of a smile. "The face of my lord—Hal—in his present avatar has a . . . a certain majesty about it."

"You can tell him also that my Hammer is now safely resting at my side."

He thought the young woman shuddered slightly, glancing

at the weapon. "You knew what it was going to do to Hagan."

"I had a pretty good idea that Myelnir would mangle whoever put on Loki's Face, as long as the order to kill was still in effect. And I thought the world could probably spare Hagan."

Alvit was contemplating him, shaking her head in private wonder. Then she gave a start. "But I am forgetting my duty! When any of us finds Thor, we are to offer him a courteous greeting from our master—there was flowery language, which I have forgotten, but it amounts to a greeting between equals."

"Really? From Wodan?"

Alvit blushed slightly. "As between near-equals, then."

"Then carry my response to Wodan, in such language as you think will not displease him. But maybe I should ride to see him face-to-face, as soon as this ritual burning is completed."

"Yes Hal, you should—but I am forgetting, there is one more thing. Along with his greeting, Wodan sends an urgent warning that he and Thor had better waste no more time, but get on with the job of slaughtering monsters and demons, the traditional enemies of all gods."

When Hal/Thor thought for a moment, he readily remembered Wodan, and the details and ramifications of Thor's relationship with Wodan, from a completely different perspective than that of Hal the downtrodden recruit. The Wodan of many avatars ago, of ages past, had often been a very different individual from the confused dreamer of today. Thor's memory in this case was encyclopedic, extending through a gulf of time that must have covered many centuries. The exact number of years was something Thor had never bothered to count.

Hal, a neophyte in his god-powers, realized that he might quickly be killed by the same power that had slain Thor's previous avatar. His vast new memory contained several possibilities regarding the precise nature of that weapon, and several suggestions as to which power of the Underworld might have wielded it. Unfortunately, there were some that even Thor knew little of.

The natural-looking flames of the funeral pyre were waning, having accomplished the necessary destruction, and there was no further reason for delay.

"Then let us go find Wodan!" Thor/Hal decided.

He took up the reins with Alvit at his side, and at his touch the Goats sprang into action, dragging the Chariot into smooth and speedy flight. The Valkyrie's Horse kept up, air-galloping obediently just behind the speeding car, as if this were another accustomed exercise, until the speed became too great, and the riderless animal fell behind. The Goats, as Thor expected, seemed ready to provide all the speed that any god could want.

22

T
he plain of Asgard," Hal/Thor mused aloud. With a
gentle, practiced tug on the reins, he brought his Goats
to a standstill in midair, so that a moment later the
Chariot drifted down to rest on solid ground. Alvit, who had
been riding beside him with her Horse following, relaxed a
little.

The god's vehicle had come to rest on the top of a bleak
hill from which Thor/Hal could survey the scene of intermittent battle spread out before him. The forces of Wodan and
his allies were no more than half a mile away, those of the
Underworld somewhat farther off, a shadowy no-man's-land
of varying width between. Beyond the enemy, some five miles
distant, a line of purple hills marked the limits of Asgard.

Alvit, of course, was not going to linger at Hal's side. Taking her leave with a few brief words, she remounted her
Horse, and in a moment was riding to report to Wodan,
whose own Chariot was visible near the center of his army's
line.

Meanwhile Hal paused to survey the scene. He was looking
over the same broad sweep of land that Sergeant Nosam had
once tried to point out to him when the two of them were
standing on the battlements of Valhalla. At the moment, the
distant walls of that stronghold were barely visible through a
notch in a wall of mountains some miles behind Thor's Chariot.

When the sergeant had been trying to tell him about the plain, the whole scene had been sunk in midnight darkness, and Hal's vision had been no more than human. So he could not recognize the landscape now—nor could Thor, who apparently had never paid much heed to Wodan's longstanding prophecies regarding a Last Battle.

The square miles of Asgard plain might once have been good for grazing, but the land looked practically worthless now, being badly scorched, either by natural fire or magic, across most of its extent. Anyone who might have been living on it when the battle started must have fled days ago. The only remaining signs of human occupancy were a couple of small and distant buildings, already knocked to ruins.

Thor/Hal spun his Hammer in his hand, his god's strength scarcely noticing the weight. It seemed to Hal that his new composite memory could show him very clearly the details regarding use of this superb weapon, the preferred techniques.

But what to use it on? Across a great span of the vague distance, wreathed and muffled in smoke and dust, were the enemy armies. Such human forces as the enemy had managed to enlist in its dark cause—some kind of army scraped together, the Fates alone knew how—were hard to make out behind a haze of smoke and dust, even to the eyesight of a god.

So far, no target worthy of Myelnir had come to Thor's attention. The enemy might well have seen his Chariot arriving on the battlefield, and the important leaders might have prudently retreated.

Another object of Hal's concern was nearer. Shifting to a closer range, Thor's divine eyesight soon discovered the All-Highest. Wodan, as anyone who knew him would expect, was of course leading his troops, taking his place at their head as they entered battle or prepared to do so. And Hal/Thor thought that even the demons of the Underworld might well be affrighted at the sight. The Father of Battles presented a terrible figure, fully armed with his helmet and spear, riding his Chariot behind his eight-legged Horse, the terrible Sleipnir, who at the moment was snorting fire.

Wodan had had much more success at mustering an army than some of his enemies had expected: his corps of fighting humans was relatively weak, but his wraiths and apparitions could frighten fleshly opponents who did not know how ineffectual they really were. This included most of the human mercenaries who now found themselves arrayed against him.

Unless you were gifted with divine eyesight or knew where and how to look for them, the solid physical presence of human beings would be all but lost in the landscape of smoke and mist and magic, among Wodan's shadowy host of several thousand wraiths, their battalions spreading out for a mile to the right and to the left. But using Thor's vision, Hal needed only a moment longer to recognize one group of the real men as his former barrack-mates. On each side of Wodan's Chariot marched, or rather shambled, a crew of a few dozen men, the Heroes from Valhalla. Beside them, extending their ranks for some distance to right and left, was a small corps of human mercenary allies, no more than a couple of hundred, somehow recruited from nearby warlords.

Wodan enjoyed the advantages and suffered the disadvantages of being really, thoroughly crazy.

His behavior became impossible for the enemy to predict, and he thought his army was much grander and more effective than it really was.

If Thor and Wodan had been able to seriously coordinate their power, victory might well have been theirs, and quickly, even against all the monsters. But that was not to be.

Above the opposing armies and between them, half a dozen Valkyries, no more, were riding proudly in the air, circling the field with Spears in hand. Alvit had told Hal that Wodan had called the glorious sisterhood together, before sending them to search for Thor, and had addressed them for what he said would probably be the last time.

The god had told his squadron of proud maidens that in this battle they must abandon their traditional role of recruiters. The last days had come, and this shabby force that he now led was all the army he would ever have. Instead, the Valkyries were to fight beside their master and, when called on, serve as Wodan's couriers.

Having surveyed the field from a distance to his satisfaction, Thor took up his Chariot's reins and drove the vehicle directly to Wodan. As he came near the place where the All-Highest waited, Hal looked around for Alvit, but she was not in sight. Either she was with her sisters over the battlefield, or Wodan had dispatched her on some urgent mission.

For the moment, the Chariots of the two great gods stood parked beside each other, Sleipnir's majestic presence in sharp contrast to the grotesquerie of the Goats.

Fixing Hal/Thor with his one-eyed stare, the senior god proclaimed in his rumbling voice: "Thunderer, I know it is a long time since we have seen each other—and yet you look strangely familiar. Have I met this avatar before?"

Thor/Hal only shook his head, and reached out for a handshake, as between equals. "I too have the feeling that it is not long since we parted."

Wodan, after a brief hesitation, accepted his hand. Immediately Hal/Thor tried to get down to business and open a discussion on matters of strategy and tactics. It seemed to Hal that there was no good reason, except for Wodan's craziness, for Thor and Wodan to fail to stand together against the threat from below the surface of the earth. Both gods were longtime enemies of the creatures from deep hell. The chief point of uneasiness between them seemed to derive from the fact that Thor was a patron god of the more numerous peasants and lower classes, while Wodan's devotees were chiefly of the elite. In the past, certain avatars of each had found this difference grounds for jealousy.

Calling on Thor's vast memory, enlisting his deep intelligence, Hal did his best to come up with some coherent plan of battle. But the effort was practically useless. At the moment Wodan was unwilling to talk about much of anything except how he was going to mow down the enemy with his Spear, when shortly he rode against them.

Suddenly the Father of Battles broke off, as if he had just remembered something of importance.

"Tell me, Thunderer, where is Loki? Have you seen him? Is it possible he's allied with the enemy?"

"In this case," Hal/Thor assured him, "he cannot be, for I have seen him dead."

Wodan was unmistakably pleased. But a moment later he asked the inevitable question: had any other mortal yet picked up Loki's Face?

It did not seem to Hal that now was the time to attempt any lengthy explanation. Sooner or later, some god or coalition of mortals would locate the Face of Loki and find some way of extracting it from its great lump of gold. But there was no point in hurrying the inevitable. The fewer who knew what had happened to the treasure, the better.

At the same time, the mention of Loki had irresistibly evoked some of Thor's more interesting ancient memories. Hal was presented with fascinating scenes involving certain antique avatars of Wodan. There had been one such who, outraged that Loki should be fighting in some ancient battle on the side of the Underworld, had caught firebomb after firebomb on the point of his magic Spear and hurled them back. Of course such missiles had failed to do Loki any harm, but they had certainly scorched his quondam allies, before the Firegod was able to take any effective countermeasures . . .

. . . but here and now, on the plain of Asgard, Wodan was waiting for an answer.

Hal cleared his throat. "My respected colleague, we can expect no help from Loki in this fight. But neither will he appear against us. Listen to me, All-Highest, it is very important that we work out some plan to follow in the battle—"

But Wodan was not looking at him or listening, and Hal had no chance to try to force him to pay attention, because here Alvit came galloping up on her airborne Horse, to report to the gods that enemy action was disrupting the ranks of Valhalla. Many wraiths had already been lost in battle, disappearing like dew in the morning sun, and the flow of replacements had suddenly been cut off. Some force was evidently damaging or interfering with the device that generated and maintained their images.

The news reached the All-Highest at one of his more lucid moments. Announcing that it would be unthinkable for he himself to leave the front line, he said he would much appreciate it if Thor could find out what was killing off his wraiths and stop the slaughter.

Before Thor/Hal could even voice agreement, Wodan had seized his great Spear and brandished it, turned his back unceremoniously on his fellow deity, cracked a kind of whip over Sleipnir's back, and went careening straight ahead, bellowing war cries, toward the center of the enemy line.

Alvit, riding her Horse beside his Chariot, directed the newest avatar to a steep-sided canyon, just below the battlements on the north side of the stronghold, opposite the plain. There, she said, the wraith-generating device was located. Only a few, even in Valhalla, knew the place.

Rounding the flank of a mountain, Hal/Thor's Chariot bore him in sight of the narrow entry to a deep cave.

Alvit might have ridden right into the cavity, but Hal/Thor

sharply called her back. His divine perception warned him that some demonic or monstrous presence was in the cavern. Myelnir was already in the god's hand, and in the blinking of an eye it sped toward its target. The narrow cave-mouth erupted in a flash of manycolored light, telling Thor's experienced eye that his weapon had wrought annihilation.

He wanted to ride his Chariot straight into the cave, feeling that way he would be better equipped to deal with whatever awaited him inside. But for the Chariot to pass the entrance, it was necessary to enlarge the opening. Myelnir proved a handy tool. Thor tossed his weapon gently, underhand, without dismounting from his Chariot. There was a cloud of dust, a hail of stones. Alvit gave a little cry and dodged as small bits of rock went shooting past her head, and when the dust cleared there was a new look to the cave's mouth. Already Myelnir's handle was snugly back in Thor's right hand. A moment later, the Chariot was inside the cave, where he who rode it could smell the faint, unpleasant residue of the creature he had just destroyed.

Entering an enclosed space many times larger than his Chariot, Hal looked carefully around, with a god's vision keen even in semidarkness. When Alvit pointed out to him the machine that generated the wraiths, he could think of nothing to compare it to, except possibly a tangle of dead or dying tree stumps, projecting from the cave floor, shorn of all branches and leaves. Even Thor had never seen anything just like this before; but his long memory retained garbled stories of a spot deep in the Underworld, where some kind of engine described as similar to this one was said to produce strange images of the dead, in pursuit of some vast project whose purpose all living minds had long since forgotten.

Alvit rode bravely right beside the strange device, whose jagged outline testified, even to one ignorant of proper shape and purpose, that it was broken.

"Hal, is there anything you can do to fix it?"

Hal made a helpless gesture with his powerful arms, limbs grown even thicker with his apotheosis. "Nothing that either Thor or I can think of." The Thunderer's divine talent for constructive building or repair was almost nonexistent, beyond some odds and ends of plain metalworking. Certainly neither god nor man were up to dealing with devices on this level of sophistication.

"Then what are we to do?" Alvit sounded desperate.

Hal didn't know, and Thor's memory was of no help. Being deprived of wraiths would cost the gods' forces one of their chief advantages over the demonic army, for wraiths could duel more effectively against demons than they could against human flesh and blood.

Again Hal was struck by how strongly the mysterious machine resembled an underground complex of tree stumps. Neither Hal nor Thor could make any sense of it—though Thor did have some memory, tantalizingly faint and remote, of having seen something like it somewhere before.

When more creatures of the Underworld suddenly appeared at the cave's entrance, Thor with a swift cast of his Hammer killed two of the latest attackers. The strange, quasi-material shapes exploded at Myelnir's touch, and others turned and fled before entering the cave.

But Thor's defense of the cave had come too late. The engine had been effectively destroyed.

"We can do no more here," he told Alvit, "let's get back to the battle."

She could only agree, and followed on her Horse as Hal drove Thor's Chariot high into the air above Valhalla to get another view of Wodan's deployment and see how the fight was going.

No more wraiths could be generated, and those already in the field continued to vanish under enemy attack, sometimes whole squadrons of them together. Thor looked about him, reveling in senses enormously keener and farther-ranging than Hal the northman had ever dreamt of having. He felt a warrior's joy on seeing that the enemy had come out of hiding and was once more on the attack.

Hal/Thor picked out a target—

And hurled Myelnir!

There had been a lull in the fighting. Again the enemy had pulled back out of contact, but no one on the gods' side could be certain if this meant a general retreat, or that the enemy was reorganizing and nerving itself for a final supreme effort.

With his strength augmented by the power of a god, Hal no longer felt the exhaustion that had drained him when he was only mortal man. But even gods could tire, as he was discovering. He had landed his Chariot again, near the spot where he had talked with Wodan, and he was waiting for the All-Highest to come back from his latest foray against the enemy.

Surprisingly, his right knee twinged as he turned round. It was a different kind of twinge than he had been trying to get used to in the last months before his chance came to be Thor. As one who had the experience of many wounds, he recognized this as a therapeutic sort of twang, part of a healing process, almost like a small dislocation popping back in place. He had no doubt at all that the knee, Thor's knee, was going to be just fine from now on.

Hal was about to look around for Wodan, when a voice right at his own Chariot-wheel distracted him.

"Hal, remember us?" There stood the youthful figure of

Holah—or was this one Noden?—one of Baldur's cousins or nephews, clinging to the vehicle in a familiar way. It was obvious that in the boy's ignorance he did not immediately grasp the fact that the man he recognized had become the great god Thor.

Meanwhile the speaker's slightly older brother was approaching. Being a little more perceptive, he must have realized the truth, for he was trying to drag his younger sibling back.

Hal gave them both a weary look. "So, you couldn't wait to get into a real fight, hey? Well, no more could I when I was your age."

Questioning the boys, Hal learned that they had experienced only a taste of fighting so far. One of them seemed eager for more, the other not nearly so enthusiastic, yet reluctant to admit the fact.

Now the elder asked: "What should we do now, sir—Hal? The men we came to this fight with seem to have disappeared."

"My advice to you both is—keep your weapons handy and don't volunteer for anything." Part of Hal wanted to tell them to go home, and had been on the verge of doing so, but another part admired their youthful daring and enterprise. Meanwhile, his Thor component hardly took notice of the lads at all.

Hal was saved from further discussion by the sudden appearance of Wodan's Chariot, the Father of Battles for once with his back to the enemy, and driving Sleipnir hard. The unaccustomed sight caught Hal's attention—Wodan was beckoning Thor to a conference.

Scouting Valkyries had brought the news that the largest and most destructive monsters of the Underworld were once more on the march just below and upon the surface of the earth.

One of the flying sisters reported the presence of the treacherous Giant Skrymir, who could surround himself with illusions as protection against the gods he feared to face directly. Thor himself had no clear memory of what Skrymir actually looked like—and when a fight was over, whether or not he had actually been present was hard to know.

Another Valkyrie claimed to have seen in the ranks of the Underworld the Giant Surt, one who continually brandished a flaming sword. There ought to be no mistaking him, at least.

Hal tried again, but with no more success than before, to work out some coherent plan of battle. But Wodan would have none of it.

The All-Highest was saying to him: ". . . and so, it is too bad, but I cannot offer most of your worshipers Valhalla. Unless of course some of them turn out better than expected, and perform as true heroes should."

Now was hardly the time to haggle over points of honor. Hal simply nodded. "My followers and I will just have to accept that as best we can."

After warning Thor to beware of treachery in their own ranks, Wodan turned, and with an elated war cry, he once more charged against the foe. Soon the Father of Battles in his Chariot was cutting a swath of destruction across the field, right through the thickest of his enemies' ranks. Humans and others fell before him, by the scores, by the hundreds, as he smote right and left with his terrible Spear, much more powerful than the similar weapons used by Valkyries.

Withdrawing slightly from the front line, Thor stayed with the tactics that had earlier been successful, getting the most out of Myelnir's long-range power. He avoided direct engagement, for the most part, killing major monsters at a distance. When one of them died, in contrast to the gods, it was dead, with no chance of a resurrection.

There was a stir in the front line now, the beginning of a retreat on the gods' side, and anxious human yells . . .

A huge shape, or shape-changer more like it, hard to see, was half-materialized behind the enemy's front rank. Skrymir, maybe?

No, no such luck. In the mosaic of legends as so often quoted by Wodan, Thor's prime enemy on the day of the last battle was beyond all doubt Jormungand, the world-serpent. And indeed Thor's memory now assured Hal that god and monster were no strangers to each other.

Hal took aim at the dim shape looming large behind the enemy front, and launched another throw. The Hammer struck home squarely, but for once the victim did not vanish in a blast, or even fall. It was Jormungand, all right.

The dull, gigantic shape, only partially visible through clouds of smoke and dust, recoiled briefly, then resumed its advance. Hal had seen this enemy only in pictures and carvings, but Thor had ancient memories of this horror in plenty. Now man and god were facing Jormungand, the greatest of serpents, who came writhing and winding his way to the attack. Red eyes the size of bushel baskets glowed in an incongruously hairy head, rising easily fifty feet above the battlefield when the long body stretched into the air. Sometimes Jormungand came rolling like some Titan's hoop, biting his own tail. Thor could recall one notable scuffle in which this creature had taken on the form of a cat; but whatever form the huge shape-changer put on, his chief weapon was spitting poison.

For a moment, Wodan seemed confused, and his Chariot was in retreat. Alvit came galloping seemingly from nowhere, to join Thor/Hal in his struggle against the poison-spewing serpent.

Hal shouted and waved a warning to her to keep clear, but on her snorting Horse she came darting in, trying to Spear the demon's eyes. Jormungand was immense, dwarfing the two human-sized bodies that dared to close with him. Hal's own purely human impulse was to turn and run, but Thor's iron confidence and long experience assured his new avatar that the odds were nowhere near as unfavorable as they appeared.

He had thrown his Hammer again, but not yet got it back, when a great fanged mouth came looming overhead, then closing like some castle's portcullis upon the man-sized god. Thor had to grab its upper and lower jaws at the same time, one in each of his two hands, and strain with all his strength to rend them violently apart. Bellowing in pain, the serpent wrenched itself free, almost dragging him from his Chariot in the process. The poisonous exhalation from the mouth would have felled a mortal human in his tracks.

Through dust and smoke and flame the battle swirled. It seemed that Jormungand had terrified the Goats, and Thor had to struggle to regain full control of his own Chariot.

On achieving this, and seeing that the monster still reeled back, Hal looked around for Alvit. He felt a surge of relief as he saw her riding through the air unharmed, Spear still ready to do battle. He told himself that if he had the welfare of the Valkyrie in mind, the best thing he could do for her would be to win this battle. And he told himself that the next time he saw her, he would tell her she was now assigned permanently as Thor's aide. He thought the chances were that if Wodan never saw her again, the old god would never know the difference.

The fact that Thor and Jormungand had come face-to-face in mortal combat made Hal wonder uneasily if crazy Wodan might be right, and the world was really going to end when this battle did.

Alvit had seen him, and came riding near. "Hal, I think that we are winning! If only Loki could be here, and fighting for us, we could destroy these dregs of hell!"

Evidently she had not arrived at the crag in time to see just what had happened to the Firegod. Briefly Hal/Thor considered telling her—because it would be impossible for her or anyone else (except maybe Wodan) to retrieve Loki's Face. But as he had with Wodan, Hal said nothing. He wanted to be sure that Alvit never got the Trickster's Face, because if she had it she would put it on to help Wodan, and it would change her much more than Hal wanted to see her changed. The world could probably get along just fine for a time, with no one wearing Loki's Face—or Wodan's, come to think of it.

The fight went on.

As a god, Hal had to admit that Myelnir's handle felt much more comfortable in his grip than any plow handle ever would.

The new avatar of Thor, slamming down row after row of his enemies with his irresistible Hammer—the enemy knew that they would have to kill Thor again or abandon the field.

Finally, the surviving great monsters and the creatures who supported them were slowly retreating, back into the Underworld. By now all of Jormungand's human auxiliaries, those who could still run or walk, had fled the field.

The powers of the Underworld had been defeated for the time being.

But the great serpent and his supporters did not withdraw entirely until there was one more flurry of combat, in which something, perhaps a last parting shot of Jormungand's poison, struck at Wodan and did him serious damage. Hal first realized the fact when Alvit came silently beckoning him, her face showing a look of gloom and doom he had never seen there before.

Thor was one of the first to know that the All-Highest had fallen, and he was first after Alvit to reach Wodan's side. The great god's body lay spilled out of his tipped and broken Chariot and clouds of steam or smoke were coming up. Some force more blunt than poison seemed to have been at work, though it had left no obvious wounds.

Hastily Hal sent his own servant powers to work. They in turn called upon surviving wraiths to form a screen around the tumbled Chariot and those who were near it.

To Alvit he said sharply: "We must keep this a secret, if we can."

As Hal/Thor turned over the old man's body, he could see that Wodan was still alive. The old man's single eye was open, showing the vacant blue of summer skies. The first words that issued from his bearded lips were threats against those the Father of Battles believed had betrayed him.

At first the murmuring was so low that even divine hearing could barely make it out. " . . . must root out . . . treachery."

Thor tried to shift the massive body into an easier position. "Can you sit up?"

Suddenly the voice was louder. "Who're you? All, all have turned against me."

"My respected colleague, that is wrong."

"One of the damned Valkyries was here. They've all failed me. Should never have trusted women. Who're you? Another shape-changer?"

"I am Thor, as much a god as you are, Wodan. We are fighting on the same side." In the circumstances it seemed only prudent to make that clear.

As usual, the All-Highest did not seem to be listening. "All mortals betray me when I trust them, especially the women. But I'll have the last laugh on the traitors."

When Hal/Thor told him that the battle was effectively won, the enemy in full retreat, Wodan reacted with alarm and refused to believe him.

"This is the day of the final battle, and they all must die. I'll see to it!"

There was a long pause. Then: "The end of the world has come!" If the fighting was really ending, then the world must too. The All-Highest could tolerate no other outcome.

Hal left the enclosure momentarily to tell Alvit that Wodan was not yet dead. When he returned, the great god was struggling to get back on his feet. With a surge of effort Wodan had grasped his Chariot and set it once more upright upon its wheels. Sleipnir looked back with the dull fear of a real horse.

Thor tried to be placating. "We have won, great Wodan. You will need your Chariot no more today."

"No, the battle cannot be over! The fighting must go on. The world is going to end. The world must end!" Then he stumbled and would have fallen, but for Thor's supporting arm.

Wodan would have it that the world must end; therefore the battle could not be over yet. Therefore he must order all his remaining forces, human and otherwise, into a suicidal charge.

"If the enemy has retreated, we must pursue!"

Hal tried arguing. "But the enemy has retreated to the lower regions."

"Then we must follow them! We'll invade the Underworld! Drive our own humans forward, Thor! Help me. Help me to my Chariot . . ."

"Maybe when our troops are rested—"

"Damned traitors! I'll give them no rest." Wodan was going to insist on rooting out and punishing the traitors in his own ranks, those who were trying to subvert the Fate of the world for their own mere cowardly survival. Faithless Valkyries! Worthless human trash! Were it not for them, the whole world could have been brought to its proper climax in destruction!

Gradually Hal was coming to the realization that once more Thanatos, god of Death, had failed to claim the god of battles. Hal/Thor knew a sinking feeling. Wodan was not really dying. If he went forward with his mad plan to invade the Underworld, death would probably claim him soon—but maybe not soon enough.

It seemed to Hal that he and Thor now thought as one, with no hint of conflict in their joint awareness.

His god-voice went out smoothly. "Of course, All-Highest. Depend on me to give you the help you really need. See, there, for instance." And he pointed. When the other's head turned, Hal with his right hand slid Myelnir from his belt. The force of the blow was precisely calibrated, getting the job done without causing inconvenient noise or mess. Myelnir was quite capable of fine precision work when such was called for. Nothing to disturb the tranquility of the mindless screen of wraiths surrounding the two gods; all of them were still staring, with great apparent interest, into some distant nothingness.

A moment later, Hal was holding the Face of Wodan in his hand, and a moment after that, he had stuffed it into the new belt pouch that Thor had already requisitioned from his powers.

With any luck at all, some considerable time would pass before the retreating enemy discovered that the Father of Battles was dead.

Now, for the third time in only a few hours, Hal had the disposal of divinity.

He shuddered inwardly to think what might happen if the powers of the Underworld should get control of the trinket he had just tucked into concealment. What would they do with it? No demon could wear a god's Face, at least Hal did not think so. No doubt they would hand it to some mortal human maniac, or truly malignant warlord. Or one of Hagan's surviving bandits. However they might dispose of the great power, it was a frightening prospect.

No. To allow that would seem to be against a northman's honor. Once again Hal could feel himself being forced to a particular choice.

Parting with a gesture the close ranks of the encircling wraiths, Hal thrust his head and shoulders out between them. A multitude of eyes were turned his way.

"Wodan and I are in conference," he announced. He had already decided that a general proclamation of the All-Highest's death had better wait, until with his next breath he could name the new avatar.

Hal's gaze went skimming along the ranks of waiting humans, pausing briefly on Sergeant Nosam. The sergeant had lived with a god so long that he might be expected to know what a good god would be like. But Alvit had been right about him—he was too small.

Moving on, Hal's speculative eye fell next on Alvit herself—but a different future awaited her, if Hal had anything to say about it. Now he called her to him with a slight gesture, and sent her to find the boys from Baldur's household.

A minute later, Holah and Noden stood before him, two boys not knowing whether to be terrified or overcome with honor.

"Lads, I am about to charge you with an extremely important mission."

Eyes wide, and rendered almost speechless by such words from Thor himself, the boys waited to hear what commission they were about to receive.

Hat/Thor said: "I am loaning you my Chariot, and you are to ride it in search of your uncle Baldur. Then you—"

"He is really our cousin," one lad murmured, as if afraid degree of kinship might make some fatally important difference.

"Whatever he is, wherever he is, you are to find him and

bring him back here to me." Hal paused for thought, then added: "If there should be a lady with him who wishes to come along—well, let her."

Seeing the beginnings of great fear in the young eyes before him, fear of their own inadequacy, he hastened to add: "Boys, I am sending help with you, in the form of invisible powers. Magic enough to make sure that you find the man I want."

"Are we to—to give him any reason, sir?"

"Yes. Tell him that Haraldur the northman appeals to his honor, and needs his help. The god Thor has a task for him, a vitally important mission, that none but Baldur can accomplish."

While Hal was speaking, Alvit had approached and looked anxiously into his face, then moved to slide past him into the enclosure of wraiths. He had let her pass.

Now she emerged again, and Hal could see that she was fighting back tears. In a low voice she asked: "And what will Baldur's mission be?"

"Wodan is asking for him," Hal told her. He could see in the woman's face that she had discovered Wodan's death, but did not realize how it had come about. Perhaps sometime he would tell her. Now he only drew her a little aside, so no one else could hear, and added: "I want him to rebuild Valhalla, and to rule there."

"Baldur?" There was grief in Alvit's voice for what she had just seen, but relief as well. "Is it wise to make a god of Hagan's son?"

"Maybe not. But can you name me a wiser choice?"

Hal could see that the Valkyrie was thinking, and he waited but she said nothing. Now it looked like Hagan's son would become the very god that Hagan had so desperately hated. Hal thought that ironic; Thor found it quite amusing.

Alvit plainly stood in need of some kind of help. Hal reached out an arm and pulled the tall young woman gently to him, so that when she slumped a little, her head rested on his shoulder. She seemed content to be there.

After a little while Hal said: "Maybe neither I nor the god in me has any true wisdom. If I did, I'd probably be a farmer. But I want to see how Baldur handles his new job."

Hal was curious.

And so was Thor.